WASHOE COUNTY LIBRARY

3 1235 03683 6976

PRAISE FOR
DOLLFACE

"*Dollface* is as intoxicating as the forbidden liquor at the heart of it. Rosen's Chicago gangsters are vividly rendered, and the gun molls stir up at least as much trouble as their infamous men. Fans of *Boardwalk Empire* will love *Dollface*. I know I did."

—Sara Gruen, *New York Times* bestselling
author of *Water for Elephants*

"Gun molls and the gangsters they love spring to life in *Dollface*, Renée Rosen's lush novel set at the height of the Roaring Twenties. Her skill at maintaining the balance between thrilling plot turns and rich character development is evident on every page. Pour yourself a glass of gin, turn up the jazz, and prepare to lose yourself in the unforgettable story of a quintessential flapper."

—Tasha Alexander, *New York Times* bestselling
author of *Death in the Floating City*

"Renée Rosen has combined her daring and vivid imagination with the rich history of Prohibition-era Chicago. *Dollface* is a lively, gutsy romp of a novel that will keep you turning pages."

—Karen Abbott, *New York Times* bestselling
author of *Sin in the Second City*

"*Dollface* sheds a new light on Prohibition-era gangsters when we see them through the eyes of the women who kept their secrets and shared their beds. Rosen's Chicago is bursting with booze, glamour, sex, and _____, author of *In Need of a Good Wife*

continued...

RECEIVED

DEC 17 2013

NORTHWEST RENO LIBRARY
Reno, Nevada

D1052330

PRAISE FOR THE WORK
OF RENÉE ROSEN

"Quirky and heartfelt."   —*Chicago Tribune*

"Beautifully written, and with larger-than-life characters, this book will remain in readers' hearts for a long time to come."
                                                  —*School Library Journal*

"A heartfelt coming-of-age story, told with the perfect combination of humor and drama."   —*Chicago Sun-Times*

"Absorbing. . . .As Rosen evokes her setting with a wealth of details . . . [readers] will empathize with the narrator's unique situation as a concentrated form of universal worries about finding acceptance, dealing with loss, and leaving home."   —*Publishers Weekly*

"An astonishingly deep and thought-provoking debut novel."
                                              —Young Adult Books Central

DOLLFACE

A NOVEL OF THE ROARING TWENTIES

RENÉE ROSEN

New American Library

New American Library
Published by the Penguin Group
Penguin Group (USA) LLC, 375 Hudson Street,
New York, New York 10014

USA | Canada | UK | Ireland | Australia | New Zealand | India | South Africa | China
penguin.com
A Penguin Random House Company

First published by New American Library,
a division of Penguin Group (USA) LLC

First Printing, November 2013

Copyright © Renée Rosen, 2013
Readers Guide copyright © Penguin Group (USA) LLC, 2013
Penguin supports copyright. Copyright fuels creativity, encourages diverse voices, pro-
motes free speech, and creates a vibrant culture. Thank you for buying an authorized
edition of this book and for complying with copyright laws by not reproducing, scanning, or distributing any part of it in any form without permission. You are supporting
writers and allowing Penguin to continue to publish books for every reader.

 REGISTERED TRADEMARK—MARCA REGISTRADA

LIBRARY OF CONGRESS CATALOGING-IN-PUBLICATION DATA:
Rosen, Renée.
Dollface: a novel of the roaring twenties/Renée Rosen.
p.cm.
ISBN 978-0-451-41920-0
1. Nineteen twenties—Fiction. 2. Young women—Illinois—Chicago—Fiction.
3. Organized crime—Illinois—Chicago—Fiction. I. Title.
PS3618.O83156E94 2007
813'.6—dc23   2012051794

Printed in the United States of America
1   3   5   7   9   10   8   6   4   2

Set in Bell MT
Designed by Spring Hoteling

PUBLISHER'S NOTE
This is a work of fiction. Names, characters, places, and incidents either are the product
of the author's imagination or are used fictitiously, and any resemblance to actual per-
sons, living or dead, business establishments, events, or locales is entirely coincidental.

For Joe Esselin, teacher, playwright, poet, and dear friend.

ACKNOWLEDGMENTS

I offer my heartfelt thanks to my friends and colleagues for their support while I was writing this novel: Jill Bernstein, Irma Bueno, Dennis Rosenthal, Chris Lee, Lauren Baratz-Logsted, Jonathan Santlofer, Craig Alton, Karen Abbott, Brian Wilson, Javier Ramirez, Stefan Moorehead, Suzy Takacs, Tasha Alexander, Andrew Grant, Nick Hawkins, Kelly O'Connor McNees, Amy Sue Nathan, Andy Gross, Jhanteigh Kupihea, Rick Kogan, Chuck Osgood, Beth Treleven, Stephanie Nelson, Lisa and Mark Fine, Lisa Kotin, Karen Call, Ron Plass, Bill Lederer, and David Lewis.

Along the way, I had the good fortune to work with Peternelle van Arsdale, who provided invaluable editorial guidance and said the magic words, "Move the men to the sidelines and give your women their due."

Had I not taken that step, my book never would have landed in the skillful hands of my editor, Claire Zion, who helped me take this book further than I ever thought possible. I'm a better writer today for having worked with you. And special thanks to my agent, Kevan Lyon. You continue to amaze me with your dedication and patience. All writers should be so lucky as to have an agent like you.

ACKNOWLEDGMENTS

My love and gratitude to Pam and Andy Jaffe; Jerry and Andrea Rosen; Joey Perilman; Devon Rosen, my father, whose memory will never fade; and especially to my mother, Deborah "Pyack" Rosen, who has been my rock and has encouraged me every step of the way—"thank you" doesn't begin to cover it.

Last, a special thanks goes to Mindy Mailman for always bringing the funny and always being there. To Brenda Klem, my "frem," for your patience and countless brainstorming sessions, for reading and always cheering me on. To Sara Gruen, my critique partner and sister separated at birth, thank you for believing and for not letting me give up on this novel. You told me so! And to Joe Esselin, this one's for you.

"We find many things to which the prohibition of them constitutes the only temptation."

—William Hazlitt

DOLLFACE

BOOK ONE

Chicago
1923–1924

THE ESCAPE HATCH

"You don't smile much, do you," said the man next to me.

"Smiling gets me into trouble."

"I'm sure it does." His eyes wandered the length of my body, from my shoulders to my shoes. I wondered if he could tell that I'd faked my stockings and that my seams had been drawn on with an eyebrow pencil. I tucked one leg behind the other, hoping to hide my ingenuity.

It was Friday night and I was at the Five Star, sitting next to this nameless man who'd just bought me my second bourbon. Glancing at my fingers, peppered with paper cuts and ribbon stains, I closed my eyes, trying to ease the headache I'd had since Tuesday. A chorus of Smith Coronas striking letterhead and the ping of two dozen carriage returns going back and forth nonstop echoed inside my head. I had just survived my first week as a typewriter for the insurance offices of Schlemmer Weiss & Unger. The job was dull—a real flat tire—and the pay was lousy. Of the twenty dollars I got in my weekly salary envelope, eight had already been grabbed by my landlady when I stopped by the rooming house to change out of my work clothes. I didn't know how twelve dollars would carry me until my next payday, but I refused to admit that my mother was right. I was eighteen years old. Other girls my age got jobs and lived on their own. They managed. I'd find a way, too.

I took another sip of bourbon. It went down easy, smooth as Coca-Cola. I'd been in only a handful of speakeasies but I could see why they were so popular. Everyone was smiling and laughing, having a swell time. From the get-go, anyone with half a brain could have told you Prohibition wasn't going to prohibit a damn thing. It only added to the allure of that forbidden fruit. People who didn't even like to drink before 1920 now knocked on unmarked doors, whispered their way inside and lingered over rows of gin and whiskey bottles lined up like tin soldiers. If the Volstead Act had outlawed chewing gum instead of liquor, what do you think we would have chomped on with our friends, spent our last dollar on, and kept hidden in our garters? We always want what's just outside our reach.

But Prohibition and speakeasies aside, I was no stranger to liquor.

"Good lord," the man said, shaking his head, "how the hell can an itty-bitty dame like you drink so damn much?"

I wasn't all that itty-bitty, not really. If I'd been standing, he would have seen that I was five-foot-three. But I was skinny. My body was as straight and sleek as my hair, which I wore bobbed to my chin with a thick row of bangs. Between my jet-black hair and dark eyes, made even darker thanks to my kohl eyeliner, I had that modern look, and it wasn't lost on men like the one sitting next to me.

"I'm serious," said the man. "How'd a little lady like you learn to drink like that?"

"My mother," I said, swirling my bourbon in my glass. "She

soaked my pacifiers in schnapps when I was a baby so I'd fall asleep."

"Well, I'll be damned." He knocked back his drink and fished a cigarette from the crumpled package peeking out of his breast pocket.

I finished that round with him, slid off my barstool and went looking for Evelyn. I was bushed and ready to go home. As I teetered across the wooden floor, I knew it was too late to re-think that second bourbon or the meager bowl of soup I'd re-garded as dinner. I perched my hand on the wall to keep the room from tilting.

The Five Star was packed, everyone sardined in, standing shoulder-to-shoulder. Couples filled the dance floor, doing the bunny hug and the Charleston while the South Side Jazzers played onstage. I went upstairs and found the second floor was just as crowded. Cigarette girls roamed the room in their short skirts and top hats, peddling trays of Lucky Strike cigarettes and White Owl cigars. Clouds of smoke floated above the blackjack tables manned by dealers dressed in red vests and matching bow ties.

Off in the corner, I spotted Evelyn by the slot machines, standing alongside a man with an unlit cigar jammed in his mouth. She'd been end-of-the-week beat when we'd arrived but not anymore. Each time the man pulled the one-armed bandit, she jumped up and down, her long brown spiral curls bouncing as she clapped, hoping the cherries lined up.

I accidentally bumped into a man at the craps table who had a floozy on either side of him. I apologized without really look-ing at him. It wasn't until after he threw the dice and his girls gave off an exaggerated round of *"Awwwwwwws"* that he got my attention. Tall, fit, and with his necktie askew and shirtsleeves rolled up, he had a slightly rumpled look about him that only truly handsome men could get away with.

"Can't win 'em all, can you?" he said, giving me the once-over along with a mischievous grin, a kind of wonky, self-assured smirk no doubt prompted by the scores of innocent hopefuls who'd preceded me. It was men like him who ruined it for the next guy who came along. And there'd be the next one and probably one after that, because men like him were never anyone's last stop on the road to happily ever after.

I was exhausted and not about to give him the satisfaction of knowing he was as good-looking as he thought he was. "Better luck next time," I said, and turned to walk away.

"Hey, not so fast, doll." He grabbed my hand, and it touched off a spark I wasn't expecting. "I was winning until you showed up. What's your rush?" He flashed that smile of his just as a few locks of hair fell forward onto his brow. Soft brown, the color of chestnuts. "If you don't mind my saying"—he leaned in closer—"you're a beautiful-looking woman. You must be a model."

"Oh, c'mon." I laughed and rolled my eyes. "Can't you feed a girl a better line than that?"

"Okay, then how about an actress?"

"Please—do girls actually believe you when you say things like that?" I crossed my arms, hoping to stop my urge to reach over and brush that lock of hair aside with my fingertips.

"C'mon," he said. "Let me buy you a drink. What's your name?"

"Vera." I looked over at Evelyn. She was still with that man at the slots, and there was no way she'd be ready to go. She'd no sooner leave his side than he'd leave a hot machine.

Even though I'd had those two bourbons already, I agreed to let him buy me a drink. He introduced himself as Tony Liolli and boy, I could tell right off he was some operator.

We had almost made it to the bar when a red light overhead flashed and an alarm sounded. I flinched, it gave me such a start.

Tony put his arm down like a crossing gate in front of me. "Oh, goddammit!" The alarm sounded again, longer this time.

"What is that? What's happening?" I gripped his arm, sobering up fast, thinking the place was on fire. My heart was racing.

"*Raid!*" someone shouted. "It's the feds! Raid! Everybody clear out!"

All at once people began hollering as they shoved past us, rushing toward the stairs. A dealer rammed into me, nearly knocking me over, while he and another barkeeper raced around, trying to get rid of any traces of liquor. I saw one of them pull a handle on the side of the bar and all the bottles on the shelves went *whoosh* and disappeared through a trapdoor. Two other men bolted past me, grabbed hold of the bar and flipped it upside down, making it look like an innocent hutch. Within seconds all the slot machines were spun around; their flip sides were disguised as bookcases.

"C'mon, we gotta get out of here." Tony grabbed my hand and weaved me through the crowd, heading for the doorway. The alarm blasted again and again while everybody charged toward the staircase, knocking tables and chairs out of the way. I trampled over someone's lost fedora and nearly tripped on an abandoned pocketbook.

"Wait!" I turned around, my heart pumping like mad. "Where's Evelyn? *Evelyn!*"

"Who the hell's Evelyn?"

"Evelyn. My roommate."

"Forget Evelyn," Tony shouted back, "unless you wanna see the inside of a paddy wagon."

"Evelyn? Evelyn!"

"C'mon. Now!"

After one last look for my friend, Tony and I were on the

move, working our way toward the front, when the direction of the crowd suddenly reversed and people started backing up, rearing into one another. The feds were heading in, and everyone who'd been trying to get down the stairs rushed back to the main room. A heavyset man wearing too much cologne stepped on my foot just as the agents burst inside with their whistles blowing shrill, high-pitched chirps.

"C'mon," Tony said, pulling at me. "Over here." He moved fast, yanking me toward the back of the room. When we dead-ended into a concrete wall, I froze. But Tony grabbed hold of a brass knob and turned it, and the wall slid to the right. It was just a facade concealing a rickety staircase. The dealers, barkeepers, waiters, and even the cigarette girls crowded in behind us.

"C'mon—hurry!"

I took one last desperate look around for Evelyn. "Evelyn? Evelyn!" It was no use.

Tony herded me and a dozen others down the stairs. There was no railing and not much light until we made it to the first-floor landing. Tony and another man unlatched a second doorway that led to another flight of stairs. We heard screams and cries coming from the upper floors. It sounded like a stampede.

When we reached the basement, Tony guided us to a long, narrow tunnel littered with garbage, smashed beer and whiskey bottles. It smelled of urine, and God knows what else. I began to tremble. I couldn't see much, but I knew we must have somehow entered the sewer tunnel. Something scurried across the floor and I yelped, watching a long, skinny tail whip back and forth before disappearing into the shadows.

Tony hustled the cigarette girls and the other men toward the tunnel's opening and one by one they vanished into the darkness. It was my turn. "Go on," he said when I hesitated. "I'm right behind you. Go!"

It was freezing and though the air was stale and sour, I gasped for breath. The tunnel grew narrower, and something was dripping from above, landing in my hair and on my shoulders. I heard the sound of shoes sloshing through the water on the floor as the others made their way ahead of us. With each step, more filthy, icy water seeped in through my soles, soaking my toes.

Each time I asked Tony where we were, he said, "Keep going. Don't stop, Vera! C'mon!"

"Okay—all right! I'm going, I'm going!" My feet inched along in the darkness, my fingers grazing the dripping, crumbling tunnel walls. The water was up to my ankles now and I could barely feel my feet; my toes had long since gone numb. Deeper into the tunnel, the shadows began to fade, eventually vanishing until everything became the blackest of blacks. I couldn't see my hands in front of me. The wall was all I had, my only source of reference. I was surrounded by the sounds of sluicing water and rodents scratching and scurrying about. If Tony was still behind me, I had no sense of him. I was alone in that endless blackness, shuffling and groping my way forward.

When I thought I couldn't take one more step, I heard the purr of automobiles and the rumble of the streetcars overhead. Shadows of the others came into view as we worked our way toward another set of stairs. A haze of light flooded down and I raced ahead, splashing through the sewer water.

Once I made it to the top, Tony was right behind me. I couldn't believe where we were: We ended up on the sidewalk directly across the street from the Five Star. Paddy wagons were parked in front and federal agents were everywhere. I saw handcuffs on the man who'd bought me the bourbons earlier. He was being loaded into a paddy wagon along with everyone else who hadn't made it out in time. I did another frantic search for Evelyn. *Oh, God, please don't let her be arrested.* What if the feds had her? How would I get her out of jail? It took money to do that and twelve dollars was all I had to my name. *Evelyn, where are you!*

More people were hustled into the paddy wagons while others raced past us up and down the sidewalk, distancing themselves from the action.

Tony checked his pocket watch. "Think you'll be all right now?"

"You're leaving?" My voice went up an octave and I shivered. Goose bumps freckled my damp arms and legs. It was December, my feet were soaking and my coat was being held hostage inside the Five Star.

"I wouldn't stick around much longer if I were you."

"So you *are* leaving?"

He leaned over and kissed my cheek. "See ya 'round, Vera."

"Yeah. Sure. See you 'round." I stared at the tops of my waterlogged shoes. I was standing like a schoolgirl, pigeon-toed. I saw where the sewer water had washed away the seams I'd drawn on the backs of my calves. When I looked up again, Tony had already disappeared around the corner.

Don't you dare cry. Do not!

Suddenly I spotted Evelyn halfway down the block, standing beneath a streetlight, hugging herself to keep warm. I began to breathe again. She searched up and down the street like a child lost at the fair, strands of her long brown curls blowing across her pale face.

"Evelyn! Hey, Ev!"

She saw me running toward her and raced in my direction. We collided, throwing our arms around each other, half laughing, half crying, both of us talking at once.

"Oh my God." She clasped a hand over her heart. "How did we end up in the middle of a raid?"

"I can't believe what just happened." I was so relieved, I hugged her again. "C'mon, let's get the hell out of here." I reached into my pocket for a dollar bill, waved it in the air and flagged down a taxicab.

DIAMONDS AND GEMS

A few weeks later, Evelyn sat on the side of my bed shaking me awake like she did most mornings. "C'mon, get up. It's ten after seven."

I groaned as I opened my eyes. It couldn't possibly be morning already.

I'd recently taken a second job so I could make ends meet. One of the girls in the rooming house had told me about it. Said I could earn two dollars a night modeling jewelry for a man who worked fancy parties for Chicago's elite.

The two dollars I'd been promised turned out to be a buck fifty, but I needed the money. That extra seven fifty or ten fifty a week, depending on if I worked every night—especially during the holiday season—meant I didn't have to choose between making my rent and going to bed hungry. Plus, I got to wear pretty dresses and real diamonds and pearls. Working those parties put me smack in the center of a lot of impressive, glamorous people and you never knew who you'd meet. The day after a party I'd always see the photographs all over the society pages. Once I even managed to get myself in a picture. I recognized the dress first and realized the shoulder and back of the head belonged to me. I clipped the photograph and tucked it up in the corner of my mirror. Someday, I told myself, I would be important enough to be the subject of a society page photograph.

"I didn't hear you come in," Evelyn said. "Was it very late?"

"After one." I yawned. "I missed my train and had to wait forty minutes for the next one."

"Poor thing." Evelyn bent down and stroked my hair. She didn't need to work a second job. She was a faster typist than I was and the best speller among us typewriters. Mr. Schlemmer insisted she proofread his most important documents, even if another girl had typed it. That right there made her weekly pay envelope ten dollars thicker than mine. Not that I begrudged her. She'd helped me plenty, lending me a dollar or two when I came up short, and it wasn't as if she had much to spare.

"C'mon, now," she said. "You have to get up! You'll be late."

"I'm always late." I rolled onto my back and rubbed my eyes with the heel of my hand.

Grabbing her toothbrush, Evelyn slung her towel over her shoulder and shuffled down the hall to the bathroom we shared with the other girls on the floor.

Evelyn Schulman and I had been best friends from the time we were seven. Hers was the house on the corner, the big one with the steep front steps. Evelyn's father owned a sporting goods store on Grand Avenue and all five of the sisters had matching bicycles, lined up one after another on their front lawn. I was jealous—not of the bicycles, but of Evelyn for having all those sisters. I didn't have any sisters or brothers. I didn't even have a father. He died when I was four years old. They found his body behind a saloon on Whiskey Row. His head, hands and feet were missing. Butchered like an animal. My mother never talked about his murder. She'd never used that word or even said out loud that he'd been killed. When she did speak of him it was always followed by, "May he rest in peace." She acted like the rest of it hadn't happened. But whether we called it by name, whether or not we acknowledged it, I slept with a light on until I was fifteen. I kept a lookout, leery of unfamiliar motorcars parked outside our house and strangers coming down our sidewalk. That was how I spent the bulk of my childhood: keeping watch, waiting for and expecting something else to happen.

Growing up it was just my mother and me, and Evelyn, my chosen sister. When we turned sixteen, our mothers sent us to the Queen Esther dances. Every Saturday night in the summertime they held dances outside the synagogue, beneath a big white tent. The music was never any good and the boys didn't know how to do the bunny hug or the black bottom. But still, we went week after week, until my mother heard that I'd been spotted behind the tent, sitting on a crate with my skirt hiked up to my knees, smoking cigarettes and playing five-card stud with a group of boys. That was the last Queen Esther dance for me. My mother was angry but not surprised. She was used to me stirring up trouble. By the time I turned fifteen I was sick of being too afraid to live. That's when I got busy, making up for lost time. There was newfound freedom in acting daring and bold, taking risks and seeing how much I could get away with.

I must have dozed off again, because the next thing I knew Evelyn was standing over my bed. "It's half past seven. C'mon. You're not even dressed yet."

I dragged myself out of bed, chilled as soon as my bare feet touched the hardwood floor. There was a draft coming in through the window where it didn't seal all the way. Our room was cramped, barely big enough for our twin beds and a set of bureaus. The faucet in the bathroom down the hall dripped, the boiler in the basement clanked all winter long and everywhere you looked paint was chipping and peeling.

Evelyn and I had moved in six weeks before. We'd both recently turned eighteen and had wanted out of our parents' homes. Evelyn's parents were strict, setting curfews fit for a child, not letting her wear makeup or date college-age boys. And I knew that unless I wanted to end up like my mother—alone and chained to a miserable family business—I had to get out of her house. So even though I was stuck in a dilapidated shack, it was still better than living with my mother. Especially since she was the main reason I'd moved out in the first place.

I dressed quickly, changing from my nightdress into a white shirtwaist and long black skirt. It was exactly the same outfit Evelyn had on, the same as all the other typewriters would be wearing that day and every day. I supposed since they called us *typewriters* it made sense to dress us like a bunch of Smith Coronas.

With three minutes to spare, Evelyn and I marched into the building and took our places at the insurance offices of Schlemmer Weiss & Unger. I yawned off and on until noon, and while the others ate lunch in the cafeteria, I curled up on a chair in the back and napped, the wooden slats pressing into my spine. I was more tired than hungry and besides, a bowl of barley soup cost a quarter. A roll with butter was a dime. Coffee was another nickel on top of that. If you wanted applesauce or gelatin, that was another dime. I figured by skipping lunch I could save two dollars and fifty cents a week. Besides, I could usually sneak some appetizers later at whatever party I was assigned to.

At five o'clock, I said good-bye to Evelyn and the others and headed from the Loop toward the Drake Hotel on Michigan Avenue. I was scheduled to work a Christmas party in the grand ballroom for a prominent law firm. Hopefully the hotel would be swarming with successful, eligible bachelors. But all I could do was look and not touch. At least not while I was working. My job was to walk through the party, smile and hand out Mr. Borowitz's calling card to anyone interested in purchasing his jewelry. I wasn't to speak unless spoken to, and I wasn't, under any circumstances, to discuss the jewelry or the prices.

When I reached the el platform, I found myself crowded in between rows of businessmen and factory workers, shopgirls and office clerks. The first train arrived and before I could inch my way toward the front of the line, the cars filled up and the doors closed.

I had time and decided to walk despite the cold wind coming off Lake Michigan whipping around and through me. Even in between gusts, I had to hold my hat in place. The sidewalks were crowded with holiday shoppers darting in and out of stores, their arms loaded down with parcels. The traffic was backed up to the bridge at Wacker with drivers blasting their horns as pedestrians weaved in and around the automobiles.

When I made my way down Michigan Avenue and arrived at the Drake, a footman, dressed in his red-and-gold uniform, held the door for me as I crossed from one world into another. I paused for a moment, rubbing the chill from my hands as I took in the garlands, the wreaths and glittery decorations on the walls. The clamor of motorcars and trolleys was replaced by the delicate clinking of crystal goblets and silver tines on bone china. The dark, winter cold was overcome by the warm hum of a healthy furnace and the glow of chandeliers hanging overhead.

Downstairs in the chambermaids' quarters, I changed from my typewriter clothes into the blue silk dress waiting for me with my name pinned to the sleeve. It was a swell number and flowed off my shoulders like it was made for me. The hem was one of those handkerchief styles that showed my kneecaps when

I walked. They even gave me a pair of matching shoes with a two-inch heel. Though my cheeks and nose were still red from the cold, I applied rouge and some lipstick. I brushed my shiny, inky black bob into place, smoothing down my bangs to cover the faint chickenpox scar above my right eyebrow.

When I was ready, I went upstairs to check in with Mr. Borowitz, an oversize man whose thick, fleshy neck doubled down, overlapping his collar. Three other girls were ahead of me and he carefully draped them in earrings, necklaces, brooches, cocktail rings and bracelets. I stood still while he trimmed me as if I were a Christmas tree, reaching over and pinching a diamond earring onto each of my earlobes before he finished decorating me, sliding an emerald bracelet onto my wrist and topping me off with a matching necklace. It was always a thrill when I heard the clasp lock into place. It meant those jewels were mine—if only for a few hours.

This was my favorite part of the job. After I was dressed and wearing my jewels, just before the guests arrived, I had five or ten minutes to wander through the busy hotel. Nobody knew that dress didn't belong to me, and that I didn't have ten others just like it hanging in my wardrobe back home. Nobody knew the gems weren't mine, either. As the heels of my loaner shoes clicked against the marble floor, I felt people watching me and in that moment I could be anyone I wanted to be.

Each night I tried on a new identity along with the gown and jewels. Sometimes I'd be a famous chorus girl—a Ziegfeld girl, or a moving-picture star like Clara Bow or Lillian Gish. Sometimes I'd pretend I was the daughter of a banker or a wealthy industrialist. Other times I was just famous for famous's sake, the type of woman men fought over and women envied.

At seven o'clock the band began playing a jazzy number, *The Uptown Stomp*, as we girls took our places inside the ballroom, trying to appear as inanimate as the gilt-framed portraits on the walls. A giant Christmas tree, with gold and red ornaments, stood in the corner of the room, its lights twinkling as the guests filtered in. The men were dressed in tuxedos with top hats and carried walking sticks; the women glistened in beaded gowns and matching cloche hats. They puffed on cigarettes and sipped champagne, their glasses kissed with ruby red lipstick. They flitted and fluttered while waiters worked through their effervescent wake, holding silver platters of pastries filled with crabmeat, butterflied shrimp, and deviled eggs topped with dollops of caviar. When no one was looking, I grabbed a few.

A photographer asked me to step aside while he arranged a group of couples standing to my left. After squaring one man's shoulders, he asked another man to crouch down while scooching his date in closer. I imagined myself as part of this group, mentally inserting myself into the shot, taking my place between the two men, looping my arms through the arm of the taller one, my fingertips gently caressing the fabric of his expensive suit. After adjusting the bellows of his camera, the photographer told them to smile as he raised his flash bag and—*poof*—released a burst of light and smokeless powder into the air. As soon as he was finished, the cluster of couples dispersed like billiard balls after a solid break. I desperately wanted to follow them.

The band struck up a new snazzy number and I watched as more couples crowded the dance floor.

"You look like a gal who'd like to dance," said a short, stocky man wearing a crooked bow tie and a Santa hat. He pointed at my shoes.

I didn't realize I'd been tapping my foot to the music. "I'm afraid I'm working here tonight."

"Oh?" His mouth dropped open as his hand reached up and pulled off his hat. "How much is a dance?"

"Oh, no." I shook my head. "God, no. Not *that* kind of working." Before I realized I'd just been insulted, I opened my silver card case. "That's my boss," I said, pointing to Mr. Borowitz's name on the card. "He'd pitch a fit if I started dancing, but thank you anyway."

After he'd replaced his Santa hat and moved on to the woman behind me, asking her to dance, I returned to my rigid modeling pose.

A young couple, looking like they'd just stepped out of a Marshall Field's display window, stopped to inquire about my necklace. I listened as they debated whether it was the right length and size for a particular gown the woman was planning to wear to a New Year's Eve ball. Evidently they weren't sold on the necklace they'd seen earlier at Cartier. The woman was about my age and I would have bet good money that she'd never worked a day in her life. No doubt she thought the handsome, wealthy man on her arm was her birthright. I would have killed to slip inside her skin for just a day. Hell, just an hour. What did it feel like to have no worries beyond choosing a piece of jewelry that some rich man would buy for you? While they contemplated the necklace, a waiter appeared with a fresh tray of deviled eggs. My stomach growled as they both helped themselves, balancing their eggs on the embossed cocktail napkins.

"Exactly how much is this necklace?" the man asked.

As instructed, I opened my silver card case, and as I handed him Mr. Borowitz's card, someone pinched my behind. I spun around, only to find half a dozen men within pinching distance who would look neither at me nor at my bottom.

"Oh, sweetie," said the woman to me, fisting up her napkin, "would you be a dear?" She placed her dirty cocktail napkin in my hand. I glanced at the napkin and back up at the woman, searching her heavy-lashed eyes, hoping she'd rethink the request.

But all I got was a dismissive smile. I made my way to the opposite side of the room, pitched the napkin and snatched two canapés from a passing tray.

The band continued to play as couples moved about the dance floor, spilling drinks and filling the air with clouds of cigarette and cigar smoke. It wasn't in my nature to stand back and watch the others having all the fun. Time seemed to pass slowly but finally the party was over and I went downstairs to change into my work clothes, which always felt rough against my skin after I'd been clothed in real silk. I had replaced the good wool coat that I'd lost in the Five Star raid with a secondhand wraparound. It had a torn lining and a hole in the pocket that I kept forgetting to mend. I'd lost a lipstick that way, and my favorite hair comb.

Upstairs in the lobby, Mr. Borowitz helped me off with the bracelet and the necklace. It wasn't until I went to unclip the earrings that I realized one of them was missing. While Mr. Borowitz impatiently tapped his foot, the panic grew inside me. I scoured the floor and patted myself down from my ears to my hips, but the earring was gone.

"You'd better hope to God you find it," Mr. Borowitz called after me as I went to retrace my steps.

I returned to the ballroom, frantically asking the waiters whether they'd seen the earring, checking with the musicians as they packed up their instruments. I went back to the chambermaids' quarters. I checked inside my shirtwaist, inside my skirt. I shook out my wrap coat and emptied my pocketbook. I scoured every inch of the vanity. Sweat broke out along my forehead as I went back to Mr. Borowitz to explain that I couldn't find it and apologize.

"You're damn right you're sorry. Do you have any idea how much those earrings are worth? Two hundred bucks! I knew the minute I laid eyes on you. I should never have trusted you. You probably stole it, you—"

"Hey!" My voice echoed off the marble floors and ceiling, loud enough to shut him up. I was so angry I was shaking. "That's enough! I'm not a thief. It was an accident. I said I was sorry. You want to fire me? Fine. Go ahead and fire me. But don't you dare accuse me of stealing. And besides, if I was going to steal your damn earring, don't you think I'd be smart enough to take the whole pair."

I heard someone behind me clapping. "Well done, young lady."

I turned around and there was a man coming toward us. He was beautifully dressed in a double-breasted pin-striped suit with a gold watch chain hanging down. His dark hair was parted in the center and slicked back with brilliantine, revealing a lovely widow's peak that pointed like an arrow toward his strong, straight nose.

"This is between me and her. Stay out of it," Borowitz said before turning back toward me. "You owe me two hundred bucks, girlie!"

"I said it was an accident!"

"I want my two hundred bucks!" Borowitz was going red in the face.

"Two hundred?" asked the man with the widow's peak. "Was that two hundred dollars you said?" He reached into his pocket and pulled out a wad of cash thick as a fist. I didn't blink once, watching as he peeled two hundred-dollar bills off the top. Stuffing them into Mr. Borowitz's breast pocket, he said, "I think that ought to cover it."

My jaw flopped open and before I could thank him, the man turned to me and said, "You seem like a nice girl. Go home." He reached into his pocket again and put a five-dollar bill in my hand. "It's late. Take a taxicab."

"But"—I held out the bill to him—"you've already done more than—"

"Take the money." He reached over and closed my fingers around it. "It's cold out there tonight."

I stared at my clenched hand and when I looked up, the man with the widow's peak was walking out of the Drake with his arm draped over the shoulder of a sensational-looking blonde. Lucky girl, whoever she was. She had a good man looking out for her. You just knew nothing bad was going to happen to her as long as she was with him. God, how I wanted to know what that felt like. This wasn't envy; it was honest-to-goodness longing.

ENTER IZZY SELTZER

I lined my eyes in front of the mirror, making them dark like the models in the fashion magazines. Evelyn and I were getting dolled up for a Saturday night on the town. It was my first day off in a week after taking a new job working the late shift as a switchboard operator. I made seventy-five cents an hour and had Saturdays and Sundays off. Because I had to work Monday night—and that was New Year's Eve—Evelyn and I decided we'd bring in 1924 a few days early.

Evelyn took a roll of bandages from her bureau drawer and wrapped them around her breasts, smashing herself down in front. Thank God I was flat-chested. I would have hated doing that. I couldn't have worn that rubber reducing girdle of hers, either. The ads said it melted away excess pounds, but all it did was make her sweat. And really, Evelyn wasn't fat. She just had those big boobs, but she didn't need to wear a rubber girdle.

While Evelyn brushed out her long brown curls, I smoothed down my bangs and combed through the blunt ends of my bob. Puckering my lips, I painted them a deep bloodred, making them look like a cherub's. I slipped into a frock and wrapped the strand of pearls around my neck that I'd borrowed from Barbara Lewis down the hall, a perky little blonde with a gap-toothed smile. Nothing rallied Barbara's support like a date or special occasion. Eager to help, she'd send you off in a dress or lend you a hat. She'd even let you borrow her jewelry and evening bags, too. Barbara was the one you went to for clothes and I was the one the girls turned to for makeup tips. I had a knack for it and showed them how to line their eyes and apply their rouge. Even Helen next door, with her bad overbite and ruddy complexion, managed to look pretty when I was finished with her.

"How's this?" Evelyn turned to face me, holding the black grease-stick liner in her hand. "Did I make them even this time?"

I tilted my head and studied her dark brown eyes for a moment. "Almost."

She frowned and looked again in the mirror.

"It's not bad," I told her, reaching for the liner. "Let me just get the outer edges for you."

By the time we were ready to leave for the night, Evelyn and I looked right in fashion, just as long as you didn't get too close to see a mismatched button here, a loose thread there, or the safety pins holding up our hems.

We rode a crowded el car, holding on to the leather ceiling straps for balance until our stop at Lawrence, where we got off and walked over to Broadway. When we arrived at the Green Mill, the hostess stood in the doorway ushering us inside. It was early, but the place was already stomping. The Green Mill had the best jazz in the city and I'd heard it was the place to meet eligible men. That was a plus since Evelyn was still hoping to find a date for New Year's. We'd barely gotten our coats checked and already a young man with a neat little goatee came over.

"How's about a dance?" he asked, looking at me.

I could tell by the way he snapped his fingers that he had no rhythm. "Maybe later," I said. "Mama needs a cocktail first."

"Well, let me take care of that for you."

Even though they weren't the kind of fellas I was looking for—no flair, no charisma, no sex appeal—I never had a problem meeting men when we went out. Not like Evelyn. It was harder for her. Usually I'd bring the guys over and introduce them to her. That's how she met Izzy Seltzer. She can blame that one on me.

I wasn't even finished with my first drink when Izzy came up to me, twisted his pinkie ring and said, "You're a doll, you know that? A living doll."

He did have those movie-star looks with his strong jawline and cleft chin, but I wasn't falling for his charms. He was just like that Tony Liolli, and something told me I couldn't trust him.

But Evelyn couldn't take her eyes off him. "Who was that?" she whispered when he walked away. "Do you know him?"

After watching her follow him around the room with her puppy-dog eyes, I finally went and got Izzy and brought him over to her.

"What are you girls up to tonight?" he asked, turning toward me, looking at my mouth first and then my body and then my eyes.

"Just out for a little fun," answered Evelyn. "What about you? What are you up to?"

"I gotta get a drink," he said, still looking at me. "You girls need another?"

Evelyn and I held up our full glasses.

"Do you think he's coming back?" Evelyn fretted after he'd walked away, craning her neck to keep an eye on him.

"Relax. He's just at the bar. And when he *does* come back, don't act so eager."

Evelyn nodded, still looking at Izzy.

"Just relax."

Izzy was skirting his way through the crowd with his drink in hand and I cringed when Evelyn waved him over. "Hey, Izzy!" she called out. "Over here!"

So while Evelyn jabbered away with Izzy, I watched a group of loudmouths at a front table playing a drinking game that involved four cigarettes and three matchsticks.

The one dealing out cigarettes saw me staring. "Wanna play?" he asked.

"What's the object?" It seemed to me that no matter what the outcome, they all took a drink anyway.

"To get as drunk as you can, as fast as you can." They cracked up laughing and started in on another round.

"Sounds swell, but I think I'll just watch."

As I fished an olive out of my martini, I looked up and noticed a short, round man coming through the doorway wearing a canary yellow overcoat, cuffed trousers, and a homburg. He was accompanied by two men considerably taller than him.

As soon as she saw him, the hostess was on her feet. "Well, if it isn't Snorky! How ya been, Al?" She held a sprig of mistletoe above his head and planted a big kiss on his mouth. She didn't bother with the other two men. Draping her arm across the short man's shoulder, she led him to the center booth that had remained empty all night despite the packed club. Obviously it had been reserved for him.

The table of loudmouths dropped it down a notch or two when he walked by. I overheard one of them say, "Yeah, that's him. That's Al Capone."

"What's he doing up here on the North Side?" the one fellow asked.

"Capone's a big jazz buff. He's a regular here."

I glanced back over my shoulder. I saw the faint scars on his face, the thick cigar clamped in the corner of his mouth. Wow, that was him, all right! I had no idea this place was Capone's hangout. He looked younger in person than in his newspaper photos. I remembered seeing one of him taken at a White Sox game where people were lining up to shake his hand, have their picture taken with him.

Not long after arriving, Capone seemed to notice something with a start. He got up, flanked by the two big guys. My pulse jumped when I realized he was heading for Izzy.

Removing his cigar, Capone said, "What's the matter? You and your girls get lost tonight?" He gazed over at Evelyn.

Izzy propped a cigarette between his lips and struck a match against the underside of the bar. "Just thought I'd see what you palookas were up to."

"Too bad you can't stay long enough to finish your drink."

Izzy took a drag off his cigarette and exhaled in Capone's face. I couldn't take my eyes off his scars. One ran from his ear to the side of his mouth. The other was etched along his jaw.

"Either show yourself out or I'll have my boys here do it for you." He gave Izzy the kind of look you didn't argue with.

Capone went back to his booth, but the two tall guys stayed with us. I glared at Izzy, wondering what the hell he was waiting for. In my mind, I was already halfway out the door.

Finally, Izzy flicked his cigarette to the floor and ground it out beneath his heel. "This place is dead. C'mon, let's go where the real action is."

"Was that really Capone?" Evelyn asked as Izzy led us outside.

"Shhh." I gave her a look.

Obviously Capone didn't want Izzy sticking around the Green Mill and I wasn't sure I wanted Izzy sticking around us, either.

"Ev." I pulled her aside as we followed Izzy down the street. "I don't think we should go with him."

"Oh, c'mon. Besides," she said under her breath, "I already blew my taxicab money and at least he can give us a ride home later."

"Here we are," Izzy said, pointing to the motorcar parked out front. It was a real sharp tan-and-black touring car with velvet upholstery. As soon as she saw it Evelyn gave me a look, her red lips growing as big and round as her eyes. We'd never ridden in a motorcar like that and while I may not have liked Izzy Seltzer, I was madly in love with his automobile. When he opened the car door I climbed into the back and Evelyn slid into the front seat, sitting as close as she could to him.

I glanced out the window as we whipped past the streetlamps, empty sidewalks and darkened storefronts. It was late; the city had turned in for the night but we were just getting started.

I ran my hand along the velvet upholstery, the leather trim. I had no idea where Izzy was taking us, but by now my reservations about him were replaced with expectations for an exciting night on the town.

Izzy took us to a place called the Meridian on the north side of town. It was a huge limestone building with a big red awning and a circular driveway filled with expensive-looking automobiles.

As soon as we stepped inside, I felt underdressed in my jersey frock. The women were all in beautiful fringed and sequined dresses. Some wore jeweled turbans, and others had plumed headdresses. The men were just as stylish in three-piece tailored suits. There was a big band up onstage and the place was jumping. Between the Christmas tree and the holiday lights sparkling about the room, it already felt like New Year's Eve in there.

Evelyn tugged on my sleeve and pointed. "Vera, look!"

"Oh my God! That's Charlie Chaplin!" He was sitting at a front table, less than three feet away. Without his funny mustache and bushy eyebrows he was a handsome man with thick, wavy dark hair and surprisingly somber-looking eyes.

We started for his table, hoping to get his autograph, but a couple of photographers cut in front of us to take his picture. Their flashbulbs popped like firecrackers, sending clouds of smoke hovering above their cameras. I stood there, unable to take my eyes off him. I couldn't believe it. First Al Capone and now Charlie Chaplin. Capone may have been a gangster, but he was famous, too. I was a believer in signs, and I took this as a big one that things were about to change for me.

After a round of drinks, Evelyn took off with Izzy while I danced with a college boy from the University of Chicago. He wore two-tone shoes that kept perfect time with my toes. While he shuffled me from side to side, other couples on the dance floor were kicking up their heels and shaking their shoulders and behinds, keeping a perfect beat with the music.

"What do you say we mix it up a little?" I said.

"Sure thing." He twirled me and lost what little rhythm he had.

In the middle of that number I broke away from him and started doing a crazy little dance step, snapping my fingers and swaying my hips. I kept my eye on the boy as my borrowed pearls swung to and fro and my bobbed hair swished to the left and then to the right. The trumpeter gave me a wink, and people turned to watch as I circled around the college boy, who stood there like a maypole.

When the number was up, I thanked him for the dance and headed to the bar. As I was catching my breath, someone leaned in close and whispered, "You always dance like that in public?"

I turned and nearly lost my balance. Standing before me was the man with the widow's peak from the Drake Hotel. I hadn't expected to ever see him again and my heart took a leap forward. He reached across the bar for my drink and placed it in my hand.

"Well, fancy seeing you here," I said, trying to play it cool by giving his martini glass a clink with mine. "You really helped me out of a jam. I never got to thank you for—"

"Not necessary." He smiled. "Just please tell me you're not still working for that *schmendrick*. You know what it is? A *schmendrick*?"

I nearly spilled my drink. "You know Yiddish?"

"What Jew doesn't?"

I looked him up and down. "You're Jewish?"

"You sound so surprised."

He was nothing like the Jewish boys I'd grown up with. For one thing, he didn't look Jewish. He had a strong chin and a slender nose. His hair was dark, almost black like mine, and he had that widow's peak that I found sexy in a strange sort of way. I decided he was nice-looking. Maybe not handsome like that Izzy Seltzer, but he had a certain something. There was an elegance to him and he was wearing another expensive-looking three-piece suit. He had style—no doubt about that. He smiled and it sent a ripple of excitement through my body.

"What's your name, Dollface?"

"Vera. Vera Abramowitz."

"Well, there you have it. We Jews have to stick together, don't we?" He rocked back on his heels, showing off his spats.

His name was Shep Green. He was older, maybe twenty-five or twenty-six. Turned out that Izzy worked for him.

"He works for you, huh? Doing what?" I couldn't help but think about Izzy's run-in with Capone earlier. If Izzy knew Capone, chances were so did Shep.

"Izzy's my right-hand man. He helps me run things around here."

"Here?" I searched around the room.

"The Meridian," he said with an easy hand gesture. "I own the club."

My jaw nearly hit the floor. "You own this place? Do you know who's here tonight? Charlie Chaplin!"

"Charlie always pays a visit when he's in town. He just left or else I would have introduced you."

"No foolin'? So you really do own this place?"

"Is that okay with you?" He smiled.

"I'll say." I did a half twirl, taking it all in, making him laugh.

Thanks to Shep, my martini was promoted to champagne and we spent the rest of the night drinking and dancing. And boy, did he know how to dance.

When the band went on break, I excused myself and went to the ladies' lounge to freshen up. Evelyn followed me. It was crowded in there with dozens of women touching up their makeup, their hair, some even painting their fingernails. The air smelled of floral perfumes, nail polish and cigarette smoke.

"Oh, Vera, wait till you hear what Izzy called me." The two of us pushed our way toward the mirror. "He said I was 'a living doll.' Do you believe that!"

"No fooling, huh? He called you a living doll, did he?" I twisted up my lipstick and shot her a glance through the mirror. "I'd watch him if I were you."

"Aw, Vera, he's the berries!"

I smiled. "Like I said, just be careful." Evelyn was always falling for the wrong kind of guys, probably just to spite her parents. They never would have let her out of the house with a fellow like Izzy.

She glanced around and lowered her voice. "Too bad he's a gangster. So is Shep, you know."

"What? What are you talking about?"

She pulled me aside. "Izzy and Shep Green—all the guys here are members of the North Side Gang."

I set my lipstick down, thinking about the bankroll Shep had on him the first night I saw him at the Drake. I knew no one legit walked around with that kind of cash on them. "Are you sure?"

"So help me God." Evelyn held up her hand and swore herself in. "I overheard some girls here talking about it. Look at what just happened at the Green Mill with Capone. And you know *someone's* supplying all the liquor here."

"That doesn't mean anything." I tried to laugh it off. "Everyone in this town serves liquor. And they're not all gangsters." And I told myself not all gangsters were thugs and criminals. Some of them, like Capone, were practically celebrities. Some might argue that gangsters like that were useful people to know as long as you stayed on their good side. So what if Shep rubbed elbows with some bad sorts every now and again. He wasn't the only one. Especially in Chicago.

I turned around, patting my hair in place. "Well, one thing's for sure, Izzy and Shep aren't your typical boring college boys, now, are they?" I ran a finger across my front teeth to clear away any traces of lipstick. "C'mon, they're waiting for us down there." I took one last look in the mirror, thinking, So what if Shep knew Al Capone, he also knew Charlie Chaplin.

STARSTRUCK

was helping Evelyn get ready for a date. It had been a week since she'd met Izzy and already they'd been out twice, including New Year's Eve. Meanwhile, I hadn't heard so much as a peep from Shep Green.

"Want me to ask Izzy about Shep?" She turned her back toward me and lifted her hair, exposing a dozen buttons needing attention. "I could find out if he's seeing anyone."

"No. No." I worked my way up her buttons, starting at her waist. "Don't say anything. But if Izzy asks, tell him I have a date tonight." It wasn't a complete lie. I had been asked out by one of the junior partners at Schlemmer Weiss & Unger but begged off, thinking a good night's sleep sounded more appealing than an evening hearing about claims and contracts.

When I was younger, immersed in romantic novels and still living at home, I couldn't wait until I was old enough to date. No one told me that all the anticipation, the trying on of outfits and the primping of hair, would be wasted on an evening of awkward silences and clumsy uncertainty. Then, to my mother's dismay, the boys started coming around—older boys—and I went along happily, expecting so much more than what I got. Oh, how many times had I sat in soda fountains with nice young men, listening to stories of how they'd run varsity track in college or were captain of their debate teams. They'd nervously bounce their leg beneath the table, making the surface of my soda water tremble as they cleared their throat, licked the perspiration from their upper lip and asked if they could hold my hand. Would Rudolph Valentino have asked Gloria Swanson if he could sweep her off her feet? Where was my leading man? That's what I wondered.

I fastened the last button on Evelyn's dress. She'd borrowed it from Barbara Lewis, who in exchange had borrowed one of Evelyn's hats for a date she had that night with her fiancé. I'd met Monty Perl only once, when he was waiting out front for Barbara. He had a good job, selling restaurant supplies, and was nice-looking with a full, dark mustache. They were getting married that spring, and Barbara was excited about quitting her job, counting the days until she could move out of our dump and into a real home.

Getting married and settling down—if that was all a girl had to look forward to, then cash me out now. I wanted to get married and have a family someday, but I planned on having a lot more fun and excitement before that happened.

Evelyn hummed to herself, irrepressibly giddy. "How do I look?" Her warm eyes fluttered at me.

"I already told you, silly. You're stunning." And she was. She wore her hair down that night, letting her light brown curls reach the center of her back, hanging loosely in a series of delicate spirals. "Your eye makeup is perfect and that shade of lipstick is going to drive Izzy crazy."

"You really think so?"

"I know so."

Evelyn never realized how attractive she was. I suppose that was what happened when you had four older sisters who'd all been crowned Queen Esther at those blasted tent dances.

"So, what are you going to do tonight?" Evelyn asked, coating her lips a second time with her beet-red lipstick.

"This right here." I patted a stack of fashion magazines at the foot of my bed, all of them back issues that I'd found abandoned on streetcars or discarded in the downstairs parlor. It was my first night off in a week. It wasn't even seven o'clock and I could barely keep my eyes open.

After Evelyn left for her date, I helped a couple girls with their makeup, including Helen, who no matter how many times I'd shown her still couldn't put her lipstick on straight.

Afterward, I went to the luncheonette around the corner, ordered a bowl of beef stew and ate my way through the breadbasket. I should have brought a book or magazine with me; I felt self-conscious sitting by myself on a Saturday night. Each time I glanced up an older woman at the counter with a wrinkled face and bags beneath her eyes looked at me in sympathy, as if we had something in common. As soon as I finished my stew, I paid the bill and hurried back to the rooming house.

No one was in the parlor and the halls were all quiet. I tried not to think about the other girls out on dates, dancing and dining. I wished I'd had the money to go to the movie house with the single girls on the floor. Here I was, working myself to exhaustion and still I couldn't spare an extra nickel for the movies. It didn't seem fair.

I got undressed, crawled into bed and leafed through last October's *Vogue*. It struck me that when that issue had been on the newsstands, I was still living at my mother's, dreaming of being on my own and moving downtown. And here I was. I'd done it. But what was next for me? What was the dream now? I wasn't ready to get married and have children. If I'd wanted that, I could have found a nice, decent fella, just like Barbara Lewis did. I wanted something more.

As simple as it sounded, I wanted to have fun! I didn't have much of that growing up. While other children were playing, my mother dragged me into work with her. It wasn't a place for children and I hated it. When I put up enough of a protest, she hired a housekeeper and left me with the emptiness of a fatherless house. I never felt safe, never felt protected, always burdened with worries and fears—both real and imagined.

But I'd broken free from my past and wanted to put it far behind me. Now I wanted just the opposite of what I'd grown up with. I wanted to lead a glamorous life filled with excitement and adventure, with fascinating people and interesting things. I wanted to find a place for myself and know that I belonged somewhere, to someone. I wanted to be important enough to command my own photographs in the society pages. I thought Shep Green might have been the answer, but clearly I was wrong about that.

I didn't want to think about him. Or anything else for that matter. It was exhausting, making my mind grind over the same rough patches again and again. I turned to an article about Coco Chanel but didn't even make it halfway through before I was out.

After another couple days had passed, I had given up on ever seeing Shep Green again, when out of the blue, someone knocked on my room door.

"Vera? Vera! Telephone call for you. It's a man!"

I went downstairs to the parlor, picked up the phone, held the receiver to my chest and took a deep breath before I answered. "Hello?"

"Is your dance card free Saturday night, Dollface?"

"Who is this?" I teased, shifting my weight back and forth.

He laughed. "Who do you want it to be?"

I caught my reflection in the mirror above the phone. I was smiling. "How are you, Shep?"

"I'll be great if you let me take you out Saturday night."

Three nights later Shep arrived out front in a fine automobile. He was impeccably dressed and I began doubting Barbara Lewis's silk two-piece with the pleated skirt, thinking I should have gone for something more formal.

Shep took me to a wonderful restaurant with crystal chandeliers and gold-trimmed plates and water glasses. The linen napkin in my lap was softer than my bath towel. I'd never dined in such grand style before and tried to keep that to myself, not wanting him to see how unsophisticated I was. I could hear my mother saying, *Ach, who needs fancy-schmancy restaurants? Nothing but a waste of money.* But oh, how I loved it, even as I fumbled with the oversize menu and later hesitated over the assortment of silverware, waiting to take my cue from the women at neighboring tables.

"I don't know about you," Shep said with a laugh, "but I never know which fork to use. I just start on the outside and work my way in."

I wondered if he'd said that because he noticed I was nervous, but it did help me relax. We chatted after placing our orders and once our dinner arrived, he told me how pretty I was and said I had a sweet voice. "Do you sing?" he asked.

"Poorly."

"I doubt that." He smiled and cut into a glistening rare porterhouse. "I do love the sound of your voice. I could listen to you read me an entire book, cover to cover."

"Oh, yeah? What book?"

He puzzled over it for a moment and changed the subject,

telling me about his childhood and mostly about his mother. "She was in a wheelchair from the time I was twelve."

"What happened?"

"A streetcar accident." He reached for his cigarette case, turning it over in his hand. "I always tried to take care of her. Did the cooking. All the cleaning. Hell, I even carried her to the water closet when she had to go. And we didn't always make it in time," he said with a sad smile. "She passed away two years ago." He stared at the tablecloth. "I go to the cemetery every couple of months. Clear the weeds. I should go more often." There was another, longer pause. He raised his eyes to mine and gave a slight shrug. "Sometimes I talk to her. Before I leave, I always place a rock on her headstone."

As he said that a dull, empty ache settled in my stomach. I realized I didn't even know where my father's grave was. I was young when he died and hadn't really known him, but still, he was my father, and I felt robbed that he'd been taken from me. Just thinking about it made me sad, even a little angry.

My mood dipped but then brightened again as we lingered at our table, nursing brandies and exchanging stories long after our plates had been cleared.

When I asked about his father, Shep gave his brandy a swirl. "He worked for the railroads. Put in sixteen hours a day and still couldn't make ends meet." He shook his head. "My older brother and I sold newspapers and shined shoes to help out. The two of us shared a bed. Well, I guess you could say it was a bed. We slept on a mattress on the kitchen floor."

"You didn't have a bedroom?"

"That *was* our bedroom." He smiled.

"Was this here in Chicago?"

He nodded, set his glass down. "Lovely part of town called Little Hell."

"Oh, dear!" I cupped a hand over my mouth. I'd heard horror stories about that part of town.

"Yep, we lived in a deluxe four-room shanty."

"Was it as rough a neighborhood back then as it is now?"

He looked somewhere over my shoulder. "Let's just say I saw a lot of holdups and murders."

"Murders!"

He looked back at me and nodded. "I saw people get stabbed and beaten to death." He opened his cigarette case and offered me one. "So, what about you? Where'd you grow up?"

"Brighton Park." I leaned in while he lit my cigarette. As I exhaled, watching the smoke drift away, I thought about the old neighborhood. Ours was the shabbiest house on the street because my mother was too busy working to notice the broken shutters or care for our lawn. I was ashamed of how our house looked, knowing the neighborhood children ran by on their way to the park at the end of our street. While other families sat down to formal dinner tables, my mother and I stood over the kitchen stove eating straight from the pot of stew or the pan of flanken the housekeeper had prepared while my mother was at work.

"Hey." Shep leaned forward. "Where'd you just go? What are you thinking about?"

"Oh, sorry." I flicked my cigarette and smiled. "It's just that Brighton Park is worlds away from Little Hell." I looked at him and flicked my cigarette ash again.

Shep told me a few more stories and it wasn't until he said his father had died when he was young that I realized we had *anything* in common.

"My father died, too," I said. "I was four years old. How old were you?" Shep didn't answer. He just reached over and, without asking permission, held my hand. His skin was soft and warm, and there was something in his touch that made me say the rest. "It was the Black Hand," I volunteered, surprised to hear those words leave my lips. "They murdered him."

Shep squeezed my fingers tighter. Part of me wanted to talk about the very thing that I could never get my mother to talk about. It was also the perfect time to ask Shep about the North Side Gang. But I hesitated, stuck between wanting to ask, but not wanting to know. Before I said anther word, he steered the conversation in a different direction. Soon we were talking about moving pictures and amusement parks.

When he drove me home, he stopped outside the rooming house and put the car in park, letting the motor softly putter away. "You know I'm crazy about you, Vera. You know that, don't you?"

"Oh, yeah," I said, rolling my eyes, "you're crazy, all right."

"I'm serious. I don't meet a lot of girls like you."

"Like me?"

"I meet a lot of floozies, showgirls. But you—you're a nice girl. You're spunky, a real pip, but you're nice."

"Nice? That's a terrible thing to say. Nice is dull. I'm not nice."

"If you say so. But I'll tell you something: You're the kind of girl I could get serious with."

And then he kissed me.

Two days later, I called in sick at both my jobs. I wasn't in any position to sacrifice a day's pay, but I couldn't resist the chance to see Shep again. When I was in his company, he made me feel special, like I was somebody and without a care in the world. He took me ice-skating on the Midway in Washington Park that day. He fastened my skates and held on to me the entire time as I wobbled from side to side.

I sat out at one point, shivering on a wooden bench, clapping as Shep sped around the rink, weaving in and out of other skaters, natural as could be. I watched him with a glowing sense of pride. He looked good on the ice, dressed in just a heavy wool sweater and gloves, his dark hair held in place with brilliantine while his scarf flapped behind him in the wind. Shaved ice sprayed off his skates each time he made a sharp turn or came to a sudden stop. I wondered if he'd brought me here to impress me, to show off a bit? If so, it was working. I eased back on the bench and waved as he whipped past me again and again.

Afterward, we sipped hot chocolates before an open fireplace at the adjacent lodge. As we listened to the logs crackling, we made plans for the upcoming weekend.

That Saturday night, he took me to a Chinese restaurant, where I tasted my first egg rolls, wonton soup, chicken subgum and fried rice. I'd never eaten with chopsticks before, and like most of the other patrons, noodles, clumps of rice and whole vegetables slipped from my grip.

"Wait, wait, wait!" Shep laughed. "What are you doing over there, huh?"

"I have no idea." I made a face. "Help!"

He laughed some more. "Try holding them like this." He reached over and placed one stick in my hand. "That's it. Hold it just like a pencil."

While he arranged my fingers, I couldn't help gazing into his dark eyes and then looking at his mouth. Something came alive inside me at that moment. It hit me and hit me hard: I was falling for Shep Green. He was everything I'd been looking for. He was charming, successful, exciting and charismatic. But more than that, he made me feel good about myself. No one else had ever treated me as if I mattered, as if I deserved to be pampered and looked after. As I watched his lips turn downward in concentration, my excitement clashed with a rush of anxiety. Was he as taken with me as I was with him? God, I hoped so.

"Now pay attention," he said, placing the second stick against my ring finger and the crook of my thumb. "Are you watching what I'm doing here?"

"Yes, sir!" I glanced down at my hands.

"Okay, now, Dollface, you're on your own."

I grabbed a piece of chicken and got it halfway to my mouth before it slipped from my chopsticks, making us both burst out laughing.

"Okay," he said, trying to compose himself, "there's only one way to handle this." Shep picked up his chopsticks, grabbed a piece of chicken subgum and fed it to me.

As we were leaving the restaurant he said he had a surprise for me. We went back to the Meridian and there he introduced me to a woman wearing a red fox stole wrapped about her shoulders, its beady eyes staring at me, its paws resting on her chest and its bushy tail draped down the side of her arm.

"Vera," he said, "I'd like you to meet America's sweetheart."

"Oh my goodness." I couldn't think of anything else to say as my cheeks burned red. Others had gathered around, trying for a closer look at Mary Pickford.

Shep gave her a kiss on the cheek, said it was good to see her *again*, said to give his best to Douglas. It was like they were old chums. I stared at Miss Pickford's glorious blond curls, wanting to tell her that I'd seen all her pictures, that I'd sometimes sat through the same one twice in a single afternoon, and that she was even more beautiful in person, that her husband, Douglas Fairbanks, was the handsomest actor in the world. . . . But I was too starstruck to say anything. I looked into her blue eyes and I so wanted to rise up, to be Mary Pickford's equal, but there were no words that could bridge the distance between us. So instead I stood and stared.

After she had moved on, Shep and I met up with Izzy and Evelyn. It must have been two, three in the morning, and the four of us were upstairs in Shep's office. I couldn't get over the fact that I'd just met Mary Pickford. The party downstairs was still going strong and we heard the faint sounds of music and laughter rising up from the dance floor beneath us. An empty bourbon bottle sat on the table next to a candle dripping wax. The air was thick with cigarette and cigar smoke, while Satchmo played on the Victrola in the corner, carrying us along. Izzy had his arm draped over Evelyn's shoulder, his fingertips dangling just inches away from her strapped-down breast. I was on Shep's lap, my arm thrown easy-like over his shoulder.

At that hour, after drinking so much, everything was funny to us. Shep was in the middle of a story that he'd been telling forever. Couldn't get through more than a line or two before we'd all bust out laughing.

". . . so this guy comes up to me, and he's a big guy—"

"Oh, wait till you hear this!" Izzy laughed, rocking back and forth, pulling Evelyn with him. Izzy must have heard this story a zillion times before.

". . . and so," Shep pressed on, "the big lug starts crying! Just bawling."

Izzy cracked up. "Tell 'em what you said. Go on, tell 'em!"

Shep could barely get the words out. "So I tell the poor sap to quit pishing from his eyes!"

"'Pishing from his eyes!'" Izzy went wild, holding his gut like it was going to burst. He must have repeated that eye-pishing line another two or three times.

We carried on as if this was the funniest thing we'd ever heard. And then the laughter dropped down a notch and then another and another, until the hilarity faded and the room fell silent. We found ourselves in a lull, happy and content. I rested my head on Shep's shoulder and nuzzled in close to his neck, taking in the soft, spicy scent of his shaving soap. I could have stayed right there forever.

THE BACKFIRE

The following Saturday night I worked another girl's shift on the switchboard. She'd come down with a bug and I'd gotten myself into a financial bind on account of calling in sick the week before, and then splurging on a two-dollar bottle of perfume and a fifty-cent pair of stockings. Besides, Shep had some business to tend to that evening but he had invited me to a Sunday matinee the next day. He said to bring Evelyn along. Izzy was going, too.

It was a tiny theater with stained carpeting. The wallpaper was peeling in the corners. There were only about a hundred seats and we were in the front row. My chair had a bad spring that jabbed me in the bottom every time I sat the wrong way.

Their friend, Vincent Drucci, had a small part—just a handful of lines. They had nicknamed him Schemer, said he was a real prankster. Halfway through the first act he flubbed his line and broke out of character. "Aw, fuck." He cuffed himself on the forehead. "Fuck, I'm gonna do it again."

I wasn't convinced that he could act, but, boy, he was something to look at: tall, with thick dark hair and dark eyes so intense his pupils were as black as his irises.

By the time Drucci took his curtain bow and we left the theater it had started to snow. We strolled two by two down a white-covered sidewalk while motorcars puttered along, rolling through the slush and fresh piles of horse manure. I looped my arm through Shep's as we walked, letting him steady me each time I felt myself slipping on the ice. It reminded me of how he'd held on to me the day we'd gone skating.

"What do you feel like doing now, fellas?" Evelyn asked, reaching for Izzy's arm.

Izzy nudged Shep. "I'd say Schemer's acting days are over."

Shep laughed. "You try telling him that."

"Hey"—Evelyn gave Izzy's arm a tug—"what do you say we go get a drink someplace, huh?"

"I'm not afraid of Drucci. I'll tell him right to his face. He can't act for shit."

"Izz." Evelyn tugged at his arm again.

"What!" He spun around and glared at her. "Can't you see I'm talking here!"

Evelyn pulled her hand away and began walking by herself, keeping her head down, snowflakes collecting on top of her hat. I dropped back and walked with her.

"No, you didn't do anything wrong," I whispered, trying to comfort her. "I'm sure he didn't mean to snap at you like that."

Eventually Shep came and joined me while Izzy packed snowballs in his bare hands.

As we made our way up State Street, the church bells rang out from Holy Name Cathedral. We passed a newspaper boy on the corner, sitting on a stack of *Chicago Daily Gazettes*.

"Any good news in there today, kid?" Shep flipped the boy a nickel for a two-penny paper. The boy looked at the coin resting in his palm and said, "Hey, mister—wait! What about your paper? Don'tcha want your newspaper, mister?"

"Nah." Shep gave the kid a wink. "You read it for me, pal."

"That was nice of you," I said, looking back at the paperboy still staring at the nickel in his hand.

"Sometimes I can be a nice guy. Oh, wait." He stopped. "Being nice means you're dull, right?"

I gave him a playful poke with my elbow.

"Hey, look who's here." Izzy pointed to two men leaving Holy Name Cathedral. The one had a big, full face, and though he walked with a limp, he had a bounce to his step. The other was younger, with a smaller build, but he moved like a man twice his size.

"Who's that?" I asked.

"Just a couple of buddies. The one guy owns this shop right here."

"The flower shop?" I looked up at the green-and-white-striped awning with the name *Schofield's* scripted across the front.

As we stood beneath the snow-topped awning, the introductions were made. The man with the limp was Dion O'Banion, owner of Schofield's Flower Shop, and his somber-looking friend was Hymie Weiss. I couldn't understand what a Jew was doing at Holy Name Cathedral, but it didn't seem like an appropriate opening question, so I let it pass. We were still standing outside the flower shop, talking about the matinee, as the snow tapered off to flurries, letting the sun break through the thinning clouds.

"You should have seen Drucci up there on that stage," Izzy said, laughing again.

"That bad, was he?" Dion chuckled.

Shep shook his head. "Yeah, well, let's just say—"

A loud bang rang out. It gave me a jolt so intense, it reverberated inside my chest. Everyone froze, eyes shifting back and forth.

"Hymie—*no!*" Shep called out as Hymie reached into his pocket, pulled out a gun and—*Oh my God*—fired off three wild shots.

"Jesus shit!" I clutched my heart, squeezed Evelyn's wrist and dropped to the ground, pulling her with me. I couldn't breathe, and I was holding on to Evelyn so tight, my nails were digging into her skin. The sidewalk was a blur of people screaming and running for cover, while Hymie stood stoic, his rosary beads hanging from his front pocket as smoke drifted from the mouth of his revolver.

"Aw, hold your horses, will ya?" Dion said to Hymie in his thick Irish brogue. "It was just an automobile backfiring is all." He pointed to the black touring car turning onto Huron. "Everybody calm down. Coast is clear. Nothing to worry about."

Just as we began to recover, we heard an anguished cry coming from a man on the sidewalk, clutching his shoulder as blood gushed out from between his fingers. The snow beneath him was already stained scarlet. I shrieked, making Hymie spin around, pointing his gun in our direction. I clasped a hand over my mouth, holding my breath, feeling each heartbeat pounding inside my head. After Hymie turned back around, Evelyn helped me up off the pavement. My knee was bleeding, scraped raw, and my new stockings were torn.

I glanced at the wounded man on the sidewalk, unable to take my eyes off him. He was pale and clenching his teeth as his eyes flashed open in alarm and he winced in pain. The blood kept coming and I could see steam from its heat rising up from the snow.

"Now look what you've gone and done," said Izzy, slapping Hymie on the back.

Dion hobbled inside the flower shop and called from the doorway to one of his clerks, "Somebody telephone for an ambulance, will ya? We've got us a man down out here."

Shep went over to the injured man and, after a quick inspection, gave his good shoulder a pat. "Don't you worry. Help is on the way. You're going to be fine," Shep assured him. "You just hang in there and you'll be fine."

The man grasped his wound, writhing in pain. The blood was soaking into his clothes fast now and he didn't seem reassured. But I could tell from the look on Shep's face that he wasn't worried. And that worried me. How could Shep be so nonchalant about a man being shot? It ran a chill down my body.

Shep walked back over to Hymie and said, "Feeling a little jumpy there?"

"Shut it." Hymie shoved his gun toward Shep.

Even with a revolver pointed in his face, Shep didn't flinch—but I did.

I wanted to get the hell out of there, and was reaching for Evelyn to leave when Dion came out of the shop wearing a big grin and holding two American Beauties. "Lovely roses for lovely ladies." He gave one to Evelyn and the other to me. By the way I was trembling he might as well have handed me a dead bird.

Dion went over to the man on the sidewalk. "It's okay there, swell fella. Just take her easy now." He crouched down over the man. "We're gonna get you fixed up in no time."

Evelyn squeezed my hand and pointed toward a cop coming up the sidewalk.

The cop twirled his billy club, sunlight glinting off his badge and the brass buttons on his uniform. "You causing trouble again, Dion?" he asked.

"Aw, just a little accident, that's all."

"Hey, Hymie," the cop said, "how many times do I gotta tell you to keep that piece of yours in your pocket?"

"C'mon," I said to Evelyn, under my breath. "Let's get out of here."

We had just turned around when Shep called after me, "Hey, where are you going, Dollface?"

It was hard for me to turn away from him when he called me that, but I froze in place, my back toward him, my shoulders up to my ears. "It's getting late," I said, trying to keep my voice even.

"It's not late. C'mon, we'll go get something to eat."

Eat! How could he eat after this? "I'm sorry, Shep. I-I don't feel well. Evelyn's going to take me home."

Shep took a few steps closer just as Evelyn called to Izzy, saying she had to leave.

"Are you sure?" asked Shep. "What's wrong? Your head? Your stomach? Let me at least drive you home."

"No. No, really. Female stuff, you know. I'll be fine. Evelyn'll take me. You stay here." I realized I didn't feel so well. I may have been hyperventilating.

"I'll call you later," he said, "just to make sure you're okay."

"Yeah, sure. That'll be swell."

Evelyn and I turned the corner and broke into a run.

THE CHASE

My legs weren't going fast enough. I was trying to run but I couldn't move forward. A scream was collecting but each cry for help was trapped inside my chest. They were after me, coming closer and closer, until I heard myself gasp and bolted up in bed, still not convinced that I was safe.

"Huh! What!" Evelyn woke with a start. The outline of her face and shoulders was silhouetted by the streetlamp outside our window.

"I'm sorry. Go back to sleep." I was bathed in a cold sweat, and my heart continued to hammer.

"Another nightmare?"

"I'm sorry," I said again. It was the second night in a row that I'd woken her up like that.

She pulled back her covers and scooted over to the far edge of her mattress. "C'mon," she said, patting the sheets.

I grabbed my pillow and climbed in beside her, easing down under the warmth of the blankets. "I'm sorry."

"Shhh." She pulled the covers up over my shoulders. Her hair smelled of lavender from her Little Dot perfume.

Ever since the fiasco outside the flower shop two days before, I'd been having nightmares—that was if I could sleep at all. During the daytime I was on edge. Loud noises—the door slamming, the radiator clanking—made me jump.

"You want to talk about it?" she asked, stifling a yawn.

I sighed and rolled onto my side, facing her. "What's there to talk about? It's over with Shep."

"You'd better tell him that. He's been calling here since Sunday."

"I know, but I don't know how to tell him I can't see him anymore. And I can't. Not after what happened the other day."

"But you're crazy about him."

I swallowed hard. My heart had stopped racing, but now it felt pinched and heavy in my chest. "But he's *really* a gangster, Ev."

"C'mon, you knew that already."

"But I didn't get it. I didn't really understand. Yes, I knew he was a gangster but not the kind of gangster who went around shooting people. None of it seemed real to me until his friend shot that guy. My God, they could have killed him. How can you keep seeing Izzy after that?"

"It's not like Izzy shot the guy. Neither did Shep, for that matter. Like you said, it was their friend." She yawned again. "Our guys had nothing to do with it."

I flopped onto my back, wishing I could justify it the way she had. My eyes were tearing up. "The funny thing is, I felt safe with Shep. Protected. Now I'm scared of him. I don't know who he is, what he's capable of. And to think I finally thought I met someone I really liked. I've never known anyone like Shep before. I knew things would never be dull with him, but I wasn't expecting guns to be going off, you know?" I wiped my eyes with the back of my hand. "But still, I miss him. I wish I didn't, but I really do miss him, Ev."

Evelyn didn't say anything.

"Ev?"

I looked over at her, watching the covers rhythmically rise up, then ease back down. She was already asleep again.

The next day, when Izzy telephoned, Evelyn hesitated for a moment or two, but in the end she couldn't say no to him. And though she wouldn't admit it, I knew Izzy's being a *real* gangster only made her like him more. It was all part of her getting a taste of the world her parents had wanted to shield her from.

Later that afternoon I was in the front parlor playing a hand of gin rummy with some of the other girls when the telephone rang. Barbara Lewis poked her head inside and said, "Vera, it's for you. It's Shep calling."

I looked up, and my heart began beating fast. God, how I wanted to hear his voice, know that he was okay, but all I did was shake my head. As hard as it was, I'd made up my mind not to see him again. The stakes were too high, the risks too great.

"You sure? It's the second time he's called for you today."

"I'm sure." I fanned out my cards and then set them facedown. "Do you girls mind if we don't finish this hand? I'm not feeling too well."

I went upstairs, flung myself on my bed and had a good cry, leaving smudges of mascara and eyeliner streaked across my pillowcase. Later that night Barbara brought me some soup from the luncheonette around the corner but I couldn't bring myself to eat it.

Shep called two more times that night. The next day I still

wouldn't take his calls, and that's when the flowers started. Bouquets of long-stemmed roses from Schofield's showed up at the rooming house. More turned up at my job, and each arrangement was more lavish than the one before. I would have bet good money that it was the first time two dozen American Beauties had ever been delivered to the insurance offices of Schlemmer Weiss & Unger. Mr. Schlemmer himself told me to put them in the back—they were obstructing his view of the typewriter pool.

I couldn't concentrate at my desk and instead shuffled through the cards that had arrived with each delivery: *I miss you, Dollface. I need to see you, Dollface.* Each one tugged a little harder at my heart.

In spite of how I felt about him being a gangster, I couldn't deny how much I missed him. And I was touched. Nobody had ever pursued me like this before. Shep Green almost had me believing I was worth the chase.

About a week later, having ignored several more of Shep's telephone calls, I found myself alone again on a Saturday night. Evelyn was on another date with Izzy. The other girls on the floor had gotten dolled up in their best outfits and had stopped by our room to have their makeup done before they disappeared for the evening. After everyone had left I called into the switchboard office, hoping they needed me to fill in. I would rather have gone into work than sit home alone. But instead I listened to *The Eveready Hour* on the radio. The Waldorf-Astoria Dance Orchestra was playing, and it made me wish I were dancing with Shep.

"... Tonight's program was brought to you by the National Carbon Company. This is your host, Wendell Hall, signing off from WEAF radio, broadcasting from New York...."

I turned off the radio and looked out the window, watching

a couple rush arm in arm down the sidewalk before disappearing around the corner. I took a deep breath, feeling the walls closing in on me. I knew if I stayed in that room, I'd start crying again.

I ended up killing almost an hour at the luncheonette around the corner, sitting in a booth with a plate of hash and eggs and free coffee refills. Someone before me had left a newspaper behind, so it kept me company. After I read the style section and the society page, a short article grabbed my attention:

Female Bootleggers
Outrun Police Again

Fanny Klem, aged twenty-four, and an unidentified female companion outran the police for the second time in two weeks. The two were last seen coming over the Indiana state line in a black Harvester truck believed to be carrying more than five hundred cases of liquor from Cincinnati. Previously arrested for bank robbery, the female bootleggers are now wanted in three states and are believed to be armed and dangerous. . . .

They showed a picture of a woman, and I had to check the caption to make sure it was her, Fanny Klem. She had a blond bob, beautiful sparkly eyes and a sweet, seemingly innocent smile. She sure didn't look like a bootlegger. But underneath that pretty exterior had to be one tough cookie, wise and cunning and not afraid to get her hands dirty. All I could think was, *She's the type of girl Shep belongs with, not me.*

After leaving the luncheonette, I wandered down along State Street to look in the store windows. That always seemed to lift my spirits and make me forget my problems, and that night was no exception. The dresses that season were dazzling and I loved how they draped off the mannequins, the hems barely reaching the middle of their calves.

It was a cold night and I stuffed my hands deep inside my pockets, my breath forming vapor clouds in front of me as I walked along. As I neared Carson Pirie Scott at State and Madison, a man walking by called to me, "Is that you? It is, isn't it?"

I looked over and couldn't help smiling. I recognized the lock of hair hanging down first and then the smile. It was Tony Liolli. He looked good, even better than I'd remembered. The tip of his collar was flipped up but somehow he made imperfection look fashionable.

"I'm sorry. Jeez—what is it? Valerie? Veronica?"

I folded my arms. "Try Vera."

"That's right. Vera." He nodded. "How could I forget?"

"I don't know, how could you?"

"Say, let me make it up to you. We'll go have a drink. I know a place around the corner."

"No, thanks." Lonely as I was, it bothered me that he didn't remember my name.

"No?" He sounded surprised, as if he'd never heard that from a woman before.

A car door slammed. It sounded like a gun going off and I turned so quickly I dropped my pocketbook.

Tony picked it up off the sidewalk. "Well, swell seeing you again, Vera."

When I reached for my pocketbook, his fingers brushed against mine and out of nowhere, a charge shot through my body. I glanced up and locked eyes with him. All of me went flush. And he knew it, too.

"You sure you won't have that drink with me?"

The next thing I knew, I was on the south side of town, at Wabash and Twenty-sixth. Tony took me to a place called the Four Deuces. It was dark and smoky inside, and the clientele seemed to fit the decor. A man with thick, wiry eyebrows and a stern expression etched on his face was talking to a man wearing a black patch over his right eye. A couple other equally menacing-looking men were sitting at the bar, huddled over teacups of whiskey, chomping on cigars. Other than a few floozies off to the side, I was the only woman in there. I was about to tell Tony I wanted to leave when the men at the bar looked up and said hello, slapping him on the back, asking where he'd been.

"So," I said in a whisper, "do you know where all the secret passageways are in this place, too?"

"Let's hope we don't have to find out."

He grabbed my hand and we went up to the second floor. I looked around at people hitting the slot machines while others leaned over the tables playing blackjack and roulette. It felt like a different establishment upstairs. A mix of men and women were laughing, singing along with the music, toasting one another with their cocktails. Halfway through my first drink I began to relax.

Tony's game was craps, and when he took to the table he drew a crowd. I didn't understand craps, but I blew on his dice and watched the bets go down and the stack of chips in front of Tony climb higher.

"See," he said, scooping up a handful of winnings, "you're my lady luck."

"So I shouldn't remind you that you lost because of me the first time we met?"

"Well, you're redeeming yourself now."

When he was up forty dollars, we went back downstairs and I was thankful he led me away from the ominous crowd at the bar. We sat in the back at a quiet corner banquette upholstered in red velvet and studded with gold rivets. Tony was talking about some Russian leader who'd recently died when I noticed one of the men at the bar getting up. I thought he was coming over to our table. I braced myself, feeling my body go stiff, but he was only going to the men's room.

"So did I tell you I just saw Houdini?"

"Huh? What?" I gazed over at Tony.

"Houdini. I saw him."

"Really?"

"Watch this." Tony flashed his hands before my eyes and produced a cigarette from behind his ear.

"Hey, how'd you do that?"

"It's magic. I'm no Houdini, but I've got a few tricks up my sleeve."

We drank scotch that night and sip by sip inched closer together. He had a way of looking at me—or I'm sure at any girl—that reeled me right in. I had forgotten all about the men at the bar. I had almost forgotten about Shep, too.

Tony was smart. As a young boy, he'd gone to private schools, and though he had been accepted to the University of Chicago, he decided college wasn't for him.

"Second semester there I got into a fistfight with one of my professors."

"Why?"

"He was giving me a hard time. Didn't want to accept a paper just because I turned it in late."

"Well, they are known to do that sort of thing, you know."

"At least I won the fight." He smiled. I melted.

Now he owned a string of tobacco stores and said he made more money than his father, who was a doctor. I was intrigued. Private schools, college—he was book smart and street smart, too. Something about that combination got me excited. It didn't hurt that he let me know he was rich, too. Plus he was the sexiest man I'd ever seen and all I wanted him to do was lean in and kiss me.

Tony pulled out a cigarette—this time from the pack of Chesterfields he'd placed on the table—and ran a hand through his hair, causing that one disobedient lock to dangle down. "I need a haircut," he said.

"No, don't cut it!" Before I could stop myself, I reached up and touched his hair. I was already blushing as I pulled my hand away.

He smiled and stroked my cheek with the back of his hand. "You are one beautiful-looking doll. I bet you must have a million guys after you."

"Not a million." I laughed, leaning into his touch. "Just one. And he doesn't seem to take no for an answer."

"Yeah, who is he? I'll get rid of him for you."

I thought that if anyone could stand up to Shep it would be Tony Liolli, but I smiled and said, "He's not the kind of guy you get rid of so easily."

"And why's that?"

"You ever heard of a guy named Shep Green?"

As soon as I'd said it, I knew that he had. Tony ground out his cigarette and looked at me, his usual easy, carefree expression replaced with one of concern. "That's him? *That's* the guy you're seeing?"

"I *was* seeing him."

He took a long pull from his scotch. "You know who he is?"

I nodded. "Yes, but I didn't *really* know. Not in the very beginning, anyway."

Just then an older, balding man with a slight frame and close-set eyes came up to our banquette and slapped Tony on the shoulder. "What are you doing hiding back here?"

The two went back and forth, and I was waiting to be introduced but that clearly wasn't going to happen, so I busied myself with a cigarette instead.

"Didn't you have some business to take care of tonight?"

"It's handled," said Tony, leaning over to produce a light for me.

"Good." The man nodded and straightened his necktie. "They tell me you were at the tables again tonight."

"Did they tell you I won?"

"Watch yourself, you hear me?" He gave Tony a severe pat on the cheek.

"Who was that?" I asked, after he walked away.

"Johnny Torrio." He paused for my reaction, as if the name should have meant something to me. "This is his place," he continued. "I do a little work for him on the side."

"He's not very friendly."

"Aw, he's okay once you get to know him." Tony finished his drink in one gulp. "C'mon, let's get out of here."

We left the Four Deuces and drove out to Municipal Pier. It was cold that night but once Tony and I started kissing we steamed up the windows good and fast. He had perfect lips, and he knew what to do with them, too. His kisses alone got me fired up. Even Shep's kisses never traveled down my legs, making my insides quiver like this. Just being in Tony's arms did something to me. I felt safe and sexy and I craved him. I'd never felt that kind of desire before. That had to have meant something. It had to have been a sign. Shep wasn't right for me but maybe Tony was.

Tony and I carried on like that until the sun came up over Lake Michigan.

WHERE IT ALL BEGAN

The next morning, on less than two hours' sleep, I dragged myself to the streetcar. After settling in, I leaned back in my seat and closed my eyes, thinking about Tony Liolli. I'd never let a man put his hand up my skirt before. I'd always had so much control with other men. I was in charge and no one went where I didn't want them to go. But something about Tony made me come undone. He couldn't have touched me there fast enough.

The conductor clanked his bell as the streetcar jolted forward, scooting along the tracks heading south. I opened my eyes and gazed out the window. At that early hour, the city was awake with motorcars crowding the streets, dodging in and around the trolleys and occasional horse-drawn carriages. People rushed along the snow-covered sidewalks with their collars turned up, hats held in place, all bracing themselves against the winds gusting off the lake. Even the buildings looked cold, as if huddling close together for warmth, block after block. As the streetcar continued heading south, I gazed out the window to the west. The Chicago River had frozen over, frosted on top like a chilled martini glass.

Farther south the skyscrapers were replaced by less imposing buildings with water tanks on their roofs, separated by alleys strung with clotheslines full of bed linens and union suits even in the freezing cold. The pungent scent of manure, guts and animal blood began to fill the air. I reached inside my pocketbook for a handkerchief to cover my nose and mouth. I was on my way to the Union Stock Yards to see my mother.

There weren't many women at the stockyards other than the ones who worked in the canning departments or the cafeterias. Some others may have done clerical work but they certainly didn't own meatpacking plants. My mother was the exception. After my father's murder, she had stepped in and taken over Abramowitz Meats.

She always assumed that someday I'd work for her and was outright offended that I'd wanted to get a job with someone else and move out. Oh, how we argued over that. There were tears and slamming doors before we came to an agreement: one visit per month. And since my mother worked seven days a week, our visits always took place at the stockyards.

The streetcar hummed along, heading straight toward the center of the stink. Even the Chicago River had not been able to escape the effects of the stockyards. I glanced into its murky waters. It was so alive with the puckering gases of dumped animal carcasses, it was nicknamed Bubbly Creek in this part of town.

The conductor clanged his bell again as the streetcar came to my stop. I got off and headed toward the main gate of the Union Stock Yards, passing underneath the cow's head that crowned the massive limestone archway, keeping watch over all four hundred and seventy-five acres. In the distance, to my left, hundreds of rail lines crisscrossed one another like a game of jackstraws. A drover tipped his cowboy hat and gave me a smile as he trotted past on his horse. Train whistles blasted as dozens of other drovers saddled up on horseback, moving the livestock from the freight cars toward the pens. Everywhere I looked there were wire-meshed pens packed with sheep, goats, lambs, cattle, and hogs. Each and every one of them waiting to be slaughtered.

Abramowitz Meats was up ahead. The company occupied two redbrick buildings. My mother's was a tiny operation compared to Swift, Armour, Wilson and the other big companies surrounding it. There was a small white sign out front with *Abramowitz Meats* spelled out in blue lettering. A Jewish star, the Mogen David, dotted the *i* in Abramowitz.

It was a kosher meatpacking house, which was ironic, seeing as we weren't observant Jews. My mother didn't keep a kosher home. But my father's father had started the business back in the 1860s. Before he became a meatpacker, he'd been a *shochet* who traveled to all the packinghouses and performed kosher slaughters. Eventually, he scraped up enough money to open Abramowitz Meats. When my father took over around 1885, he grew the business, married a young bride twenty-three years his junior, and had a baby.

Four years later, in 1910, he was murdered during what we thought was a dispute among the stockyard workers. After a group of laborers had walked off their jobs one day, violence broke out between the meatpackers and the workers. My father's torso was found two days later. It was only the scar on his left shoulder—caused by a meat hook accident—that allowed my mother to identify him. The police thought the disgruntled workers did it. At the time of his death they didn't know about the Black Hand Gang. That didn't come out until later.

And I didn't find out about the Black Hand Gang until later still, when I was twelve. That was when I came across the cigar box my mother had hidden beneath some old blankets in the front hall closet. I found the letters inside. All six of them were addressed to my father. They were yellowed and worn at the folds, as if my mother had read them many times over. As I started to read the first one, my mouth went dry and a lump gathered in my throat. They'd written to my father, threatening to *make you a very sorry man* unless he delivered a hundred dollars to them the next day. The second letter demanded two hundred *or else your wife and child will never see you alive again*. It went on and on like that, up to fifteen hundred dollars. I remembered sitting on the floor, leaning against the closet door with my knees up close to my chest, reading through the letters one at a time.

When I was finished, I couldn't move. I stayed like that on the floor, staring at the wall as the sunlight coming through the window slipped away. Each letter was signed the same way, with a black handprint and a dagger.

When I asked about the letters, my mother was furious and told me it was none of my business. But it was my business. He was my father and I had a right to know how he'd gotten involved with those people. And were they done with us, or were they coming back for more?

I later found out that the Black Hand Gang had disbanded years earlier, but had been replaced by street thugs and gangsters. It was a struggle for control, and whoever had the most power was in charge. That was one of the reasons I was so drawn to Shep. I thought he could protect me from people like the Black Hand Gang. But that was before I'd met his friends, Vincent Drucci and Hymie Weiss. They scared the hell out of me.

Having made my way to Abramowitz Meats, I climbed the stairs of the slaughterhouse and went inside. Ida Brech was there, seated at her desk, where she'd been for as long as I could remember. As a young girl I considered her the original Gibson girl with her glossy brown hair pinned up and her bright, hopeful smile. Funny, I always thought she was so pretty and I wanted to be like her when I grew up. But the years had left Ida behind and she'd been sitting at that desk—where my mother would have gladly made a place for me—all this time. Instead of letting young men court her, show her a good time, maybe learning to paint or play piano and one day getting married and having children, Ida had been working at Abramowitz Meats. Now her hair was streaked with gray and the lines around her mouth were set in a deep, resigned frown. Ida represented everything I feared I'd become if I'd stayed with my mother.

"Your mother's on the kill floor," she said as she spun a fresh sheet of paper in the typewriter. "She told me to send you over when you got here."

It was cold on the kill floor and I could see my breath before me. Hundreds of carcasses were strung up, hanging from the track of meat hooks in the ceiling, their guts split open, innards sticking out, stomachs looking like slimy gray balloons. On the far end, a dozen cattle were hanging upside down with blood pouring from their throats while their bodies twisted, kicked and thrashed. It would go on like that until they bled out. That was the kosher way.

A few of the men looked up from their work, acknowledged me and said my mother was in the back. I found her standing on a worktable over a giant vat of animal gizzards and hearts and God knows what else.

"Ma? What are you doing up there?"

"Oh, good, you're here! Hand me that wrench over there, would you? This pipe's leaking."

"Why don't you have one of the men fix it?"

"They're busy working. It's dripping right into the meat."

"So hire a plumber."

"Ach, a plumber. Listen to you. Miss Big Shot! Working girl! So quick to throw your money away."

Thanks to my mother I couldn't cook a brisket, knit a sweater or bake a cake, but I knew how to fix a flush toilet, feed a furnace, and drive a truck. At seven, I learned to braid my own hair, since my mother had no patience for things she deemed frivolous or tedious, such as housecleaning. In between housekeepers—of which we had many—dishes piled up in the sink, food soured in the icebox and clumps of dust blew across the hardwood floors like tumbleweed. After school I went to Evelyn's until my mother came from work to get me, filling the Schulmans' pristine foyer with her repugnant stink of manure, blood, and animal rot. Once she hadn't had time to do the wash and had pulled something from the hamper for me to wear to school that reeked so from her dirty clothes, the other children refused to sit near me in class. I was forced to stand in the back—just like the children who'd wet their pants—tears of shame running down my cheeks. For years afterward, my schoolmates plugged their noses and stuck out their tongues each time I walked by. From that point on, I vowed that no matter what, I would give people reason to envy me rather than humiliate me.

I handed my mother the wrench, and after she'd tightened the pipe, she climbed down from the table and took a moment to brush herself off. She was a petite woman who still wore a corset and drab gray *schmattas* that hung to the floor. She kept her long dark hair pinned up in a bun. Her smile was spoiled by a discolored front tooth that reminded me of an old yellowed piano key. Her hands always looked rough and chapped, her fingernails cracked and brittle. I noticed a smear of animal blood on the front of her dress and when she went to hug me hello, I cringed and tried to pull away.

"Tell me now," she asked, "did they get the radiator working at your place yet?"

"Why? You want to come over and fix it?"

"Don't be smart. I've worked all my life to make a nice home for you, and it was so awful there that you'd rather go live in that dilapidated shack with your girlfriend?"

She didn't know that I'd taken on a second job, or that I preferred to be broke and in a dump than live with her. How could I tell her that even after she bathed, she still stank of the stockyards? She wouldn't have understood why it bothered me that she never did her hair, wore nice clothes, or bothered to file her fingernails or at least clean the slaughterhouse filth out from underneath them.

Terrified that I'd end up like her, I had swung hard the other way, losing myself in fashion magazines, primping before the mirror with the makeup I'd stolen from the five-and-dime and kept hidden in my room.

Back in her office, my mother pulled her pocketbook from her bottom desk drawer, and as she buttoned her wool coat, she glanced at my wraparound jacket and made a face, as if she'd just noticed it for the first time. "What are you doing wearing a *schmatta* like that? You'll freeze to death in this weather."

"I thought it was going to be warmer today."

"You should know better." She shook her head. "And what? No one in the city wears a scarf and gloves anymore?"

"Ma, I'm fine." I stuffed my hands deep inside my pockets, the fingers on my right hand poking through the torn seam.

We wandered over to Garfield's, a lunch counter on Halsted and Forty-seventh Street. The smell of grease and fried onions hit us when we stepped inside, fortunately overpowering the stink of cow manure and decay outside. It was crowded, but we managed to find two seats together at the end of the counter. We sat side by side on red swivel stools and studied the menu scribbled on a blackboard hanging above the grill. I could still feel the scotches from the night before sloshing about in my belly, and the sausage links sizzling up made my mouth water. I ordered flapjacks, fried potatoes and a rasher of bacon.

"It's good to see you have an appetite," she said, reaching for the pitcher of cream for her coffee. "You're getting too thin. Don't you girls eat?"

"Of course we eat. I'm just hungry today, that's all."

My mother lifted her coffee cup and blew through the steam, her pale gray eyes narrowed as they traveled over my face. "You look tired, Vera. Are you getting enough rest?"

"I'm fine. I just didn't sleep well." I thought about Tony and me in his car the night before as a rush of heat flushed through my body.

"Why aren't you sleeping well?"

"I'm sleeping okay. I just didn't get a lot of sleep last night."

She gave me a suspicious look, or maybe I just thought she did. As she sipped her coffee, I glanced about, studying the giant clock on the wall. It was half past nine. I had another six hours until I could go back downtown. The breakfast crowd was thinning out and the silence between my mother and me was growing more unbearable.

"I see you decided to cut your hair again," she said eventually. "It gets shorter and shorter every time I see you."

I reached up and touched my bangs. "It's not any shorter than it was the last time."

"Ach, *genug shayn*. Enough already." She waved her hand through the air.

"I swear, Ma. I haven't cut it since you saw me last." It was true. I hadn't.

She shook her head and we lapsed into another silence. Her

disappointment in me was palpable. A pang of guilt settled in my gut. This not speaking was maddening. I felt I owed her conversation, but couldn't think of anything worthwhile to say.

A woman stepped out of the water closet and we noticed that she had accidentally tucked the back of her dress up inside her bloomers. I glanced over at the woman, and from the corner of my eye, I saw the expression on my mother's face. I turned and looked at her. She was trying not to laugh, but her shoulders were shaking. That's when I surrendered and started laughing, too.

"Stop that," she said, wiping a tear from her eye. "It's not nice. We have to help her. Go tell her." My mother was still laughing.

"Me? You go tell her." I was holding my sides, I was laughing so hard.

"Okay, fine. I'll tell her." My mother composed herself, fighting to keep a straight face when she went over to the woman and whispered in her ear. The woman's face turned red as my mother helped get her untucked. When she came back to the counter, my mother started laughing all over again and that got me laughing, too. Despite our differences, my mother and I had the same silly sense of humor.

At the end of the day, when it was time to leave, she insisted on walking me to the streetcar stop even though it was bitter cold outside. As I was about to get on board she reached inside her handbag for two dollars.

"Just in case." She pressed the bills into my hand, worn and soft as scraps of fabric.

"Ma." I made a halfhearted show of rejecting her offer.

"Take it. Go on."

I nodded, stuffed the bills inside my one good pocket. My mother wouldn't splurge on a plumber, but she'd give me two dollars like it was spare change. I gave her a hug, and for a moment she stood there, her body stiff with surprise. My gesture had caught her off guard. I started to pull away but she drew me in closer, tightening her embrace. This was the nature of our relationship; we were always out of step. When I wanted nothing to do with her, she wanted me nearby, and when I grew desperate for her approval, for her attention, she was too busy for me.

"Go—go," she said, still holding me tight.

After I boarded the streetcar, I stared out the window, watching her walk toward the slaughterhouse. Before the streetcar started up, she turned back and waved to me. I pressed my hand to the glass and felt a tear forming. I hated when I felt sorry for her. Seeing her make that walk back by herself made me feel as if I'd abandoned her, and maybe I had. But I didn't mean to hurt her; I was only trying to help myself. No matter what, I couldn't let myself end up like her. I just couldn't.

When I got back to the rooming house that night, I rushed to the message board to see if Tony Liolli had called for me.

I plucked the folded piece of paper with my name across the outside and looked at the message: *Shep Green telephoned. 2:10 pm. Shep Green called. 4:27 pm.*

I crumpled up the note and threw it into the fireplace in the parlor.

THE INTOXICATING LIFE

"Vera—Vera! C'mon. Time to get up."

"Five more minutes." I rolled over and hugged my pillow.

"C'mon." Evelyn pulled back the covers. "You can't afford to be late again."

I crawled out of bed and reached for my black skirt. "It can't be Monday morning already. It just can't be." I groaned, dying to tell her about Tony but I was too exhausted to speak. I knew she'd have a million questions and it was all I could do to get myself dressed and out the door.

I couldn't imagine finding the energy to go from the insurance office to my switchboard job. As it was, I'd nearly fallen asleep on the el ride into the Loop and had conked out completely during my lunch break. I probably would have gone on sleeping through the afternoon if Evelyn hadn't nudged me awake.

At half past two, one of the partners stormed out of his office and stood over my station. "I can't send this out!" He shook the letter I'd handed him earlier in the day. "It's full of mistakes and spelling errors. It's an embarrassment. Have you ever heard of a dictionary, Miss Abramowitz?"

"I'm—I'm sorry," I mumbled, feeling everyone's eyes on me. "I'll fix it."

"You're on thin ice, young lady. I expect this retyped, proofread and back on my desk by three o'clock."

I looked at what I'd handed in. It was a mess. I hadn't realized it. "I'm sorry. It won't happen again." My chin was trembling and my eyes were glassing up.

As soon as he went back into his office and slammed the door, I stood up and rushed to the ladies' room and into the last stall. I leaned against the latched door and cried—and not because I'd fouled up. I was crying because I was so tired. My eyes burned; my back ached. All I wanted to do was sleep.

Because of my typing errors that day, I ended up working late and didn't finish until ten after five. I was going to have to rush to make it to my next job on time.

When I finally left the insurance office, the last person I expected to find waiting for me was Shep Green. He was standing outside the building, leaning against his shiny black Oldsmobile, looking smart as usual in a dark overcoat and fedora.

"Did you get my flowers, Dollface?"

"I did. Thanks." I glanced over his shoulder and then down the street, looking anywhere but at him. I didn't know what to say.

"Thanks? That's it?" He grabbed my hand. "C'mon now, you've got me chasing after you like some putz." He reached up and touched my chin. "I've been calling you for the past two weeks. What gives?"

The desperate look in his eyes made me feel cruel, as if I'd been punishing him. I stalled for a moment and when he asked again, I said, "You want to know the truth? I'm scared." A wind gust kicked up and I folded my arms across my chest. "Your friend's a little quick on the trigger. I don't want to sneeze at the wrong time and end up with a bullet in my brain."

"Is that why you won't see me now? Because of Hymie?"

I stared at the ground, my eyes shifting from his spats to my shoes. The tops of mine were scuffed, looking more gray than black, and my laces were fraying.

"Don't worry about Hymie," he said. "I don't want you to worry about anything. I would never let anything happen to you. Just give me another chance. That's all I'm asking for."

I looked at him and bit down on my lip. "I have to go. I'm late for work."

"Don't go. Not tonight. Please?" He reached for my arm. "I don't want to lose you because of some silly misunderstanding. I'm not Hymie. I'm nothing like Hymie. You have to let me prove that to you. At least let me take you to dinner."

"Shep . . ." I didn't know what to say. Even if I left right then—without stopping to grab something to eat on my way, like I normally did—I still would have been late, and they would have docked my pay for every second.

"Come with me, please? I know a great place. It's quiet. They have a big fireplace and the best steaks in town. We'll have a nice meal, some good wine, and you'll be home safe and in bed by eight o'clock. I promise. You have nothing to be afraid of with me." When I didn't say anything, he reached for my hands. "I can't stop thinking about you, Dollface."

He had me in tears when he said that. Maybe he was feeding me a line, maybe I was a fool, but I was tired and broke and hungry. And I'd missed him. Shep Green was the type of man a girl like me dreamed about. He may have scared me, but he also thrilled me. He could bring me into a world I'd only read about in magazines and seen in movies. If I were his girl, I'd never have to model jewelry again to get into a fancy party. Instead I'd be at the top of the guest list.

"C'mon, Dollface, give me a chance. That's all I'm asking for. Just one more chance."

I didn't go to my second job that night.

Or the night after that.

My popularity soared during the winter of 1924. One night I'd be having dinner with Shep Green at a white linen restaurant, meeting movie stars and famous musicians and all kinds of interesting people. The following evening, I'd be in the balcony of a dark movie house with Tony Liolli, the two of us necking and pawing at each other through the entire show.

I'd never dated two men at the same time, but I knew plenty of girls who did. Those girls always said, "You're free to do as you please until somebody puts a ring on your finger." So far neither Tony nor Shep had staked their claim on me, but still, I knew I was playing with two men that nobody messed with. The whole thing made me feel sneaky and uncomfortable.

Of the two, Shep was more likely to get serious with me than Tony. I knew that. Shep looked into my eyes and told me straight out how much he cared for me, whereas Tony cracked jokes and wiggled his way out of any serious conversations I tried to have about our future together. I adored Tony but I knew this thing with us wasn't going anywhere. So finally I told him it was over.

"I'm sorry," I said to him on the telephone, keeping my voice low so the girls sitting in the parlor wouldn't hear. "But I can't see you anymore."

"Are you kidding? Just like that, huh?"

"Just like that." I hung up the phone, wiped a tear from my cheek, and whispered, "Good-bye."

The following week, one night after my switchboard shift, I was coming up the sidewalk when a man stepped out from behind a tree. My heart dropped to the pit of my stomach until I saw the smile.

"What are you doing here, Tony?" I clutched my chest, waiting for my pulse to stop racing.

He reached for my hand, kissing my fingertips. "I couldn't stay away from you." He ran his other hand across my cheek and it felt electric. "I dare you to tell me you don't miss me."

I was breathing hard, staring into his eyes. "I don't. I don't miss you."

He stepped in closer and traced his fingers over my lips. "I don't believe you."

I couldn't speak. He leaned in closer still, his eyes never leaving mine. "Tell me," he said. "Tell me you don't miss me."

"Tony," I whispered, trying to turn away, but he cupped my face and made me look into his eyes.

"Tell me. Just tell me you're not feeling it, too."

I knew all the reasons I shouldn't be with him, but just then none of them mattered. I grabbed him by the nape of his neck and pulled him into my kiss. It was all over after that. We were right back where we started.

A week or two later, when I realized that dark theater balconies and a lot of moaning and groaning in his automobile were all I could depend on Tony for, I cut it off again. That time it took him only two days before he came around with a bouquet in his hand and a promise to start taking me on proper dates. I knew he was just telling me what I wanted to hear but still, when he looked at me with those sexy dark eyes, I couldn't resist him.

Meanwhile, Shep was doing his best to convince me that I was perfectly safe with him. The more time we spent together, the more inclined I was to believe him. Other than Hymie Weiss and sometimes Vincent Drucci, Shep's friends didn't trouble me. Dion O'Banion was as kind as could be, always smiling, laughing, offering me flowers.

When I went out with Shep, we went to the best places. One night he took me to see Fats Waller perform at Ebenezer's, a popular downtown jazz club. The line outside the door stretched halfway around the block.

"It's okay," I said, trying to hide my disappointment. "We'll see him play another time."

"Come with me." Shep slipped his arm around the small of my back and led me toward the front of the line. I felt people glaring as we walked by. Someone said, "Who do they think they are?" I turned around and there was a burly man with his hands on his hips, ready for a fight.

I held my breath, watching Shep walk over to the man who was a good three inches taller and fifty pounds heavier. I couldn't believe it. Shep hadn't said a word, and I saw the man drop his hands to his sides, already backing down. He must have realized who he'd started up with. That was the thing about Shep: He never raised his voice, never acted hostile. He just had a way of letting people know they didn't want to mess with him.

"I suppose you think this is very rude of me," Shep said to the man as he reached into his pocket. I watched the color drain from the man's face. He must have thought Shep was reaching for a gun, but instead Shep pulled out a roll of bills. Peeling a twenty off the top, he stuffed it into the man's hand. "You're right. It was rude of me. I apologize."

Meanwhile, the doorman had approached us and now got Shep's attention. "Good evening, Mr. Green."

"How are you tonight, Ralphy?" He handed him a twenty.

"Good to see you tonight, sir," he said, holding the door for us. "Have a wonderful evening."

Part of me felt embarrassed but a bigger part of me felt wildly excited to be on the arm of such a powerful man. And okay, so Shep was a gangster, but he wasn't hurting anyone, and the guy waiting in line was twenty dollars richer for it all. We waltzed right inside and were seated at a front table.

Another time I met Shep at a café in the Loop. When I got there, I couldn't find him. Noticing me searching around the room, the maître d' approached me.

"May I help you, miss?"

"I'm looking for Shep Green."

He smiled. "Ah, yes. We've been expecting you. Mr. Green is running a few minutes late, but please follow me." He helped me off with my coat and showed me to a corner table. I had just sat down and a waiter appeared with a glass of champagne. As soon as I took out a cigarette, a young waiter appeared with a match. Later, as I drew my last puff, he quickly whisked away the dirty ashtray, replacing it with a fresh one.

Although I loved the attention, at first I felt foolish about their making such a fuss over me, treating me like I was a motion picture star. But as the weeks passed, I became comfortable being waited on and fawned over and it didn't take long for me to think I deserved this special treatment. I couldn't help it: Being with Shep was intoxicating. He'd walk into a room and people would turn and stare. Women—beautiful, stunning women—would bat their lashes and push out their hips, doing their best to catch his eye. But he wasn't looking at them; he was only there for me. Sometimes I couldn't figure out what he saw in me. But when his eyes landed on me and he said, "Dollface, I couldn't be more proud than to be with you," my self-doubt vanished. It was there, in his reflection, that I found my worth.

Shep said I needed to be spoiled and he was just the man to do that. He loved to surprise me with flowers, a new hat, a pair of leather gloves. I'd never thought anyone could get such pleasure from making me happy. It made me feel lovable in spite of my past.

THREE-DIAMOND LEGS

Thanks to Shep, by the end of February I was able to quit my night job. Amazing how much money a girl could save when she got taken out for dinner four or five nights a week. And it didn't stop there. I never asked for money but whenever I was with Shep I'd find a ten-dollar bill in my coat pocket, or a twenty next to my pocketbook.

"What's this for?" I asked the first time I pulled a five from my pocket.

"Go treat yourself to something nice." He winked.

"Just like that, he gave me five dollars," I said to Evelyn later that night when I got home. We were sitting cross-legged on her bed, looking through a fashion magazine. "If my mother knew about this, she'd call me a prostitute."

"It's okay to take the money," Evelyn said, closing the magazine. "Lots of girls let their boyfriends buy them fancy dinners and clothes, even jewelry. They take money from them, too."

I stretched out and yawned. "If only our mothers knew . . ."

She laughed. "And they thought suffrage was a big deal. Imagine if they knew what we consider freedom nowadays."

"You mean it's not just about getting rid of corsets?" I teased, placing a hand over my chest.

She laughed. "They thought girls drinking liquor and bobbing their hair was daring."

"My God, a bare shoulder or kneecap is mild compared to what's *really* going on."

Night after night the girls in the rooming house stayed up late, swapping stories about boys and the things they did with them.

"So when he unbuttoned his trousers," explained Betsy Freelain, demonstrating with a banana, "I grabbed it like this." She had firm hold of the fruit, making the rest of us roll around on the parlor rug, giggling until our sides ached.

"So that's all there is to it?" someone asked. "How long did you hold it like that?"

"No, silly. I didn't just *hold* it. You have to go like this, see?" Betsy ran her hand up and down the banana, setting off another round of giggles.

Another night I was in Barbara's room polishing her toenails when Evelyn and Helen burst through the doorway, howling. "We just heard that Ginny Sparkus put Aaron's penis in her mouth and then she turned around and put it right here!" Helen bent over and pointed to her rear end.

"No!" Barbara gasped, clasping a hand over her mouth.

I almost dropped the bottle of nail polish. "I didn't even know you could do that."

"I don't think you're supposed to," said Evelyn.

We were laughing so hard that Barbara Lewis snorted, which only made us laugh harder.

I knew most of the girls were more conventional. Sheila

Schwartz told me it hurt only the first time and that lots of girls hardly bled at all.

"Everybody's doing it, Vera," she said. "You ought to try it."

One night not long after that, Tony and I were parked along the lakefront in his car. It was the beginning of March, still wintertime in Chicago, and we should have been freezing, but we were generating enough body heat to steam up all the windows. The lighthouse was off in the distance, dancing its spotlight on us from time to time. Tony had a way of touching me in all the right places. In between my moaning I heard the waves breaking along the shoreline. His breath was hot on my neck when he put his hand under my dress.

He murmured, "God, you make me crazy. You gotta let me have you."

I heard the passion in his voice, felt the urgency of his touch. It made me want him as badly as he wanted me. I couldn't hold out anymore. I needed to feel him inside me. My mind went blank and my body took over. As he unbuttoned his trousers, I reached for him. With my back pressed against the door handle, my dress hiked up to my waist, and my stockings sliding down my calves, he entered me. I gritted my teeth to keep from crying out and as he moved on top of me, a thick wetness oozed from between my legs. Once the initial pain subsided, my hips rose up to pull him in closer, and I no longer cared that my back was banging into the door or that his motorcar was rocking back and forth from the rhythm of our bodies.

After that night, we didn't bother with movie houses or the backseat of his car anymore. Instead I'd go straight to the Hotel Twenty-nine, where he was living. I saw him fully naked for the first time in his room. His body was as perfect as his face, lean but solid, and his skin was smooth as marble. I never thought a

RENÉE ROSEN

man's body could be beautiful, or could be something that I'd want to touch and kiss, but just the feel of his muscles gave me a thrill. And when I cried out his name, it was because I never knew a man could do that for you—give you such pleasure.

The next time I saw him, two nights later, he answered the door and pulled me inside. "Wait till you see what I've got in here for you." He grabbed the bulge in his trousers with one hand and reached under my skirt with the other.

"Well, maybe I've got something for you, too," I said, coaxing his fingers toward me. He closed his eyes and let his mouth drop open as he ran his fingers through the slick, wet parting between my legs.

Afterward, as I lay in his arms, Tony lit a cigarette and blew out the match, filling the air with the smell of sulfur. The bedsheets were damp with our sweat.

"I have to get going." I sat up, but he pulled me back onto the bed.

"Oh, no, you don't. Stay. It's early."

"It's *late*, and I have a long day tomorrow."

"Long day—you're going out with *him* tomorrow, aren't you?"

Tony wouldn't say Shep's name. I wasn't sure how he figured out that I was dating Shep again. But he'd asked about it once and I didn't deny it.

"I don't get why you're still seeing him," said Tony.

I twisted around and reached for the cigarette propped between his lips. "Because you disappear on me for days at a time." And it was true. No telephone calls. No messages. When I left his hotel room I never knew when I'd see him next. For all I knew, Tony was dating other women, too. I didn't ask. I didn't want to know. I took a draw off his smoke.

"I don't disappear. I'm working."

I placed the cigarette back between his lips. Whenever Tony said he was working I knew that meant he was probably at the racetrack or else at the Four Deuces playing poker or craps. In his mind, gambling *was* working. It was easier for him to say that than admit he had a weakness. Especially to me.

Tony leaned back and laced his fingers behind his head. With the cigarette still bobbing in his mouth, he said, "You think he has any idea you're seeing me?"

"No."

"You're sure about that?" Tony sat up and rubbed out his cigarette in the ashtray.

I looked at him, at his beautiful body, his lips and eyes, and I knew I had it bad. "No one knows I'm seeing you." I didn't tell a soul, not even Evelyn. I was afraid she'd slip and say something to Izzy and that it would get back to Shep.

It wasn't so much that I was afraid of losing Shep, but rather, I was just afraid, period. I had no idea what Shep would do if he found out I was seeing someone else. And I did understand Tony's concern. Tony may have been a tough guy who could take care of himself but still, Shep was a gangster.

A few nights later, Shep took me back to his apartment for the first time. Moonlight flooded in through the bay window, casting an ambient glow over the mahogany furniture, the Tiffany lamps, and the plush Persian carpets.

"This is some place you have here, Shep. It's beautiful."

"I'm glad you like it."

As if by magic, the Victrola cranked out a soft jazz number and the candles seemed to have lit themselves.

Slowly Shep came over to me. I was breathing hard and standing motionless while he unbuttoned my dress, slipping it off my shoulders and down my hips.

He reached for my hands, brought them to his lips. "You're beautiful, Dollface." Taking a step back, he studied my body, his eyes moving from my shoulders to my flat chest and down the length of my body. "You've got three-diamond legs."

I glanced down. "I have what?"

"They're rare." He started at my ankles and slid his hand in the opening between my shins, making my insides tingle. "There's one diamond." His hand rose up to the opening above my knees. "There's two." And ever so slowly he inched his hand up higher, slipping his fingers through my thighs as I trembled. "And here's diamond number three."

Then he kissed me and led me to his bedroom.

Afterward I was quiet, staring at the ceiling, feeling a little sad, or maybe disappointed. Making love with Shep wasn't what I'd been expecting. With Tony, he didn't let up until I was dizzy and my ears were ringing and my legs were too weak for standing. But with Shep I hadn't reached a climax. I kept waiting for it, but it never happened.

He did hold me afterward. Oddly, with Shep, that part—the cuddling and the kissing—was in some ways just as satisfying.

A GANGSTER'S GIRL

Saturday nights could have been tricky, but as luck would have it Tony had a standing poker game, and by ten o'clock, he was either broke, passed out or both. That freed me up to go out with Shep. No excuses, no explanations required.

It was a damp rainy Saturday night. I had been seeing Shep again for almost six weeks when he took me to dinner with some of his friends at Legends down on Monroe and Dearborn. I'd passed by that restaurant hundreds of times, wondering what kind of people could afford to dine there, and now I was about to find out. The interior did not disappoint. There was a harp serenade as you walked inside and a fish tank, big as a bathtub, loaded with lobsters. The waiters all wore tuxedos and carried silver trays with folded monogrammed towels strung over their forearms. It was crowded when we arrived with customers waiting a good hour or more for a table.

"You think you can fit us in?" Shep reached into his pocket and held out a fifty to the maître d'. "There's six of us. We're just waiting on the other girls."

"Of course, Mr. Green." He smiled and bowed slightly.

Was there anyone Shep couldn't sway with money? I wasn't sure if I found this trait of his annoying or incredibly sexy.

"Good." Shep tore the bill in two and slapped one half in the maître d's palm. "You get the other half when we get the table."

Shep's buddies busted out laughing but I was still shocked that he'd torn a fifty-dollar bill in two. Meanwhile the maître d' made the people at the front table move, and a buxom woman eyed us, saying we had some nerve. Her companion whispered something that made her jaw clamp shut as she pressed her fingers to her mouth like she was blowing herself a kiss.

"Ah, here comes Dora and Basha," said Shep, gesturing toward a tall blonde and petite brunette coming our way. "Wait till you meet these two. You're a cream puff compared to them."

"Is that Chanel?" Basha asked, eyeing my dress after we were introduced. She leaned over and pinched the fabric of Barbara Lewis's favorite loaner dress with the beading down the front. "Oh, well." She frowned.

"Oh, cut it, Basha." Dora snickered. "You wouldn't know Chanel if it bit you in the ass."

"I'll have you know," said Basha, "this is a Jeanne Paquin."

Dora rolled her eyes and pulled out a gold compact and a tube of crimson lipstick from her pocketbook. She didn't notice—or maybe she didn't care—that people were staring. I stared, too. It was the sort of behavior reserved for the powder room, and I couldn't believe she was doing it in the middle of an elegant restaurant.

Dora was married to a man named Nathan Sloan but everyone called him Knuckles. "He's my little roly-poly, aren't you, sweetie?" she said with a wink.

Knuckles was short and thick around the middle with a bald

head and a bulbous nose. But Dora, she was something else. She was a tall, striking blonde with fluttery blue eyes that rivaled a kewpie doll's. The rock on her finger was enormous, and so was the diamond in her matching necklace.

Basha stood next to me, barely coming up to my nose. I thought she had something on the side of her face before I realized it was a beauty mark. And she was beautiful, but not in the same way as Dora. No, Basha's beauty sneaked up on me, and I noticed then that a lot of men were looking at her, too, admiring her permanent marcel-waved hairdo, or maybe it was the mink stole draped over her bare shoulders. She had a cigarette holder with so many gems on it, it practically blinded me each time the light caught it just right. Basha was with Stanley, a handsome man they called Pip Squeak, or Squeak for short.

"How long have you and Stanley been married?" I asked.

"Oh, boy!" Knuckles started to laugh.

"Shut it," Basha snapped, and with her jaw set and her lips barely moving, she said, "I'm *not* the wife."

"Oh, I'm sorry," I said, feeling my face flush red. "I didn't know. I'm so—"

"Shep"—Knuckles was still laughing—"didn't you tell her Squeak's double-breasted?"

I turned to Shep, bewildered.

"Squeak here's got two sets of breasts," said Shep. "One set belongs to Basha and the other pair belongs to his wife."

Basha drew a long, luxurious puff from her cigarette before dramatically tilting her head back as she blew a stream of smoke toward the chandelier.

As I looked at Dora's sparkling diamonds and Basha's mink, I felt like a schoolgirl in comparison. I was still cursing myself over my earlier blunder with Basha, afraid I was making a horrible first impression. I hoped I hadn't embarrassed Shep.

Dora poked her platinum blond hair with a handful of red-lacquered fingernails and said, "What's taking them so long to get our table ready?"

"What's your rush?" said Basha. "You gotta train to catch or something?"

Just then, the maître d' came to seat us, and everybody in the restaurant turned and looked, thinking they were somebodies. I felt like a tagalong, someone's kid sister who had wandered in behind them.

I watched how Dora sat, so easy-like, her elbow resting on the back of her chair, her fingers dangling down, fluttering as she flashed her rock. Basha was just the opposite. She leaned in on one elbow, keeping her chin cradled in the heel of her hand. In her other hand she held her cigarette holder, using it as a pointer each time she talked. I liked the effect. It made everything she said seem important.

The restaurant owner came over and shook Shep's hand. "I'm gonna take special care of you and your party." Without our even ordering, two waiters brought out big round trays hefted on their shoulders, loaded with fancy salads, lobster tails, and prime rib. The food kept coming and the men dug in.

Everyone was clowning, having a swell time, until a tall, dark-haired man came into the restaurant. He was well dressed and wore a bright red bow tie with a matching handkerchief peeking out of his jacket pocket. The blonde on his arm sported half a dozen strands of pearls, one of which had lassoed her left breast.

"What the hell's he doing here?" said Knuckles.

"Shit!" Squeak threw his napkin onto the table.

"Who's that?" I asked.

Dora silenced me with a look.

Shep, Knuckles and Squeak stood up as the manager rushed

over, waving his arms. "Please, Shep, eh? No trouble tonight, huh?"

"C'mon, ladies." Basha dabbed the corners of her mouth with her napkin and rose from her chair. "Time for us to powder our noses."

I followed Basha and Dora into the ladies' lounge, a big pink velvet room with gold statuettes mounted on marble pedestals and a long, mirrored wall. We were the only ones in there aside from the bathroom attendant, a middle-aged black woman in an aproned dress to her ankles. She'd just cleaned the sink and was standing to the side with a bar of soap in one hand and a towel in the other. Her tip jar was filled with nickels, pennies and a few dimes.

Sitting on one of the pink settees, I pinched open my pocketbook. "What was that all about?" I asked, reaching inside for my face powder.

Basha turned to the attendant. "Give us a minute in here, will ya?" She dipped into her satchel and dropped a quarter in the tip jar. After the attendant left, Basha lit the cigarette sticking out of her gem-studded holder.

"What's going on?" I asked again.

"One of Johnny Torrio's men showed up, that's all."

I remembered meeting Torrio when I was with Tony at the Four Deuces. I hadn't liked him either. But the men's reaction seemed like more than simple dislike. "Why's that a problem?" I got up and set my lipstick on the ledge below the mirror.

Dora shot me a look. "Do you *know* who Johnny Torrio is?"

"Yeah, he owns that place—the Four Deuces."

"Girlie, you'd better wise up." Basha gripped her cigarette holder with her back teeth. "Torrio owns a hell of a lot more than just the Four Deuces."

Dora pulled me aside. "Here's the story. You got the north

side of Chicago and the south side. Johnny Torrio and Al Capone run the south side, and Dion O'Banion and our boys run the north side."

Basha checked herself in the mirror and said, "The whole city's in on it. Dion's got the cops, the politicians, even the judges on the payroll."

"Don't look so surprised." Dora glanced at me. "It's true." She said the Meridian was a front for Shep, just like Schofield's Flower Shop was a front for Dion. "But that's not where they get their money from—not their serious money, anyway."

The Black Hand flashed through my mind. I got that woozy, detached feeling, like when a drink hits you too fast, too hard.

"Schofield's is the North Siders' headquarters," said Dora. "And the Four Deuces is the South Siders' headquarters."

I almost lost my balance and stumbled, banging my hip into the ledge. The Four Deuces was Tony's hangout. I closed my eyes and rubbed my fingers across my brow. My head was suddenly throbbing. *Damn him!* He didn't just own a string of tobacco stores. He didn't go to the Four Deuces just to gamble.

Basha knocked her cigarette ash into the sink that the attendant had just cleaned. "The thing to remember is the North Siders and the South Siders hate each other's guts. So when one of Torrio's lugs shows up on Dion's turf—like that punk out there tonight—it gets the boys cranky."

"C'mon," Dora said, giving me a wink. "Let's get back out there before they kill the poor bastard."

I snapped my pocketbook shut. I felt like such a fool. What did Tony take me for—some silly girl from the stockyards who let him have his way with her? And what about Shep? I believed him when he said he owned a nightclub. *Now I find out it's just a front.* I couldn't look at Basha or Dora. If what they said was true about the South Side Gang and the North Side

Gang, I was in trouble. Real trouble. Somehow I had gotten myself in the middle of all this, and now I had to find a way to get myself out.

I closed my eyes, willed myself not to cry and told myself to breathe. *Just breathe.*

BEHIND ENEMY LINES

"I did not lie to you!" Tony held my wrists back, pinning me to the wall in his hotel room the next afternoon when I confronted him.

"Liar!" I strained to get free but he had a grip on me.

"Calm down, Vera. It's not the sort of thing you go around talking about." He dropped his head to my shoulder and whispered, "I didn't lie to you."

"I should have known the minute you took me to the Four Deuces. How could you have taken me in there when you knew I was dating Shep Green! How could you have put me in that position?"

"That was before I knew about him. And I *never* took you back there."

"You told me you own tobacco stores."

"I *do* own tobacco stores."

I continued to struggle against the weight of him. "What kind of a fool do you take me for? You work for Torrio and Capone, you son of a bitch!"

He moved in closer and had my back flush against the wall, his body pressed to mine. I could feel the heat coming off him, the warmth rising up inside me, but still I wanted to hit him, slap him, push him away.

"C'mon, don't be like this. Nothing's changed."

"*Everything's* changed."

"Don't say that." He started to kiss me and I bit down full-force on his lip. He reared back and touched his mouth and his fingers came away red. His eyes moved from his fingers to my face. He kissed me again. I twisted and thrashed, trying to pull away but he kept kissing me. The metallic taste of his blood was on my lips and then my tongue. He had me and he knew it. As much as I tried, I couldn't fight it anymore. In that moment, all I wanted was him—right there, against the wall, I gripped onto Tony while my body shook, trembled and surrendered.

Afterward, the two of us sat slumped on the floor, our backs leaning against the closet door. A draft blew across our naked bodies. We shared a cigarette, and as I watched the smoke wafting above our heads, my mind began to drift.

The night before, after we left the restaurant, Shep and I had gone back to his apartment. I was quiet and when pressed, I questioned Shep about Dion O'Banion and the North Side Gang.

"Just how involved are you?" I had asked, hands on my hips, my toe tapping his plush Persian carpet. "Basha and Dora said the Meridian's just a front."

"If all I needed was a front, believe me, there's a hell of a lot simpler setups I could have gone for. Do you have any idea what it takes to keep that place going?" Shep removed his hat, passing it from hand to hand. "Vera, I don't know what Dora and Basha told you tonight, but I do run a nightclub. And you can't have a nightclub without serving liquor. It's as simple as that. So yes, I bring in liquor and I can't do that without the help of someone like Dion. Every hotel, every restaurant, every speakeasy in this town is doing the same thing."

"So that's it? You buy liquor from Dion? That's all?" It made sense. Or maybe I just wanted it to.

He sat me down on the couch and cradled my chin in his hand. "Listen to me, Dollface. I'm crazy about you." He paused and shook his head. "No, I'm not just crazy about you. I'm falling in love with you. Don't you know that?"

When I let my eyes meet his, I had to blink back the tears. I wanted to be loved. I wanted to be loved by him, but it was too complicated now. I felt torn. How could I love him back when I'd been cheating on him this whole time—and now I find out it's been with a member of the South Side Gang.

"And you don't have to say it, Dollface. I know you're falling for me, too."

A single droplet leaked from my eye. He stopped it halfway down my cheek with his thumb. "C'mon now, you're supposed to be happy. You know the kind of guy I am. This has nothing to do with what happened to your father. You have to trust me on this."

He didn't say the words, but he knew what I was thinking. If he was as involved in the North Side Gang like Dora and Basha said, then Shep could be just like the members of the Black Hand.

"You have to trust me, Vera," he said again.

I looked into his eyes. They were warm brown and clear, with seemingly nothing to hide. How could I look into those eyes and doubt what he was saying?

He got up, went to a cabinet and came back with a small velvet box. "I was going to wait and give this to you later," he said, handing it to me.

I held the box and looked at him.

"Go on, open it."

When I lifted the lid, I saw a diamond drop necklace almost

as big as the one Dora had. I traced my fingers over the smooth edges of the stone. For the longest time I just stared at it. No one had ever bought me jewelry before. I wanted the necklace, but I knew I didn't deserve it. I'd cheated on him, and with his enemy. But what could I do, refuse it?

"Well, turn around. Let me put it on you."

I hesitated for a moment and then held my hair up off my neck while he fastened the hook. Reaching up, I touched my new necklace and turned back to face him. "I don't know what to say."

He fingered the diamond at the base of my neck. "I'm always going to make sure you have nice things. But you have to trust me. You have to trust who I am. I have a complicated life. If you don't want to be part of it, you have to tell me. I'll understand, don't worry. And even though it would break my heart, I have to tell you that if you can't handle it, you should walk away now."

Something had caught in my chest when he said that. I didn't want to lose him. I didn't want to walk away. Shep loved me. He would look out for me, make sure I never wanted for anything. I wasn't convinced I could say the same for Tony. I knew then that I had to end it with Tony. I reached up and stroked Shep's face. He sat down beside me, covered my hand with his and kissed my palm.

"But if you stay, no more questions. You understand?"

I leaned over and wrapped my arms around his neck and kissed him. With his lips still touching mine, I said, "I understand."

"What are you thinking about?" Tony asked, grinding out his cigarette.

His voice brought me back to the present. I reached for my necklace, remembering I had come here to end it with Tony once and for all. So what the hell was I still doing with him now? Was

I that weak? That attached to him? Or was this my way of saying good-bye? "My head's all over the place. I'm confused."

"It's like I said, nothing's changed. You and me have a good thing going. You see what happens when we're together. What we have is special."

"But I can't keep doing this. Not now."

"Then dump him. Get rid of him." Tony gave the ashtray a shove, knocking cigarette butts across the floor.

"I can't. He's falling in love with me."

"And what about you? Are you falling in love with him?"

When I didn't answer, Tony got up and hoisted his trousers up on his slim hips. With his back toward me he said, "I don't suppose my feelings enter into this at all. It doesn't matter that I love you."

I looked up at him, stunned. I had no idea he felt that way. What was I supposed to do now? I thought this was just fun and games for him. I didn't know it was love. Tony had shown me a side of myself I never knew existed. He had freed something in me and I discovered I was bold and sensual and powerful enough to render a man like him helpless.

"Don't you get it? I've never felt this way about a woman before." He looked at me. "But that doesn't matter, does it?"

"That's not fair, Tony."

"Fair?" He turned around with fire in his eyes. "You want to talk about what's fair? I'm the one in the shadows here. I'm the one who's second best."

"That's not true." I got up and looped my arms about his waist, kissing his chest and neck. "I didn't know how you felt. I didn't know you loved me."

"Then you need to figure this out. I do love you, but I'm getting tired of playing this game."

I kissed him full on the mouth and slipped his unbuttoned

trousers down off his hips. I knew I was complicating matters but he loved me and that blurred everything.

An hour later, as I started to get out of bed, Tony said, "No, not yet."

"Five more minutes," I said, lying back down with him, surrendering.

He leaned over and grabbed a cigarette, reaching for his lighter on the nightstand. "Just stay here with me."

"It's tempting," I said, reaching for his cigarette and taking a deep drag. I glanced at the clock and passed the cigarette back to him before resting my head on his chest. I could hear his heart beating, his skin smooth beneath my cheek.

I couldn't have found two men more different and their true natures came out when they made love to me. Tony was a ravenous lover, like he couldn't get enough of me. He took charge of me. He took me and turned me weak, whereas Shep was soft, tender and full of feeling. He would kiss and touch me like I was fragile, breakable. I couldn't make Shep see that I wanted to be broken, and broken by him. While I'd thrash and buck beneath him, he would only cup my face in his hands, hushing me, saying, "Just relax. It's okay. Relax. . . ."

It was clear to me. Tony Liolli was my lover. Shep was my protector, my keeper.

I rolled onto my side and looked again at the clock on the nightstand. It was a quarter to four. I should have been home an hour ago. Tony ran his fingers from my hip up to my neck and I squeezed my eyes shut. All I could think about then was Shep.

"Tony, I have to go."

"No, c'mon." There were his fingertips again, grazing down the length of my body. Those same fingers that had thrilled me moments before now felt like razors on my skin. All pleasure was replaced with confusion and guilt. I couldn't breathe.

"I have to." I shrugged off the covers and sat up in bed, scanning the room for my clothes. "I have to go now."

He reached for my arm but I pulled away, grabbed my dress off the floor and hurried into the bathroom. Over the sound of the running tap, I heard Tony talking about some horse race and some beef he had going with Capone, but I wasn't listening. With one foot planted on the edge of the sink, I soaped up a washcloth and wiped away the traces of Tony between my legs. I glanced again at the clock in the outer room. If I left in the next few minutes, I'd have time to bathe properly before I had to meet Shep.

I came out of the bathroom and scampered around the room looking for my stockings as I smoothed the wrinkles from my dress. Tony was still going on about Capone. I didn't say a word. I just wanted to get home. I reached for my earrings on the dresser and as I stared at my reflection in the mirror, fixing my hair and applying my makeup, I couldn't bring myself to look at Tony. I could hardly look at myself.

As soon as I left Tony's hotel room, I rushed home, grabbed the bottle of Lysol and the coiled syringe from my bottom drawer and sneaked into the bathroom down the hall. After I had used the douche, I had just enough time to bathe before Shep picked me up.

When he held the car door open for me, I barely offered him a peck on the cheek before I slid into the passenger's seat.

My head was spinning while he told me about a new act he'd booked for the club. I didn't even know where we were going. I didn't care.

"You'll love this band," he said.

"Sounds great," I said, staring out the window as we turned onto Harrison Street, distracted by how I'd left things with

Tony. I'd gone to his hotel room furious, ready to end it with him. Now I felt like I'd just gotten myself in deeper.

Yes, Tony loved me, but now that I wasn't in his arms and could think clearly again, I could see that he wasn't good for me. Not for the long haul. He was restless and impulsive—two traits that didn't bode well for a gambler. There was no reasoning with the risk taker in him. He was drawn to the excitement, and at times I wondered if that explained his attraction to me. Was I just another wager, a pretty prize wrapped up in dangerous stakes?

So I knew he wasn't good for me but that didn't make me want him any less.

"They've got this one song," Shep said, "and as soon as I heard it, I thought to myself, 'I can't wait to get Dollface on the dance floor for this.'" Shep reached over and placed his hand on mine. I flinched at his touch, as if he had acid on his fingertips. I couldn't stand the feel of him so fresh on my skin after Tony had just been there.

Shep frowned, pulled his hand away and gripped the steering wheel tighter.

I stared out the window, the silence between us growing. I knew that someone would get hurt in all this, but I always assumed it would be me. I never realized that I had the ability to hurt Shep or Tony, or both of them. These two virile, powerful men—gangsters, no less—were now at my mercy. It was an unexpected shift of power, and one that I hadn't asked for. Or had I? Whatever the case, I didn't want it. I was going to have to end it with one of them, maybe both of them. It was too much responsibility, holding someone's heart in your hands.

We pulled onto South Federal Street and up to Fontaine's, a new restaurant Shep had been wanting to take me to. You could tell from the uniformed doormen, the velvet rope out front, the men with their top hats and walking sticks and women in their gowns and fur stoles that it was an elegant place to dine. I looked over at Shep and the thought of giving him up made me want to cling to him all the more.

Before he opened his car door, I scooted closer to him. "Wait!" I leaned over and looked into his eyes. "I do crazy, stupid things sometimes," I said, reaching up to touch the diamond necklace he'd given me. I kissed him first on the cheek and then on the lips. "I'm sorry. Forgive me?"

"What's there to forgive, Dollface?" He kissed me back. "You didn't do anything wrong."

THE INDOCTRINATION

By the time spring arrived, Basha and Dora had taken it upon themselves to indoctrinate me into their gun moll club. I had introduced them to Evelyn right away. They thought she was swell, though they couldn't understand what she was doing with Izzy Seltzer.

"He's plenty handsome to look at, but honey, keep your eye on him, 'cause he's watching every skirt that walks by," said Basha one afternoon, when we were on our way to meet Dion O'Banion's wife, Viola, and Vincent Drucci's wife, Cecelia. Both were regarded as something of gangster gal royalty.

Viola O'Banion was not what I was expecting. "Pleasure to meet you both," she said, in a soft, quiet voice. "I'm so glad you could join us for lunch." She was petite like Basha, but had mousy brown hair and unremarkable eyes that seemed all but lost on her face. The whole time we spoke, she never once looked me in the eye.

"And this, of course, is Cecelia Drucci," said Basha.

Cecelia was a stunning flapper, tall and very blond. She and

Dora could have passed for sisters. The two of them towered over Basha and Viola.

Cecelia reached out and shook my hand with a grip as firm as any man's. "Heard a lot about you two," she said with a nod.

Evelyn and I had heard a lot about her, too. According to Basha, one night in the middle of a crowded restaurant, Cecelia pulled a steak knife on a woman who was "making eyes at her Vinny."

"You were right, toots." Cecelia winked at Dora. "They're just precious." Then she snapped her fingers to get the waiter's attention.

During lunch the rest of us had doctored our soda waters with gin, but not Viola. Like her husband, she never touched a drop of liquor.

Instead, Viola talked about that Sunday's sermon at Holy Name. She spoke in a low murmur, forcing me to lean forward just so I could hear. "It was so moving," she said, shaking her head, still marveling over it.

Cecelia changed the subject, told us that Vinny had gotten a new acting role. "He landed a part in a blue movie. It's called *Bob's Hot Story*. And guess who's going to play Bob . . . ?" She seemed as happy about her husband being in a dirty movie as Viola had been about the church sermon. Cecelia went on talking. She had something on her lip but I didn't feel comfortable enough with her to say anything. Apparently no one else did either.

Evelyn and I had nothing in common with these women, but following our lunch with Viola and Cecelia it seemed that Basha and Dora had decided to take us on like you would a craft project or special assignment.

The next day, they took Evelyn and me to a beauty parlor in the Loop. It was a frilly place with lace curtains and pink floral wallpaper set against a black-and-white checkered floor. A sign above the cash register listed the prices: *Shampoo 15¢, Haircut 75¢, Permanent Wave $1.50, Manicure 50¢.* The air smelled of hair tonic, talcum powder and borax.

A woman was hooked up to a curling machine whose wires reached from her scalp to an apparatus suspended from the ceiling. Another woman was getting a marcel wave, sitting patiently while her hairdresser carefully wrapped a small section of hair about a hot metal rod the length of a ruler. After each section, she stopped to reheat the rod over a burner.

Evelyn and I were seated side by side in chairs that swiveled this way and that. Our freshly shampooed hair dripped onto the capes that the beauty operators had draped over our shoulders.

Dora contemplated the nail polish colors. "What do you think would be better? This red or one of the orange shades?"

"Oh, red. Absolutely." Basha admired her perfectly coiffed brown waves in the mirror as she called to the shop owner, "We're gonna need the works today, Stella. We gotta give these two gals updated looks." Basha went on to instruct our beauticians as if Evelyn and I were merely mannequin heads. Circling around Evelyn, she said, "This one's gonna be the biggest challenge."

Evelyn looked at me and frowned.

"And this one"—she turned her focus to me—"needs to get those eyebrows of hers plucked before you do anything else."

Up until that moment, I'd never given my eyebrows a second thought, especially since they were hidden by my bangs. Now I felt ashamed of them.

When I first bobbed my hair, on my seventeenth birthday, I'd gone to the barbershop in Brighton Park. As I walked inside the men looked up from their newspapers, puzzled. They snickered, muttered and puffed on their cigars when I sat in the empty chair, telling the barber to cut my waist-length hair to my chin.

When I got home that day, my mother said I looked like a boy and wouldn't talk to me for the next two days. Since my visit to the barbershop, I'd been trimming my hair myself but apparently I wasn't doing a sufficient job.

"She needs those bangs evened up," Basha said, pointing to my brow with her cigarette holder.

"And even up her ends while you're at it," Dora suggested, shaking a bottle of bloodred polish.

Basha took another puff off her cigarette and turned to Evelyn. "Now, for this one here," she said, "let's give her the shingle bob."

"A shingle? Really?" Evelyn bit down on her lip.

A shingle was the most severe cut and the latest thing. Her parents were going to kill her. They'd read Fitzgerald's "Bernice Bobs Her Hair" in the *Saturday Evening Post* and had forbidden Evelyn to cut her hair. If putting your elbows on the table was cause for discipline in the Schulman household, I couldn't imagine the reprimand a shingle cut was going to cause.

"Would you look at those cuticles," said Dora while the manicurist scooted about on a low stool, filing and polishing my nails. "Honey, you gotta start taking better care of your hands."

I nodded as I heard the *snip, snip, snip* of the scissors working their way around the nape of my neck. I was told to close my eyes and felt the cold blade of the shears press against my forehead as tiny wisps of black hair rained onto my cheeks and nose. It tickled at first and then made me sneeze.

I glanced over at Evelyn. Half her hair was gone. The checkered floor was covered with foot-long strands of her brown curly locks, lying there like fraying ropes.

"Don't worry," I said. "It's going to look great."

By the time we left the beauty shop, my bangs were a good

half inch shorter, and Evelyn walked out with her hair cropped to her ears.

"Excuse me," I said, looking her over, "but have you seen my best friend?"

We both burst out laughing, ruffling our fingers through each other's new hairdos with our red-lacquered nails the same shade as Dora's.

Next stop was to see Irwin Ragguffy. Irwin was an attractive man in his late twenties and already a widower after only two years of marriage. About a year or so before, two members of Detroit's Purple Gang had come looking for Irwin and had shot his wife by mistake. When they told me that, I went numb. If it happened once, could it happen again? Were we all just one gangster away from a bullet? And how was Shep going to protect me from that? I didn't want to think about it and forced my mind to brush it aside.

When he wasn't working for Dion—doing God knows what—Irwin ran a garment factory down on West Van Buren, where he made brassieres and women's undergarments.

"I've never seen so many sewing machines under one roof before," said Evelyn as we walked through the main floor.

"And to think I thought the typewriter pool was noisy," I added.

The women sat side by side before their Singer machines, their lace-up boots working the treadle, their hands guiding the sheer fabric beneath the needles. When they'd finished their part of the job, dozens of other women reached in, then took the garments to the opposite side of the room, where they sewed hooks and eyes, hooks and eyes, hooks and eyes. It was quite an operation.

Irwin led us into a showroom off to the side, filled with mannequins displaying brassieres, bloomers and the occasional corset.

"Help yourselves, ladies. Pick out whatever you'd like." He gestured toward bins filled with lacy garments.

"What do you think, Irwin," said Basha, draping her arm around Evelyn's waist. "You make anything big enough for these bazoombas?"

The following Saturday, with my new brassiere and undergarments hidden beneath last season's jersey frock, I headed down to Marshall Field's. Basha and Dora had invited Evelyn and me along for some shopping and lunch, followed by the Basque fashion show. Evelyn, who'd been out all night with Izzy, was meeting us there.

I boarded the el, shimmying side to side on the tracks, and rode it to the Loop. It was the second week in April and the sun was beating down, heating up the city. It was unseasonably warm. The radio that morning had predicted a record-breaking high for the day of seventy-seven. After winter's punishing cold, everyone was taking advantage of the break in the weather. People on the sidewalks moved slowly; women hid beneath parasols; men fanned themselves with their newspapers. The fruit and vegetable vendors had temporarily come out from hibernation and had their pushcarts parked on the street corners underneath storefront awnings, borrowing their shade.

I got off at the Washington Street stop and made my way over to Marshall Field's, breaking up a flock of pigeons clustered and cooing on the sidewalk. Dora, Basha and Evelyn were waiting for me on the corner, beneath the giant green clock. Dora was wearing a gorgeous drop-waist blue dress that had pleats along the bottom. Her stockings matched the dress perfectly. Basha wore a light green sleeveless number that belted at her hip, accompanied by an extra-long strand of pearls knotted in the center. I still wasn't used to Evelyn's new hairstyle and almost didn't recognize her at first. She looked terrific, right in style. A man outside the barbershop across the street was getting a shoe-shine while giving Evelyn the up-and-down.

"I think you got yourself an admirer," Dora said, rolling her eyes in his direction.

"Oh, yeah?" Evelyn turned to look as Basha told the man to keep his eyes to himself.

"Ladies, let's go." Basha removed the cigarette from her holder, dropped the butt to the sidewalk, and ground it out beneath the ball of her Mary Jane.

Marshall Field's was a palace inside, with white marble columns and crystal chandeliers. The polished hardwood floors gleamed and the vaulted ceiling made of Tiffany Favrile glass was museum-worthy.

We worked our way from floor to floor, starting in the dress salon. Shep had given me an extra twenty, told me to have fun. Without even looking at the price tags—a first for me—I went to a rack of dresses to investigate. A beautiful purple gown stopped me. I had a blouse in a similar color that Tony said he liked.

Tony. Tony. Tony. I couldn't keep my mind off him. One day, when I was missing him so, I went into a tobacco shop. I knew it wasn't one of his stores, but as I gazed into the display case, admiring the pipes and cigars resting on red velvet risers, and breathed in the rich scent of aromatic tobacco, I was instantly calmed.

I wished I were strong enough to end it with Tony, but I didn't want to let him go. When I was away from him, I grew restless, my head filled with a haze of memories: nights in his hotel room, crumpled sheets sweaty with the heady scent of sex, the ashtray filled with smoldering cigarette butts. I pictured the bottle of whiskey uncapped on the nightstand, my silk stockings strung through the bedposts, my wrists still tender from where he'd bound me.

Holding the dress to my chin, I let the silk crepe fabric flow the length of my body. "What do you think?"

"Oh, gawd, no! That color's awful. Just overpowers you." Basha snatched the dress from my hands and flung it over the rack carelessly so that it fell to the floor.

Before I could catch it, the shopgirl darted over and picked it up. Basha stepped around her and continued sorting through the rack, screeching the hangers to the left, to the right. The shop-girl was about my age and severely knock-kneed. I offered a sympathetic smile, which she returned as she hung the dress back up and tried to get out of Basha's way. When she thought no one was looking, I saw that shopgirl's smile go sour. She must have hated waiting on women like Basha.

Our entourage moved on to purses and hats. We unbuckled, unsnapped, pinched open every pocketbook on display, reaching for every trinket that intrigued us. We each grabbed a hat, crowding in on the three-way mirror in the corner, pulling the cloches down past our eyebrows, raising our chins just enough so we could see how we looked.

Before we were finished, hatbox lids were tossed about, tissue paper was crumpled up and overflowing from the boxes stacked on the counter. The two shopgirls waiting on us couldn't keep up with Basha, who couldn't decide between two cloches, one with a slight brim, the other with a feather shooting out the side.

"Aw, nuts." Basha made a clucking sound and swept the feathered hat off her head and flung it onto the counter. "I don't like any of 'em." She patted her dark waved hair in place, looked at us through the mirror, and then announced, "I'm starved. Time for lunch!"

The shopgirls exchanged looks as they began collecting the merchandise to put back on the shelves. I felt sorry for them. After all that, no one even made a purchase.

As we approached the escalator, something tugged at me. I paused. "You know what? I forgot something. Go on. I'll be right there." I dashed back to the counter and when the shopgirls saw me coming they glanced at each other and then at me.

"Can we help you?"

I grabbed the first thing I saw, a red coin purse. I didn't like it or need it. Maybe I'd give it to my mother. "Can you ring this up for me, please?"

When I caught up with the others in the Walnut Room I wasn't hungry. It was warm inside even with the floor-to-ceiling windows thrown open. But the room was spectacular. It was my first time at the Walnut Room, and I was so taken by the crystal wall sconces, the velvet draperies, the thick carpets, and the intricately carved armrests on the chairs that I hadn't been listening to the conversation at our table.

". . . I could push her off the bridge at Wacker Drive," Basha was saying. "I'd do it right at Wacker and Michigan. Only I'll have to wait till wintertime, so she'll freeze to death."

"Oh, that's a good one," said Dora, glancing up from her menu, her blue eyes sparkling. "Or you could *accidentally* knock her off the el platform. She'd either be run over or electrocuted."

Basha doubled over, laughing so hard she nearly fell off her chair. Her pearl necklace was practically touching the floor. "Or," she said, sitting up straight and raising her salad fork in a clenched fist, "I could just stab her with one of these!"

Evelyn and I smiled dutifully while Dora and Basha laughed, going back and forth on the many ways Basha could eliminate Mrs. Squeak. This little game of theirs continued until the waiter came by for our order.

I wiped the perspiration from the back of my neck. I was hot when I'd arrived but now I felt like the temperature inside the Walnut Room had just shot up ten degrees. I was clammy. Even my mouth was sweating. When the waiter turned to me, I ordered the Walnut Room special, even though the thought of food turned my stomach.

"I'm not kidding," said Basha without skipping a beat. "I wish I could do it. Just get rid of her." She lifted her knife, holding it like you would a compact while she inspected her teeth in the reflection of the blade. "Let me tell you, she's got it coming. She's making Squeak miserable and me, too. She's been in our way since I first set eyes on him. It's true," Basha went on. "I was a waitress working at a lunch counter when Squeak came in there with that bitch wife of his."

"So you met her?" asked Evelyn.

"Oh, yeah. She's a redhead. Looks just like Raggedy Ann."

"Oh, my! You've actually seen her!" Evelyn leaned forward.

"Sure. And while she was looking at the daily specials, I was looking at her husband." Basha laughed. "I put my name and telephone number on the check and handed it to Squeak."

Evelyn's jaw dropped. "Did his wife see you do that?"

She shrugged. "I wouldn't have cared if she did. All I can tell you is that he telephoned me that night and I've been with him ever since."

The waiter came back with our lunches: pot pie, scoops of crab salad and tuna salad. As beautiful as it looked, the pungent smell of fish and mayonnaise was making me queasy.

"Well, did you hear?" asked Dora. "Johnny Torrio's in jail."

"Isn't that something!" said Basha. "It was all over the morning newspapers."

Contemplating my tuna salad, I lifted my fork. "What happened?"

"There was a big raid at his brewery. Last night they arrested him and thirty of his men."

Thirty men! I set my fork down in a panic. What if Tony Liolli had been there? What if he'd been arrested? *What if he's in jail right now?* I patted my mouth with my napkin as a trickle of sweat worked its way down my chest, sliding between my breasts. I fanned myself with my hand.

"They say Torrio's gonna do time, so I guess that means Capone'll be in charge." Dora's smile vanished when she looked at me. "Hey, Vera—sweetie, you okay? You're looking a little green around the gills there."

"You know," I said, dabbing my mouth again, "actually, I'm not feeling too well." By now I was flat-out nauseous. "I'm just going to go up to the ladies' lounge for a while. You girls don't mind, do you?"

"How about I come with you?" Evelyn offered.

"No, no, I'll be fine." But when I got up from my chair, the room started spinning. I stumbled as a wave of nausea rose up inside me.

They got me out of the Walnut Room and into the ladies' lounge just in time. I barely made it into the stall before I retched. Another wave shot through me, giving me the dry heaves. After I'd turned my stomach inside out again, the girls made me stretch out on the chaise and Dora placed a cool, damp cloth on my forehead.

That was the end of our lunch.

I felt better the next day and chalked it up to something I'd eaten the night before. But by Monday morning, I was back at it again. I had to call in sick to work, having spent a good hour in the bathroom down the hall. My stomach muscles ached and I'd broken the blood vessels in my right eye from vomiting so hard. I rinsed the sour taste from my mouth, dabbed the sweat from my brow, and returned to our two-by-four of a room.

Once I crawled back into bed, my eyes traced the spider cracks on the ceiling, from the doorway to the naked bulb overhead and back again. I listened to the ragman down in the alley crying out, "Any bottles, any rags today? Any bottles? Any rags today . . . ?" I picked at the stem of a goose feather poking out of my pillow, plucked it clean, and then searched front and back for another one. When there was nothing else I could find to distract myself, I threw off the covers, went over to my bureau, and reluctantly pulled out my date book.

I frantically flipped through the pages, forward and back, counting and recounting the days. After the third count, I thought I might faint. I dropped to the side of the bed and threw the date book halfway across the room. I had skipped my monthlies. I was almost three weeks late and I was never late. Not ever. I squeezed my eyes shut and winced, holding my head in my hands. How could I be pregnant? I always remembered to douche as soon as I got home, and besides, Tony and Shep almost always pulled out in time. *Goddammit!* I didn't even know which one was the father.

Curling myself into a ball, I grabbed a pillow to muffle my sobbing and my screams. I cried so hard I gave myself a headache and made myself sick, grabbing the waste bucket just in time. I flopped onto my back, the tears continuing to pour from my eyes, landing in my ears.

AND BABY MAKES FOUR

I sat in silence with my news for several days. I was in bad shape and nonstop nauseous. Everything smelled like fish to me, making me even queasier. All day long at the insurance offices of Schlemmer Weiss & Unger, I forced down soda crackers, praying they wouldn't come back up and land on my Smith Corona.

I didn't tell anyone, not even Evelyn—who assumed I had the stomach flu and kept her distance, hoping not to catch it. I didn't dare correct her. She didn't know about Tony Liolli, but even if he hadn't been in the picture, I didn't want Evelyn discussing my condition over a round of pillow talk with Izzy. I couldn't risk having Shep hear the news before I'd had a chance to tell him myself.

With each day I grew more confused, acting as if there were choices to make—Tony, Shep, Shep, Tony—when really, the only choice was deciding when to tell Shep. I knew he loved me and he'd once said he wanted children. He'd be thrilled if he knew I was pregnant and we'd get married. End of story. End of my affair with Tony.

But then I'd turn weak. What if Tony wanted to marry me? I knew that was an unlikely scenario. Tony loved me, but he wasn't the marrying kind. But still, even if he would have me, I wasn't ready to pick one man over the other. I questioned whether I knew either one well enough to marry them. I didn't know Tony's birthday or Shep's favorite movie. I couldn't have told you what size shirt they wore or if they still had their tonsils.

And in turn, neither one of them knew that purple was my favorite color or that all my life I'd dreamed of falling in love with a handsome man who would get down on one knee, profess his love for me, place a diamond on my finger and whisk me away from my ugly past. Maybe I'd read too many novels, seen too many moving pictures, but that was how it was supposed to happen. Not like this.

And, yes, I wanted to have a baby someday—three, to be exact—but how could I bring a child into a crime family? Was that fair? Especially when my own father had been murdered by men like that.

There was one other option, though I told myself I could never go through with it. But I was scared and desperate and each time I pushed the idea aside, it boomeranged back with greater force.

So I decided to call Tony.

When I arrived at his hotel room, Tony took one look at me and said, "What's wrong? What's the matter?"

I tossed my pocketbook onto the bed and just came out with it. "I'm pregnant."

He pulled a matchstick from his pocket and slipped it between his lips. I went over and sat on the side of the bed and Tony joined me. Neither one of us said anything just then. I glanced over and I could see by the way his eyes went wide and then narrow that the news was sinking in. The elevator dinged out in the hallway and we heard a couple laughing until they keyed into their room.

"So am I the father?" he asked.

"I don't know. . . ." *God, I honestly don't! How did I let this happen?*

Tony pitched the matchstick onto the nightstand. "Does *he* know?"

"I haven't told him yet."

He lowered his head to his hands and sighed. "So what do we do about this?"

"I don't know. I don't want a baby. Not right now. I'm not ready." After a week of wrestling with myself and weighing options, I had my answer. "Tony, you have to help me. Tell me you'll help me!"

"Help you? How?"

"Don't you know someone?" I reached over and clutched his lapels. "You must know someone who could . . ."

"You mean like a doctor?" Prying my fingers off his suit, he stood up, padded over to the dresser, poured himself a whiskey and studied my face.

"Please don't look at me like that. What else am I supposed to do?" I dropped my head and cried into my hands.

Tony threw back his drink, polishing it off with one gulp. He looked into the bottom of his empty glass and then gazed back at me. "Yeah, I probably know of someone."

"Will you help me?" I wiped my nose on my sleeve.

Tony set his glass down, came over, and stood in front of me. "You're sure this is what you wanna do?" He sat down beside me.

Once I felt his arms around me, I dropped my head to his shoulder, the fabric of his jacket rubbing against my cheek. "I'm not sure about anything right now."

. . .

Tony made the arrangements. All I had to do was meet him at his hotel room that Thursday and he'd take me to a doctor on Fullerton Parkway. Afterward, I'd tell Shep I wasn't feeling well. Female problems. He wouldn't ask questions. Not his department. I'd recover and life would go on.

But it would be different now. It had to be.

The time had come for me to make a choice. I couldn't continue carrying on with both men. So I pictured my future with Shep and then with Tony, and then, in rare, fleeting moments, I saw myself walking away from them both. I felt more confused than ever.

By the time I showed up at the Hotel Twenty-nine, I was light-headed and a little tipsy from draining my flask on the el ride over. Stepping off the elevator on the twelfth floor, I went to room 1201. As I knocked on the door, I opened my compact to check my lipstick one last time before I knocked again. And then a third time. Still no answer. I was about to knock once more, but heard the elevator car coming and left before anyone caught me hovering outside Tony's door.

I rode down to the lobby, staring into the iron pull gate, ignoring the elevator operator who'd been asking about the weather. I was dazed, wondering where Tony was. He said Thursday afternoon. It was Thursday, wasn't it?

The lobby was crowded with men seated in oversize chairs, reading newspapers, talking quietly among themselves. The faint smell of Clubman talc hung in the air. I knew it was Clubman because Tony used it and the back of his neck was always scented with it. I glanced about, certain he'd be standing nearby, but I didn't see him anywhere. Maybe he was running late. Maybe something had come up.

I went to the front desk to see if he'd left a message for me. After I pinged the little brass bell, I stepped out of one of my heels. I wore a new pair of pumps that day, and they were smarting. The marble floor felt cool and soothing beneath the ball of my foot.

A stocky man with a pockmarked face stood off to the side at the front desk. "Hey, you—toots—looking for your boyfriend?" He stuffed the stub of his cigar into the corner of his mouth.

I didn't know who he was or if he knew who I was. Keeping my eyes straight ahead, I tried not to let anything register on my face.

"You're looking for Liolli, right?"

My heart was pounding as I clutched my pocketbook and turned toward him.

"I've seen you here before with him," he said through a haze of smoke. "Yeah, I've seen you before." He buttoned his double-breasted suit coat, his sapphire pinkie ring sparkling in the light. "I've seen you here with him."

I broke out in a clammy sweat and fidgeted with my bracelet and then an earring and then my bracelet again, wondering if he knew I was also Shep Green's girl. It was for this very reason that I never lingered in the lobby. I told Tony we should meet someplace else. This hotel was too risky, too close to the Four Deuces, but he had said I was worrying for nothing. I should have trusted my gut. Not a doubt in my mind that this guy worked for Capone. He drew down on his cigar, and I busied myself with something in my pocketbook, but I could still feel his eyes on me.

When the desk clerk turned up I asked if there was a message from Tony.

He gave me a vacant look.

"Tony? Tony Liolli. He's a guest here."

"Oh! Mr. Liolli. I'm sorry," he said, consulting the registry, "but Mr. Liolli has already checked out."

"He what?" The room turned upside down as I gripped the edge of the counter.

"Just this morning. I'm afraid you missed him."

I felt the smile on my face stiffen in place. I couldn't breathe. "Where'd he go? Do you know?"

"Oh, miss, Mr. Liolli doesn't tell me things like that," the clerk said, leafing through the pages of the registry.

"But I need to find him. This is important!" I was calling too much attention to myself. The floor turned wobbly beneath my feet. I was woozy as I worked my foot back into my shoe.

"I'm sorry, ma'am, but I can't give out any personal information about our guests. It's the hotel's policy."

A bellhop handed the clerk a room key and I slipped through the lobby, making it less than a block away from the hotel before I started to cry.

Tony Liolli had run out on me. He saw his way out and he took it. It was over. He was gone and now there would be no doctor. I was pregnant and I was going to stay pregnant. My future flashed before my eyes: a crying swaddled child on my hip, dirty diapers piled on the bathroom floor, bibs and baby bottles everywhere I turned, me dressing in *schmattas* like my mother wore, my body stretched out beyond recognition. A new life inside of me was growing, but at the same time part of me was dying.

I ducked into an alley, trembling as I doubled over, sobbing. People walked by, looked in, looked away. One young man stopped and asked if I was okay. *Was I okay?* No, I wasn't okay. I was never going to be okay again.

I was in a fog and hardly remember how I made it back to the rooming house that day. What I do remember is a sensation that I had a sickness inside me that I had to get rid of. And I tried everything I could think of. I called in sick the next day, and while the others were all at work, I drank quinine and castor oil, remembering that had worked for one of the girls in the rooming house. Next I soaked in a scalding hot bath, gulping down gin. I didn't even feel a cramp. Nothing. I didn't know how long it was supposed to take, and I was so desperate I climbed out of the tub, reached for Evelyn's tennis racket and swatted myself in the stomach until I cried out in pain and dropped to the ground.

The next morning when I still hadn't miscarried, I called in sick to work again.

"You're not warm," said Evelyn, feeling my forehead. "You're going to get fired if you keep this up."

"I don't care!" I snapped. "I can't go in there right now. I'm sick. I'm really sick!"

"Okay." She backed off, her hands raised in surrender. "I believe you."

I felt horrible not telling her the truth. I just couldn't bring myself to tell her about Tony and the baby. I was terrified she'd say something to Izzy and it would all get back to Shep.

When all the girls had left for the day, I went downstairs to the parlor. My hands were shaking and even before I picked up the telephone, I knew what I was about to do was a mistake.

Someone answered on the third ring. "Four Deuces."

"Is Tony Liolli there by any chance?"

There was a long pause and the knot in my stomach tightened. I could hear whoever was on the other end of the line taking a drag off his cigarette or cigar. I was sweating, my fingers gripping a porcelain vase that rested on top of the desk where the house phone was stationed.

"Ah, sorry, Tony isn't here. You, ah, you wanna leave a message?"

I slammed down the telephone and batted the vase, watching it land on the floor, furious when it didn't shatter into pieces. Not even a chip or a scratch. God, how I'd wanted the satisfaction of destroying something other than my own life.

I looked at the telephone again, hating myself for still thinking about Tony. And what would I have said if he'd been there? I didn't know if I still wanted Tony to take me to that doctor, or if I really just wanted to hear him say it—say that he didn't love me anymore.

After that I went upstairs and grabbed the bottle of bourbon I kept stashed in my bureau. I went to the closet and took out a knitting needle and headed for the bathroom at the end of the hall. Hanging my robe on the hook behind the door, I stood naked on the cool tiled floor, trembling. I didn't know if I was more frightened of the pain or the consequences. I wasn't proud of what I was about to do, but I couldn't see another way out for myself—or for this child who deserved a better start in this world. I knew this would haunt me for the rest of my life. Wondered if I would ever be able to forgive myself. Worried that I might do permanent damage to myself and not be able to have children when the time was right. It all weighed on me. But the thought of being rid of *it*, of being free to get on with my life, canceled out every doubt, every fear, every worry.

I sat on the edge of the bathtub, set my drink on the floor and reached for the wooden knitting needle. My thighs quivered as I spread my legs. *Just do it! Just get it over with already.* But I couldn't. I grabbed my drink again and that time gulped down the last of the bourbon and took a deep breath. *Now! Do it now!* I clenched my jaw as I inserted the tip of the needle and paused. Collecting myself, I attempted another few inches. I'd gotten only three or four inches in when I heard someone coming down the hallway. I froze in place as my pulse raced and my heart hammered against my ribs.

"Vera? Vera—you okay?" Evelyn pounded on the door. "I

ducked out during lunch to check on you. I brought you some soup."

"I'm fine. Just, um ... Just give me a minute. I'll be right out." I threw the knitting needle across the floor and buried my face in my hands. Tears streamed down between my fingers and mucus bubbled from my nostrils as my body shuddered in shame. If Evelyn had come home just five minutes later I would have gone through with it. I know I would have. She'd stopped me. It was a sign.

I knew what I had to do. The decision had just been made.

I DID AND NOW I DO

Facing myself in the cheval mirror, I studied my long white satin gown and gauzy lace veil. It had been a rush job from the dressmaker, the same designer who made Dora's wedding gown. It had mother-of-pearl buttons and hand-stitched embroidery. It cost a fortune but Shep didn't mind. He just wanted me to have the dress of my dreams. It was perfect and yet I didn't look anything like the bride I wanted to be. I turned to the side and flattened my hands across my stomach to see if I was showing. Not yet. It was the first week of May and according to the doctor I was only in my seventh week. I pursed my lips, studying myself in the mirror. There was no sparkle in my eye, no joy in my heart; I felt heavy and weighed down. I was not the sweet object of affection who had waited patiently for her man to propose. No, I had cheated my way into matrimony. I didn't deserve to be a bride.

"It's starting to fill up in the synagogue," said Evelyn, coming back into the dressing room.

"God, I don't want to be the center of attention right now," I said, squeezing my eyes shut and rubbing my temples.

"Oh c'mon now." Dora stepped in and hugged me. "This is just typical prewedding jitters is all. Here," she said, handing me her glass, "have some champagne."

I nodded and took a sip, but it wasn't just the wedding; it was everything—it was the mess I'd made of my life. It hurt to breathe.

I hated Tony Liolli, but goddammit, I also missed him. Everything reminded me of him. A crumpled package of Lucky Strikes resting on the vanity made me think of Tony—not because that was his brand, but just because he smoked. Earlier in the day a deck of cards got me thinking about his magic tricks. Anything Italian ,or just the mention of the South Side, made him flash through my mind. Everything led me back to Tony Liolli, including the baby I was carrying.

"Oh c'mon now, honey," Dora said. "You're gonna be just fine. You should have seen me before I married Knuckles." She smoothed out the crepe fabric of her dress and jangled her bracelets until they slid down her forearm, settling at her wrist.

"I've never been so scared in all my life," I said, taking another sip of champagne. The girls all knew I was pregnant and not one of them judged me for it. "I've never changed a diaper, never fed a baby." My voice began to crack. "I don't know the first thing about raising a child."

"When the time comes, you'll know what to do," said Dora, stroking my arm.

"Kids—I hate 'em. No good comes of them." Basha reached for her flask tucked inside her garter. She took a long swig and dragged the back of her hand across her mouth.

"What's eating her?" I asked.

"Squeak," said Evelyn, adjusting her pearl necklace. "Squeak's here with Mrs. Squeak."

"Oh, no, Basha, I'm sorry—"

"Why the hell did you invite her, anyway?"

"I didn't. We invited Squeak—not her. You know I wouldn't do that to you."

"It's all because of his damn kids," said Basha. She slurred her words, weaving in her high heels. It wasn't even three o'clock yet.

"Keep an eye on her, will you?" I pleaded with Dora and Evelyn. "I don't want her to make a scene. And tell her to go easy on the sauce."

"Don't you worry, honey," Dora said with a smile. "We've got everything under control."

Just then my mother came into the room and the girls clammed up. "Can I have a moment alone with my daughter?"

Without saying a word, my friends each kissed me on the cheek and excused themselves, sidestepping their way around my mother. She stood in the doorway studying my gown, twisting her mouth into a pucker that brought out every line around her lips. "This isn't the way it's supposed to be," she said finally.

I thought she was talking about the baby, the marriage, Shep—*everything*. She must have asked half a dozen times if I was pregnant, and half a dozen times I told her I wasn't. She knew I was lying. She just wanted to make me admit it out loud.

"This isn't right," she said again.

I almost started to cry until I realized she was pointing at my gown.

"I don't like the way it's hanging." She bent down and tugged on one end of the dress, then fluffed out my train. "There! That's at least a little better. . . ." She stood up and dusted her hands off each other.

I stared at her. "Aren't you going to say something? *Anything?*"

"What do you want me to say?" My mother folded her arms

and tapped her fingertips along the sleeve of her dress. "You want me to say that I'm happy for you? That I think you have a wonderful future ahead of you? That I couldn't have asked for a better son-in-law?"

Even before I'd taken Shep home to meet my mother, I knew she wasn't going to like him. When I'd introduced them she narrowed her eyes, took in his slicked-back hair, the pinstriped suit, his spats, the gold watch chain, the pinkie ring— all the things I had first noticed about him, too. But those were the things I'd liked. She had the opposite reaction. I thought he would at least have scored some points for being Jewish but she didn't care.

Afterward she said, "Only a gangster wears that much jewelry and aftershave."

My mother looked at me in my wedding dress and brought a hand to her throat, running her fingers along her neck. "Just look at you—do you think you're fooling anyone about your condition? They know. Believe me, they know. And maybe it doesn't matter with this crowd, but I didn't raise you to end up like this. You break my heart, you know that? After everything we've been through—after what happened to your own father—why would you allow yourself to get involved with someone like that?"

It was one of the only times she'd ever referenced my father's murder. I looked down at my shoes and then gazed up at my mother. I couldn't help it; I couldn't fight the tears any longer. "I'm scared, Ma."

"Well, I would imagine you should be." My mother went to the door and then turned around. "I hope you and your gangster will be very happy."

I glared at her. Something about her calling him a gangster set me off. It didn't matter that it was true. It was that she'd said it. "He's a nightclub owner, Ma!" I shouted as she closed the door. "Not a gangster. *A nightclub owner!*"

The reception was held at the Meridian. We had close to three hundred guests, a combination of gangsters and every crooked politician in Cook County, all the corrupt lawyers and judges in the city, even the chief of police and the fire chief. People I didn't know hugged and kissed me, wished me well and told me I was a beautiful bride. If it weren't for the handful of girls I'd invited from the rooming house, I would have felt like a complete outsider at my own wedding.

"This is the most beautiful wedding I've ever been to," said Helen, squeezing my hands as she eyed the room. "Everything's so glamorous. You're the luckiest bride I've ever seen. It's like a fairy tale come true."

The other girls from the rooming house were circled around us and while they joined in, agreeing with Helen and congratulating me, something opened wide inside my chest. Wasn't this what I'd asked for? In that moment, regardless of the circumstances, which they knew nothing about, I was the luckiest bride. Those girls were going back to the rooming house that night and back to their old lives, while I was staying in a penthouse suite at the Palmer House Hotel, ready to embark on a whole new beginning. A server came by with a tray of champagne. We each took a glass and I smiled while they toasted to my happiness. Maybe it was the champagne I'd had earlier, or all the admiration heaped upon me from those girls, but whatever the reason, I was beginning to believe in my own fairy tale.

Shep had brought in Bix Beiderbecke to perform, and when his orchestra played *Hava Nagila*, they had everyone up, dancing the hora. I drifted off to the side, watching as all the guests held hands, forming a circle within a circle, spinning clockwise, then counterclockwise. Shep, Izzy and Irwin Ragguffy were in the center doing the *kazatsky*, their arms and legs kicking in time with the music.

I happened to gaze over at my mother. She was still punishing me, sitting by herself in the back of the room, scooting her untouched wedding cake toward the center of the table. No one would have guessed that she was the mother of the bride.

I was talking to Barbara and Monty when I looked up and saw that Basha had cornered Squeak. When she began hollering, I excused myself, rushing over to her. "Basha, please! Not here— please!"

She ignored me and went on shouting. "You'd better think twice before you show up on my doorstep tonight!" I cringed as she flailed her arms, stomped her foot and pointed her finger in his face. "I'm not kidding, if you fuck that bitch ever again, don't bother coming back to me. . . ."

People were staring, whispering, and looking back over their shoulders as they passed by. I glanced at Mrs. Squeak, who stood off to the side and adjusted her hat, ignoring it all.

I couldn't take it anymore. I had turned to walk away when two men grabbed me and then Shep, swooping us up in chairs and dancing like they did in the old country, holding us high above everyone, a handkerchief joining us together.

"You've made me the happiest man in the world, Vera!" Shep shouted above the music and the clapping. "I love you!"

I loved him, too—but I couldn't get the words out. It was as if I were stuck inside a kaleidoscope, everything whirling around me, changing shape and form, changing my life before my eyes. I was Mrs. Shep Green. I had arrived, no longer the pitiable, fatherless girl from the stockyards. A smile spread across my face, making my cheeks ache. Gripping the handkerchief that connected me to Shep, I found my voice. "I love you, too, Shep Green. I really do!"

After the dance was over, Shep threw my garter and I tossed my bouquet, aiming for Evelyn, though it was intercepted by a young woman I'd never seen before. Evelyn grabbed me afterward and we went upstairs to the powder room. She was upset with Izzy.

"Just as well I didn't catch the bouquet," she said as we sat on the settee. "We've been fighting all day. He's practically ignored me ever since we got here."

"I'm sorry, Ev." I scissored my fingers, waiting for Evelyn to pass me her cigarette.

"He just about bit my head off when I asked him to dance with me."

"Izzy doesn't deserve you."

She dropped her elbows to her knees and planted her chin in the heels of her hands. "Ah, to hell with him. This is your day."

I slipped off one of my shoes and curled my foot under my rump. "Do you think everyone knows I'm pregnant?" I asked, exhaling toward the ceiling.

"No. Just us. We're the only ones." Evelyn crossed her legs, pointing her toes.

"My mother said everyone can tell." I took another puff and passed the cigarette back to Evelyn.

"But you're not even showing yet."

"No, I mean, she thinks everyone knows because we decided to get married so fast."

There was a commotion building out in the hallway. "You got some nerve showing up here tonight, lady," I heard Basha saying.

"Oh God no," I said to Evelyn, "please don't let her start in!" I was just beginning to think I'd fooled everyone—including myself. I didn't need Basha turning my wedding into a fiasco.

The powder room door swung open and in walked Mrs. Squeak.

"Hey—get back here!" Basha charged in behind her. "I'm talking to you!"

"Basha—" I tried to step in but she barked at me and told me to mind my own business. For such a tiny little thing she could be scary at times.

"Don't you ever walk away from me!" Basha went red in the face as she cornered Mrs. Squeak. "Don't you ever—do you hear me?"

"I have nothing to say to you." Mrs. Squeak went to the mirror to check her makeup and adjust her beaded cloche.

"I'm not finished with you!" Basha reached for Mrs. Squeak's shoulder and spun her around, putting the two in a face-off. "You know what he says about you? He can't stand to touch you anymore. You make him sick to his stomach. He thinks you're nothing but a nag."

"And he thinks you're nothing but a whore!"

That's when Basha threw the first punch, clipping Mrs. Squeak right on the jaw. Much to my surprise, Mrs. Squeak swung back, catching Basha on the side of the head with her pocketbook.

Evelyn and I sprang to our feet, trying to get out of the way. The two of them were going at it. Evelyn and I grabbed hold of Basha. I had her by the waist and Evelyn had her arms but we couldn't pull her off Mrs. Squeak. She popped Mrs. Squeak a good one, right in the face. It must have stung, and instantly her freckled cheek turned red.

I left Evelyn holding Basha and raced back down to the reception to get help. By the time I returned with Dora, Evelyn was cowering in the corner, looking like she'd gone a few rounds herself. Basha straddled Mrs. Squeak across the chest and had her pinned to the floor. The sleeve of Basha's dress was torn and the two of them were calling each other names. Fists were flying as Mrs. Squeak kicked and screamed and reached up, grabbing a handful of Basha's hair. I heard something awful and I saw Mrs. Squeak's fingers come away with a clump of Basha's marcelled waves.

"For chrissakes, you two!" Dora grabbed hold of Basha, but she twisted out of Dora's grip. Dora lost her balance, landing on her rear end. One of her platinum-colored curls escaped from its updo and fell above her shoulder. It took all three of us to pull Basha off Mrs. Squeak. But Basha was still steaming and as soon as we let go of her, we heard the scream. That's when we saw that Basha had reached into her pocketbook and pulled out a pistol.

"Oh my God! Please, Basha, don't!" I begged.

"Aw, shit, Basha!" Dora shook her head. "What are you doing with that thing? Jesus! Somebody go get the fellas!"

Evelyn bolted out of the powder room. I stood still, paralyzed.

"Fuck you, Dora! Fuck you, too!" Basha said to me, waving the gun all around.

Mrs. Squeak got back up to her feet but didn't say a damn thing. Her eyes were locked on the pistol. Mrs. Squeak took a cautious step backward and then, without warning, she lunged toward Basha. Her fingers gripped Basha's wrist as the gun swayed back and forth until we heard the *pop!*

Basha's eyes grew wide. Mrs. Squeak looked stunned. Neither one of them expected the thing to go off. None of us did. Then slowly Mrs. Squeak's knees buckled and her body folded as she sank to the ground. She clutched her side, watching the blood gushing forth. When she removed her hand, repulsed and confused, she stared at the blood dripping from her cocktail ring and bracelet onto her dress.

"You shot me?" She looked at Basha in shock and then back at the crimson puddle spreading across her dress, trying to pat away the blood. She brought both blood-drenched hands to her mouth. "You *shot* me?"

We heard the men out in the hallway and when the door swung open, Squeak, Shep, Drucci and Dion all looked on in disbelief.

"Holy shit, Basha! What'd you do!" Squeak leaned over Mrs. Squeak, whose freckled face was smeared with blood, the tips of her hair looking more scarlet than its natural orangey-red. Squeak stared up at Basha, bewildered.

Basha brushed her hair off her forehead and drew a deep breath. "She's gonna live. I didn't kill her."

The guys looked at one another and then Dion slapped Squeak on the back. "That's a couple of hotheaded women you got on your hands, swell fella!"

Hymie and Drucci were trying to calm down Basha even as the ambulance drove away.

I was relieved that Barbara, Monty, Helen and the other girls from the rooming house had already left by then. But as I stood on the street watching the ambulance go, my mother looked at the blood streaked across the front of my wedding gown. "Nice friends you have, Vera. Very nice friends."

MARITAL BLISS

Right after the wedding, Shep took me to New York City for our honeymoon. We stayed at the Waldorf Astoria, on Fifth Avenue. The lobby was graced with displays of fresh flowers in oversize urns and vases. The staff stood at attention when we walked by, as if we were the hotel's only guests. Every morning they brought us the *New York Times* and a sterling silver pot of coffee, which they poured into bone-china cups and served with fresh-baked muffins. I adored the opulence of the Waldorf as much as I enjoyed our visit to Coney Island, where we strolled along the Boardwalk, stopping for nickel hot dogs with tangy mustard.

"You want to go on the merry-go-round or take an elephant ride?" Shep asked.

I looked up at the sky. It was full of squawking seagulls, their wings spread wide as they swooped in for landing. "The roller coaster," I said, pointing to the people screaming in terror as their cars whipped up and over the hilly tracks. "The roller coaster! I want to ride the roller coaster."

"You got it, Dollface."

I held on to him the whole time, keeping my eyes closed. When the ride was over, I wanted to go again.

That night we had icy cold gin martinis with his friends Charlie Luciano and Meyer Lansky, at a place called Club Fronton.

"We always knew it would take a special gal to get this one to settle down," said Meyer. "Mazel tov to you both!"

The following night Shep took me to see the Eight Little Notes at the Music Box on West Forty-fifth Street. We had such swell fun in New York, and for the first time in weeks I hadn't dwelled on the pregnancy. At least I hadn't until we went shopping our last day. Everything I tried on fit, but for how long?

"I won't even be able to wear this in another three months," I said, stepping out of the dressing room in a blue satin frock.

"So you'll have it for three months," said Shep, motioning to the shopgirl to start ringing up the dresses I'd already tried on. That day he spent more than a thousand dollars on clothes that I'd soon be too pregnant to wear.

It wouldn't hit me until later, when we were heading for the train station, that I hadn't thought about Tony Liolli once the entire time we'd been away.

When we got back to Chicago the honeymoon continued. Shep went on spoiling me. We spent our first weekend home looking for a new place to live.

After a day of walking through houses and apartments that were either too small, too old, or too far away from the city, Shep pulled up to a gray stone on State Parkway. "What do you think of this one?"

I looked up and pressed my hands to the passenger window. "Shep!" I stared at the cornices and the exquisite detail on the bay windows. Crocuses and tulips were blooming in the gardens, and the lawn was that perfect shade of new spring green.

"Well," he said as he cut the motor, "shall we go inside?"

I turned and looked at him. "Are you serious? I thought we were going to look at bungalows, or maybe just a larger apartment."

I smiled, a hand over my heart as he held the front door for me.

"Four bedrooms. A nursery," he said casually as we walked through the foyer. "There's also a butler's pantry and a maid's room. And look at this staircase." He grabbed hold of the banister. "Not too shabby now, is it?"

"Shep—look!" I marveled at the loggia off the living room. "And did you see this view?" While I peered out the floor-to-ceiling windows overlooking the park, Shep asked the owner about the roof, the furnace, the boiler, and things I wouldn't have thought about.

"Well, Dollface"—he smiled—"you think you could be comfortable in a place like this?"

"Are you kidding me!" I wrapped my arms around him and kissed him hard on the mouth. I was in love with the house and Shep promised we'd be moved in by the time the baby arrived.

When we got back to the apartment that afternoon I wandered about our place with a new perspective. Shep's apartment had once seemed so magnificent to me compared to the rooming house, and even my mother's house, but we had outgrown the space. I had already taken custody of the closets and the bathroom. My camisoles and hosiery hung over the side of the tub, drying. I hogged the medicine cabinet with my perfumes, my face powder, rouge, and lipsticks crowding in alongside Shep's bicarbonate, the bottles of liniment, his supply of aspirin and aftershave.

"Why are you throwing this out?" I asked, walking into the bedroom, reaching for a necktie that I saw him put in the trash.

"There's a stain."

"Where?" I held up the tie, inspecting it front and back.

"Right there." He came over and pointed to a speck, barely visible.

"You don't need to throw it out. Just hide it with a tie bar."

"But I'll know it's there."

He had done the same thing a few days before, throwing out a perfectly good undershirt at the first sign of a hole.

I loved our life together, but sometimes I worried that Shep and I were mismatched. Every day I discovered new habits of his that baffled me. Like whenever he bathed, even if he was home alone, he'd lock the bathroom door. And then there were the floor-to-ceiling bookshelves in his living room. He'd arranged the books in the oddest fashion. Not alphabetical, not according to subject, not novels versus nonfiction, but rather by color and size. All the tan spines lined up with the burgundies next to the green covers beside the pale blues and so on. And, of course, each color graduated accordingly from the tallest to the shortest.

"How can you find anything this way?"

"I think they look neater when they're organized like this," he said. "And besides, once you've read a book, you don't go back to it."

"Maybe you don't. And you said you haven't even read most of these yet."

"That's because I'm waiting for you to read them to me."

So far we'd made it through *Great Expectations*, *This Side of Paradise* and *Sister Carrie*. We had a long way to go.

The following day, after Shep had left for the Meridian, I wandered around the apartment, roaming from the bedroom to the living room to the kitchen and back to the bedroom again. I never would have thought it was possible, but now that I didn't have to work anymore, I was bored.

Fortunately, that day I had a distraction: I was meeting Dora for lunch. One thing about Dora and the others—they were very big on lunching. And shopping. It seemed as though that was all I'd done since I'd become Mrs. Shep Green.

Dora was looking smart as usual when I met her at a tearoom down on Adams and LaSalle. Her blond hair was held in place with a beautiful ivory comb, and the pale pink frock she wore made her baby blues more luminous than ever. Unlike Basha and Cecelia, who looked and talked like gun molls no matter what, Dora knew how to tone it down. She was ambidextrous when it came to dipping in and out of both worlds.

The tearoom however was decidedly art deco, with black onyx tables and cobalt blue and gold mosaic tiles lining the walls. Nearly every table was taken, occupied by wealthy women who, like me, didn't need to work or worry that a simple finger sandwich and a cup of soup cost two dollars. Dora and I sat at a corner table in oversize chairs with silk cushions. A bud vase with a fresh daisy served as the centerpiece.

"You're looking just swell," Dora said after we were situated. "How are you feeling?"

"So far so good. At least there's no more morning sickness." I opened my menu and scanned the entrées.

Dora sighed, setting her menu aside. "Oh, what I wouldn't give for a little morning sickness."

"Yeah, that's what you think."

"I'm serious. Knuckles and I have been trying for years."

"Really? You?" I didn't know why this surprised me. I closed my menu.

"Well, sure. What woman wouldn't want a baby?"

I opened my menu again and changed the subject.

Halfway through lunch the woman at the next table removed a series of miniature perfume bottles from a crocodile attaché case. She carefully uncapped each one and took turns dabbing a bit onto the wrists and forearms of her two companions.

"I can't believe she's selling Little Dot in here," I whispered, leaning forward.

"It is tacky," said Dora, smoothing her thumb across her shiny red nails. "But, you know, it's never a bad idea for a woman to have her own money."

"I suppose, if you're single."

"Not necessarily." She hiked up her eyebrows and leaned forward on her elbows. "I hope you don't mind if I give you a little piece of advice."

"You're not going to suggest I go out and sell perfume, are you?" I smiled.

"I'm serious." She leaned in further, letting her diamond necklace sway back and forth like a pendulum. "You're married now. You've got a good man who brings home good money. But take it from me, start putting a little stash aside for yourself."

"Oh, I don't need to do that. Shep's always been generous with me."

"This isn't about generosity." She sat back in her chair and dabbed her mouth with her napkin. Her ruby red lipstick was still perfect. "Trust me on this. Our husbands aren't ordinary working stiffs. You need to have your own money. If something happens to Shep, you'll have to fend for yourself."

A sense of dread crept over my shoulders, but I used that trick I'd learned from my mother and swept it aside, telling myself that Shep was strong and smart and wouldn't let anything happen to him.

"You just never know." She signaled the waiter and placed a

ten-dollar bill on the table. "It's something Cecelia told me when I married Knuckles, and I never forgot it. Every week Knuckles gives me spending money and the first fifty, right off the top, goes into my own pocket. Just in case." She crossed herself as soon as she said it.

A BLUFF OR THE BULL'S-EYE

I knew something was wrong with Evelyn. We were supposed to take in the new Buster Keaton moving picture, *Sherlock Jr.*, but she'd telephoned at the last minute to say she wasn't feeling well. I could tell she'd been crying, so as soon as we hung up, I jumped on the el and went straight to the rooming house.

When I first stepped inside what was once my room, I glanced around, wondering how I'd managed in such a small space. You could fit four of these rooms inside Shep's living room alone. It was the end of July, sweltering outside, and she had the only window in the room closed. She didn't even have a fan running.

"Aren't you hot in here?" I asked, and when she didn't respond, I opened the window anyway.

Evelyn's new roommate was out so I went and sat on her bed, running my fingers along her crocheted and embroidered spread. Two bath towels, one blue, the other beige, hung on the hooks near the door and I ached a little thinking of Evelyn dragging her soap and toothbrush and that blue towel to the bathroom down the hall.

Evelyn was on her bed, lying on her stomach with her ankles crisscrossed. She was reading a fashion magazine and without looking up, she asked what I was doing there.

"You sounded upset on the phone. I wanted to make sure you were all right."

"I'm fine." She looked up from her *Vogue* and I saw the bruise on her cheek, swollen reddish purple and spreading a good four inches across her face.

"Jesus, God! What happened to you?"

"Nothing. It's nothing." She squinted as if she were staring into a beam of sunlight. "Is that dress new?"

"Don't say it's nothing. What happened? Did Izzy do this to you?"

"It's nothing. I bumped into the door."

"Baloney."

Evelyn got up, tossed her magazine on the dresser and burst into tears.

"Did you two have another fight? He did this to you, didn't he?"

She nodded and sank down onto her bed. "It all started because I took him home to meet my family."

"Are you crazy? You took him home?" If my mother hated Shep, there was no way Mr. and Mrs. Schulman were going to approve of Izzy Seltzer.

"I had to." She blew her nose carefully, so as not to bump her swollen cheek. "I told my sister Reba about Izzy and she went and told my parents." Evelyn brought her hand to her bruised cheek. "They said they needed to meet him—" She choked on a fresh round of tears. "My father said Izzy was no good. Said he was to blame for me cutting my hair and dressing like a vamp. I don't dress like a vamp, do I?"

"No, not at all. You're right in style. Your father doesn't appreciate fashion, is all."

"He said I couldn't see Izzy anymore, and that if I did, not to bother coming home again."

"Oh, no. So you broke it off with Izzy?"

"No." She wiped her hand across her nose. "I left. I said good-bye to my mother and I left with Izzy. We're walking out the door and my father calls after me, telling me I'm dead to him, and starts reciting the mourner's kaddish. I feel like I've been disowned."

"Oh, Ev . . ." I couldn't make her see that Izzy wasn't worth it. I'd heard him call her names, and I'd seen him gawk at other women, even in front of Evelyn. She'd pretend not to notice, and it drove me crazy.

Evelyn blew her nose again and shook her head. "After we left—that's when Izzy went nuts. He started hollering and then . . . I don't know what happened. He just snapped and then he hit me."

"I'll kill him. I swear I will."

"No, Vera." Evelyn shook her head. "It's okay. I just . . . It was my fault."

"How was this possibly *your* fault?"

"He didn't want to meet my parents. He told me he didn't want to go but I made him. I begged him to."

I put my arm around her and hugged her to my side. "Ah, Evelyn, you have to stop doing this to yourself."

"Doing what?" She sniffled.

I turned and brushed her hair aside, careful of her bruise as I tucked a lock behind her ear. "You always take the blame for everyone else."

"No, I don't. Not really."

"C'mon, Ev." I gave her a look and cocked my eyebrow. "You took the blame for every one of your sisters. Reba left the bathroom a mess and you said you did it. Marlene left dirty dishes in the sink and you'd say it was you. Why did you always do that? Was that just so they'd let you tag along with them?"

"I didn't *always* do that. Not *always* . . ."

"You even did it with me. You always took the heat. Remember the time we got caught sneaking into the movie house? Or what about the time we got caught pinching lipsticks from the five-and-dime? I talked you into it and you said it was all your idea."

"I just . . ." Even she couldn't explain it.

"And now here you are again, blaming yourself for the way Izzy treats you. Don't you see? You deserve so much better."

She hung her head and started to cry.

Was this the price for a lifetime of hand-me-downs, of watching her older sisters get the new dresses and toys? It was her sisters whose piano and dance recitals her parents attended, not Evelyn's. It wasn't that her parents didn't love Evelyn, but after already raising four daughters, it seemed as if Mr. and Mrs. Schulman were just plain tired by the time she came around. She once told me that the only thing she ever had that was brand-new was her bicycle. I could still picture it parked on their front lawn next to the four others belonging to her older sisters.

Evelyn wiped her nose with her sleeve and sniffled some more. "I don't know what gets into Izzy sometimes. You've heard the things he says to me. But then, you know, when it's just the two of us, he's real sweet. He tells me I'm pretty. And he doesn't even mind that my chest is so big." She sniffled some more. "But when we're around other people he thinks he's a big shot if he can boss me around and make me look like a fool."

"He's a snake. You could do a lot better for yourself than Izzy Seltzer."

"But I love him. You don't understand—I really do love him!"

"This isn't love, Evelyn."

I stayed with Evelyn until she had fallen asleep and as soon as she was out, I headed over to the Meridian in search of Izzy.

When I walked inside the club, the driving beat of the Stompin' Juniors had the dance floor packed. Shep was seated at the end of the bar, nursing his whiskey, looking over the place.

"Dollface!" He lit up when he saw me, and kissed my cheek. "This is a nice surprise. I thought you were going to the movie house with Evelyn."

"Change of plans." I set my pocketbook on the bar. "Is Izzy around?"

"Izzy? Yeah, he's here somewhere. Hey," Shep called to the barkeeper. "Let's get a bourbon over here for my gal." He smiled, pulled out the stool next to him and gave it a pat.

I sat down and scanned the floor for Izzy. Table lamps glowed from all corners of the room. A couple seated up front swayed in time with the music, while a raucous party of four next to them clinked their glasses in a group toast.

Shep said something while I absentmindedly glanced at the square containers behind the bar filled with olives, syrupy maraschino cherries, lemon and lime wedges. Glasses resting upside down were lined up two rows deep. The bartender smiled, making a show of pouring a thin stream of amber liquor into a lowball glass for me.

"Hey," Shep said, placing his hand on my arm, "I asked if you're okay."

"I'm sorry, what?" I had just spotted Izzy standing off to the side, talking to a blonde with a violet feather headdress protruding from her hair. The bartender had barely set my glass down before I grabbed it and took a big, burning gulp.

"What's the matter with you?" Shep asked. "You seem upset."

"What's he doing over there?" I gestured toward Izzy. He was sliding his fingers up and down the blonde's arm.

"Aw, just ignore him."

I took another pull from my drink. "Evelyn should keep him on a leash like the dog that he is."

"She's just a girl from the club. She doesn't mean anything. You know how Izzy is."

I kept my attention on my drink and as soon as Shep got called away to the back room, I went over to Izzy and the blonde.

I tapped him on the shoulder. "Can I have a word with you?"

Izzy motioned to the blonde. "Give me a minute, will ya, hon?"

She wasn't out of earshot before I lashed into him. "What do you think you're doing? You slap Evelyn around and then start snuggling up to someone else?"

"Whoa—take it easy. Just slow down. What are you talking about?"

"You know exactly what I'm talking about. And if you ever lay a hand on Evelyn again, I swear, I'll kill you."

"You're making a lot of assumptions here. I don't know what you're talking about. I never slapped Evelyn."

"There's no point in denying it. You should see her face! I know all about you, Izzy."

His eyes turned to narrow beams and I saw something cold and mean and evil lurking inside. With a smirk he said, "Well, I guess I could say the same about you."

"What's that supposed to mean?"

"I think you know exactly what I'm talking about." He

stepped closer to me and it took all my will not to retreat. I could smell the cigarettes and whiskey on his breath. My pulse was doing double time. "You may have Shep wrapped around your little finger, but you don't fool me for a minute. I know all about you, Vera. So if I were you, I'd watch my step."

I forced myself to meet his gaze, not to flinch or back down. He didn't know anything about Tony. He had to be bluffing. Wasn't he?

We were at a standoff. Izzy wasn't about to crack.

Finally, I mustered the words, barely managing to keep my voice even. "Don't threaten me, Izzy."

"Then don't push me and we'll get along just fine."

I turned and walked away, the clicking of my heels sounding off as I stormed the stairs and headed for the ladies' lounge. My heart was racing and I'd broken out in a cold sweat. I splashed water on my face and sat on the bench in the corner smoking a cigarette, one deep puff after another. Each time the door opened, my insides jumped. It took another cigarette and another ten minutes before my pulse settled down and I was able to go back downstairs and face Shep.

JUST LIKE NORMAL

Did Izzy have anything on me? I doubted it. Tony and I had spent most of our time in his hotel room. When we did go out, it was always on the south side of town. And after I'd started dating Shep again, we were always discreet. But still, the threat of Izzy lingered. I couldn't forget him saying, *"I know all about you, Vera. So if I were you, I'd watch my step."* His words were circling inside my head just as Shep called to me from the other room.

"You're not using my razor again, are you?"

"Um . . . what? I can't hear you." I was in the bathroom and could hear him perfectly well, but it was too late. I was already shaving my legs in the sink. After I ran his razor under the tap and wiped the blade dry, I switched legs. It was getting harder and harder to lift my foot to the ledge of the sink now that my belly was ripening.

When I was finished, I went into the bedroom and found Shep standing in his BVDs with sock garters hugging his calves. He held up a towel. "How many times do I have to tell you not to leave your wet towels lying around on the furniture?"

I lowered my head and raised my eyes. "Where'd I leave that one?"

"On the bed."

I went over and took the towel from him. "Oh, it's not even wet."

"It's damp. And you left it on a silk bedcover. How hard can it be to hang it up when you're done with it?" He grabbed the towel from my hand, ratted it up, and gave me a playful snap along my bottom.

"You think I'm a slob, don't you?"

"Oh, I *know* you're a slob." He laughed and snapped the towel at me again as I darted to the closet.

Sorting through my clothes, scooting hangers this way and that, I muttered, "Where is that dress . . . ? I just saw it. . . ."

"I don't know how you expect to find anything in there." Shep pulled a pair of trousers from under the mattress and stepped into them, hoisting them onto his hips. He always kept his pants there overnight so they'd be nice and creased for him the next day.

I turned back to the closet. You could tell which half belonged to Shep. His shirts and trousers, suits and neckties were hanging straight and neat, all hangers going in the same direction, shoes lined up on the floor, standing two by two. My half was packed with skirts and dresses jutting out. My high heels were kicked off all over the place, wadded-up stockings here and there, a hat or two that had toppled off the shelf that I'd never bothered to pick up.

Shep went into the bathroom and a few minutes later he marched back in with his razor in his hand and two scraps of blood-soaked toilet paper stuck to his chin. "I don't believe it! You did it! You used my razor again."

"Aw, Sheppy, it was just a quick touchup." I looked at his chin and frowned. "And, c'mon, you want me to look nice tonight, don't you?"

We were having dinner that evening with my friend from the rooming house and her husband. I had run into Barbara Lewis—Barbara Perl now—the week before on Chicago Avenue. She was on her way to a meeting for the Jewish Women's Council.

"It's a wonderful group of women," she said. "You'd really like these girls. Harriet Wagner is a member, too. You should come join us sometime. We meet every week." She said they worked for various Jewish charities, sponsored luncheons and held fund-raisers. It sounded mildly interesting, and I thought it would be a nice break from all the lunching and shopping I'd been doing with Dora and Basha.

Barbara and I had stood outside for the better part of twenty minutes, catching up. When I told her I was pregnant, she hugged me, congratulated me, and asked how far along I was.

"Just four months," I said, wondering if she'd figured out that I was already pregnant at my wedding.

"Well," she said, "we need to go out and celebrate. I know Monty would love to see you and he never really did get a chance to know Shep."

So we set a date for the following Saturday evening. Just the four of us.

We met at a quaint restaurant on the near north side. It was small, with just a dozen or so tables. The specialty of the house was leg of lamb served with mint jelly.

Monty and Shep hit it off just swell.

"Barbara," Monty said, turning to her as he chomped on a bread stick, "you didn't tell me Shep here owns the Meridian."

"That was my fault," I said, ducking my head playfully. "I don't think I mentioned it."

Monty had a few crumbs stuck in his mustache and Barbara

reached over to casually brush them away while he kept talking. "You get some big names in there. Al Jolson, Louis Armstrong."

Shep raised his martini. "Anytime you want to see a show, just say the word."

"Frankly," said Monty, "I'd rather get in there to show you *my* act. I'm in restaurant supply sales."

"Vera," Shep said, turning to me, "you didn't tell me that."

"Guilty again." I shrugged.

"I can always use glasses and table linens. Why don't you come by the club this week?"

"I'll give you the friends and family discount," Monty said with a wink.

While the men discussed business, Barbara told me a bit more about her women's group. "Promise me you'll come to our next meeting."

"Okay, I promise. And I'll try to bring Evelyn along, too."

By the time the main course was served, it seemed like the men had been friends forever. And I could tell Barbara adored Shep. She flashed her gap-toothed smile, asking him about all the celebrities he'd met.

"What about Sophie Tucker? What's she really like?" Barbara asked, leaning in on her chair.

"Just as risqué offstage as she is on," he said. "Just ask Vera."

"You met her, too?" Barbara grabbed my wrist.

"She's a pip, all right," I said. "Who would have thought she's just a nice Jewish girl under it all?"

We laughed, and when Shep slid his arm around the back of my chair, I placed my hand over my swelling belly and smiled. I was married and pregnant and just plain happy, like I'd planned it this way all along. Shep and I could have been any normal married couple out with our friends on a Saturday night.

. . .

I t was a beautiful summer evening so after dinner the four of us went for a walk along the lakeshore. The waves were lapping onto the sand, and a bonfire was going, with a group of teenagers huddled around it. *Teenagers,* ha—they were probably my age, but they seemed like kids in comparison now that I was married, getting ready to have a baby and about to move into a big house on State Parkway.

"What do you say we grab a nightcap?" suggested Monty. "There's a jazz club not too far from here."

By the time Shep and I finally arrived home that night it was after midnight and we heard the telephone ringing as we stepped off the elevator. Just as we walked into the apartment, the caller hung up, but not a minute later, as I set down my pocketbook, the telephone rang again.

As soon as Shep answered, I knew there was trouble. I could hear it in his voice. Could see the color draining from his cheeks.

"Aw, shit!" Shep moved away from the window and drew the drapes shut. "Where was he? When did this happen?"

My stomach tensed up as I inched closer, reaching for his arm, trying to figure out what was going on.

He looked at me and shook his head. "Anyone else hurt?" Pinching the bridge of his nose, he closed his eyes. "Okay—I'm on my way."

Shep set the telephone down and ran a hand over his face and along the back of his neck.

"What is it? What happened?" I was holding my stomach along with my breath.

"It's Izzy. I have to go." He reached for his hat. "He's been shot."

S hep took off to meet Dion and Hymie and the others. Meanwhile, I flagged down a taxicab outside our apartment building and headed for Cook County Hospital. When the driver wasn't looking, I uncapped my flask and took a pull of bourbon. Until that night, I'd thought our men were invincible. If someone got shot, I thought it was our boys pulling the trigger. I didn't realize that the danger was a two-way street. If something like this happened to Izzy, it could happen to Shep, too. None of it had seemed real to me, like a grown-up game of cops and robbers, cowboys and Indians. I'd been kidding myself, thinking there was an invisible shield protecting our men and, therefore, us. Now it was clear: We were all on the line, exposed and left wide open. Irwin Ragguffy's wife flashed through my mind—killed by bullets meant for her husband. Then I thought about my father. My God, what kind of broken world were we living in? An ache settled into my gut. What if something happened to Shep? To Evelyn? To me? To my baby? I hadn't been this shook up since the day Hymie shot that man outside of Schofield's Flower Shop. I took the last sip of bourbon and stuffed the empty flask back inside my pocketbook.

When I arrived at the hospital, Evelyn was in the waiting room, her eyes swollen from crying, her face pale and drawn. An antiseptic scent hung in the air, and the harsh overhead lights glared off the white tiled walls. One of the seat cushions had ink scribbled across it, perhaps the work of an impatient child.

As soon as Evelyn saw me she began to cry again. After a history of playing with paper dolls and having sleepovers, I never imagined that Evelyn Schulman and I would find ourselves in a hospital emergency room because one of our mobsters had been shot.

"What if he dies, Vera?"

I squeezed her hand and looked at the empty nurses' station. God knows there was no love lost between Izzy and me, but I didn't want him to die. "Want me to get you some coffee? How about some water?"

She shook her head as fresh tears rolled down her face.

I felt helpless. I didn't even have a handkerchief for her. But before long, Dora and Basha rushed into the waiting room and took charge. I was relieved.

Dora threw her pocketbook on the spare chair, drew Evelyn into her arms and hugged her, saying, "It's okay. We're here. It's okay."

"How's he doing?" Basha asked, stepping in, grabbing hold of Evelyn by her shoulders.

Evelyn shrugged. "I don't know. They haven't told me anything."

"Okay," Dora said. "Basha, see if you can track down Squeak and the boys. See what you can find out. I'm gonna go talk to the doctors. You"—she looked at me—"stay here with her." Dora stormed past the nurses' station and down the corridor while Basha darted into the telephone booth.

We could hear Basha on the telephone as she sat in the booth, swaying back and forth on the swivel stool, firing up a cigarette as she talked nonstop, going, "Uh-huh? Yeah. Okay, uh-huh . . ." She took a deep puff, clouding up the booth with her smoke. Basha finished her call, stepped out of the telephone booth, and came over to us.

"It was Capone and his goddamn greaseballs. They're the ones who did this. Shep, Hymie and Drucci are out looking for them now."

Evelyn covered her face with her hands and cried some more. Everything went numb inside me. Shep was out looking for the men who tried to kill Izzy? I would have expected that from Hymie and Drucci, but not Shep. The knot tightened in the pit of my stomach. How long could I go on trying to convince myself that he wasn't like the rest of them.

"C'mon, now, Ev!" Basha pulled her flask from her pocketbook and nudged her with it. "Go on now," she said, instructing her to take a good long sip. "That's it, honey. Take another. It'll calm you down."

I could have used a drink myself but Evelyn needed it more. Besides, I'd drained my flask earlier on the cab ride over.

Dora's heels clicked and clacked, marching down the hallway. "Okay," she said, "they're telling me it's not life-threatening. Looks like he's gonna be okay."

Evelyn's knees buckled with relief as she collapsed into Basha's arms.

"He's in surgery now," Dora said.

"He's gonna be fine." Basha nodded and held on to Evelyn.

"Please don't leave me here," said Evelyn. "I'm so scared."

"It's okay." Dora rubbed Evelyn's back, guiding her over to the couch. "We're here with you, honey. Don't you worry. We'll be right here with you for as long as you need us."

"We gals stick together," said Basha, squeezing Evelyn's hand. "We're like glue. We'll stay here all night if that's what you want. We're not going anywhere."

I couldn't think of a better place for Evelyn to be at that moment than sitting in between Dora and Basha. They had her surrounded, taking turns stroking her hands, her hair, wrapping their arms around her. They handed her their handkerchiefs and passed their flasks back and forth.

Standing to the side watching the three of them, I felt a pang of jealousy. And yet I knew if it had been Shep—God forbid a million times—Basha and Dora would have rallied around me, too. They would have dried my tears and held me and rocked me in their arms, assuring me that everything was going to be okay.

And that's when I got it. It was there in that waiting room that I realized that what Evelyn and I shared with these girls went beyond friendship. Evelyn already had sisters, so it may not have meant as much to her, but for me, these were the sisters I'd always wanted. I knew that no matter what, I'd have these women by my side. For the first time in my life I understood what it meant to be part of a family, even if it was a crime family. I finally belonged somewhere, and what the outside world didn't understand about gangsters was that it wasn't all about violence and muscling your way through life. We operated according to our code of ethics, based on camaraderie and loyalty. I looked at Evelyn, sitting with Basha and Dora, and the whole thing choked me up.

"What the hell's wrong with you now?" Basha said, handing me a handkerchief.

"Nothing. Nothing. I'm fine." I dabbed my eyes.

A BREED APART

The Jewish Women's Council met every Wednesday afternoon from one o'clock until three. I'd wanted Evelyn to come with me but she was still working at her typewriter job, and besides, these women were all married and she said she'd feel out of place.

The women took turns hosting the meetings, and by September of that year, I'd been to four homes that, like the family dog and their masters, resembled their matriarchs to a T. Adele Markey, the council president, had a house with a dark, masculine interior and heavy mahogany furniture that fit her short, stout stature and serious disposition. Harriet Wagner, on the other hand, had decorated her home in floral prints, from the sofa cushions to the draperies, right down to her china pattern. She even had floral artwork that seemed every bit as peppy and bright as Harriet herself. Esther Bloomberg's home was a confused ensemble of art deco touches mixed in with nicked-up end tables and faded lampshades that had probably once been in her mother's home. She served lukewarm coffee in mismatched cups and saucers. No wonder poor Esther couldn't make a decision about anything, whether to serve coffee cake or *schnecken*, or whether to vote for or against whatever issue was on the table.

"Welcome, everyone! Please, please come make yourselves at home," said Janice Kaufman, our hostess that afternoon. Like Janice, with her formal ballet training, her home was designed for perfect posture, with uncomfortable high-backed chairs and a hard, straight-edged sofa. The twenty or so of us sat in a perfectly choreographed semicircle, with cups and saucers balanced on our laps.

"Does anyone have any new business to discuss?" asked Adele Markey, looking at me.

Even after a month of meetings and my five-dollar dues in her coffer, I still felt more like a guest than a member. I don't think I'd said more than a handful of words at any one meeting. This was my chance to be part of something legitimate, and I wanted to fit in, but I didn't know how. On the surface we had so much in common. These women were all in their late teens or early twenties and many of them were young mothers or pregnant like me. But that was where the similarities ended. Their husbands were doctors and lawyers, accountants and salesmen. Being married to a nightclub owner was beyond their comprehension, and God forbid if they knew the nightclub owner also happened to be a gangster. How could they ever understand my world? I wrestled with it enough myself. Some days I longed to be like these other women: simple, normal and uncomplicated. Other times, I found their very existences mundane and boring to the point of madness.

"Very well then," Adele Markey continued. "At our last meeting we were still divided over the central design for the new stained-glass windows for the synagogue. Should it be the Torah or the Star of David . . . ?"

Five minutes later it was clear that the divide hadn't been

resolved. Adele felt that it should be a depiction of the Torah and half of the others agreed, while Harriet, Barbara and the other half preferred the Star of David. Esther Bloomberg, of course, couldn't decide.

"Ladies, ladies." Adele Markey raised her voice above the clamoring. "Can I just remind you that we have five windows and there are five books of the Torah."

"Adele does have a valid point," said Janice.

Adele nodded and stood up. "Now, I say we end this foolish bickering and put this issue to a vote. All in favor of the Torah raise your hand."

I didn't care one way or the other, and after Adele had swayed the group and gotten her Torah design, the meeting was adjourned.

The women stuck around for an hour or so afterward, drinking coffee, noshing on rugelach and pound cake. They gossiped and discussed the upcoming Jewish holidays and shared their recipes for noodle kugel and farfel and their main dishes.

"I've found that if you just add some stewed tomatoes to your brisket," Barbara said, slicing a sliver of pound cake, "it'll keep the meat extra moist."

"Does it still need gravy then?" asked Harriet, setting her coffee cup in her saucer and crossing her legs. I noticed she wore thick stockings that had bunched together around her ankles.

"Oh, of course you have to add gravy," insisted Adele as she scooped a forkful of cake into her mouth, letting a cluster of crumbs fall onto the front of her jacket.

She caught me staring and I turned away and gazed into Janice's kitchen, mesmerized by her canisters and rolling pins, her egg beaters and other shiny gadgetry that I didn't own or know how to use. I had a beautiful kitchen in our new home and yet I didn't cook at all. If we ate in, which was rare, Shep would fry up some hamburger meat or else scramble a few eggs. The first time he did that, he was appalled when I began eating from the pan, standing over the stove like I did in my mother's home.

"Can we at least sit down and pretend to be a civilized couple?" he said, reaching inside the cupboard and taking down two plates.

It had never occurred to me to set the table or fill the water glasses. Here I was, a married woman, living in a luxurious new house on State Parkway, about to have a child, and I didn't know the first thing about making a home. I needed to start picking up after myself, making an effort to keep the place clean and presentable. I glanced again at Janice's kitchen, fascinated by her row of cookbooks and measuring cups that fit one inside the other like Russian dolls.

"And don't forget," I heard Esther saying. "Use a good meat bone for your beef broth and you'll see what a difference it makes."

I nodded, taking note, trying to picture myself in an apron, standing over my stove, stirring a pot of beef stock.

I supposed the conversation was dull, but compared to what Evelyn had recently gone through with Izzy and his brush with death, it was refreshing to be preoccupied with something as basic as stained-glass windows and holiday recipes. I sat back and sipped my coffee, thinking, *So this is what regular, normal married women do.*

One thing I knew regular normal married women didn't do was attend parties for gangsters. But that very evening there was a celebration at the Meridian in honor of Dion O'Banion. What they were celebrating, no one said and I didn't ask.

I was six and half months pregnant and none of my other dresses fit, so I'd bought a special outfit for the occasion, not that there was much to choose from. I had my pick of a drop-waist in brown or beige, with no beading, no fringe, no nothing. Did dressmakers expect us to stay home and hide like our mothers did when they were pregnant? It wasn't like that anymore, but the thought that a pregnant woman might actually need an evening dress was still outlandish to some. "Help? Please." I turned my back to Shep so he could button my dress.

Following him into the kitchen, I watched as he reached for the bottle of cooking oil on the counter and took a swig. "You really think that's going to do something?" I asked, making a face as he swallowed another gulp of oil.

"Been doing it for years, Dollface. Just a little barkeep wisdom."

I shook my head. The first time I saw him do that, he said that the oil coated your stomach, kept you from getting too drunk.

"Gotta keep my wits about me tonight," he said, dabbing his mouth on a dish towel. "Can't afford to get sloppy."

"You, sloppy?" I laughed. "Never." I arranged the new pearl necklace he'd given me and smoothed the front of my dress.

He took another swig of the oil.

"Well?" I said, arms out to my sides, on display for him. "How pregnant do I look?"

He wiped his mouth again and placed his hand over the slope of my belly. "You look just pregnant enough."

As soon as we walked into the party, I spotted the one person I'd been hoping to avoid. Izzy was leaning against the end of the bar with a drink in one hand, a cigarette in the other. The last time I'd seen him, he'd just come out of surgery and was so groggy he didn't know who was in his hospital room. Considering that he'd been on a gurney just six weeks before, Izzy was doing surprisingly well.

I could feel his eyes on me, watching as Shep helped me off

with my coat. I looked straight ahead, willing myself not to turn his way. From the corner of my eye, I saw Izzy set his drink down. As he took a step toward me, I rushed over to Basha, Dora and Evelyn at the other end of the bar.

I saw right away that Basha was in a mood. She had a look on her face as she drummed her fingers on the marble top of the bar, her bracelets clanking off one another.

"What's with her?" I whispered to Evelyn after Shep and Izzy had gone into the back room where the party was already under way.

"Dora and Knuckles had dinner last night with Squeak and his wife."

"Ooh, no . . ." I made a face and ordered a bourbon, neat.

"All I'm saying is that Squeak's wife might be here tonight." Dora threw up her hands. "That's all. That's it!"

"She's not gonna be here because I'm here with him!" Basha drew hard on her cigarette. "And what the hell were you doing out with her anyway? You're supposed to be my friend. Not hers."

"C'mon, Basha," Evelyn said. "You know how it is."

"That's right!" Basha was all over Evelyn. "And you'd better get used to it. 'Cause Izzy's chasing after every skirt he sees, and he don't care if you know about it or not. Even when he was in the hospital he was feeling up his nurses. At least Squeak shows me some respect. Izzy don't give a damn about you."

Basha wasn't wrong about Izzy, but I couldn't sit back and let her talk to Evelyn that way. "Basha, back off!"

"Oh, listen to you!" She laughed, looking like she wanted to spit at my feet. "Now you wanna start in on me? You—Little Miss Nothin'. All of a sudden you think you're a somebody. You go and get yourself knocked up and marry Shep Green, start dressing with some class, you move into that big fancy house and you think you're better than the rest of us."

I felt smacked down, exposed as a fraud. I couldn't bring myself to look Basha in the eye. It was like she knew that underneath it all, I was still that same scrappy little girl from the stockyards trying to outrun my past.

"Hey!" Cecelia hissed from the opposite end of the bar. "This is Dion's party in case you forgot."

We got the message. Even Basha, who cleared her throat and climbed down off her barstool.

Dora whispered to no one in particular, "I was just saying that Squeak's wife might be here. That's it! That's all I was saying!"

"I know. I know." Basha held up a hand to silence her.

The four of us entered the party, packed with every major figure in the Forty-second and Forty-third wards, along with judges, representatives from the mayor's office, the teamsters union, and a group of trusted policemen. I pasted on a phony smile that was too wide, too bright. My face felt like it was about to crack.

Dora and Basha took off in opposite directions and Basha came over and sat with me, acting as if a cross word had never passed between us. "Would you get a load of that one?" She pointed across the room where this guy, Buster, was fooling around, juggling shot glasses.

"Hey, Buster!" Shep shouted with his hands cupped like a megaphone. "You break those and I'll break your neck!"

"No sweat!" Buster called back, tossing another glass into the air, chomping on a wad of chewing gum.

Buster was what Shep liked to call one of his Little Pishers. The Little Pishers were a dozen or so young thugs Shep let hang around the club. Whenever he needed someone to wash his motorcar or run his errands, he would say, "Have one of the Little Pishers do it." Buster was just a punk, maybe sixteen or seventeen, but he wanted to be a big shot already. He was wearing the same flashy pin-striped suit and fedora that I'd always seen him in.

"What a goddamn goof," said Bugs Moran, pulling up a chair, flipping it around, and sitting backward, sailor style. I didn't know much about Bugs at the time, other than that he hated being called Bugs. His real name was George and he struck me as a bit of a buffoon, a big lug of a guy who wasn't all that bright. I was surprised later when the girls told me he was third in command of the North Side Gang, right behind Hymie and Drucci.

"Hey, Buster," Bugs called to him, "why don't you run out and get me some smokes."

"Sure thing. I gotta go meet my girl anyway." Buster set down the glasses and was on the job.

Meanwhile the party lingered on and I sat back, drinking, watching Evelyn and Izzy. He had her on his lap with his arms looped around her waist. I'd been avoiding him all night but just then he caught me staring. We locked eyes for a moment before I caved and turned away.

Shep came over, set my drink down, and led me onto the dance floor. We were in the middle of *My Baby, She's So Good When She's Being Oh So Bad* when Buster walked in with a package of cigarettes for Bugs and a buxom redhead on his arm. The woman was a good three inches taller than him and wore a bright red dress with lots of feathers sticking out of it.

Shep sighed. "Son of a bitch—what's that Little Pisher up to now?" He kissed my cheek. "Give me a minute, Dollface."

He broke away and went over to Buster and his redhead. "Nice to see you again, Sally," I overheard him say.

"Oh, hey, you twos know each other?" Buster cracked his chewing gum.

"Sally and I go way back. Don't we, Big Red?"

"Hi, Shep." The redhead lowered her eyes, fluttering her lashes.

"So where'd you twos meet, anyway?" Buster asked, chomping away.

Shep smiled. "If memory serves me correctly, we met over by the Four Deuces—that piece-of-shit hole-in-the-wall."

Buster stopped chewing. His face went still and you could see him shrinking. That flashy suit of his now looked two sizes too big. "Hey, Shep—Sally here, she's—"

"She's leaving is what she's doing." Shep said this with his smile intact, his voice calm, steady. By now Hymie, Drucci and Bugs had made their way over to Shep's side.

"C'mon, Shep. Sally's not—"

"Sally's not staying." Shep tilted his head. "Good of you to stop by, Big Red. Be sure and give my best to Capone." Bugs held the door for Big Red while Shep and Hymie escorted her out.

I wandered back over to my table. As soon as Shep was gone and Evelyn was distracted, talking to Irwin Ragguffy, Izzy got up and walked over to me. His icy cold stare reached me before he did. *He couldn't know about Tony. Could he?* I kept reminding myself I hadn't even talked to Tony in months.... Still, my nerves were fraying. Beads of sweat began forming along the nape of my neck.

"Can't avoid me all night," he said.

"Looks like you've all but recovered," I managed to say, ignoring his comment. I took a sip from my drink, hoping the tremor in my hand wasn't obvious.

"Good as new." He held his hands out to the side and then lit a cigarette, holding it overhand style.

He must have smoked a good third of it down before he said anything else. If Izzy said anything to Shep about Tony, if he even suggested anything about my past, I'd be ruined. I was sure of it.

Izzy continued torturing me with silence. I looked at the doorway, hoping Shep would hurry back. Looking around, I saw Buster pacing, fidgeting first with his hat and then with his shirtsleeves.

"Listen . . ." Izzy set his cold, black eyes on me.

My pulse jumped. *Here it comes. . . .*

"I wanted to thank you for taking care of Evelyn while I was in the hospital."

"Oh . . ." I didn't know how else to respond. It felt like a trick.

He leaned over and planted a kiss on my cheek. "You're a good friend to her." Then he turned and walked away.

I stood there, dumbfounded. All I could think was that maybe the shooting had scared some sense into the man. Evelyn kept saying he was behaving himself. Maybe she was right.

When Shep and Hymie came back inside, Buster rushed up to them, hands flailing and head shaking. Shep smiled and placed what looked like a reassuring hand on Buster's shoulder. After motioning to Dion, I watched the three men lead Buster toward the back room.

I had another bourbon and made small talk with Irwin about the baby and the move to the new house. After a bit he excused himself and disappeared over by the bar. It was getting late and the party was thinning out. I hadn't seen Shep in a while. I was tired and figured I'd go find him, see how much longer he'd be.

When I pushed through the swinging door in the back and made my way past the cases of liquor, I heard the men below, in the cellar. I was halfway down the stairs when Buster began whimpering. "I swear, I didn't know. I swear it. Oh, c'mon! Please, no more. *Please!*"

My body went stiff as the cry of his *please* echoed through my insides. I inched along on the balls of my feet, keeping my body flush with the railing as I leaned forward, peering into the room. Buster was seated in a folding chair and Hymie had him by his hair, holding his head up. Blood trickled from Buster's lip like a drunkard's spittle, and his left eye was bruised shut. A puddle had collected beneath his chair, and the inside seam of his trousers was wet. Dion stood to his side, his fist tinged red from blood.

"It's getting late, Buster," Shep said, leaning against a ledge with his arms crossed. "How long you want this to go on?"

"I swear to you"—Buster was panting—"I didn't say nothin'. We didn't even talk about the Sieben Brewery raid. I swear it."

Shep lit a cigarette and took a long inhale. Hymie grabbed Buster by the hair again, violently jerking back his head. Buster let out a yelp as more blood spilled from his mouth. I winced, inching closer, not believing what I was seeing.

"You've already lost a couple of teeth," said Shep, pacing back and forth. "But we can keep going."

"No." Buster raised his hands. "Please, no more teeth. Please."

Shep examined the tip of his cigarette. "I'm only going to ask you once more."

"I swear on my life, I never told her about the Sieben Brewery. I didn't say a word about the raid. I swear it."

Shep took a final drag off his cigarette before grinding it out on the floor. He looked over at Dion and gave a nod. Buster let out a begging cry that rippled through me as Dion picked up a pair of wire cutters. Dion took hold of Buster's middle finger with the wire cutters and the more Dion tightened his grip, the louder Buster howled. I held on to the banister, squeezing it as Dion applied more pressure. The blood gushed out below Buster's knuckle. Even above Buster's screaming, I heard the snap of the bone. I closed my eyes and when I dared to open them again,

Buster's finger was lying on the floor in a pool of his own piss and blood.

Shep crouched down by Buster's side and said something else as Dion started on another finger. *Oh dear God!* I gagged as my stomach rose up. I cupped a hand over my mouth, swallowing my own vomit while I made my way back up the stairs.

I paused for a moment when I reached the top step. Ever since I'd married Shep I'd been so smug, thinking I'd come so far, that I'd escaped the blood and gore of the stockyards. But look where I'd landed. I'd had my suspicions before, but now the truth was staring me down. How much more could I pretend not to know, not to see? Especially after I'd just witnessed something that would haunt me the rest of my life. *How did I get mixed up in all this? And how do I get myself out of it?*

When I walked back into the party, Dora asked if I was okay.

"Yeah, sure. I'm fine. Just had a little too much to drink."

couldn't sleep next to Shep that night. I faked a headache and went out to the living room and lay awake on the sofa until the sun came up. Watching the shadows creeping in through the windows overlooking the park, I questioned if I knew Shep at all. I looked around our beautiful new home, taking note of the velvet cushions on the Queen Anne sofa, the Victrola housed in its beautifully carved walnut cabinet, the player piano and all the expensive artwork on the walls. As I ran my fingers over my silk bathrobe and admired my oversize diamond ring, all I could think was, *Is all this worth it?* If I hadn't been pregnant, I would have left him. That's what I told myself that night.

But the days passed and I didn't question Shep about what I'd seen him do to Buster. What was the point of confronting him? What would I do if he lied to me? What would I do if he told me the truth? I had a baby coming. Was I really prepared to leave? Leave my baby fatherless, the way I'd grown up? How could I ever take care of a child on my own? So I never asked Shep about the incident. Each time I had the opportunity, I lost my nerve, telling myself it was none of my business, or that it wasn't that bad. That at least they hadn't killed him. Or had they?

And then, just like everything else I didn't want to look at, I swept it aside, and over time the episode faded until its memory had all but vanished, just like Buster. I never did see him again at the Meridian after that night.

THE HANDSHAKE
AND THE SIN CAKE

It was the tenth of November. I was in my eighth month, sitting comfortably in the front parlor, when I heard a car door slam. Parting the drapes of the bay window, I saw Izzy coming up the walkway. He'd left the gate open behind him. It was eleven o'clock in the morning. Shep wasn't even awake yet. What was he doing here? My old fears began to surface. He was coming to tell Shep about Tony and me. That was the thing about a guilty conscience: It always expects the worst.

I waited for Izzy to knock or ring the bell, and after a few moments, I got up and opened the front door. Izzy stood on the threshold looking confused, as if he couldn't remember why he was there.

"Izzy?"

The blank expression on his face didn't change.

"Izzy, are you okay?" Whatever it was, I knew it wasn't about me and Tony.

He was pale and his eyes looked sunken.

"What's wrong?" I reached for his arm, trying to coax him inside.

"Get Shep for me, will ya," he said, stepping into the foyer but not bothering to close the door behind him. The cold winter chill rushed inside, skirting about my legs.

I went upstairs and woke Shep and by the time I came back downstairs, Izzy had fixed himself a drink. A few moments later, Shep came downstairs with his bathrobe flapping open, his dark hair rumpled.

"What's going on, Iz?" he asked, rubbing the sleep from his eyes.

"It's Dion," Izzy said, staring into his drink, shaking his head, a deep line furrowed along his brow.

"Dion? What happened?" Suddenly Shep was wide awake.

Izzy glanced up, his lids heavy and dark. "They got him, Shep. They shot him. Dion's dead."

I let out a gasp as Shep's legs gave way. He practically collapsed, but Izzy dropped his glass, stepped in and held him up.

"No! No! Not Dion! Jesus Christ. No!" Shep squeezed his eyes shut and grabbed onto his hair, tugging so hard his fingers turned white. His face was racked with anguish. It was the first time I'd ever seen him cry.

I knew then that we'd crossed a line that Shep wasn't prepared for. Even before I understood the ramifications of Dion's death, I had a sense that everything had just come unhinged and I was frightened down to my bones.

was too young to remember my father's murder, but what happened to Dion left me numb. Maybe I was reliving my past. All I knew was that the cold, heartless act of murder was beyond my comprehension. Anyone, anywhere could be taken from you. It would have been better if I could have cried, gotten it out of my system, but the fear was lodged so deep within me, I couldn't bring it to the surface.

I didn't find out what had happened to Dion until later that night. Basha had telephoned me after she'd gone to see Viola and told me to come over. "The guys are going to be out all night looking for Capone. No reason why we gals should be all alone worrying. I just called Dora. She's calling Evelyn now."

I was the first to arrive. Basha opened the door with a martini in one hand, a cigarette propped between her lips. She sauntered into her living room in her stocking feet.

"How's Viola?" I asked, unbuttoning my coat. I felt like it was ready to burst open, the buttons were straining so against my belly.

"She's a mess. Just destroyed. Help yourself," she said, pointing to the bottle of gin and a bucket of ice as she wandered over to the settee. "I'm almost out of vermouth, but at least there's plenty of olives."

I went and sat beside her.

"You don't want a drink?"

"Just tell me what happened."

"It's pretty much because Mike Merlo died," she said, shaking out her bracelets.

"Who's Mike Merlo?"

"He was a big to-do with the American Italians. He just passed away two days ago. Cancer." She shrugged and took a long sip from her martini. "Supposedly Merlo was the only one who's been able to keep Capone in line. Rumor has it that Capone blamed Dion for the Sieben Brewery raid—remember? That was what landed Johnny Torrio in the slammer. Anyway, Merlo told Capone to take the high road, but as soon as Merlo was gone, Capone was set loose."

"So Capone did it?" I asked.

"They're saying he hired Frankie Yale—some big-time New York gangster—to come into town and take care of Dion." She paused for another sip and danced her olive through her martini. "Apparently right after Merlo died, Capone sent Frankie Yale and another guy over to Schofield's to order flowers for the Merlo funeral."

"Why would Capone get his flowers at Schofield's?"

"You gotta understand how it works," Basha said, taking a puff off her cigarette. Her ashes were growing longer and longer, but she didn't seem to notice. "If you're a gangster and you need funeral flowers, there's only one place to go in Chicago. And that's Schofield's. Doesn't matter if you're a South Sider or a North Sider. Doesn't even matter if you're the one who whacked the guy."

"That doesn't make any sense."

"Doesn't have to make sense. Gangsters have a way of doing things. Especially when it comes to whacking someone." Basha dropped her cigarette ash on her settee cushion. She looked at it lying there and just went on talking. "So like I was saying, everyone went to Dion for funeral flowers, and Schofield's was working 'round the clock to fill all the orders for Merlo. For the really big orders, like the one Frankie Yale placed, Dion always made up the arrangements himself. He always liked Merlo and Viola said he wanted the flowers to be real nice, see. So this morning Dion goes to mass at Holy Name like he always does, and then goes back to the flower shop to put the finishing touches on the wreath for Merlo. At about ten o'clock this morning Frankie Yale and two other greaseballs go into Schofield's. Dion—you know how friendly he always was—went over to welcome Frankie Yale. He holds out his hand and that's when Yale grabbed him and held him in place. Dion didn't have a chance. They put six rounds in him." She looked at her martini glass and popped the olive in her mouth.

Basha was so icy cold in her delivery, like she was talking about a stranger, not Dion.

Does she not feel anything? At all?

I got up and fixed myself a drink.

Dion O'Banion's wake was a two-day citywide event. Reporters hovered outside Sbarbaro's Funeral Chapel in the chilling wind and rain, hoping for a comment or photograph. They hounded Shep when we arrived at the chapel that morning, practically chasing us up the front stairs. Aside from the first few rows of pews reserved for family and close friends, all the chairs were taken, leaving lines of people standing in front of the stained-glass windows along the back wall and out in the hallway. Everyone came to pay their last respects: union leaders, city clerks, aldermen, judges and cops. I glanced about the room: ministers and churchgoers sitting side by side with bootleggers, gangsters and hit men. It was a strange ensemble of mourners, and I wasn't sure if I was in the safest place in the city or the most dangerous.

It was all over the newspapers that Viola O'Banion had spent ten thousand dollars for Dion's casket. Some said it was nicer than most automobiles. Nicer than some homes. I didn't doubt it. That casket was made of solid silver and bronze, lined in white satin, with fourteen-karat-gold handles.

I'd never seen an open casket before and my first glimpse of Dion frightened me, sending a chill down my body. I turned away and nearly gasped. But then, when I looked back, when I really looked at him, I saw something I wasn't expecting. If ever I believed in a soul or an afterlife, it was in that moment. Dion looked like a wax figure, and all his life force, that jovial, dynamic spirit that defined him, had left his body. It wasn't Dion lying there; it was just a corpse.

The shell of him was laid out inside the coffin, dressed in a beautiful black three-piece suit, a silk necktie, and a rosary in his breast pocket. Next to that, resting on his chest, was an odd-looking cake the size of a silver dollar.

"What is that?" I whispered to Basha as we stood side by side in front of the casket.

"Some Irish tradition," she whispered back. "From the old country. I think they call it a sin cake. They say whoever eats it takes on the dead man's sins, so that way he can go to heaven with a clean slate." She sighed and shook her head. "He sure was a walking contradiction, wasn't he?"

I nodded. Dion O'Banion was a bootlegger who didn't drink, a devout Catholic who as a child had been an altar boy by day and a petty thief by night. . . .

"How many men you know who carry two short-barreled Bolos, a revolver *and* a rosary?" Basha smiled as if she'd always admired him for that. "He really loved the Church. And God, too." She ran her tongue across her front teeth and made a sucking sound. "You know that's why he never got into the whole cathouse racket. He thought prostitution was immoral. God wouldn't have approved."

"Apparently he didn't worry what God thought about murder. All the newspapers said he killed more than sixty men."

"Aw, he probably bumped off more than that. To him that was just business."

I glanced again at Dion's casket. I wouldn't have believed he was capable of murdering even one man if I hadn't seen what he'd done to Buster that night.

And then there were his flowers. Everywhere I looked I saw carnations, lilies, tulips and American Beauties, all of them in huge arrangements, oversize bouquets, baskets and gigantic wreaths with satin ribbons and glittery bows. The room had that waxy, mossy smell, just like Schofield's.

"Don't you think some of these flowers are a bit garish?"

"Nah," said Basha. "Not for Dion O'Banion. And I'll tell you, Squeak ain't impressed with the arrangement from Capone. He says it's too chintzy."

"I'm surprised Capone sent flowers in the first place."

"Ah, that's just the gangster way. First they kill you, then they send you flowers."

We'd been at the wake all day and my lower back was sore, my feet swollen. The baby was restless that day and I rubbed my stomach in big lazy circles until it found a place and settled. Wearing the only black maternity dress I could fit into, I felt like a whale sitting next to Evelyn. How was I going to handle another month of this?

I glanced over at Evelyn with her stylish hairdo, dressed in a smart tailored dark suit and a fur stole. She'd never looked better. In what came as a shock to us all, Evelyn had finally managed to rope in Izzy. They were playing house, and according to Evelyn, he was being a good boy. You had to hand it to her: She'd hung in there and put up with more baloney than any woman I knew, and in the end, she got her man. And at least she was able to quit her typewriter job. I was beginning to think I'd underestimated Izzy. Ever since he'd taken those slugs to his gut, he appeared to be a changed man. As long as he was good to Evelyn I was willing to give him the benefit of the doubt.

When the service began the priest called Shep to the podium to give the first of what turned out to be a series of eulogies and memorials.

Shep gripped the sides of the stand and took a moment to collect himself before he began speaking. "Dion practically raised me," he said. "He was like a brother to me. Deanie taught me everything. He appreciated art and music, especially opera. He always believed in surrounding yourself with good books. He taught me the important things—that you always open a door for a lady, you always shake a gentleman's hand." He paused for a moment, his eyes filling with tears; I knew he was remembering that it was the handshake that had done Dion in. He covered his eyes and took another moment. "I loved Dion. He was my family and he will be missed." He took his hand away as tears slid down his face.

Then Shep walked over to the casket and picked up the piece of cake resting on Dion's chest. A lump collected in my throat. I didn't know if I believed in the notion of sin cakes or not, but I looked at that cake in Shep's hand and I felt afraid for him. *Don't do it, Shep!*

"And so, Deanie," he said, raising the cake to his mouth, "this I do for you. May you rest in peace. May God bless and keep you." Shep bit into the sin cake and tainted his soul.

I t was late, going on midnight, and most of the visitors had already left the funeral home. Drucci and Cecilia had taken Viola home hours before, and so there was just a handful of us left when Al Capone showed up.

Dressed in a pale yellow overcoat and bold matching necktie, he waltzed in accompanied by a short, stocky man with a pock-marked face. As soon as I saw the sapphire pinkie ring and the stub of a cigar in his hand, my blood went cold. He was the cigar man, the one who'd asked me about Tony the day he'd run out on me at the Hotel Twenty-nine. I lowered my head and held my breath, trying to be invisible. I hadn't been showing when that man saw me last. Now I was fat and hardly recognized myself so there was a chance that he wouldn't recognize me, either. But still, my palms were damp, my throat was dry.

Shep and Hymie stopped Capone and the cigar man just inside the doorway. "You got some nerve showing up here."

"Well"—Capone motioned toward Dion's casket—"I had to come by and make sure he's not still breathing."

Hymie lunged forward but Shep stopped him. "Not here," Shep said, keeping his eyes on Capone. "Not now."

I buried my face inside my pocketbook and waited it out with my pulse ready to jump out of my skin. As soon as Capone finished viewing the body, Hymie and Shep escorted him and the cigar man out of the funeral parlor.

"What was he doing here?" Evelyn asked.

"Oh, I'm not surprised," said Basha, toying with her bracelets. "You wait and see, all those South Siders'll be at the funeral Friday."

"Even though they killed him?"

Dora nodded. "Makes no sense, but they think it's an act of respect. Go figure."

When Hymie and Shep came inside, the men huddled together in the back of the room. We girls were standing well within earshot but for once the men didn't seem to care.

Hymie lit a cigarette and exhaled two thick streams of smoke from his nose. "The day those greaseballs went into Schofield's to whack Deanie," he said, picking a fleck of tobacco off his tongue, "was the day Capone gave himself a death sentence."

Shep ran his hand back through his hair, smoothing over his widow's peak. "Gentlemen," he said, "we're in the middle of a gang war now."

BOOK TWO

1926–1927

THE WAR HITS HOME

The front door slammed and woke me with a jolt. It was almost two in the morning and the other side of the bed was empty, the sheets smooth and cool against my open palm. I heard Shep and Hymie going at it, even from upstairs, even while I was still half asleep.

It had been a little over a year since Dion's murder and everything had shifted. Hymie, Drucci, Bugs, Shep and the rest of the North Siders were like those shooting galleries at the penny arcade: One got gunned down and the others all moved up a notch.

Now it was Hymie in charge and he had one goal, one obsession, and that was to kill Al Capone. I knew Hymie had already made several attempts but Capone had always gotten away. Rumor had it that every morning for the past year, Hymie had been going to Holy Name, getting down on his knees, and praying for a clean shot at Capone.

I used to question why a Jew would go to Holy Name Cathedral. Then Shep explained that Hymie wasn't Jewish. Turned out

Hymie Weiss came into this world as Earl Wojciechowski and was as Catholic as could be, though he did the most unholiest of things. I wondered why he paraded around as a Jew. Why not say he was Irish or Italian? We Jews had enough problems without being adopted by the likes of him. But for whatever reason, Earl wanted to be called Hymie Weiss.

I rolled onto my stomach and tried to go back to sleep. I was exhausted. Hannah had just turned one year old the month before, but she still wasn't sleeping through the night. I couldn't remember the last time I'd gotten more than a few hours' sleep at a stretch. I wasn't yet able to wean her off nursing, and there were feedings and crying spells and times when I woke with a start and raced into her nursery, only to find her sound asleep. Plus, I'd been running around the day before, getting ready for the Jewish Women's Council meeting that I was hosting the following day.

I'd never entertained before. Ever. Here it was, more than a year and half since we'd been married, and I finally had an occasion to use our wedding china. I wanted everything to be perfect. While the housekeeper polished the silver and the samovar and ironed the tablecloth and napkins, I set out my china and serving platters on the table and sideboard for the buffet. In addition to purchasing *Mrs. Wilson's Cook Book*, I had enrolled in a correspondence cooking course out of Scranton, Pennsylvania. I had five books of instruction, complete with examinations at the end of each chapter. I was only a quarter of the way through book one, which focused on kitchen utensils, cooking terminology and kitchen safety.

For my first stab at home entertaining, I turned to a recipe for upside-down pineapple cake in *Mrs. Wilson's Cook Book*. I'd made a practice cake the day before that had fallen as soon as I'd removed it from the oven, so I'd started over, measuring the flour and baking soda from my newly purchased canisters. I prepared the shortening and with my new hand beater blended the ingredients into a fluffy, frothy batter. After it came out of the oven, I was so stinking proud of myself. The cake on my counter looked not too different from Mrs. Wilson's photographs. I set it in the center of my buffet, carefully covering the top with a glass cake dome.

I had almost fallen back asleep when the baby started crying. Such a tiny thing, but Hannah tested me in ways I never expected. She also opened my heart further and faster than I thought possible. The instant the nurse placed her in my arms I burst into tears, because she was perfect and beautiful. And mine.

Hannah wailed again and I threw off the covers, grabbed my robe, and padded down the hall to the nursery. I turned on the night-light, and as soon as she saw me she stopped crying. Her need for me went straight to my heart. How could I forgive myself for thinking I hadn't wanted her? *My God, I made her.* This beautiful, perfect little being came from me. Part of me—part of my heart—was in my arms and there was nothing that could separate the two of us. I loved to kiss every finger, every toe, to lean over and play the trumpet on her belly. I couldn't imagine my mother ever feeling that way about me. But I was sure she'd had all the answers when I was born. She and every other mother in the world knew what they were supposed to do. I was scared to death. Did I change her diaper in time? Did I feed her too soon, too late? Why was she crying? Why *wasn't* she crying? There wasn't a single thing I didn't question. I wanted to be a good mother. I wanted her to love me. I never wanted anyone's love before like I wanted the love of my baby.

After she fell back asleep, I stood over her crib, studying her face, scrutinizing her dark curls, hoping that was a sign that she belonged to Shep.

Meanwhile, Hymie and Shep were still arguing, their voices growing louder. I worried that they would wake Hannah and headed downstairs to tell them to knock it off.

"I'm running the show," I overheard Hymie saying. "I'm the one calling the shots and I'm telling you, I want Capone backed into a corner. I wanna make him pay for what he did to Deanie. I want that cocksucker's blood splattered all over this town."

"I've been greasing every palm I can. We'll get him. I promise you. I've got people on the lookout for Capone from Cicero all the way up to Rogers Park. I know when that son of a bitch goes to the barbershop. I know every restaurant he's been to in the past twelve months. I know when he takes a crap—"

"Then just fuckin' do it already!"

"Jesus Christ, Hymie—get a grip."

"You need to get the fuckin' job done. *Now!*"

"Oh, that's just great. Sure, pull out your gun. Shoot me, Hymie. That'll help matters."

Hymie let out a low growl.

A second later I heard a scuffle and something crashed to the ground. Sounded like the samovar and half my wedding china. The two of them were calling each other names and in the midst of all the chaos, I heard a gun go off.

I screamed as I tore into the living room and found Hymie and Shep looking up at the hole in the ceiling, plaster showering down onto the dining room table. While I stood there trying to put my heart back inside my chest, what were they doing? *Laughing!* I could have killed them both, especially when Hannah started crying.

"Great! You scared the baby! And me, too. Thanks." Half the coffee cups and saucers were shattered on the ground. I looked at what was left of my upside-down cake, now broken in two, the pineapple slices strewn across the rug with flecks of plaster stuck to them. Kicking a piece of china out of the way, I stormed up-stairs to the nursery.

Hard as I tried, I couldn't find the balance between being a gangster's wife and a mother. How was I supposed to raise a child in the middle of all this? It was times like this that the truth about our life poked through the illusion of normality I tried to create. I knew what it was to be fearful as a child and I didn't want that for my daughter. I wanted her to know she was safe, no matter what. But how was that possible when a gun had just gone off inside her home? And as she grew older, what would I tell her? Would I lie to her about her father, the way I'd lied to myself?

After I'd gotten Hannah quieted down and Hymie had left, Shep came upstairs.

"What was that all about?" I glared at him.

"Hymie just got a little hot under the collar. That's all. Don't worry about it."

"Don't worry about it? Hymie just fired a gun in my house! It scared your daughter half to death! My dining room is in shambles thanks to the two of you." I slapped my hands against my thighs. "I'm having a meeting here tomorrow afternoon. How am I supposed to explain a bullet hole in my ceiling! I've had it. You tell Hymie he's not welcome here anymore."

"I can't do that. You know I can't." He stepped out of his trousers, lining up the creases and folding them neatly in half before tucking them under the mattress. "Hymie's going through a rough time. It won't happen again."

I went to my dressing table. Made a big show of brushing my hair too hard, opening a drawer and then slamming it shut.

He came over and met my eyes in the mirror. "You have to understand, I'm under a lot of pressure right now. I'm trying to keep Hymie in line, trying to keep everything glued together."

I turned around on my vanity stool. "We have a baby now. I'm trying to make a real home for us. You're supposed to protect us, Shep, and instead you're putting us in danger."

"I'm not going to let anything happen to you and Hannah."

"How can you be so sure? I can't have guns going off inside my house. Jesus, I'm surprised the neighbors didn't call the police."

"I get it." He leaned in closer to me. "I'll talk to Hymie. It won't happen again. Okay?"

We looked at each other, but his eyes were empty. He was someplace else and I felt a chill in his fingertips as he traced them across my shoulders.

The next morning, even before the baby awoke and the housekeeper had arrived, I was up, cleaning. I swept up the broken china pieces and the plaster dust, trying to salvage my buffet setup. Since half a dozen cups and saucers had been casualties of the previous night's ruckus, I had to fill in with my everyday dishes. My cake was ruined and I didn't have the ingredients to make a new one. All I had to serve my guests was coffee in mismatched cups.

After getting the house ready, I went upstairs to freshen up and get dressed. Fifteen minutes before the women started arriving Shep wandered downstairs in just his BVDs, with his bathrobe flapping open, the belt hanging from the loops, dragging behind him.

"Shep!"

"What?"

"My meeting. Remember? They'll be here any minute."

He raised his hands in surrender and went back upstairs.

By the time the women arrived, I was thankful that Shep was properly dressed and tucked away inside his study.

It took Adele Markey all of thirty seconds to ask about the ceiling.

"Oh," I said, trying to lead her away from the scene of the crime, "we just had a little accident, that's all. It was nothing. . . ."

I must have fielded another dozen similar inquiries by the time everyone arrived. The bullet hole had upstaged everything I was so proud of: my beautiful Jean-Michel Frank carpets, my velveteen rococo settees and the Chippendale chairs. The women paid no attention to my favorite pieces. Instead they helped themselves to coffee while I apologized, explaining that I'd dropped the cake that morning. They didn't seem to mind half as much as I did.

A good twenty minutes into it, Adele started the meeting. The topic of the day was a book drive for the needy.

"Forgive me for asking," said Esther, "but can the needy read?"

Adele and Harriet were debating the issue when Hymie Weiss, Bugs Moran and Vincent Drucci, in all their pinstripes and brawn, barged through the front door, letting in a rush of frigid January air along with a trail of snow and slush behind them. It gave the women quite a start and I apologized as the men let themselves into Shep's study.

"Well"—Adele Markey cleared her throat—"as I was saying, we need to stress that all the books must be in good condition. . . ." Adele continued, gradually raising her voice to compete with the commotion coming from the men down the hall. "Are you getting all this down, madam secretary?"

"Absolutely," said Harriet, taking copious notes.

Filtering through the walls we heard, "Goddamn motherfuckin' greaseballs! Those fuckin' slimeballs!"

I spoke up, trying to deflect their attention. "We'll need to organize them in some way, either by author or by—"

"Cocksuckers!"

The word hung in the air, reverberating like a bell, ringing out over and over again. I shifted my eyes about the room. The women looked like they'd been assaulted.

"I'm sorry, ladies. Excuse me." I got up, my cheeks burning red as I rushed down the hall.

"Will you guys knock it off! Jesus! We can hear *everything* you're saying!"

I had barely made it back into the living room when the telephone rang. Not a minute later Shep's office door swung open and the men moved into action. They stormed into the living room, oblivious to the twenty women staring with their mouths agape. The men were whooping it up, slapping one another on their backs, squaring their fedoras on their heads as they spit out a few more obscenities and bolted out the door. From the picture window I saw them pile into Shep's automobile and drive away.

"Shep doesn't usually work from home," I said, forcing a laugh. "I hardly even know those other men—thank goodness. They work down at the nightclub," I said, hoping they looked more like the nightclubbing sort than a group of mobsters.

"Oh . . ."

"I see. . . ."

"Uh-huh . . ."

The women seemed understanding enough, considering that the only disruptions we'd ever had during our meetings were an occasional child waking up from their nap, a rare telephone call, or the time Thelma Glick suffered a migraine and we had her lie down on the sofa with cold compresses applied to her forehead.

The next morning it was all over the newspapers. *Deadly Gunfire Opens on Alphonse Capone.* I glanced at the photograph on the front page. It featured the remains of an automobile, polka-dotted with bullet holes from the hood to the trunk. The windshield was shattered like confetti, and a body was slumped over the steering wheel.

I shoved my coffee aside and reached for a cigarette as I sat at the kitchen table reading about the *unidentified assailants* who blasted Capone's car. Those *unidentified assailants* had congregated in my home just moments before. A witness claimed that a black sedan closed in on Capone's Packard at State and Fifty-fifth streets. He said he saw the tommy guns sticking out the windows of the car just moments before he heard the first shots. The real news was in the next paragraph: "The driver was killed instantly; however, Mr. Capone himself escaped uninjured. . . ."

I couldn't finish the article. I crumpled up the newspaper and stuffed it in the garbage pail.

As hard as I tried, I couldn't straddle both worlds. What happened to the man I married? When did he become this cold-blooded hit man who'd run out the door at the drop of a hat to chase down Capone?

SMALL WORLD

looked out the window as my streetcar swept along the track. Trees were in bloom, the grass was green again and spring was alive and thriving. We'd made it through the bulk of the winter without incident, and I was beginning to think the North Side Gang's obsession with killing Capone had run its course. I couldn't remember the last time I'd heard Shep mention Capone's name.

Covering my nose and mouth with my handkerchief, I continued to watch as my streetcar hummed past the familiar brick buildings and the long stretch of railroads. It was my third visit to the stockyards that month. Ever since Hannah was born, I found excuses to see my mother. It was hard leaving Hannah, even for a few hours. I'd miss her and worried that I was missing something: her putting new words together, learning to play by herself with a toy. But if I didn't get away I was no good for her. Exhausted from lack of sleep, I'd grow irritable and short, bursting into tears over the slightest little things. So, reluctantly I'd leave my baby with the housekeeper or Dora, who was forever volunteering to stay with Hannah. My mother always wanted me to bring Hannah along, which surprised me at first. I hadn't expected her to embrace her "illegitimate" granddaughter, but apparently she liked being a grandmother more than she liked being a mother. As for me, I wasn't about to expose Hannah to the stockyards. She was only fifteen months old, and she'd already seen enough things I wished she hadn't.

Maybe it was guilt that brought me back to my mother's, or maybe it was because I understood her more now that I was a mother myself. My mother had to have had her share of sleepless nights, raw, chafed nipples, fatigue and frustration, and yet all of that would have been set aside for the needs of me, her child. I understood that now and it choked me up. She may not have known how to show it, but how could I have doubted that she loved me as much as I loved Hannah?

I got off the streetcar along with a cluster of other passengers and waded my way through the main gate of the Union Stock Yards. A young girl wearing a babushka and tattered shoes lumbered her way alongside me. She had the posture of an old woman, and when I caught her eye, she gave me a smile without a speck of resentment for my cloche hat or my new Mary Janes. But still, I couldn't look at her again and was relieved when she veered off the path, heading in the opposite direction.

I walked past a group of men unloading flatbed wagons full of cowhides piled on top of one another, stacked up like carpets. Flies swarmed everywhere, huge ones, buzzing around my head, loud as bees. In between each cowhide there was a layer of salt. Four men grabbed hold of a skin, two at one end and two more at the other, and together they lifted it above their heads, shaking the hide like they were airing out a blanket. Pellets of salt flew in all directions, landing on the sidewalk at my feet.

As I walked by, someone called to me, "Vera? Hey, Vera?"

"Buster? What are you doing down here?" I was surprised to see him and relieved that he was still alive. Instead of that flashy suit he always wore, now Buster was in a pair of dusty bib overalls and a graying undershirt. His fedora was replaced by a soft cap and he was missing a couple teeth and two fingers on his left hand. I glanced at the knobby stubs, stopping at his knuckles.

"Well, how have you been, Mith Vera?" he asked, walking over to me. He spoke with a lisp on account of his missing teeth.

"What are you doing here, Buster?"

"I'm working at the thockyards now." He took off his cap and put it back on riding backward on his forehead. He chomped hard on a piece of gum and it struck me that, aside from that night when Dion knocked his teeth out, I couldn't remember when he wasn't chewing gum.

"Yep," he said, "working real hard down here at the thock-yards."

"No fooling, huh?"

"Yeah, I got out of the rackets." He stared out at the livestock pens. He asked about Shep and before I could answer, he said he'd recently gotten married himself. I pretended not to notice when he glanced down at what should have been his ring finger.

"Did you now? Well, that's real swell, Buster."

"Yeah. I married Thally."

Sally? I was blank for a minute but then I remembered Sally—Big Red, the redhead he'd brought to Dion's party.

"She's a good girl. Her father's worked down here for years. He's the one who got me a job here." He pointed toward the Abramowitz sign.

"Here? You work here?"

"Yep. Been here 'bout thix months now."

"Six months, huh? Doing what?"

"I drive a truck. Make deliveries. Mostly I run hides over to the thanneries. Make a few runs to the butcher thops around town, that thort of thing." He reached in his pocket for a stick of chewing gum and offered me a piece of Juicy Fruit.

I shook my head and looked at the delivery trucks with *Abramowitz Meats* stenciled along the back and side panels. There were two of them, parked by the loading dock.

He folded a fresh stick, and before he shoved it into his mouth, he spit out the wad he'd been chewing. I glanced at the ground and noticed Buster's shoes. Brand-new, expensive-looking. More than he could have ever afforded on a deliveryman's salary. Those were rich men's shoes, and only someone like Buster would have been stupid enough to wear them around the stockyards with his overalls. I looked up at Buster, noticing the gold chain on his watch dangling down from his pocket.

Buster was a nothing in Dion's outfit. Nothing but a Little Pisher. They used him as a driver, had him load and unload cases of liquor and barrels of beer, but not much more. He wasn't making the kind of money at that point that he could have afforded shoes like that, not to mention his watch. He was getting his money from someplace now, though. And if he was married to Big Red, then his connection had to be with Capone. I glanced back at the trucks parked along the side of the building.

"What brings you down here, anyway, Mith Vera? Or should I say Mithess Green?"

When he said that, I got a funny feeling. He'd called me Mrs. Green with such disdain. Could he have possibly seen me standing on the stairwell that night, watching everything that Shep and the others had done to him? "Visiting a friend, that's all." I forced a smile and shrugged. For some reason I didn't want Buster knowing that my mother was his boss. Buster never knew my maiden name, and he wasn't going to find out now.

"Well," he said, turning back toward the others, gesturing to the flatbed of bloody cowhides, "I'd better get back to work."

We said our good-byes and I went inside.

My mother sat at her desk, talking on the telephone. A stack of papers had collected at her side and the day's mail was fanned out before her. Four men stood around, talking softly among themselves, waiting to speak with her about a salt order, how many head of cattle they needed to purchase, how much ice they needed for the cooling rooms. She'd been complaining that business was slow, but it didn't look slow to me.

I stood back watching while she finished her phone call and issued orders to her men. "And don't come back here without that contract signed, you hear me?" she called to one of them as he was leaving. "Jessie," she said to another worker, "remember I want that cattle pen fixed before you leave here today."

As I observed my mother, something struck me at my core. I realized that she must have been about my age when she took over my father's business. I tried to imagine what she must have gone through back then. My mother, like me, had been an only child. She'd married my father, twenty-three years her senior, just three months after his first wife died, which set off a scandal. His family didn't approve of the marriage and by the time I was born, they wanted nothing to do with me—even after my father was killed. My mother had no family to help her, and I'm certain she was terrified that the Black Hand would come back looking for more money.

How dare I complain about anything! I didn't work. I went to lunch and shopped. I went to meetings with a bunch of women who believed a cookie could solve the world's ills. And while I may have been learning to cook, I had a housekeeper who did most of the cleaning and helped with the baby. The two days each week she wasn't there, I could barely get the beds made. But here my mother had stepped into a man's world, learned how to run a business and mastered all the ins and outs of an ugly industry.

I'd seen her negotiate a heard of cattle for an unheard-of price. I'd seen her throw many a salesman out on their ear because they came in thinking they could swindle a woman. I'd seen her scold a grown man, reducing him to tears. My mother could be every bit as tough as a man and God knows she was a hell of a lot smarter than most of them.

After her workers had left and she'd sent Ida down to the kill floor, I wanted to tell her I was proud of her, but instead I said, "Since when do you hire bootleggers?"

"Bootleggers?" The corners of my mother's mouth turned downward as she gathered the papers strewn across her desk. "What are you talking about?"

"That guy, Buster, out there"—I gestured toward the front door—"he used to make liquor runs for the North Side Gang."

"Oh, that's nonsense. He's a nice young man. His father-in-law's worked here for years."

"Yeah, well, I'd keep an eye on him if I were you. And your trucks, too. I wouldn't be surprised if he's using one of them for bootlegging." I sat on her desk, letting my legs dangle down in front, my heels knocking against the side panel like I used to do when I was little. Thinking about Buster's shoes and his watch, I said, "Looks like Buster's lining his pockets pretty good, Ma."

She checked some totals on her ledger. "At least someone's getting rich down here. All I'm doing these days is losing money." She opened a file drawer, dropped the ledger inside. "If your friend out there wasn't such cheap labor, he'd be out of a job."

"Are things really that bad? You seem so busy." I leaned back and looked at her.

My mother went into a full stretch and yawned. "At least the bank gave me another extension on my loan—that'll buy me some time."

"An extension? Ma, if you need money, why don't you come to me? I'll ask Shep for it."

My mother sat up straight and shot me a look like she just ate something rotten. I should have known better than to make that kind of an offer. Usually Shep's money made me feel superior; now it made me ashamed. My mother knew Shep's money was dirty, and I felt dirty for having it.

THE BALANCING ACT

Judging by the half dozen cigarette butts in the ashtray, Basha must have been waiting at the café for half an hour or so. She uncapped her flask and poured a splash of bourbon into her teacup and then mine. It was a gorgeous summer day and it was just the two of us, seated outside at a garden café, surrounded by ladies who probably had never added anything to their teacups other than a wedge of lemon or a teaspoon of sugar.

"So what is this all about?" I asked. She'd called earlier, saying it was urgent. She needed to meet with me privately.

"I need your help."

"With what?" I opened my menu.

"I'm gonna do it." She nodded as she examined her cigarette holder, rolling its bejeweled stem between her fingertips. "I'm gonna off her."

"Oh, Basha." I shook my head and laughed. "So what's it going to be this time? Are you going to throw a bomb through her kitchen window? Or maybe just set her house on fire?"

Lighting up a fresh cigarette, she leaned back and exhaled. "There's this poison I can get."

"Uh-huh . . ." I closed my menu, setting it aside.

"She'll never even taste it. It's this white powder. It dissolves right away. Costs a damn fortune but it'll be worth it. They said it takes about four hours to work. All I have to do is find a way to get it in her coffee or her food. And I need you to—"

"Wait a minute. Hold it." I leaned forward and lowered my voice. "Are you serious?" I looked into her eyes. Her long dark lashes didn't flutter; her heavily lined lids didn't blink. "Oh, good lord. You *are* serious, aren't you!"

"I can't take it anymore. I can't stand the thought of Squeak being with her. He doesn't love her."

"But he loves his children."

"But he loves me more."

As a parent I could have set her straight on that score, but I didn't.

"She'd meet with you. You could call and invite her out for lunch. Or coffee. I'll do the rest. I just need you to help me so I can put it in her food."

"Basha, put this crazy idea out of your mind."

"You don't know what it's like for me. It's different when you're a wife. I'm only the moll. It's not the same. And yeah, sure, Squeak's got me in a nice place but he's with her two, sometimes three nights a week. And when do I get a Saturday night? Hardly ever. And the holidays, forget it. I'm the one sitting home alone while he's with her. It tears me up inside."

"Then maybe you should look for a man who's single and available."

She winced, making her face look as though it were cast in plaster and on the verge of cracking. "I have to do this, and I can't go to Dora—she's friends with the bitch. So is Cecelia. The old wives' club. And Viola's still a mess over Dion. I can't ask her. Squeak's wife's doesn't really know Evelyn, so you're my only hope."

I reached for my bourbon and took a burning gulp. "I'm not going to be any part of this."

"You don't understand. Squeak's everything to me. I never had a family. My father was a drunkard. My mother went crazy, thought there were spiders crawling on her all the time. She picked her arms and legs raw trying to get the spiders off. I hated being in that house with them. I was miserable until I met Squeak." Her eyes began to glaze over. It was the first time I'd ever seen her close to showing any real emotion, let alone shedding an honest-to-God tear. Under that rough, brash exterior was another lonely romantic. "I love him," she said. "I can't stand to be away from him. It hurts. It makes me ache for him. Do you have any idea what it's like to love a man that much?"

I stared down into my bourbon. There he was, right in the center of my thoughts. Tony Liolli.

After an hour and a half of talking Basha out of poisoning Mrs. Squeak, I arrived fifteen minutes late for that Wednesday's meeting of the Jewish Women's Council.

With a girlfriend plotting murder and a gangster for a husband, my weekly meeting was the only thing that made me feel normal. Whether we were discussing making challah for the temple bake sale or donating books to the Yeshiva library, attending those meetings was my anchor, helping me keep one foot planted in reality.

The topic that day was helping Jewish war widows.

"I've given this matter a great deal of thought," began Adele Markey, "and I suggest that we give the Jewish widows yellow carnations to commemorate the anniversary of the Great War."

Adele pressed on, "Wouldn't that be a lovely gesture for those lonely widows whose brave husbands perished?"

When she'd finished, I surprised myself by speaking up. "A carnation? That's it?"

Everyone turned and looked at me, shocked that I would question the great Adele Markey.

"What would you prefer?" Adele challenged me, narrowing her eyes, pursing her lips.

"I can only speak as a daughter who grew up without a father," I said. "He may not have died in the war, but I know what a struggle it was for my mother without him. And having a child to provide for made it especially difficult. We can't forget that these women have children. It takes money for their shoes, clothing, doctor visits—housekeepers to look after them while their mothers go to work. With all due respect, Adele, we can do better than giving them a carnation. Why can't we hold a fundraiser in their honor? These widows don't need flowers—they need money." I paused, noticing that all the women had scooted forward in their chairs, their bodies turned toward me. "I'm sorry," I said. "I didn't mean to ramble on like that."

"No, no," said Harriet, "please go on."

I shifted in my chair and smoothed the front of my dress, feeling all eyes upon me. "It's just that there's a hole in the heart of these families. Their lives have been shattered and these widows are left to pick up the pieces." The women were nodding, encouraging me. "I know that money is never going to take the place of the love and security that only a husband and father can give, but money—even a small amount—could make their lives a little easier. . . ."

The whole time I was talking, I found myself missing my father, though I hadn't really known him. I told myself that if Abe Abramowitz had lived, he would have gotten out of the meatpacking business and taken an office job. If he had lived, my mother wouldn't have had to work. We wouldn't have lived beneath the Black Hand's shadow, haunted by the unspoken trepidation that had settled over our house.

By the end of my sermon, all the women—even Adele Markey—agreed that it was a splendid idea and that I should chair the event. At first I resisted. It was too much work. The thought of it overwhelmed me. But then I realized this was a chance for me to redeem myself with the Jewish Women's Council after the disastrous meeting I'd hosted. It was also a chance for self-redemption. I wouldn't be just a gangster's wife anymore. This had nothing to do with who I'd married. It wasn't about Shep's money, his influence, or his connections. This was about me and what I could do to make a legitimate place for myself and my daughter in this community.

I left that day with half a dozen invitations to dinner parties and luncheons and I'd never felt better.

As soon as I got home, I telephoned my mother. I wanted to make her proud, to show her that she had raised a strong, independent-minded daughter after all. ". . . I was telling them all about you," I told her.

"My goodness, what on earth did you tell them?"

"Nothing bad, don't worry. I just told them how hard it was for you, raising a daughter on your own."

"Oh, that." She sighed. "*Nisht geferlech*, it wasn't such a big deal. I did what I had to do. That was that." I could picture her dusting her hands, one off the other, as she said that.

"Yes, it was a big deal." It was so hard to give her a compliment. I told her about the fund-raiser. "And guess what? They want me to chair the whole event." I held my breath, waiting for her response. I felt like a little girl again, showing her my marks from school.

"And why shouldn't they pick you? You're certainly capable."
She sounded as if she believed this, as if she believed in me. But
all I could think was, Where was this mother when I did show
her my marks from school?

There was a long silence and I heard the ruckus going on
behind her, the banging of typewriter keys, the squeaking of filing cabinets being opened and shut.

"I'm just glad you're not associating with that Basha woman
or the others anymore."

I didn't dare say that I hadn't forsaken Basha and Dora for
the members of the JWC.

"Those other women were trouble, believe me. You're better
off without them. Now if you could just get rid of that gangster
husband of yours, you might stand half a chance."

I gripped the base of the phone and when she started to
speak again, I cut her off. "The baby's crying, Ma," I lied. "I have
to go." I hung up before she'd even said good-bye.

MADAM CHAIRMAN

With Hannah asleep in my arms, I spent hours on the telephone talking with committee members and discussing possibilities. I kept a booklet at my side, filled with numbers, meeting dates and notes for the Jewish Women's Council's event.

We agreed that we would hold a luncheon and charge five dollars a person, half of which would go to our cause. But five dollars a head wasn't going to amount to much of a fund-raiser, so we schemed and decided to hold an auction with all the proceeds going to the Jewish Women's Council's Widows' Fund.

On the days my housekeeper looked after Hannah, I visited venues where we could hold our luncheon. I must have met with every café and tearoom owner from the Loop up to North Michigan Avenue. I worked on the invitations, the flowers and other decorations.

All was coming together except for the auction. The luncheon was less than six weeks away when Esther telephoned to say they were having trouble getting items donated.

"I'm sorry," she said, "but we're just not having any luck."

"You're telling me we have nothing!" I said. "We're running out of time and we have nothing to auction?"

"We're trying, but no one wants to donate merchandise when they can sell it."

As the chairwoman, the auction was ultimately my responsibility, so I had no choice but to step in. The next day I went out and called upon merchants myself.

I started in the neighborhood and went from store to store in the sweltering August heat. When I asked the owner of the millinery shop around the corner if she'd like to donate a hat to our cause, she politely asked me to leave. The stationers' shop wasn't much more receptive, but at least the owner let me get through my spiel before he escorted me to the door.

After a week of similar encounters, out of desperation I turned to Irwin Ragguffy, a widower and Jewish. I knew he'd be more sympathetic to our cause.

"You sure you don't need anything more?" he asked when I went to see him.

"You're too generous, Irwin." My arms were loaded down with brassieres and undergarments. I could just picture those prim and proper women bidding on a pair of lacy silk bloomers.

"I'll tell you what." He reached for his fountain pen and jotted down a list of names and addresses. "You go see these people. They'll donate to your cause. And if they don't"—he winked as he handed me the paper—"you just let me know."

Benny Alberts was my first stop. He was a middle-aged man, bald-headed, with a silver horseshoe hairline and a gold ring the size of a sealing wax stamp. I introduced myself and explained that I was hosting a charity luncheon and in need of merchandise for the auction.

"Let me see what we can do for you," he said, unlocking one

of his glass display cases. "Just tell me what you'd like. I've got brooches and bracelets. I've got rubies and emeralds. Maybe some sapphires?" He couldn't have been more helpful. "Now this," he said, draping a diamond bracelet about my wrist, "is a one-of-a-kind. A real treasure, but it may be a little more than you were looking to spend."

"Mr. Alberts," I said with a laugh, "I'm not looking to spend anything. This is for charity. I'm looking for donations for the auction. For our *charity* luncheon."

"Sweetheart"—he unclasped the bracelet and put it back on its velvet tray—"what do you take me for? I don't stay in business by giving away my jewelry. Now, if you want to pay, since it's for charity, I'll give you a nice deal."

"Hmmm . . ." I traced my fingers over the brooches he'd laid out on the counter. "That's really not going to be an option."

He leaned forward, planting an elbow on his display case. "Then I'm afraid you've come to the wrong place. I can't help you."

"That's a shame, because Irwin Ragguffy was *sure* you'd be more than happy to donate an item or two."

"Irwin?" Benny Alberts dragged a hand over his face and straightened up. "Irwin Ragguffy told you that?"

"Oh, yes." I batted my lashes and dropped my chin, holding it in place with my fingertip. "He said that if you gave me a hard time, I should just let him know."

"Well, you should have said something sooner." He cleared his throat. "Irwin's a very good customer. Why didn't you tell me Irwin sent you. . . ."

I walked out of Alberts's jewelry store with a jade hatpin, a necklace, and a ruby brooch.

Thanks to Irwin, within a few days, I had donations of clothing, area rugs and picture frames, a Brownie camera, brass candlesticks and an RCA Victrola.

. . .

One week later, I arrived home after a lengthy committee meeting where we'd reviewed all our plans. The housekeeper answered the door before I'd even turned the knob. She had Hannah asleep in her arms and a worried look on her face.

"You have company, Mrs. Green," she said in a whisper.

I followed her into the living room and there were Evelyn, Dora, and Basha waiting for me. One look at their faces and my knees went weak.

"What's wrong? What happened to him?" I reached for the back of the chair to steady myself. I felt faint.

"There *was* some trouble today," said Dora, taking me in her arms. "Some of Capone's boys opened fire on Vinny, Hymie, and Shep down at the Standard Oil Building."

"Oh God! Just tell me—was he shot? Is he dead?"

"No. He's fine. They're all fine. But the cops picked him up."

"I need a drink." The room was spinning.

"Right here." Basha handed me a glass and I knocked back most of it in one gulp.

"Hymie got away, but the cops caught up with Shep and Vinny." Dora took hold of my hand and led me over to the settee. "They arrested them."

"So they're in jail? Shep's in jail?" My stomach clenched up. I finished off my drink.

"Hymie's probably down there now posting their bail."

"You wait and see, the boys will be home in time for supper," said Basha.

And they were. It wasn't even dark out yet and Shep was home, sitting on the edge of the divan, a scotch in one hand, a cigarette in the other. His shirt was unbuttoned at the neck, sleeves rolled up to his elbows, his necktie hanging down loose. I was standing by the window, staring outside, watching the sun slip below the horizon.

"So when the cops caught up with me," Shep explained, "I was holding a tommy gun in my hand."

I turned and looked at him. "So that's why they arrested you?" But what I really wanted to ask was, *Why in the hell were you carrying a Thompson submachine gun?*

"No." He shook his head. "No, a tommy gun's legal. You could walk down the street with one in broad daylight and the coppers couldn't touch you."

"Then why did they—"

"Because they found the Colt .45 in my pocket."

"What?" A chill came over me. A tommy gun in his hand, another gun in his pocket? He was turning into Dion O'Banion. I went and sat on the ottoman across from him.

"They charged me with carrying a concealed weapon." Shep ground out his cigarette. "And when they thought that wouldn't stick, they slapped me with assault, attempt to kill and a slew of other bullshit charges."

I hugged myself around the middle and rocked back and forth. It was worse than I thought. "What happens now?"

"We've got a hearing next week."

"What about Drucci?" I asked, staring at the rug.

"Nah, they're not interested in him. He's off the hook. It's me they're after." Shep didn't seem fazed by it. If anything, to him it was an annoying inconvenience. "Hey." He paused until I looked up, tears in my eyes. "It's gonna be okay."

I leaned in and kissed him hard on the mouth. "You scared the hell out of me today, you know that?" I wiped my eyes with the back of my hand. "I don't know what I would have done if something happened to you."

"Don't you worry, Dollface. Nothing's ever gonna happen to me."

"But what about the hearing? Couldn't that—"

"That's just standard routine. We've got the judge in our pocket. Everything's fine. I promise you."

TRIALS AND ERRORS

t was the day before Shep's hearing and I was a wreck. But not Shep. He was up early and had already left the house for a meeting down at Schofield's.

With a cup of coffee in one hand and a cigarette in the other, I sat at the table and stared until nervous energy kicked in and I couldn't sit still another minute. I got up, did the breakfast dishes, scoured out the sink and polished the silver. I cleaned out the icebox and ironed the bedsheets. After rinsing the dirty diapers in the upstairs toilet, I gave Hannah a bath and clipped her fingernails and toenails, swabbed out her ears. Having no luck in weaning her off her bottle, I even let her have it early, just to have something to do. As I rocked her in my arms, she stared up at me, hardly blinking. It was as if she knew something was wrong.

"Don't you worry," I said in a whisper. "Mommy's just being silly, that's all. Just a silly worrywart . . ."

Halfway through her bottle I felt Hannah's fierce grip ease up as her tiny mouth went slack. Her thick lashes fluttered once before her eyes closed. She was out. I gently set her down in her crib for her nap, half wishing she'd wake up. I felt so alone just then.

Tiptoeing out of the nursery, I stepped into a flood of sunlight coming in through the hallway window. How was I going to make it through the day?

Half an hour later Shep returned with Hymie. I wanted to talk about the hearing. I wanted to know what to expect but the two of them went into Shep's study and closed the door.

I tried to keep busy but couldn't focus on the council luncheon. None of the members knew a thing about the hearing and the thought of going over menu selections with Adele Markey or reviewing the centerpiece flowers with Janice Kaufman was more than I could have pulled off.

When I had just about come out of my skin, I knew I needed my girls with me—my sisters. So I got on the telephone and asked Dora, Basha and Evelyn to come to the house.

"Gin rummy," said Dora with a nod after they'd all arrived. "That'll do the trick. It's the best for taking your mind off things."

I got some playing cards and fixed everyone drinks while we waited on Evelyn. She'd been on the telephone ever since she arrived. With her shoes kicked off and her feet up on my divan, she blathered away to Cecelia, asking if she'd seen Izzy. Unfortunately, it hadn't taken long for him to revert back to his old ways. He hadn't come home the night before and somebody said they saw him snuggling up with someone named Maxine earlier in the evening. Evelyn had already been on the phone for almost twenty minutes, whining about Izzy, but never once saying that she was going to leave him. She knew better than to come crying to Basha, Dora or me. Cecelia was a fresh audience.

"What about a pitchfork," said Basha. "You think one of those would do the job?" Basha was back to plotting Mrs. Squeak's demise. "I was thinking about a chainsaw but it's too messy." She let out a giggle that I could only hope meant this was said in jest.

"Hey, c'mon already." Dora leaned back in her chair, calling to Evelyn. "Are we gonna play cards here or not?"

Evelyn held up her just-a-minute finger and kept talking to Cecelia. ". . . But when it's just the two of us alone, it's different. . . . Yeah, he's real sweet then. . . ."

Dora shuffled the cards. "Why in the hell does she put up with him?"

"It's not like he's even got her in that nice of a place," said Basha, scooting the tip of her nail through a bowl of mixed nuts, hunting for cashews.

"Oh, I think it's nice," said Dora. "She's got that view, don't forget."

"Yeah, but she's got no doorman," said Basha.

"There's a doorman at night," Evelyn called over, then went back to her conversation with Cecelia.

"I've got a twenty-four-hour doorman," Basha said, sorting through more nuts, knocking a pecan or two overboard. "And I got a real nice lobby, don'tcha think?" Basha looked at Dora and me and popped a cashew into her mouth.

"I tried to warn her about Izzy," I said, shaking my head. "He's the type who'll go for a different girl every night."

"He's Humpty-Dumpty," said Basha, snorting. "First he humps 'em and then he dumps 'em."

Dora and Basha burst out laughing. They even got me giggling on that one, and we were still cackling away when Evelyn finally got off the phone.

"Very funny!" She pulled out a chair and plopped down. "You know, he's not always like that. When it's just the two of us—"

"Yeah, yeah, yeah, we know, we know—he's real sweet when it's just the two of you." Basha howled.

Dora chuckled as she dealt the cards. I couldn't stop laughing, either.

Evelyn fanned out her cards and slapped them down on the table. "What do you expect me to do, Basha? Leave him? Give up my apartment? You expect me to go back to a rooming house and get some crummy job? Would you do that? Would any of you do that? I know I put up with a lot of baloney. I know it. And I know you all think I'm a fool, but I'm getting something out of this, too. I don't go around judging the rest of you, so just back off!"

There it was. Evelyn had just stated our truth. I wasn't laughing anymore.

"Aw, Ev, don't be upset." Basha got up and put her arms around Evelyn, giving her shoulders a squeeze from behind. "We're just worried about you, that's all."

"Yeah, honey, that's all it is." Dora reached over and gave Evelyn's hand a pat.

"And I do so have a doorman at night," Evelyn sniveled. "I do!"

"Oh, sweetie, we all know Izzy's got you in a swell place," said Basha, still hovering over Evelyn. "And you do have a great view—we all think so, don't we?" Basha looked to me for backup.

And then, out of nowhere, Izzy himself charged through the front door with a wild look in his eyes.

"Jesus," I said, "don't you people ever knock?"

"Where's Shep? Is Hymie still here?"

Evelyn jumped up and ran to his side. "Izzy, where have you been? I was worried sick about you."

"Where are they?" he asked again. "Hey, Shep—"

Shep and Hymie came out of the study.

"We found him!" Izzy said. "We found Capone. He's down at the Hawthorne Arms. They just spotted him in the restaurant."

Hymie was already heading for the front door.

"They said I just missed you guys at Schofield's," said Izzy. "I kept calling you here at the house but the line was busy."

Shep grabbed his hat and squared it on his head. Watching him bolt outside with Hymie and Izzy, I closed my eyes and said a silent prayer: *God, please forgive him and keep him safe.* When I opened my eyes, I saw Evelyn still standing at the door long after they'd left. Izzy hadn't said one word to her.

Basha went over and put her arm around Evelyn. "Aw, Ev, you know how the guys get about Capone. Izzy didn't mean nothing by it."

"Oh, yeah," Dora joined in. "You should see how Knuckles ignores me whenever they start talking about Capone."

Evelyn nodded and looked at me, waiting.

"Ev, what do you want me to say, huh? I'm not going to lie to you. You know what I think of Izzy. He's no good for you."

Evelyn stood there, crying.

"Aw, Jesus . . . I'm sorry, Ev." I worked my way out of my chair and went to her side. "Don't you know, it's just because I love you. I just don't want to see you get hurt."

"It's too late for that." She sobbed into my shoulder.

After we'd calmed Evelyn down, we tried to get back to our gin game, but we were all preoccupied.

Dora leaned forward and pressed the tips of her fingers to her temples. "I really hope they kill that son of a bitch this time so we can get on with our lives. I can't take it anymore."

Basha nodded. "Revenge is all they care about these days."

I looked at the others and wondered how they could live with it—knowing what their men had done. I thought I'd found a way to justify it. I told myself that Shep was different from other gangsters, that he would never hurt anyone unless it was in self-defense, that underneath it all, he was a kindhearted, loving man. But what was I supposed to tell myself now that he'd been arrested and was out hunting down Capone? I wanted to ask Dora and Basha how much bigger the lies could get.

Over my coffee the next morning, while Shep was getting dressed for his hearing, I read about the attack on Capone in the newspaper.

Alfonse Capone, the Target of Hawthorne Arms Shooting

Gangster Alphonse Capone was dining yesterday afternoon at the Hawthorne Arms in Cicero when witnesses said they spotted a motorcade of ten black touring cars with Thompson submachine guns visible from the rear windows. Gunshots rang out for two minutes without interruption. Chaos erupted as people on the street ran for cover. By the time the caravan had passed by the Hawthorne Arms, they had razed the first floor of the hotel and restaurant. "Everything was destroyed in under two minutes," said an unidentified witness. Despite the destruction, Alphonse Capone was able to walk out of the Hawthorne Arms unharmed.

Shep came downstairs and I folded the newspaper in half and tucked it under my plate. He had said earlier that he didn't want me at the courthouse that day. He didn't want me to be subjected to a bunch of lies and false accusations.

"Are you sure you won't change your mind?" I asked as I got up to pour his coffee. "Dora said she'd watch Hannah for me. Please, Shep, let me be there for you."

"I can't. I can't let you sit there and listen to them attack me. I'll be fine. I'll call you as soon as it's over."

I placed the coffee down before him and leaned over and kissed the top of his head.

I spent the day waiting by the phone, sipping bourbon and smoking cigarettes. While listening to the radio, I rocked Hannah in my arms, whispering, "It's going to be okay. Everything's going to be okay." She looked up at me with those big brown eyes and reached out with her hand. I grasped those precious fingers and kissed each one. I swear, she understood what I was saying.

Despite my hopes and prayers, when Shep came home later that night, I learned that something had gone terribly wrong. The judge turned on them. The case was going on trial.

"Trial!" I became light-headed, the room going dizzy on me. "You're going to be on trial? What are you going on trial for?"

Shep poured a glass of whiskey and took a long pull. "It's nothing but a bunch of trumped-up charges. They'll never hold up."

He didn't have to say it. Trumped up or not, I knew Hymie and the boys would do whatever they had to do to the judge and the jury to get Shep off. *I don't care! Whatever it takes, God, I don't care. Let them do what they have to. Just let Shep be cleared.*

"Hey, c'mon now." He reached for his handkerchief and dabbed the tears streaming down my cheeks. "Everything's going to be okay, Dollface. Sometimes these things happen. But I'm not worried, so don't you be worried."

FOR EVELYN'S SAKE

Evelyn was in bad shape by the time I got to her apartment. It was almost noon when I got there and she was still in her bathrobe. Her hair was up in a net except for a few escaped strands hanging down in front. The apartment smelled sour, like milk turning bad, and the drapes were drawn, making the place dark and dreary inside. It was the end of August and hot as a coffin inside her place. I went and opened the windows, pulled back the drapes.

"I know you can't stand Izzy," she said, squinting at the sunlight, "and I didn't want to bother you with Shep's trial starting, but I'm terrified. Izzy's never been gone this long. I keep thinking he's either with that woman or else something's happened to him."

"Aw, Ev . . ." I tossed my pocketbook onto the coffee table and held out my arms to her. I felt her tears bleeding through the sheer fabric on my shoulder as I held her.

"He's never stayed away this long. It's been two days." She stepped into the middle of the room and paced before the bay window, tugging on the belt of her bathrobe.

I moved a pile of newspapers and magazines from the divan to a spare chair and sat down. I sucked in a deep breath, reached for my pocketbook and took out a smoke, tapping the cigarette on the coffee table. "When was the last time you ate anything?"

"Who can eat?"

"Well," I said, getting off the divan, "I'm going to fix you something anyway. You need to put something in your stomach—even if you don't feel like it." I lit my cigarette and tossed the box of matches onto the table.

"I keep thinking I'm going to end up like Basha. He'll never marry me and I tell you, it would kill me—just kill me—if he turned around and married someone else. It would just kill me. . . ."

Her kitchen was a mess. Dirty plates were stacked in the sink. Damp dish towels were bunched up on the counter, garbage overflowing from the trash. With my cigarette propped between my lips, I scouted through her icebox and found some cheese, a chunk of salami and a loaf of moldy bread. "Where are your knives?"

"What if he's with her now? What if he loves her? What if Capone got him?"

"You can't think like that." I opened the top drawer and found one knife, a carving knife with a dried-out wooden handle.

"I can't take the pressure anymore. I'm so tired and all I do is sleep all day."

I was sawing through the salami when I heard the front door open. I walked into the other room just as Izzy stumbled inside and slammed the door behind him.

"Oh God, where have you been?" Evelyn ran to his side. "You had me worried sick."

I knew Izzy was drunk. His hair was a mess. His shirttails were hanging out. His suit coat looked like he'd slept in it and he smelled of cigar smoke and whiskey.

She put her arms around him but he shrugged her off.

"Izzy—don't be like that. I've been up for days worrying about you!"

"Well, I'm home now, aren't I?"

"I thought you were dead somewhere."

"Aw, not again. Shut up with that shit already. Why do you think I stay out all night? I can't listen to your whining anymore."

I looked at the expression on Evelyn's face. "Hey, Izzy," I said, "lay off her."

"Shut it, Vera. This is between me and her."

I spun around and went back into the kitchen to finish slicing the cheese and salami.

"Look at this place," I heard him say. "Look at you. You're not even dressed yet. You're a goddamn mess and this place is a goddamn pigsty."

"I was so worried about you, Izzy." Evelyn sobbed. "That's why I didn't get dressed today. That's why I didn't clean up. I couldn't."

"Well, I'm back now, so why don't you fuckin' start cleaning this place up."

"Izzy—no! C'mon . . ."

"I said, clean this place up! *Now!*"

"Izzy, you're hurting me. Stop it!"

Evelyn screamed and I raced into the living room. Izzy was standing over her, holding her down, pushing her head against the floor. She struggled to stand up and that's when he struck her in the face with his fist. When I saw him winding up for a second time, I snapped.

"Stop it!" I screamed as I grabbed his arm.

"Stay out of it, Vera." He shrugged me off and struck her again.

I still had the carving knife in my hand and like a reflex, I charged toward him and plunged the knife into his rear end. It all happened so fast and the blade went in so easily. It cut through his trousers and skin like it was nothing. The salami had been harder to slice up than Izzy's ass.

Izzy let out a scream and I yanked the blade out as he whipped around. "You fuckin' bitch!" He drew back his hand, fingers balled in a fist, ready to let me have it.

I looked him in the eye. "C'mon, Izzy, hit me. Hit me and Shep'll kill you. Go ahead, Izzy. I dare you to." I taunted him, dancing the knife before him in a lazy airward crazy-eight. "C'mon—"

"Vera, no!" Evelyn got up off the floor. Blood trickled from her nose and mouth.

Izzy held his ass, staring at me, speechless. I had him and he knew it. He knew he couldn't touch me.

"Now, I want you to apologize to me and then you're going to apologize to Evelyn. And I swear, if you ever say another disrespectful word to her—if you ever lay another hand on her—I'll come back and slice your balls off." I stopped the knife's slow dance. I looked at it for a second. It was already tinged with his blood and I inched it closer to him. I don't think I ever blinked.

"Vera, don't!" Evelyn was at my side, begging.

Without taking my eyes off Izzy, I shouted, "Say it! Say you're sorry."

He studied the knife and rolled his eyes.

"Say it, goddammit!" I moved the blade in closer.

He mumbled something. Could have been an apology or, knowing Izzy, an obscenity.

"I didn't hear that." I touched the blade to his shirt collar.

"I said I'm sorry. Okay?"

"Now tell her."

"It's okay, Vera," Evelyn cried. "He didn't mean anything by it."

"No, Evelyn! It's *not* okay!" I grabbed a vase—the first thing I could find—and slammed it to the ground. "It's not okay at all. Now, Izzy, tell her. Tell her you're sorry."

His eyes moved from mine to the blade before he jerked his chin away. "Sorry."

"Louder!" I swooped in with the tip of the knife under his chin. One move and I'd pierce his throat.

"I fuckin' said I'm sorry."

"Now tell her you're a piece of shit. And you don't deserve her." I raised the knife higher, nicking him so that a pinprick of blood sprouted on his chin. *"Say it!"*

"I'm-a-piece-of-shit-and-I-don't-deserve-her."

"Evelyn, c'mon." I threw the knife onto the table, reached for her hand, and pulled her close. "You're coming home with me."

GUN MOLLS ON PARADE

The trial got under way right after Labor Day, and just like with the hearing, Shep had asked me not to come down to the courthouse. It was agonizing to stay away, but again he said he didn't want me subjected to the prosecution's lies. All day I'd wait for news, for updates of any kind, but by the time Shep came home at night, he said he didn't want to talk about it.

During the first days of the trial, we sat silently through dinners—pickled tongue with green beans, beef croquettes with creamed corn, a rack of lamb with scalloped potatoes—recipes that I'd spent the day preparing in hopes of distracting myself. When we did talk, it was nonsense.

"I heard the Farmer's Almanac is predicting the worst winter in over a decade," I said one night, leaning over to wipe the creamed yams off Hannah's fingers. "Isn't that something?"

Shep nodded, pushing a clump of meat around with his fork. "I guess we should brace ourselves for a rough couple of months."

I leaned back in my chair and glanced at my plate. "Yeah, it's going to be a bad one." I stabbed a piece of brisket but couldn't bring myself to eat it. Instead, I set my fork down with a loud clank. Hannah let out a quick shriek and went back to sticking her fingers in her yams.

Shep tossed his napkin onto the table and scooped up Hannah, sucking the creamed yams off her fingers one at a time, making her giggle so that her belly shook.

I pushed my plate away and cradled my head in my hands. I couldn't look at the two of them just then.

"Remind me," Shep said, "I need to ask the neighbors to trim their hedges back."

I looked up. "Dammit, Shep! I don't want to talk about the neighbors' hedges! You have to let me in. You have to tell me what's happening."

"Relax." He set Hannah back down even as she continued to grope for him, her fingers outstretched and straining. She wanted more of him. So did I.

"Everything's under control," he said, reaching for his wineglass, draining it with one gulp. "We've got nothing to worry about."

But all I did was worry. In the days that followed, time passed in slow motion. The ticking of the kitchen clock pounded into my skull like a hammer; the shrill of the telephone made my heart stop.

Not knowing that my husband was on trial, committee members called nonstop with details for the luncheon that was coming up at the end of the month. I tried to focus but I couldn't concentrate. Meanwhile Barbara and some of the others from the JWC invited me to play bridge or else join them for coffee. I made excuses, took rain checks, and feigned sore throats and headaches. I couldn't pretend that all was fine and I wouldn't dare speak about Shep's trial outside our circle. The boys had managed to keep it out of the newspapers and even my own mother didn't know what was going on. The only ones I turned to were the women who knew me best.

The girls did whatever they could to distract me, keeping me busy with shopping sprees or Walnut Room lunches and double features at the movie house. And more shopping. I distracted myself with one purchase after another, foolish things I didn't want or need: an extra set of china, crystal candlestick holders, new linens and a telephone table with an attached chair, along with dresses and shoes, hats and pocketbooks.

Evelyn came by one day after I'd put Hannah down for her nap. She brought me the new issue of *Vogue* and a box of my favorite peanut brittle.

"What's all this?" she asked, looking at the racks of cookies and pies I'd baked the night before and earlier that morning.

"You should see what's in the icebox."

She peeked inside. "Who's going to eat all this?" Earlier in the week I'd made stuffed peppers, a standing rib roast, deviled eggs and two gelatin molds.

"I'm sick of shopping, and cooking's the only thing that's keeping me sane right now." I had *The Metropolitan Cook Book* along with *Mrs. Wilson's Cook Book* and half a dozen others sprawled out across the kitchen table. The radio was on, but I wasn't paying any attention to the program.

"What are you looking for?"

"Trying to find a recipe for pull taffy. I just saw it the other day," I said, leafing forward and back, scanning through the pages.

"You know how to make taffy?"

"Of course not, but it'll give us something to do— Ah!" I marked my place with my finger. "Found it."

I cleared away the other cookbooks and looped an apron over Evelyn's head, tying it behind her waist.

"Well"—she turned to face me, arms out to her sides—"how do I look?"

"Like a real *balabusta*," I said with a smile. "A real Yiddishe homemaker."

Evelyn peered over my shoulder while I mixed the sugar, corn syrup and butter in a saucepan. While it boiled, I took down two glasses and poured us each a drink.

"You're drinking an awful lot these days," she said.

"Not as much as I'm shopping and cooking!" I clinked my glass to hers.

We sat and made small talk and smoked cigarettes until it was time for the water test. "Come." I motioned for her as I spooned a droplet of the taffy mixture into a cold glass of water and waited for a ball to form. "Does that look like a hard ball or a soft ball to you?" I asked, rolling the mixture between my fingers.

"What's it supposed to be?"

"A hard ball."

"Then I say it's a hard ball."

"If this doesn't work, it's your fault," I said, removing the taffy from the stove to let it cool.

We went back to the table and I poured another drink. "So how's Izzy?" I asked.

"I was wondering how long it was going to take you to ask about him."

Evelyn had wasted no time getting back together with him. Though we never discussed it, I knew she resented me for stabbing him. After that incident she stayed in our guest room for two days. Two lousy days was all it took before she crawled back to that bastard.

"Ready to pull some taffy?" I asked when the mixture had cooled down. I took a clump of butter and slapped it into her hands. "Butter up, baby!"

Reaching into the saucepan, I took out the blob of taffy and plopped it into Evelyn's slippery hands. "Now just stand still." I grabbed a fistful of taffy and while she held on to it, I started stepping backward until I was about two feet away.

Over and over again we did that, stepping farther apart each time, until I was on the other side of the kitchen and the taffy looked like a giant wad of chewing gum. It began to sag in the middle and almost touched the floor. I dived in to save it, landing on my rear end. Evelyn plopped down on the kitchen floor beside me, giggling as she held her half of the taffy up over her head. It was the first time I'd laughed in days, maybe weeks. We were howling, doubled over, holding our sides, and in the middle of all this, my laughter turned to tears. I dropped the taffy on the floor and broke down and sobbed.

By week two of the trial, Shep was in good spirits. He waltzed through the front door that Monday night, wrapped his arms around me, and gave me a deep kiss. "The defense busted the prosecution's case wide open," he said, moving over to the bar to pour himself a drink. "Now we just have to go through the motions. But this'll all be over within a week, Dollface, and we can get back to normal."

Normal. Now, that was a relative term.

The Jewish Women's Council luncheon was just a week away, and feeling optimistic about Shep's case, I threw myself into the final planning stages. I met with the committee heads, reviewed menus and seating charts, inventoried all the donated items for the auction, and telephoned the wealthiest Jewish women in Chicago to remind them about the event.

On day ten of the trial, I was walking home from a meeting at the Palmer House Hotel where we had reviewed the details for the luncheon. It was a crisp autumn day, and I thought I'd take the long way home and stroll along the lakeshore. I'd always found the waves washing up along Oak Street Beach to be soothing, relaxing.

I passed by the newspaper boy on the corner of Michigan and Walton. He was holding up the afternoon edition, waving the *Chicago Tribune* in the air for all to see. One look and my heart stopped.

Shep's picture was on the front page. I reached for a newspaper and my mouth went dry. *Assault . . . Carrying a concealed weapon . . . Transporting illegal liquor . . . Attempted murder . . .* I couldn't finish the article and set the paper back on the stack. I walked away briskly and then broke into a run.

The next morning, after I'd tried to explain what could not be reasonably explained to my mother, I hung up, and two minutes later the telephone rang again. It was Adele Markey on the line.

"What do you mean, you have concerns about the luncheon?" I was distracted, wrestling with Hannah on my hip, who was reaching for the teddy bear I'd set on the table when I answered the telephone. Hannah was at that stage where she was getting into everything and I was afraid that if I set her down I wouldn't be able to keep an eye on her. "What kind of concerns do you have, Adele?"

"Well, are you still planning on attending the luncheon?"

"Of course I am." I laughed and hoisted Hannah up further on my hip. "Why wouldn't I be attending?"

"Well . . ." She sighed.

"What's this all about, Adele?"

"I don't know how else to put this, but, well . . . I've heard it from several of the members. . . . If you're going to be at the luncheon, we should expect cancellations."

"What? Why?" I set the baby bottle back down on the table.

There was a long pause. I pictured her standing in her dark, cavernous hallway where her telephone sat on the mahogany table.

"Adele, who said they wouldn't go?"

"All of them."

Another long pause hung on the line. I couldn't speak.

"Vera, you have to understand. . . . This business with your husband . . . It's not good for the council's image."

"But Shep hasn't done anything wrong. It's all a bunch of nonsense. He's being falsely accused."

"That very well may be true, but it's been all over the newspapers and the radio, too. I'm afraid we just can't tolerate that sort of association with the Jewish Women's Council."

"And if I cancel?"

"Then the other members said they would be happy to attend the luncheon."

"But I chaired this event. I've planned the whole thing." Hannah was wiggling in my arms, straining for her teddy bear.

"I'm sorry, but the members are just too afraid to let that sort of element into the council."

"Afraid? Afraid of what?"

"Vera, the Jewish Women's Council doesn't associate with gangsters. I'm sorry."

After Adele Markey hung up, I was stunned. I dropped the telephone and almost dropped Hannah as she lunged for her bear on the table. It was as if I'd been struck with polio or influenza. I was infected. Guilt by association. I hoisted Hannah up higher in my arms and held her as close as I could. As soon as I felt her tiny arms cling to me, my eyes went blurry.

My one chance to prove myself and it had been pulled out from under me. I wanted to blame Shep, but that wasn't fair. But if not Shep, then whose fault was it? The very person who had propped me up in this town had also knocked me down.

. . .

The girls stopped by the house that afternoon to check on me and as soon as I let them inside, they knew something was wrong. Something beyond just the trial.

"I spent the past three months working my tail off on this and now they're taking it away from me. And why? Because they're *afraid* of letting this *element* into the council."

"They're afraid?" Basha fired back, grounding out her cigarette. "We'll give 'em something to be afraid of, won't we?"

At ten past noon on Saturday, September 25, 1926, Evelyn and I threw open the French doors of the Palmer House ballroom and walked into the Jewish Women's Council's luncheon followed by our *shiksa* girlfriends, Dora, Basha and Cecelia. It was gun molls on parade. We made some entrance in our short beaded dresses, our even shorter bobbed hair, cloche hats, feather headdresses and our biggest, flashiest jewelry.

I quickly scanned the room. Barbara Perl nearly dropped her fork when she saw me and Esther's mouth hung open as she elbowed the woman next to her. Another woman gasped, knocking her teacup off the table. The sound of china shattering echoed through the room. Within a matter of seconds, the eighty or so members all looked up from their chicken salads and watercress. Their ladylike prattle and the clatter of their silverware came to a halt. All was quiet except for the sound of our high heels clicking against the marble floor and the clanking of our bracelets.

It had taken a bit of convincing on the part of Basha and Dora before I agreed to any of this. But they were right: I had nothing to lose. I would never be allowed back into the JWC. I was the wife of a gangster and now everyone knew it.

Adele Markey excused herself from the head table and rushed up to me. "Vera—I thought I made it perfectly clear when we spoke on the telephone."

"Oh, you did. You made it *perfectly* clear, but you forgot one thing. I planned this event so we could raise money for a good cause, and that's exactly what we're here to do." I turned to my posse. "Ladies?"

And with that, my girls dispersed around the room, pulling up chairs at the various tables. The women's faces turned the color of their chinaware and they were all on *shpilkes*, pins and needles. Barbara's hands were trembling as she dabbed her napkin to her mouth.

"Well," I said to Adele, "what are we waiting for? Let's start the auction."

"You heard her," said Cecelia. "Let's go. Chop-chop!"

The entire room gasped for the umpteenth time since we'd arrived, and Adele, always the picture of grace and dignity, looked as though she'd soiled herself.

When everyone calmed down, the auctioneer took the podium and presented the first item, the jade hatpin from Benny Alberts. "Ladies," she began with a tentative bang of her gavel, "can we start the bidding at two dollars? Do I hear two?"

Cecelia turned to Janice Kaufman, seated to her right. "You want that hatpin, don't you?"

Janice looked at her, bewildered.

"Toots, this is no time to be shy."

"But I don't want a hatpin," said Janice.

"I guess I didn't make myself clear." Cecelia smiled. "I don't really think what *you want* matters."

"But I—"

Cecelia grabbed Janice's hand and raised it high in the air. "This woman right here bids twenty-five dollars!"

After this latest round of gasps hushed down, Basha turned to Esther Bloomberg, who was seated next to her. "You're not gonna let her have that hatpin for twenty-five bucks, are you?"

"What?" Esther lifted her coffee cup with both hands.

"I'd say it's worth at least thirty, wouldn't you?"

"But I can't . . ." Esther set her cup back down, nearly missing the saucer. "My husband would never let me spend that much for a hatpin—"

"You think I give a crap about your husband? C'mon, now. Don't make me ask again."

Esther's voice was cracking as she raised her hand and said, "Thirty dollars."

Dora turned to Barbara Perl. "That's a crime to let it go for only thirty bucks."

"Just . . . just, ah, just tell me what you want me to do." Barbara's voice was quavering as lines of worry etched across her brow.

"Hmmm . . ." Dora drummed her red nails along the tablecloth. "Bump it up to forty-five bucks."

And so she did.

Evelyn was next, and she was all over Adele. "What do you say we spend some of your money?"

"I refuse to be intimidated by you."

"Aw, c'mon now, you're the president of this group. You can't let your members down. All it takes is fifty bucks, Adele. Fifty and we leave you alone."

Adele cleared her throat and raised her hand.

It went back and forth like that, item by item, as my girls used the force of their presence to drive up every bid. At the end of the luncheon, we had exceeded our overall goal of raising one thousand dollars by a good measure and ended up raising five thousand dollars.

All in the name of charity.

As we walked out of the Palmer House we were laughing, our arms slung around one another's shoulders. I'd climbed up the social ladder and tumbled down the other side in one fell swoop. I looked at Cecelia, Basha, Dora, and even Evelyn. I was one of them now. There was no turning back.

As we walked five abreast down the sidewalk, I threw my head back and let the autumn sun wash over my face. I felt like I owned the streets. Yes, my husband may have been on trial, but he was going to beat the charges. I was Mrs. Shep Green, and I was a force to be reckoned with. From now on, nobody was going to mess with me.

This gaiety followed us back to the house. We were still toasting with a round of bourbons when Hymie and Drucci came to the door, letting a gust of wind blow dead leaves into the foyer as they stepped inside.

I knew it. Even before they said a word, I knew it. My legs grew shaky as Hymie removed his hat and Drucci lowered his head.

"The jury reached a verdict," said Drucci, clenching and unclenching his fists.

I sank into a chair and dropped my head to my hands. "Just tell me."

Hymie delivered the blow. "Guilty. On five counts. The judge sentenced him to eighteen months."

I kept my head low, didn't say a word. Someone asked if I was okay but I didn't respond. All that power I'd felt just moments before had vaporized. I was deflated and lost. Everything inside me grew still and quiet. The tears were immediate, running down my cheeks and leaving dark marks as they landed on the front of my dress. I didn't know what this meant for me and for Hannah, only I knew that our world had been turned upside down.

FINDING OUT WHAT
YOU'RE MADE OF

There was a cold, dank smell that clung to everything, like limestone after a rainstorm. In some ways I found that odor harder to take than the stench from the stockyards. It bothered me that this hellhole was attached to the courthouse with its majestic marble walls and floors, its intricately carved wooden seats and golden inlays.

Peering through the cast-iron bars running floor to ceiling, I couldn't bring myself to look at Shep. Instead, I stared at the concrete floor, the cinder-block walls, the metal bench hinged to the wall along with a cot. The mattress wasn't more than an inch thick, and it was covered with yellow, brown and gray stains. My eyes landed on a bucket in the corner and, next to that, a couple of flies hovering over something dark and runny on the floor that I realized was a pile of shit.

I drew a deep breath and dared to look at him. Within minutes, I broke my promise to myself and began to cry. Shep Green, the most meticulous man I knew, was unshaven, dressed in work overalls, his hair a tousled mess. He'd no sooner sleep on that filthy mattress than he would have lain in a sewer.

"C'mon now, Dollface," he said. "I've been in worse places." He laughed, trying to reassure me by drawing comparisons to his childhood in Little Hell. When he saw it wasn't helping, he changed his tone. "Listen to me, everything's going to be okay. I met with my lawyer and we're going to appeal. I'll be back home before you know it."

I just nodded. There were no words.

"And in the meantime, if you need anything, you just tell Hymie. He'll take care of you and Hannah. You don't have to worry about anything. You understand?"

"I brought you some books," I said, sniffling. "But they wouldn't let me give them to you. I brought you *Babbitt*. We only made it to page fifty-seven. I thought you'd want to finish it. And you said you'd never read *Frankenstein*, so I brought you that, too, but they're with the guard. Maybe they'll let you have them after I leave. Make sure you ask them about the books, okay?"

He nodded. "Listen, I want you to do something for me."

"Anything." I don't know why, but I thought he was going to ask me to visit his mother's grave.

"I don't want you coming here again. Okay?"

"But . . ." My chin began to tremble.

"I don't want you seeing me like this."

"But, Shep—"

"I mean it. This isn't good for you and it's not good for me. I'm going to be home soon anyway."

I squeezed the bars tighter and closed my eyes.

"You just take care of yourself and Hannah and I'll be home before you know it." He reached through the bar for my hand. His fingers were covered in black ink from where they'd taken his prints.

. . .

One week later, when I was feeding Hannah, trying to get her to use her spoon, Bugs and Hymie stopped by to tell me Shep had been moved to Chicago's House of Corrections on Twenty-sixth Street and California.

"But why?" I asked, looking up just as Hannah plastered a handful of creamed corn into her hair. I blew out a sigh so deep it fluttered my bangs. "If he's supposed to be coming home, why are they taking him farther away?"

"This is routine," said Hymie. "It happens whenever someone *goes away.*"

That was how they referred to it. *Going away.* No one ever spoke about anyone being in jail, as if the word were taboo. Instead they all just *went away.*

"They only keep you in the Hubbard County Jail for a couple days—a week at the most," said Bugs.

"Why didn't someone explain that to me?" I wiped the paste from Hannah's hair and took the bowl of creamed corn away, which only made her fuss more, running her fingers through the slop on her high chair tray. "I want to talk with his lawyer." I stood up and wiped my hands on the front of my apron.

"That's not gonna do any good," said Bugs. "Shep doesn't want you getting caught up in all that. We're talking to the lawyer every day and as soon as we hear anything, we'll come and tell you."

"In the meantime," said Hymie, reaching into his breast pocket for an envelope, "here."

"What's this?" I looked inside.

"Two hundred," Hymie said before I'd had a chance to count it. "That should hold you."

"For how long?"

He shrugged. "If you need more, you come see me."

I wasn't even aware that I was pacing until Bugs grabbed hold of my shoulders. "It's gonna be okay, Vera. We're making good progress on the appeal and we're gonna lean on the judge. Don't you worry about them moving him. Shep's gonna be out of there any day now."

I nodded. Couldn't speak.

Hymie and Bugs let themselves out and I called to the housekeeper, told her I was going out and to watch Hannah until I got back.

As I was walking out the door, Hannah cried out, "Da-da! Da-da!"

Twenty minutes later I arrived at the law office of Henry C. Brice, Esquire. His secretary tried to stop me, saying he was on a telephone call but I barged into his office anyway. Brice looked up from his desk and, as if we'd had an appointment all along, he stood up, crossed the room and welcomed me in.

"Come sit down. Can I get you some tea? Coffee? Water?"

I shook my head. "I just want to know what's going on with Shep's case. Why did they move him? Why is this appeal taking so long?"

"Just come sit down and I'll explain everything."

He tossed out a lot of phrases like *petition the court, plaintiff in error, the appellee's plea, the series of injunctions....* He said the courts were overloaded and we were on a waitlist for Shep's case, but it was solid. We had nothing to worry about.

When I got home that afternoon, I fixed myself a drink, lit a cigarette and resumed my pacing—right in the same spot where I'd paced earlier that day. Back and forth I went until the housekeeper came and stood in the doorway.

"Mrs. Green?" She hesitated when I looked up. "It's Friday and . . ."

"And?"

She cleared her throat. "This is the day Mr. Green pays me."

"Oh, I see." I went over to my pocketbook, propped my cigarette between my lips and squinted to keep the smoke from my
eyes. I took out a five. The housekeeper looked at the bill in her
hand and then looked up at me. I had no idea what Shep paid her
each week but clearly it was more than that. I went back to my
pocketbook and gave her another five. She thanked me and went
upstairs to give Hannah her bath.

I stayed in the living room, watching the shadows grow longer as the sunlight slipped away from the windows. Finally I
went into Shep's office and poured myself another drink. When
I'd worked up the nerve, I began to shuffle through the bills for
the electric, the water, the telephone, the mortgage and car payments. There were bills from Marshall Field's, Carson Pirie
Scott, my dressmaker, Shep's tailor and Hannah's doctor. I made
a list of all the other household expenses and finished off my
drink. I had no idea how much coal we needed every month or
what arrangements Shep had worked out with the iceman and
the milkman. What did he pay the gardener each week?

Whenever I needed money for groceries or anything else,
Shep gave me plenty with more to spare. We lived well—very
well—I knew that much, but until Shep *went away*, I had no idea
what it cost to be us.

I collected the bills and stuffed them in the top drawer, un-
willing to look at them anymore. My neck was stiff with tension
and from leaning over the desk all afternoon. When I couldn't sit
there any longer, I went and checked on Hannah. She was fast
asleep, without a care or worry and I wanted to keep it that way.

As more time passed, I tried to remain optimistic. I wrote to
Shep almost every day—sometimes twice a day—filling up two
and three pages, front and back. Every day I checked the mail-

box, hoping for a letter from Shep, but instead, all I found were more bills. Bugs and Hymie assured me that Shep was doing fine and that the appeal was moving forward. When I said I was running low on money, Hymie produced another envelope and on top of that, he reached into his own pocket and handed me a couple extra twenties.

One afternoon Cecelia came over and told me about the first time Vinny *went away.*

"I think it's harder on us than it is on them," she said, looking over the bottles on the bar before selecting the scotch and pouring us each a glass.

"Shep doesn't want me to go see him."

"Ah, sometimes they get like that. Stupid pride. Vinny said the same thing, but I went anyway. It's not so bad. Really." She handed me a glass. "Just be glad he's out here on California and not downstate at the penitentiary. That was worse. I wouldn't put a dog in there. Maggots this big." She spread her fingers three inches apart. "They got no toilets. There're two and three men to a cell. They just piss and shit wherever they want. And they only let them bathe once a week. . . ."

I set my glass down and reached for a cigarette.

"The main thing is to keep busy. But I'm not gonna kid you. When Vinny *went away,* it was a long six months."

Six months! "I won't make it six months." I shook my head and took a long pull from my drink. "I don't know what I'll do if he doesn't come home soon." Even as the words left my mouth, I thought of my mother going it alone all those years after my father had been killed. *God, please don't let me end up like her.* "I won't be able to make it without him."

"You'd be surprised, toots. You're a lot tougher than you think. It's this sort of thing that shows you what you're really made of. . . ."

.   .   .

Later that evening Basha called, asking if I wanted company. It was the third night in a row that she'd come to see me.

After I'd gotten the baby to sleep, I came back downstairs. "Feel like playing gin?" I asked.

"I don't know what I feel like doing." Basha went over to the bar and fixed herself another gin martini, reaching into the ice bucket with her fingers. "Squeak was supposed to come over tonight and at the last minute, he calls and cancels. I didn't get to see him last night or the night before, either."

"Oh, so now I get it!" I lit a cigarette and drew a deep puff. "That's why you're here—because Squeak's at home with his wife."

"Ah, no. It's not just because of that. I wanted to come over tonight. No, really, I did. I'm here for you, you know that."

"It's okay, Basha. I get it." I held up my hand to cut her off. "It's okay. Spare me!" Basha's visits may have been more about consoling her than me, but still, she was company; and at night, after Hannah was in bed, the house grew so still even my favorite radio programs couldn't fill the quiet.

Basha finished her drink and contemplated another one while she told me her latest plans for Mrs. Squeak. "I was reading up on black widow spiders. Turns out even a bite won't kill her if she gets to a doctor in time."

"So what do you hear from Viola these days?" I had to change the subject. Basha may have been my friend, but I was a wife just like Mrs. Squeak. At times, I took Basha's vindictive spirit toward her as a personal affront.

In the days and weeks ahead, Basha was company whenever it was convenient for her, but it was Evelyn and Dora who were my rocks. Especially Dora, who was always helping out with Hannah. There were plenty of afternoons when the housekeeper had the day off that Dora would encourage me to get out of the house.

"Go do some shopping or take a walk. I'll watch Hannah for you."

"No, I shouldn't. She's been fussy all day."

"She'll be fine. Go on. Don't worry about us."

After going back and forth, Dora would persuade me to take some time for myself, listening patiently as I'd remind her which toys were Hannah's favorites and what blanket she liked to nap with and which pacifiers to use.

"I know. I know," Dora said each time, ushering me to the door. "Now get out of here. We'll be fine."

Usually on those days I'd escape to the picture show, hoping to lose myself in the dark theater for an hour or two. But as the screen flickered in the blackness all I could do was fret over whether Dora had remembered to put Hannah down for her nap, if she'd given her an extra blanket in case she was cold, if she'd put the ointment on for her diaper rash. . . . I'd shift in my chair, trying to follow the movie, but all I did was worry about Hannah, and then Shep. By the time the picture was over and the lights came up, I couldn't have told you what the movie was about.

woke in the middle of the night and reached for Shep—a habit I couldn't break. I was always surprised at first to find his half of the bed empty, the sheets cool beneath my hand. Grabbing Shep's pillow, I hugged it to my chest. This time of the night was the hardest for me. I was used to Shep being gone during the days and in the evenings, but at two or three in the morning, I didn't know what to do without him. I took him for granted, always assuming he'd be here for Hannah and me. He was our cornerstone; he was what made our life together work.

A chill swept through the room and I reached for Shep's bathrobe and covered my shoulders. I knew it was a silly thing to do, but each night before I turned in, I always put his robe at the foot of the bed, just like he used to do when he was home. In the mornings, before the housekeeper would see, I'd hang it back in his closet. I pulled the robe up to my chin, smelling the collar, still alive with the spicy scent of his shaving soap.

I was about to drift back to sleep when I heard Hannah crying. I pulled on Shep's robe and went to her.

"What's the matter, sweetie," I asked, turning on the night lamp and scooping her up in my arms. I brushed the dark curls from her eyes and saw that her long black lashes were webbed with tears. Those curls and dark eyes had to belong to Shep. They just had to.

"You miss Daddy, too, huh?" I held her as I sat in the rocking chair that squeaked each time we pitched forward and back. "When you're older," I said to her, "you're going to hear a lot of unkind things about your father, but don't you believe them. He's had to do a lot of things—terrible things—that he didn't want to do. No matter what people tell you, just remember your father's a good, decent man." I was saying this as much for myself as I was for her, maybe more so. "And he loves you. He'd be here with you right now if he could. So don't listen to what people say, because they don't know him like we do."

Hannah gurgled and cooed, and as she reached up with her tiny outstretched hand, a tear ran down my cheek and splashed against her fingers. I rocked her and before long she was back asleep and so was I.

CHANGING OF THE GUARD

It was a brisk October day. The air smelled of burning leaves and manure from a carriage that had just clomped by. I was on my way to Schofield's to talk to Hymie and ask for more money. I was already behind on most of my bills. Plus, Hannah, whose weight had more than doubled in the past six months, was outgrowing her clothes as fast as I could replace them.

I was at the corner of Superior and State, waiting for a streetcar to pass, when I spotted Hymie coming up the sidewalk. He was with another man and his two bodyguards. Those oversize thugs with their thick necks and broad, burly shoulders had been sticking close to Hymie ever since the Standard Oil Building shootings. His bodyguards had started out as Little Pishers. Now they were just bigger Little Pishers.

As Hymie crossed the street a few yards in front of me, I heard a loud bang. It sounded like an automobile had backfired, but not a second later there were screams and a long, steady eruption of noise. Clouds of dust billowed up, coming off the limestone on the front of Holy Name Cathedral. It took a moment before I realized I was in the midst of gunfire. It was machine gun fire, rattling off round after round after round. I went stiff. Couldn't move. I heard the bullets soaring past my ears as more dust kicked off the limestone facade of Holy Name.

Both the bodyguards were down, one lying in a pool of blood in the middle of State Street, the other collapsed just steps away from Schofield's. Hymie was running for cover when he froze, arched his back and stretched his arms out to his sides as his legs buckled and he dropped to the ground. His eyes were wild, bulging open as blood trickled from his nose and mouth.

I heard myself cry out, "Nooooo!"

Hymie tried to get up but another round of bullets flattened him on his back, making his body jump as each new round pelted him. The pavement was sprayed in blood and the bullet holes in his suit coat were smoldering.

I gagged when I saw bits of brain coming out the top of his head. I couldn't look anymore. My legs gave way beneath me, and the next thing I knew the sky was spinning overhead and someone was shaking me.

"Miss? Miss? Are you okay? Were you hit?" A man stood over me with blood splattered down the front of his shirt. There were screams and the sound of tires screeching around the corner.

"Have you been shot?" he asked again.

I didn't know. I didn't think so. I was numb and later would vaguely remember him helping me to my feet. I heard the sound of sirens growing louder, approaching the scene as a flurry of people gathered around the bodies lying in the street and along the steps of Holy Name Cathedral.

I gathered myself together as the ambulances arrived to tend to the dead and wounded. By the time they were leaving, I had made it inside Schofield's, where I telephoned Evelyn. Cupping my ear against the whine of the sirens, I explained to her very matter-of-factly what had happened.

"Stay put, Vera. I'm on my way."

I hung up the telephone and stared at the floorboards. They were worn and uneven, and some looked charred in spots, as if they'd once caught fire; others had splits running down the length of them. I realized that I could have been standing in the very spot where Dion O'Banion had been gunned down almost two years before. It seemed wrong, standing there, like I was standing over his grave. I stepped to the side and when that didn't feel like it was enough, I moved to the opposite end of the room.

There was chaos inside the shop with police officers and reporters coming in and out, asking questions. Some I answered; some I knew I shouldn't. The heavy scent of flowers was nauseating me.

As soon as Evelyn arrived, I took one look at her and began to cry. By the time she got me home, I was hysterical.

"His body was full of bullet holes," I said as she helped me into bed and placed a cold compress on my forehead. I covered my mouth and sobbed. "I can't believe I'm crying like this. What's the matter with me? You'd think Hymie Weiss was my best friend." I sat up and bawled into her shoulder.

The doorbell sounded and she pulled away. "I'll be right back," she said. "That must be the doctor. I asked him to come by and give you something to help you sleep."

Even after the doctor left, I was restless. When I did finally fall asleep I had nightmares filled with the *rat-a-tat-tat* of machine gun fire going off.

The next day I slept until noon, and though I was still groggy from the sleeping pills, something about me was different. I couldn't explain it. It was as if all those tears I'd cried for

Hymie and for myself had hardened into a shell around me. You'd think it would have been just the opposite, but after seeing a man gunned down, after having my husband taken away, nothing was getting through my skin anymore. It was just like Cecelia said. I was tougher than I realized. And if all this hadn't broken me, there was nothing else that could.

With Hymie dead, Drucci was now in charge of the North Side Gang. And he was also in charge of me. Every few days he came by the house with an update on Shep's case, which as far as I could tell was at a standstill. He'd pacify me with promises that all was moving forward and hand me an envelope, which seemed to be getting lighter by the drop.

One time I looked inside the pouch and then back at Drucci. "Where's the rest of it?"

"That's it."

"Vinny!" Dread moved over me.

"That's all I got to spare right now," he said without apology, checking his pocket watch, as if I were keeping him from something more important.

"But I can't live on this. I have a child. I have bills. What about the Meridian? There has to be money coming in from the club."

"The Meridian's been sold," he said.

"Sold? To who?"

"Look, we had to, okay. Izzy couldn't run the place by himself without Shep. We had no choice."

"But what about the money from selling the club?"

"Gone."

"What do you mean, gone?"

"Vera, you weren't the only one depending on the Meridian for your income. Now listen to me. I'm doing what I can for you, but you gotta understand, Hymie's gone now. Over the past few weeks a dozen of my best men have been taken out by Capone. I don't have enough men left to keep the sauce moving. I got warehouses packed to the gills and thirsty customers, so unless you wanna start hauling hooch," he said with a laugh, "I can't keep you in the grand style that Shep did."

"But what am I going to do? I'm running out of money." I was on my feet, reaching for my coat and pocketbook. I called to the housekeeper, told her I needed her to stay with Hannah.

Drucci stood in front of me, blocking my way. "Where are you going?"

"I have to go see Shep. I have to."

"Now, wait a minute. I know you don't want to hear this, but the worst thing you can do for Shep is go see him. He's gonna take one look at you and all it's gonna do is remind him of everything he can't have right now. Trust me on this."

But I didn't trust Drucci. I knew what was best. I knew what I had to do.

As soon as Drucci left, I grabbed Shep's keys from his desk drawer. The car was brand-new and had been sitting idle since Shep had gone away. I'd never driven that car before and wasn't all that keen on driving to begin with. Still, I got behind the wheel of Shep's new Cadillac and made my way to a part of town I'd never been to before and hadn't even known existed. I accelerated on the gas, moving past the broken sidewalks and unpaved roads that led to California and Twenty-sixth Street.

I parked outside a stretch of windowless brick buildings with a tower in the center. There was a chill in the air and a cloudless sky. The sun was trying to work its way through the golden autumn leaves and it was an oddly beautiful sight, given that I was standing outside a prison gate. There were guards positioned all around with all their guns and badges, their billy clubs and handcuffs.

After looking inside my pocketbook, the guard had me empty my coat and dress pockets before leading me back to see Shep. The hallways were narrow and poorly lit. Cigarette butts littered the filthy floor, along with spit, clumps of dust, and God knows what else. The smell was horrendous, a combination of body odor, stale smoke, urine, and shit.

I stared straight ahead, though I was aware of the men perched at the edge of their cages, gripping the bars, watching me walk past, escorted by a guard who thwacked the iron bars every couple of cells when the men whistled and made lewd comments.

Finally, I arrived at a small concrete room with a wooden table and two chairs in the center. The guard stood by the door, and from the opposite end of the room, a second guard appeared through another doorway. Behind him was Shep.

I felt like someone had kicked me in the gut. I bit my lip and held my breath to keep from crying.

When he saw me, Shep perked up. "They didn't tell me it was you, Dollface. I would have cleaned myself up if I'd known." He smiled and tried to shrug but his hands were cuffed behind his back.

All I could do was stroke his unshaven face. I couldn't speak.

"C'mon now. This is why I didn't want you to come here," he said, after I'd lost my fight and broke down in sobs. He kept saying things were going to be fine. Said his lawyer was going to get his case before the judge by the end of the month.

"Hey, Leon." He turned to the guard. "Do you mind?" He gestured as best he could to the handcuffs.

Leon looked around, making sure the other guards were out of sight, and then unlocked the cuffs. Shep's wrists were raw with fresh cuts. Scabs had already formed over his previous wounds.

"Do you have a cigarette?"

My hands were trembling as I reached inside my pocketbook and took out one for him and one for myself. His guard, Leon, stepped in and produced a light for us both. Shep inhaled deeply and asked about Hannah. He asked about the girls and my women's group meetings. He even asked about my mother. When I told him we were running out of money, he assured me he'd talk to Vinny.

"I know things are tight now, but don't worry, Dollface. You're gonna be fine."

I grabbed hold of his hands. They were blistered, chapped and dirty, but still I brought them to my lips while he leaned forward and kissed the top of my head. I squeezed my eyes shut and said a prayer asking that he'd be home soon. He was right in front of me and already I was missing him. He didn't deserve to be locked up like an animal. I didn't want to leave him behind. I wanted to take him home with me. I wanted to wrap my arms around him, and for once I wanted to be the one protecting him.

We smoked another cigarette together and with tears streaming down my face I watched the guard put the cuffs back on, making Shep wince as the metal rubbed against his open cuts. He kissed me good-bye, told me to be strong and was walked back out the door and into one of those awful, crowded cells.

When I left Shep, my head was pounding. I could smell leaves burning in the distance, a scent I normally loved, but now it was too sharp, too much. The sun was glaring in my eyes and my legs felt like they were made of rubber. I was dizzy and queasy. Once I made it to the car, I leaned over and vomited on the side of the road.

MAKING DO

I could tell by the look on Shep's face that the news wasn't good. His case was supposed to have gone before the judge that week and I was holding my breath, waiting to hear the outcome.

Shep grasped the iron bars and hung his head. "They said it's gonna be another month."

"Until you're released?"

"Until the judge hears my case." Shep squeezed the bars even tighter.

"But, Shep—"

"Nothing I can do about it." He shook his head. "But the lawyer promised it would go before the judge next month."

"Oh, Shep, I'm sorry." I reached over and ran my fingers through his hair.

We stood there side by side, saying nothing. There were no words to comfort him. Or me. Eventually I wrapped my arms around his waist and we held each other until the guard told us our visit was up.

"It's okay, you're going to be okay. We'll get through this, Shep," I told him.

"You're coming back next week?" Though initially Shep had asked me not to visit him, I knew he needed to see me.

"I'll be back. I'm not going anywhere."

For the past month I'd been going to see Shep once a week, sometimes twice. The guards, especially Leon, got to know me and they let me bring Shep pictures of Hannah, a few books, a blanket, cigarettes, and even some cigars—as long as I had a few extras for the guards as well. I was almost getting used to our routine when they moved Shep again.

"They moved him?" I glared at the lawyer. "Why did they move him?"

"Cook County's too crowded. They needed to make room for more inmates."

"So where did they take him?"

Henry Brice bobbed his head, staring at his polished shoes.

"Henry? Where?"

He glanced up, steepled his fingers and said, "I'm sorry, Vera. They transferred him downstate to Southern Illinois Penitentiary."

I went home and drank for the next day and a half. He was so far away now, down along the Mississippi, and worst of all, he was in the state penitentiary. I remembered what Cecelia had told me about that place. And Drucci and Bugs begged me not to go see him there. They said Shep specifically had asked me not to come.

"Not down there," said Bugs. "It's no place for you."

I went back to Shep's lawyer but again got no real answers. So I went home and wrote more letters and sent care packages that I knew would probably never reach him.

The next couple of months were rough. What little savings I had deteriorated rapidly.

Each time I asked Drucci for more help, I heard the same thing: "Be patient. Shep'll be home soon. Learn to make do."

Making do meant cutting back everywhere I could. For the first time in years, I threaded a needle and sewed loose buttons onto my dresses and Hannah's clothes. I canceled my weekly beauty salon appointments and went back to trimming my own bangs, tweezing my own eyebrows and polishing my own fingernails. Much as I hated to do it, I had to let the housekeeper go. Even an extra ten dollars a week was more than I could manage. Thankfully Dora was happy to look after Hannah whenever I asked, always willing to give her baths, read her bedtime stories—whatever she needed. And Dora was good enough not to say, "I told you so," about not having my own money.

Money. That was all I thought about. Winter was coming and the buttons on my daughter's coat were straining to close, and her shoes were so small they hurt her feet.

I went to a pawnshop and got a pittance for my jewelry, at least for the jewelry I was willing to part with. Though it wasn't a time to be sentimental, I couldn't pawn my wedding ring or the first diamond necklace that Shep had given me. The pawnshop put some cash back in my pocket, helped me cover some bills, but there were more bills coming and I had new fears forming.

Finally I realized I had no choice but to put the house up for sale, along with Shep's car. Almost immediately people came in droves to see the house. I stood by feeling violated as strangers and even some neighbors romped through my home, opening closets and cupboards, going into my bedroom and Hannah's room. A young married couple stood in the drawing room, staring at the photographs on the fireplace mantel. "That's him," I heard the wife say, pointing at a picture of the three of us, taken the summer before, Shep and me with Hannah on my lap. "He's the mobster."

I stepped in, snatched the photograph from them and put it away, but the couple hardly seemed to notice. The husband turned around and said, "Let's get a look at the upstairs. I want to see where he slept at night."

I stormed out of the drawing room and headed for the parlor where I overheard two women clucking. "So this is the way a gangster lives. Not bad, huh? Do you think anyone was killed in this room?"

"Not yet," I said furiously. "But there's always a first time."

The women looked at me, the color draining from their faces.

I was through being the neighborhood spectacle. "Ladies," I said, "this showing is over." I turned to a roomful of gawkers and calmly addressed them all. "Everyone, if I could please have your attention. This house is no longer on the market."

After I'd shooed all of them out, I marched outside and found a group of men circling Shep's Cadillac, talking nonstop among themselves.

"I tell ya, this is the car," said one of the men, his hand on the hood. "This is the one they went after Capone in."

"Actually, gentlemen," I said, "that one's in the garage. It's not for sale, and neither is this one anymore." I folded my arms across my chest and said, "I think we're done here."

They looked up at me, stunned.

"I said, I think we're done." I went up the front stairs and when I turned back around they were already scurrying off the grounds.

The next day I went to the grocery store and when the cashier rang me up, I counted my money and realized I was a dollar and seven cents short. The woman behind me sighed as I removed the bacon, a sack of flour and a jar of jam from my bag.

"Still need another forty-seven cents."

My cheeks burned red as I pulled a loaf of bread and a dozen eggs from the bag and set them on the counter.

When I returned home that afternoon the telephone was ringing. It was my mother calling. ". . . You know I'd help you if I could," she said.

"I'm not asking for your help," I said. "You've already told me your business is struggling." I peeled back the drapes and gazed out the window.

"I still think you should reconsider selling the house. There's plenty of room here for you and Hannah. . . ."

I closed my eyes and held the phone away from my ear. Every time she mentioned this it made my head throb. I'd never wanted to sell the house in the first place. I loved my home, and besides, to give it up made it seem like Shep was never coming back, like he was gone for good. "I'll figure something out."

"Don't be so proud, Vera."

But I was proud, and I'd left Brighton Park once and that was for good. I couldn't raise my daughter in that house, not if I wanted a better life for her. I didn't want her nose filled with the stockyard rot. I didn't want neighborhood children teasing her that her grandmother killed stray cats and cooked them for supper. I didn't want my daughter to be the fatherless girl others felt sorry for.

After I hung up with my mother, I fixed myself a drink and wondered what I was going to do. Out of desperation I went on a mad search through the house, thinking that perhaps Shep had an emergency stash tucked away somewhere. I looked everywhere, checked where he kept his guns, his cuff links and tiepins. I scoured his office, reaching inside the porcelain jars he had arranged on the fireplace mantel, along his bookcases and behind photographs on the walls, even inside his cigar humidor. Nothing. Then I turned to his desk, a sturdy oversize rolltop mahogany that he'd had specially designed.

He'd kept the bottom drawers locked at all times, but I knew where he hid the key. I fixed myself a drink and got busy, unlocking each drawer one by one. Hoping to find an envelope bulging with fresh, crisp bills, I pulled open the top drawer, sorting my way through loose papers and letter openers and scissors. I found discarded fountain pens and rubber bands. Then I unlocked the last drawer, housing dozens of file folders dating back to January of 1920.

I pulled out the first folder and leafed through it. The pages were divided into columns filled with names, addresses and dollar amounts—all typed and very official looking. At first I couldn't decipher any of it but then I realized that some were customers and others were suppliers. And the merchandise in play was liquor. As far as I could tell, Shep and the North Siders were bringing in liquor from as far away as Detroit, Philadelphia, Cincinnati, even Ontario. Some of the names were scratched off, with new ones typed in underneath. The dollar amounts were staggering, ranging from fifteen dollars a case to forty-five dollars a case. Drucci's words echoed in my mind: *Unless you wanna start hauling hooch....*

I pushed away from the desk and poured myself another bourbon.

SUPPLY AND DEMAND

Drucci had promised to drop off some money by the end of the week. "But just so you know," he'd said over the telephone, "it ain't gonna be much."

In the meantime, I'd run out of coal for the furnace, and there was such a chill inside the house that I kept Hannah bundled up in her coat and mittens while I tried to stay warm in one of Shep's sweaters and two pairs of his socks.

I had chopped up a cheese sandwich in fine bites for Hannah, but she had already refused that, along with the gelatin, and was fighting me on the mashed-up banana.

"C'mon now, honey, just try it. Just try one bite."

She clamped her lips tight and turned her face away.

"Please, Hannah! Just one bite!"

But each spoonful was met with angry protest, and in the time it took me to reach for a cigarette, she had made a mess, running her fingers through her food and then through her hair. I wanted to scream, but when I looked at that face, how could I be angry? She was smiling and so proud of herself. It was the first time I'd laughed in ages.

The next day the sun was shining despite the bite in the air. I bundled Hannah up and put her in her buggy for a walk. She was getting too big for the buggy, but when she got fussy it was the only thing that calmed her down. We made our way past the black cast-iron finial gate in front of the house and moved on toward the neighbor's. It had begun to snow lightly, and Hannah looked up at the sky, fascinated by the few snowflakes floating down. We'd made it halfway around the block when the front wheel of the buggy came loose, wobbling from side to side until it came off. The buggy tilted to the side and I lunged for Hannah, for fear she'd tumble out. The loose wheel took off and rolled into a slushy pothole in the street.

My hands were freezing as I retrieved the wheel and crouched down beside the buggy, trying to fix it. Hannah was watching, leaning over the edge to see what I was doing. My fingers were stiff from the cold, and each time I tried to tighten the wheel, it just flopped off, landing on the sidewalk. It was no use. It wasn't going to work. So I set the wheel inside the buggy, lifted Hannah up, and hoisted her onto my hip, holding her bottom with one hand while I dragged the broken buggy behind us. She was heavy, the buggy was heavy and it was one of the longest few blocks I'd ever walked. I felt the tears building up with each step. I was a failure. I couldn't even take my daughter for a walk without messing up. When we turned the corner and I saw the house, that's when the tears let loose. Hannah looked at me and started to cry, too.

That night, after I'd gotten her bathed and put down for bed, I went downstairs to fix her buggy. My arms and shoulders were already stiff when I reached for Shep's toolbox. With a wrench and a screwdriver and sweat coming up on my brow, I sat on the drawing room floor surrounded by nuts and bolts and stripped screws. In another few months she'd probably outgrow the buggy anyway, but I wouldn't give up. It was as if mending that wheel would have fixed my other problems, too. In the end, it was hopeless and buying a new buggy was out of the question. I threw the wrench across the room and capsized the broken buggy with a good hard shove.

I tried to get a job. Hell, I even dragged myself back to the office of Schlemmer Weiss & Unger, but they wouldn't have me on account of how I'd walked off the job once Shep started paying my way. So I knocked on other doors, and after I met with a dozen or so merchants and office managers, it was clear that I wasn't qualified for anything paying more than twenty dollars a week, and that just wasn't enough.

One night, after tossing and turning, I got up, went downstairs to Shep's study, and turned on the desk lamp. I hadn't wanted to look at the bills sitting on his desk. The pile was growing, and the time had come to face it. If Shep were still home, our creditors never would have bothered us. Of course, they would have also been paid in full. But since they knew Shep was in prison those bill collectors had become fearless and relentless, sending notices every week, calling the house, refusing to let me shop on credit anymore. They made me feel like a thief.

I poured myself a drink, took a deep breath and began to sort through the envelopes, one at a time. I was overwhelmed by the mortgage and car payments. Plus, I still owed Marshall Field's and Carson's more than four thousand dollars for the items I'd bought months before while Shep was on trial. Shep had never questioned my spending; he'd never wanted to say no to me and now I wished that he had.

As I began making a list, trying to prioritize what needed to be paid first, my fountain pen started to leak. The sight of that black ink covering my fingers and the butt of my hand infuriated me. I didn't know where this sudden rage came from, but it boiled up inside me. I slammed the fountain pen down, causing more ink to escape from the reservoir and it made me so angry that with a sweep of my arm I cleared the desktop, sending the bills flying to the floor along with the lamp, cracking the base in two. I was breathing hard, practically panting as I looked at the mess. I dropped my head to my hands and gave way to heaving sobs. The tears poured out of me, hanging from the tip of my nose, falling one by one onto the empty desktop.

When I was all cried out, I dried my eyes, blew my nose and gathered up the bills. The broken lamp would have to wait. The tears helped, and I was calmer now, able to face what I didn't want to look at.

Among the envelopes were three letters addressed to Mr. Shepherd Green from Mr. Warren Steel in Milwaukee. Thinking they were urgent, I opened the letters and read through each one. Essentially they all said the same thing: He'd been trying to reach Shep for several weeks and had finally tracked down his home address. The long and the short of it was that Mr. Steel had a warehouse of liquor. Canadian whiskey. "The real stuff," as he put it. He needed to move the merchandise. He'd been cheated in the past by some associates of Capone's. "But I've heard you're a fair businessman and that you cut a level deal. . . ." Obviously he hadn't heard that Shep had *gone away*—apparently that news hadn't traveled across state lines.

I set the letters aside, eased back in Shep's oversize chair, and gazed out the window into the night. The wind kicked up and I listened to the tree branches scraping against the side of the house. It gave me a chill. I wondered if my mother had felt this frightened and helpless after my father was killed. What made her think she could have stepped in and learned to run his business? If I were a man—or if I were more like my mother—I could have taken up Warren Steel's offer and told him I'd do it. I'd be the one who'd cut him a level deal. I leaned back and closed my eyes. Just how much was a warehouse full of "the real stuff" worth?

I got up and got the key to Shep's desk. Unlocking the bottom drawer, I pulled out all the folders dating back to January of 1920. Scooting closer to the desk, I traced my finger down and across each column. The total revenue from importing liquor reached into the thousands, even the tens of thousands. I looked at the list of suppliers and the list of customers. One or two names sounded familiar, restaurants I'd either been to or had heard of. By the time I got to the 1925 file, there was a whole new set of customers and suppliers and still more new entries in 1926. Since the early 1920s, at the start of Prohibition, the dollar amounts had tripled, even quadrupled.

I finished combing through Shep's files just as the sun was coming up, sending a haze of pale morning light through the windows. I should have been exhausted but instead I made a pot of coffee and paced back and forth in the kitchen, the wheels turning. . . . If I could make even a fraction of the money indicated in those files, I'd be okay. Hannah would be provided for.

I had watched Shep long enough to learn a thing or two. And my mother, too. In a lot of ways, the liquor trade was no different from the meatpacking business. Or any business, for that matter. It all came down to supply and demand.

It was crazy. Too risky. Women didn't do this sort of thing. But then again, women didn't run meatpacking plants, either. And there were those women bootleggers I'd read about in the newspaper, the ones who'd outrun the police. . . .

Another cup of coffee, two more cigarettes.

I was about to telephone Evelyn when Hannah let out a shrill cry. I dropped the phone and raced up to the nursery. Hannah's face was red and blotchy. Her beautiful brown eyes were teary and unfocused. I felt the heat coming off her body even before I checked for a fever. She was burning up.

I lifted her from the crib just as she threw up on the front of my bathrobe. Balancing her on my hip, I rushed her into the bathroom and dabbed cool tap water on her forehead and the back of her neck. She continued to cry, and with each heaving shriek, I felt another stab to my heart.

Other than some teething pain and a stuffy nose or two, she'd never really been sick before and I couldn't afford to have the doctor come. I laid her down on my bed while I rushed to the kitchen. With a pick, I frantically broke off chunks of ice from the icebox and wrapped them in a towel. For the rest of the day I kept ice packs around her but they weren't doing much good. Her cheeks were still red and her tiny body was drenched in sweat. Poor thing couldn't keep anything down. All I could do was rock her in my arms, saying, "I'm sorry, baby girl. I'm so sorry I can't make this better."

I was failing her. Again. And even though she was so young and probably wouldn't remember any of it, I would never forget.

Six long hours later her fever finally broke. I went downstairs and made myself a fresh pot of coffee. While the percolator was brewing I went into the powder room and cleaned the dried vomit off my robe. I looked at myself in the mirror, disgusted by the dark purplish circles beneath my eyes, the grayish cast to my skin. It was the first time I saw a resemblance between my mother and me.

I couldn't look at myself any longer. My child was sick and I couldn't even afford a doctor's visit. I couldn't go on like this. I had to do something.

Was the idea of selling liquor really that absurd? Especially when the plan had practically fallen in my lap. Wasn't that a sign? Thanks to Warren Steel, I had a source for the supply. All I needed to do was find customers. Customers who weren't doing business with the North Siders. But I had the list, dating back to 1920. I knew who to stay away from and who was fair game. I knew that some former customers hadn't been profitable enough for the North Siders, but they would be plenty big enough for me. The key to making this work was keeping it small, contained, and inconspicuous. If I could resurrect just one of those accounts, I'd be okay. I knew I could do it, but I couldn't do it alone.

Evelyn thought I was kidding. I showed her Warren Steel's letters, and once she realized I was serious, she set them on the table, glanced into her coffee cup, and said, "I'm afraid I'm going to need something stronger than this."

"I've got it all figured out," I said, taking down a couple glasses and a bottle of whiskey. "I have a list of speakeasies, hotels, restaurants, and private customers we can sell to."

"What's this *we* business?"

"I know it sounds crazy, but we can do this. We can. There're plenty of small outfits out there—too small for anyone else to bother with, but it'll put money in our pockets. Good money. And the other day when I asked if I could borrow a few dollars, remember you said you were tight? Remember? You said Izzy was cutting back on your spending money?"

"He doesn't have the Meridian anymore and you know things have been tough since Hymie's been gone, but—"

"Listen to me." I reached over and grabbed her hands. "Dora tried to warn me a long time ago, but I didn't listen. And now I'm telling you—if something happens to Izzy, you'll be in the same boat as me. Do you want to go back to being a typewriter, counting every penny? You have to start making your own money."

Evelyn freed her hands and took a long sip of whiskey. "It's too dangerous."

"Believe me, I know there's risk involved in making liquor runs, but I've given this a lot of thought. I have a child and I'm not going to do something foolish. We just have to be smart about this."

"Smarter than the guys?"

"Yes."

She shook her head. "Are you forgetting that Izzy was shot driving a truck of liquor? They could have killed him."

"This is different. Capone's men were waiting for Izzy. And he was leading a caravan of trucks. I'm not talking about doing anything on a scale like that. All we'd need to sell is just ten or fifteen cases at a time. We'd put them right in the backseat of Shep's car and throw a blanket over the top. Nobody would even notice us. And who would ever suspect a couple women of transporting liquor? I'm telling you, they wouldn't even bother with us for ten or fifteen cases. It would be no different from you and me driving up to Wisconsin to see your aunt Millie."

"Only I don't have an aunt Millie." Evelyn cocked her eyebrow and took a pull from her drink.

I gave her a jab with my elbow. "Let's just go up there and talk to Warren Steel. For all I know he's already found someone to work with. He may not need us. But let's just meet with him."

She stared into her glass, refusing to look at me.

"Please, Evelyn." My voice began to crack. "I'm dying here. I'm flat broke. I have to do something. I won't make it through the winter. I don't know when Shep's coming home. I don't . . ."

"Shhh . . ." She gave me the same look she'd served up all our lives when I'd been able to convince her to do something she didn't want to do, like pinch a chocolate bar or perfumed sachets from the corner store. "Okay," she said, setting down her empty glass. "We'll go *meet* with him."

The next day, I pulled out a map and laid it down flat across the dining room table. Evelyn and I held down the corners with the heels of our hands and traced the roads we needed to take.

When we were set, I bundled up Hannah and dropped her off at Dora's house.

"There's my baby!" Dora picked Hannah up, bouncing her on her hip.

"We'll be back late tonight," I said, stroking Hannah's curls.

"We're going to visit my aunt Millie in Milwaukee," Evelyn blurted out.

I shot her a look, though Dora didn't seem fazed. She was busy fussing over Hannah.

"Well, we should get going." I planted kisses on Hannah's forehead and cheeks and waved good-bye.

Evelyn and I climbed back inside Shep's car and headed toward Milwaukee.

"See," I said to her as we were leaving the city limits, the skyline fading into the distance, "this is what it would be like. This is exactly what we'd be doing. Doesn't seem so dangerous now, does it?"

After getting lost twice, we finally turned onto a long country road lined with evergreens, with shacklike houses peppered here and there. The street dead-ended at what looked like an abandoned barn.

"Are you sure this is it?" Evelyn asked.

I double-checked the address on one of Warren Steel's letters. "This is the place."

We found Mr. Warren Steel inside. He was a short man with

a slight frame and a Dr. Grabow–style pipe planted in his mouth. I would have guessed him to be in his mid- to late thirties. He was clean-shaven with sprigs of reddish brown hair sprouting up from his glossy scalp. He wore coveralls and mud-caked work boots.

"You girls lost?"

"No." I held out my hand and introduced myself using my maiden name. "I understand that you have some liquor that we could buy."

He took a step back, pulled the pipe from his mouth. "This isn't a speakeasy, miss. If you want a drink—"

"No, no, I realize that. But see, I have some people looking for whiskey and I've heard you have some you'd like to sell."

"Where'd you hear that from?"

"Let's just say I have some people looking out for me." I had to keep Shep and the North Siders out of it.

He closed his hand around the bowl of his pipe and took a puff, squinting one eye. "I may have what you're looking for." He took another couple slow puffs and looked at our automobile parked out front. I hadn't thought about it before, but I supposed pulling up in a new Cadillac hadn't hurt our cause. "Follow me," he said.

He led us to a musty back room, and when he reached up for the string hanging from a naked bulb, the scene came to life. There were rows of wooden crates stacked floor to ceiling, each plastered with a "Baker's Flour" label on the side.

Opening one of the crates, he pulled out a bottle of whiskey, wiped off the dust, uncapped the top and handed it to me.

I held the bottle, studying the label: Distilled in Canada. Imported Genuine Canadian Blend . . . I looked up and gave him a nod.

"I assume you want to sample the merchandise," he said.

"Of course." I took a sip. It was the real stuff, just like he'd said. I passed the bottle to Evelyn, who looked like she could have used a good belt of whiskey. She hadn't said a word since we'd arrived.

Warren Steel rocked back on his heels and eyed me first and then Evelyn. "I've never dealt with a couple of women before."

I nodded. "I understand your hesitation." I took a step forward and handed back his bottle. "But remember, I've never dealt with *you* before, either."

He snickered.

I peered into the case he had uncrated and then looked him in the eye. "Mr. Steel, I know you've been cheated before, but you'll find that I'm more than fair. I'm not out to chisel you. And between the two of us"—I gestured toward Evelyn—"we'll get your merchandise moving. Unless, of course, you'd rather it just sit in your warehouse collecting dust."

He struck a match and fired up his pipe, filling the musty air with the sweet smell of tobacco. Squinting from the smoke, he said, "I'll let you have it for twenty-five dollars a case."

I hesitated the right amount of time before I said, "That'll be just fine."

I detected a smile.

"Did you hear yourself in there?" Evelyn said once we got back to the car. "You sounded like a regular bootlegger. Where did you learn to wheel and deal like that?"

I pulled out a cigarette and tapped it to the center of the steering wheel. "Helps to have a mother who's dealt with men all her life." I sounded coy about it, but I was damn proud of how I'd conducted myself in there. I struck the match, holding it while it burned for a second or two.

"My lord." Sinking down in the passenger seat, Evelyn

propped her feet up on the dash and began to laugh. "Wow—was that ever fun!"

I lit my cigarette and shot her a surprised look. "Just remember, now we have to find some people to sell his liquor to."

Before we'd left, Warren Steel and I had shaken hands and I was given a bottle for sampling. I told him we'd be back in touch to set up our first pickup and delivery.

Evelyn and I spent the rest of the week going over the list of customers from Shep's files.

After a long drive to the west side of the city, we arrived outside a dilapidated building with boarded-up windows and a splintered sign that said, "Gaylord's Fine Dining."

"Well," I said, putting the car in park and looking at Evelyn, "what's next?"

Next came a string of abandoned saloons.

"How are we going to find a customer when everybody's out of business?" said Evelyn, fishing a piece of chewing gum out of her pocketbook.

"Don't lose hope. We still have more places to try."

Twenty minutes later we pulled up to a modest-looking brick building on Sheffield near the el tracks. There was no sign outside, but the address matched up.

I pulled out my compact and a tube of lipstick. "Now just follow my lead," I said, giving myself a quick touch-up.

Evelyn finished her cigarette and we headed inside, letting a wedge of daylight pierce an otherwise dark tavern. It smelled of stale beer and tobacco. A film clung to the glasses behind the bar and it looked as though they hadn't been washed in a year. My shoes were sticking to the floor.

Three grisly-looking men at the bar stared us up and down.

One of them stood up and circled around us. "You gals wanna drink?"

I shot a sideways glance at Evelyn. My pulse was racing.

"What'll it be?" asked the bartender, a pudgy middle-aged man with pockmarked cheeks and gray stubble along his chin.

"Ah, I'm sorry," I said. "I think we have the wrong place."

I grabbed Evelyn and as soon as we cleared the doorway, we ran for the car.

Once we were a safe distance away, I pulled onto the shoulder of the road and threw the car in park. Resting my head on the steering wheel, I sighed. "You were right. This is crazy."

"Don't be discouraged. Who's left?" Evelyn reached for the list and scanned down the names. "We haven't tried this place yet." She shoved the paper before me.

"It's all the way up in Northfield." I blew out another sigh. I was tired and my legs were stiff from sitting in the car all day. "I just don't think this is going to work."

"But there're still at least half a dozen places to try."

"I'm sorry I dragged you into this, Ev. You were right all along. This was a dumb idea."

"Oh, c'mon! Don't give up. We can't quit now. All we need is one—just one person to give us a chance." She cocked her eyebrow and gave me her best Billy the Kid. "C'mon, what do you say? I know we can do this. I know we can."

I shook my head. "I'm sorry but I don't see how this is going to work." Feeling defeated, I put the car in gear and headed back onto the road.

I dropped Evelyn off and then stopped at Dora's to get Hannah. It was already dark, and the streetlamps were glowing like globes hovering over their neighborhood. I hoped Dora had fed Hannah, maybe even given her a bath.

When Dora answered the door I apologized for being so late.

"Don't be silly. Hannah's been a little angel. C'mon in."

I walked into the parlor and there was my daughter, dressed in a new pretty pink outfit and a pair of new shoes. There was a teddy bear next to her on the rug.

"Well, don't you look beautiful," I said, reaching for Hannah and hoisting her into my arms, freckling her face with kisses. "Where'd all this come from, huh?"

"Just a little something from her auntie Dora." Dora stroked Hannah's dark curls. "We girls did a little shopping today."

"I can see that. You shouldn't have, Dora."

"It was nothing." Dora picked up the teddy bear and held it up so Hannah could see. "She just loves her new teddy. Don't you?"

Dora dangled the bear and Hannah reached for it, grabbing hold of its paw, her tiny face bursting into a smile as she giggled. I couldn't remember the last time I'd seen her laughing like that. Seeing my daughter so happy, I should have been grateful to Dora, but instead I felt stung and somehow I twisted Dora's generosity into a declaration of my shortcomings as a mother. I hated feeling like that. I knew I was being self-centered and selfish and now, on top of everything else, I had reason to be ashamed of myself, too.

"I hope you don't mind," said Dora, still prancing the teddy bear before Hannah's outstretched fingers. "I just put her old clothes in a bag. If you want, I can throw them out. Everything was so small on her anyway. Besides, she's far too pretty to be dressed like a pauper."

I couldn't bring myself to say thank you or even smile, because I was buckling under the weight of my failures. And at the same time, I had a premonition: Hannah as a young girl, sitting with her friends and laughing at me, making fun of me just as I'd done to my mother.

"C'mon, honey," I said, clutching her closer, an ache spreading across my chest. "We have to go now."

While I walked to the car, I pressed my lips to Hannah's ear and whispered, "I promise you, we're going to be okay. I'm going to take care of you. I promise. I promise."

After we got home and I had put Hannah to bed, I telephoned Evelyn. "Are you free tomorrow?"

HAULING THE WEIGHT
OF THE WORLD

The next day Evelyn and I went back out in search of a customer and met with a man named Simon Marvin. When we told him what we were up to, he backed off, saying, "I don't deal in liquor anymore. Been raided one time too many."

I thanked him for his time, and as Evelyn and I were walking out of his office, he called to us. "But"—he came over and removed his hat—"if you're sure you've got the genuine article there, straight from Canada, you should go talk to my brother, Felix."

Twenty minutes later we turned up on Felix Marvin's front steps. I noticed the mezuzah nailed to the doorjamb.

He looked at us and smiled. The first thing he said was, "Two nice Jewish girls. That's a new twist. Come." He motioned us inside his office. "Simon told me you were on your way."

He made us coffee, offered us some strudel that his wife had baked that morning. He was kind, well dressed with manicured hands and a gleaming wedding band. There was a prayer book on the corner of his desk along with a tallis bag. I took it as a sign. Something about a Jew doing business with another Jew put me more at ease.

After I'd poured him a taste of Warren's whiskey, he took a sip and a reflective moment later he nodded. "I have almost a dozen speakeasies out in the suburbs. Your Canadian whiskey would make for a nice addition."

"It's top-shelf."

"This I can tell." He raised his glass.

"I can let you have it for thirty dollars a case."

"Thirty?" He rubbed his chin and nodded. "Your price is fair. You seem like a couple of nice, *hamishe* girls. What you're doing in this line of work is beyond me," he said with a shrug. "But if I can help you and you can help me, why not, eh?"

So after a cup of coffee and a little *kibitzing*, Evelyn and I had our first customer. He ordered twenty cases—more than I'd been expecting—but if we had to, we could stow a couple cases in the front seat. My only stipulation was that he had to give us half the money up front.

It was a deal, and by nightfall, Evelyn and I both had twenty-five dollars in our pockets.

Evelyn was nervous on that first run. But surprisingly, I wasn't. No, I had surpassed fear months ago. Now I was determined to do whatever I had to do in order to survive. The ride up was a breeze and this time we didn't get lost.

When we made it to Steel's warehouse in Milwaukee, Warren and his men were waiting for us. After questioning where our truck was and learning that we were taking only twenty cases, Warren dismissed his men in disgust.

"It's hardly worth the trouble," he said as he unlocked the back gate.

I tried to assure him there'd be many more runs in the future but he waved my words away as if they were gnats buzzing about his head.

While Evelyn and I hefted each case of liquor in our arms and wobbled our way to the car, he leaned back and smoked his pipe. After watching us struggle for a few minutes, he finally decided to lend a hand.

It was a tight squeeze. We had to take the bottles out of the cases just so they would fit. Twenty minutes later, all but one case made it into the backseat, slumbering under a heavy wool blanket. The last case rode up front on the floor beneath Evelyn's feet.

The drive back to Chicago was fortunately uneventful, despite the rattling of the bottles in the back. I was thankful not a single one broke. When we made it to Felix's dropoff point, he was a bit miffed when we began handing over individual bottles, so I lied and said the cases had all come in broken. He accepted this and we were on our way.

By midnight, the two of us were another twenty-five dollars richer and even Evelyn had to admit, "This is easy!"

When I stopped by Dora's to pick up Hannah, Dora showed me the blanket she was knitting for my daughter.

The sight of the wooden needles stabbed me through the heart and made my mouth go dry. "It's beautiful." I couldn't look at those needles. "Sweetheart," I said, calling to Hannah, "you ready to go home?"

Hannah looked up at me just as Knuckles came through the back way, slamming the door with a bang so loud it frightened her. Her eyes grew wide as she let out a high-pitched scream and ran to Dora.

I felt clobbered. Dora scooped my child up in her arms and patted soothing circles on her back. "It's okay. Uncle Knuckles didn't mean to scare you."

I pasted on a smile, overcompensating for my heartache by thanking Dora with the kind of enthusiasm reserved for heroic acts while she fastened on the new coat and hat she'd purchased for Hannah.

"Oh, wait, don't forget your new baby doll!"

I reached for Hannah's free hand as she grabbed the doll from Dora. Even though Hannah was too young to know the difference, I knew I'd have to upstage that doll with a better one.

And it didn't stop there. I went on a shopping spree the following week. After I'd spent all but five dollars on toys and clothes for Hannah, Felix Marvin called and ordered another fifty cases.

"Fifty cases!" Evelyn's eyes grew wide with alarm. She'd been sitting in the living room, listening to a radio program while I'd taken the telephone call from Felix. "We can't fit fifty cases in the car. Why did you tell him we could do it?"

"Because I'm broke again and I need the money."

"What are we going to do, make two trips up and back?"

"I thought about that, but it'll take too long and I don't think Warren and Felix are too crazy about our methods as it is." I lit a cigarette and turned off the radio. "We've come this far. We can't turn back now." I smoked down half my cigarette, thinking. "What if I . . . I borrow one of my mother's trucks?"

"A truck!"

"I'll tell her I'm having car trouble. She won't question it. Business is slow, so I know there's a truck just sitting there. Besides, Buster's already been using the other one for liquor runs."

The truck was my mother's 1925 Ford Runabout, a black Model T pickup. She'd paid two hundred and eighty-one dollars for it and if my calculations were right, Evelyn and I would be making almost that much delivering liquor one day a week. If I'd thought for one minute that we would be making regular liquor runs, I would have suggested getting our own truck. But this was temporary, just something I had to do until Shep came home.

"What if something goes wrong?" Evelyn asked when I picked her up.

"It's not going to."

"But what if it does?"

I reached across for the glove compartment and pulled out two of Shep's handguns.

"Oh, Jesus, Vera!" Her eyes nearly bulged from their sockets.

"They're loaded, so be careful. One for you." I handed her the six-shot. "And a Browning Hi-Power for me."

"I don't know how to shoot a gun!" But even as she said this, I saw Evelyn grip that six-shooter like she'd held a dozen guns before. She angled it this way and that. "It's so heavy," she said, not taking her eyes off the barrel.

"You can put it away now," I told her.

It took another few minutes before her fascination wore off and she was able to part with the gun and put it back in the glove compartment where it belonged.

When we arrived at Warren Steel's warehouse, he wasn't waiting for us like he had before. But he must have heard the truck pull up, because it didn't take long before we saw him standing in the doorway, arms folded across his chest. When I said we were taking fifty cases and promised him an extra ten dollars if he had his men load the truck for us, he didn't exactly smile, but I did see his top lip curve upward ever so slightly.

"I told you, Mr. Steel, I'm more than fair."

We pulled the truck up to the dock and fifteen minutes later all the whiskey was loaded on. We kept the liquor hidden beneath layers of cowhides and rigged a heavy canvas tarp over the top and fastened it down to the sides and back of the cargo box.

It was only as we pulled away from Warren Steel's warehouse that the realization of what we were doing began to sink in. The drive up hadn't fazed me. I'd driven my mother's trucks plenty of times before. That morning we'd just stepped onto the running boards, climbed into the cab and were on our way. Just two women in an empty truck. But now that the truck was loaded with liquor it was a different story. I could feel the weight of the whiskey in the cargo box. It was like I was hauling the weight of the world behind me. I sat up close to the steering wheel, my fingers gripping tight with both hands.

Twice I thought I saw a police car and my heart all but stopped. Turned out it was only my mind playing tricks on me but it didn't help that Evelyn kept telling me I was driving too fast.

"You're only drawing attention to us," she snapped.

"I am not! I'm going twenty-five." I gripped the wheel tighter. "Stop making me nervous!"

"This was such a stupid idea," she hissed under her breath.

"What did you just say?" I turned and glowered at her.

"We should have stuck with smaller runs. In the car."

"Why are you bringing this up now? We agreed to do this, so just shut it!"

"Don't tell me to shut it."

"Shut it! *Now!*"

We didn't have much more to say to each other until we reached our dropoff point in Chicago, where two of Felix Marvin's men were waiting for us. They unloaded the truck, sending crate after crate down the coal chute.

As we were driving away, I turned to Evelyn. "I'm sorry I snapped at you."

"I'm sorry I was making you nuts."

I rubbed the back of my neck, feeling the tension going away. "You do that really well, you know—make me nuts!"

"Years of experience." She laughed. "So how much did we make today, anyway?"

"Let's find out." I pulled off to the side of the road and removed an envelope from my pocketbook. "Let's see. . . ." I counted out a stack of bills on the front seat: two hundred-dollar bills and the rest fifties and twenties. "After Warren takes his cut, we've got a hundred and twenty-five. Plus the first hundred and twenty-five we already got from Felix."

"Not bad for a day's work."

And it got even better after that.

A few weeks later, Felix increased his order to seventy-five cases, and then one hundred cases, and by the end of our second month, we were up to five hundred cases. His business was up, Warren was happy, and Evelyn and I were making money. Turned out that selling illegal liquor was easier than I thought it would be.

One night we were driving a truckload back to the city and Evelyn and I were sharing a cigarette—the last one either of us had—passing it back and forth, me scissoring my fingers, waiting for the handoff.

"Will you let me drive on the next run?"

"No! What do you think I am, crazy?" I took a drag and handed her cigarette back.

"Please?" She looked at me all wide-eyed and hopeful.

"You barely know how to drive a car, let alone a truck."

"Well, it's not like you're such an expert driver. Remember when we first took the truck out? You wouldn't even let go of the wheel. You were such a nervous Nellie."

"That's because I didn't want to get us killed."

"Yeah, and look at you now. You just slouch back in the driver's seat. You remind me of my father when we'd drive to the lake house in Michigan. It doesn't look so hard. C'mon. I just want to try it once. It'll be fun."

"Maybe I'll let you do a practice run one day. Maybe!" I reached up to adjust the rearview mirror and caught myself smiling. Really, it was just as Evelyn had said: *This is easy!*

"So what did Felix want to talk to you about?" she asked.

He'd pulled me aside as we were leaving earlier. "Oh, he just mentioned that he has some friends who need liquor."

"That's good, right? We should do it!" She sat up, eager, her eyes dancing. "Why wouldn't we? Warren's got an endless supply of whiskey looking to find a good home."

"I know, but I don't want to get greedy. We have a good thing going right now. It's manageable. I'm afraid that if we take on more jobs—if we get any bigger than we are—word could get back to the boys. We can't risk that. And besides, I'm comfortable dealing with Warren and Felix." I glanced at Evelyn, trying to get a bead on her. I didn't want to let her down. "I just don't think it's a smart idea. We're doing great right now. I don't see any reason to ball things up over a couple extra dollars here and there."

"Whatever you say. You're the boss." She smiled, and even if she wouldn't admit it, I could tell she was relieved. Evelyn was no more a gangster than I was.

That night after I'd picked up Hannah and put her to bed, I went to my room and counted my bills, separating the hundreds from the fifties. I even had two five-hundred-dollar bills from a previous run, and I put those on top of the stack.

In exchange for the calculated risk we were taking, I had been able to make sure there was coal for the furnace and plenty of food and warm clothing for my child. I was even able to hire back my housekeeper, something that hadn't met with Dora's approval. She'd wanted me to save my money and let her watch Hannah, until I asked if she wanted to clean my house as well.

"Don't worry," I assured her. "I only have the housekeeper three days a week. I'll still need a babysitter from time to time."

In addition to the housekeeper, I also went back to my weekly hair appointments at the beauty salon and treated myself to some new outfits. I even paid a visit to the pawnshop and was able to buy back the pieces of jewelry that were still there.

I'd restored my credit and my reputation with the department stores around town, and I'd done it on my own. It was one thing to be surrounded by money, and another thing entirely to know that you generated it yourself, even if it wasn't through the most legitimate channels. That was the one part of the equation I didn't want to look at. I was a mother and a businesswoman. That was how I chose to see myself. I wasn't a bootlegger, and I certainly wasn't a gangster. But I had my own money, and I felt as powerful as any man.

"I don't know what you're up to," Basha said, eyeing my new cloche hat, "but you'd better be careful."

"I'm not up to anything." I'd just arrived at Carson's where she'd been saving me a seat for a fashion show.

"Baloney." She leaned in closer to whisper, "New shoes?"

"Oh, you've seen these before." It was the first time I'd ever worn them.

"All I know is you've been crying the blues, saying you're broke, and now you're living the high life. And I know it ain't coming from the fellas. Squeak's even had to cut me back."

"My mother helped me out."

"Mm-hm. Sure she did. . . ." She shook her head and looked again at my shoes. "Just watch yourself; that's all I'm saying. While Shep's away, you're on your own. You get yourself into trouble and you'll have to fend for yourself. You might want to pass some of this advice on to Evelyn, too. . . ."

Dora also had her suspicions. "Where are you and Evelyn off

to this time?" she'd asked when I'd dropped Hannah off at her house.

I'd invented a sick aunt up in Milwaukee.

"I see. All of a sudden you and Evelyn sure do have a lot of aunts up there, don't you. Say hello to Aunt Millie for me."

THE MARKED RIG

I t may have been April, but Chicago winters didn't always coin-
cide with the calendar. The snow started at daybreak and was
already accumulating. By nine o'clock that morning there were
five inches on the ground, with heavy winds producing snow-
drifts peaking twice that high.

As Evelyn and I climbed inside the Ford Runabout, I knew it
was going to be a tough run. The Wrigley Building had all but
disappeared against the white sky and traffic crawled along the
snow-covered roads. Even the el moved slower than usual. But
still, Felix needed his delivery, and I didn't want to lose our mo-
mentum or give him reason to think that if we were men we
would have done better.

As we inched along, the wipers swished back and forth,
clearing away another fresh dusting of snow. Evelyn and I were
both quiet. I was tired from a restless night of sleep and she was
upset over an argument she'd had with Izzy. For a long while the
only sound we heard was the rattle of the empty cargo box and
the crunching of our tires rolling over the snow-covered road.

"Do you want to talk about it?" I asked, breaking the silence as I used my glove to wipe away a clean porthole on the window fog.

"No," Evelyn said with a sigh, but then launched into it anyway. "I can't stand how he talks to me sometimes. Just because he's drunk doesn't give him the right to call me names—tells me I'm an idiot. *Me*"—she gave off a bitter laugh—"*I'm* the idiot here!"

"I've never heard you talk about Izzy like this before."

"Well, I'm fed up. I'm sick and tired of the way he treats me. The way he pushes me around."

"You know you'll get no argument out of me. I think you should have left him long ago."

"I didn't say I was going to leave him." Evelyn lit a cigarette and cracked her window, letting the smell of sulfur and tobacco fill the cab, along with a few snowflakes. "Let's talk about something else. . . ."

When we made it to Warren Steel's warehouse, Evelyn and I stayed in the truck to keep warm while his men loaded up the liquor. Forty minutes later, we were back on the road. It was still snowing, coming down hard. It hadn't let up all day.

The truck bounced up and down over the bumpy back roads, the bottles rattling inside their crates in the cargo box. Everything was dark except for the beams from our headlights, snow pouring into them like sheets of rain. We were nearing Kenosha and still had a long drive ahead of us.

Evelyn had picked up her diatribe. ". . . He's the idiot. If Izzy only knew what we're doing right now he'd *plotz*—I tell you, he'd faint and drop to the floor."

"I just don't understand why you stay with him." I took my eyes off the road just long enough to glance at her.

She turned away and looked out the passenger-side window. "Let's just say he's got his virtues."

"Oh, yeah? Like what? Name one."

She laughed like a naughty schoolgirl. "None of your business."

"Oh, none of my business! Ooh-la-la!" I slouched down in the driver's seat and started singing "T'Ain't Nobody's Bizness If I Do. . . ." I drummed my fingers along the dash with my free hand, tapping out the melody.

Halfway through the second verse, Evelyn looked at me. "Vera, what'd you do with that money I gave you?"

"What money?"

"The money I gave you for singing lessons."

We burst out laughing as Evelyn imitated my singing, making her voice crack and go flat.

The two of us were howling, wiping the tears oozing from our eyes, when I glanced up and spotted a pair of headlights in the rearview mirror. They were coming over the hill behind us, moving fast, shooting off a spray of fresh snow on either side.

The road was icy, and I put both hands on the wheel to keep us moving steadily. Evelyn went on humming that Bessie Smith song, and every few minutes or so I'd eye the rearview mirror. They were inching closer, narrowing the distance between us.

Evelyn eventually noticed the headlights, too. "If they're in such a hurry why don't they just go around us?"

"I'm already going twenty as it is."

Those headlights stayed on us as we bounced around, the engine grinding, the wheels hitting every icy patch and every snow-covered gully. Finally the other car made a move and whipped past us, kicking up a blinding spray of snow that forced me to swerve off the road. After a series of skids, I brought the truck to a screeching stop as Evelyn and I lurched forward in our seats.

Two men got out of the car and I swallowed hard. The panic was mounting inside me as they walked toward us with their fedoras and tommy guns silhouetted in the glare of the head-lights.

I saw Evelyn going for the glove compartment. "No! Keep the guns hidden," I said. "Keep them out of sight."

When the first man reached our truck I stared at his tommy gun, my voice trembling as I asked what he wanted.

He didn't say anything. He just eyed the truck and then me. My heart was beating so hard, I was sure he could see it pounding even through my coat.

The only thing in our favor was that we were women and that threw him off. But not entirely. There were female bootleggers, not many of them, but they were out there. I looked straight ahead, watching as the second man came toward the truck. It was freezing outside but I was sweating, clutching the steering wheel.

I looked again at the man coming toward us. There was something about his walk that seemed familiar. Or maybe it was just that tough gangster gait they all had. But as he cut through the headlights and came closer, I got a feeling in my gut. An absolute certainty. I knew this man.

He came over to my side, leaned toward the window, and said, "What seems to be the problem—" Tony Liolli got a look at me and stopped midsentence.

I didn't say a word and prayed the expression on my face wouldn't betray me. The other man told me to roll down my window and I did, letting in a gust of frigid air. Tony Liolli had his tommy gun raised, gripped with one gloved hand. He was a gangster, and gangsters were loyal to their gangs, not to women they'd run out on. If he knew we had liquor in the back, there was no question what he'd do to us.

Tony and I looked at each other, our breath hanging before

us, suspended in the freezing air like rolling plumes of smoke. I didn't want to die. I didn't want Evelyn to die.

The other man walked around the back of the truck and over to Evelyn's side. "This is the rig," he said.

"You sure?" Tony hadn't taken his eyes off me.

"C'mon," the first guy said, yanking open Evelyn's door. "Get out!"

I reached across the seat and squeezed her hand. She was trembling. I didn't know if she'd recognized or even remembered seeing me with Tony Liolli that first night I met him at the Five Star.

Tony's eyes burrowed through me. He wasn't just looking at me. No, he was studying me, searching for a crack in my composure, to see if I was hiding something—that something being booze. He kept his tommy gun raised and I stared into the barrel. The metal was shinier at the tip, like a bronze statue that'd been rubbed too many times for luck. I felt my bottom lip quivering and knew the tears were building up behind my eyes. Even in the freezing cold, beads of sweat formed along my brow and upper lip. I didn't move; neither did he. A vein in the side of his neck was pulsing as he rolled his tongue inside the pocket of his cheek, something I'd never seen him do before. We were at a standoff, and he was starting to wear me down. I was losing my nerve. I didn't know what he might do.

Just as I was about to crack, Tony lowered his chin and then the tommy gun. "Let 'em go," he said.

I clutched my chest and drew a deep breath, my shoulders dropping back down in place.

"But this is the rig," the other man was saying. "There's a run coming through here and we know Buster's been short-changing us. They're probably driving this for him."

"Look at them!" Tony shook his head, like we weren't worth the bother. "Do they look like they got anything we want?"

"But I tell ya, this is the truck—it says right here, 'Abramowitz Meats.'"

"I said, let 'em go." Tony looked at me and then turned and walked away.

After they had returned to their car and after it was clear that they weren't going to kill us, I began to breathe again. Evelyn gasped, as if she'd been holding her breath the entire time, too.

I pulled the truck around and we got back on the road. I drove fast, even in the snow, my face close to the wheel, hands squeezing tight.

"Are you okay?" I asked.

"Are you?"

I didn't answer her. The snow continued to shower down. Visibility was next to null. It didn't matter though. All I saw the whole drive back to Chicago was Tony Liolli's face.

WHAT HAPPENS WHEN YOU CAN'T SEE STRAIGHT

The following day I stood on the el platform shaking snow off my scarf and the sleeves of my coat. The bitter cold seemed to mask the stench of the stockyards, so it was almost bearable that morning. Nothing like in the summertime when the rot and decay wafted for miles in all directions.

I had just dropped off my mother's truck—which was what I did after all our runs. Now I was heading back up north, where I planned to pay a condolence call to a young widow whose husband had been gunned down outside a pool hall, and then I was going to sleep away the rest of the day. I was so exhausted, even my bones ached. I wondered if I had the nerve to make another liquor run after what had happened to us.

When I got home the night before, the first thing I did was check on Hannah. Dora had brought her to the house earlier and had fallen asleep in the rocker in the corner of the nursery. I placed a blanket over her shoulders and went back to Hannah, asleep in her crib. I couldn't help myself; I had to pick her up and hold her. I had to. Nothing had ever felt so good to me in all my life. She stirred and fluttered her eyes open, looking at me for a moment. Her mouth curled into a faint smile as her tiny hand reached out to touch my cheek. I blinked back my tears as I stroked her dark brown curls. Not a moment later, she fell back asleep, resting her head on my shoulder. I could have stood there and held her all night.

A gust of cold air struck me, cutting into my thoughts as I stood on the el platform. The winds shifted and I was hit with that peculiar scent of creosote on the railroad ties and the dank smell of wet, cold limestone mixed with the faint odor of the stockyards. Another *whoosh* of cold air rushed toward me as the train approached, slowing, slowing, and finally coming to a stop. The doors slid open and I was about to step inside when someone grabbed hold of my arm and pulled me away from the train.

I tried to scream, but nothing came out. Worried they were after my pocketbook, I clutched my bag with both hands. A tall man had hold of me and at first all I could see was his dark over-coat, his face hidden by the brim of his hat. Then he looked up.

"How you doing, kid?"

I froze for a moment, taking him in. "Tony?"

"I've been looking for you. I've been waiting at this stop most of the morning. I was counting on your having to return that truck."

He looked at me and I felt that dull ache for him trying to resurface.

The next thing I knew, we were outside a doorway tucked beneath the el tracks at Lake and Randolph. I should have re-sisted, should have fought him on it. The two of us had no busi-ness being seen in public together. The last thing I needed was word getting back to Shep that I'd been spotted with Tony Liolli. He assured me no one would bother us here.

Two quick knocks and a circular cutaway in the door flipped

open. A man scanned Tony and a moment later the door creaked open onto a dark, cozy den with wood and brass accents. Luckily it was quiet inside. A handful of older men who took no notice of us sat at the bar, puffing on cigars, sipping whiskey and scotch from teacups. Tony led me to a banquette way in the back.

"So, Vera," he said after we sat down, "what in the hell were you doing on that road last night? And how'd you get ahold of Buster's truck?"

Buster's truck! I wanted to set him straight, but I wasn't ready to answer him yet. Seeing Tony scrambled everything inside my head. As much as I'd once wanted him, now that I was face-to-face with him, all I felt was anger. I was that pregnant girl again, left standing in a hotel lobby, scared and all alone. I glanced around the room, my heart thumping, the blood pounding inside my ears.

"At least tell me how you've been."

"I've been fine, no thanks to you." My voice was cold, but shaky; my hands trembled. I stuck my elbow in a sticky spot on the table.

He didn't acknowledge what I said or how I'd said it. He pulled a pack of cigarettes from his breast pocket and slapped them on the table. "The thing I can't figure out is how you got hooked up with Buster in the first place. He's one of our boys now. You know that, don't you?"

"Oh, please. Do you think I'd give Buster the time of day?"

"Well, you didn't just magically appear in his truck. He had that rig loaded up with eight hundred cases of gin."

"And if you'd bothered to check, I bet you would have seen that he made his delivery just fine. Jesus! What makes you think it was his truck, anyway? That truck belongs to my mother. Abramowitz Meats—Vera Abramowitz. Put the pieces together. Buster works for my mother. And no, she doesn't know he steals

285

her truck at night." My mouth was dry; my breathing turned heavy. "If you think I'd have anything to do with a putz like Buster, then you're a bigger fool than I thought you were. And if you were so damned sure we were driving liquor, why didn't you search the truck? How come you let us go?"

"You really have to ask? You know what would have happened if we'd found something? I couldn't have saved you then. Not without hanging myself." Tony signaled the barkeeper. "Hey, Frankie, bring us a round over here, will ya?" He turned to me. "Still a bourbon drinker?"

I nodded.

"Two bourbons."

He latched onto me with his eyes and it got to me. I was angry and couldn't hold back: "You said you loved me. Said you couldn't keep away from me. I was pregnant, dammit. You said you'd help me and instead you left me! What kind of cruel bastard does a thing like that?"

He looked at me, but said nothing.

There it was, out on the table like a spilled drink running over the edges. It came out all wrong. Too emotional. But I couldn't help that now. "How could you do that to me?"

"I messed up." He surrendered with his hands. "I got scared. I panicked."

"*You* got scared? How do you think *I* felt?"

The front door opened and Tony and I paused, both of us holding our breath, worried that it might be someone who would recognize us. But it was just another older gentleman going to take his place at the bar.

"Listen"—Tony scooted in closer—"I was going through a rough time back then. I had a couple of bad bets. Got myself into some trouble. I owed a lot of money. Capone was breathing down my neck. And then you got pregnant and . . ."

"Well, I'm sorry if it wasn't convenient timing for you."

"That's not what I'm saying. You wanted me to find you a doctor and I did. But I didn't know if he was reputable. And it wasn't like I could go around asking about him." He shook a cigarette from the pack and pulled a matchstick from his pocket, striking the tip against the sole of his shoe. "I didn't know anything about this doctor. What if something went wrong? What if something happened to you?" He lit his cigarette and blew a stream of smoke toward the ceiling. "It's a small circle we move in. Christ, Shep was one of Dion's lieutenants. You think he wouldn't have found out? You think he wouldn't have put a bullet in my head? Yours, too." He took another drag off his cigarette. "I admit it—I panicked. I fucked it up. But I never meant to hurt you. And even if Shep never found out, you would have regretted not having that baby. You would have blamed me for it. You would have made me take you to that doctor, and we both know I would have, 'cause, baby, I can't say no to you."

He made it *almost* seem logical, as if leaving me was the only thing he could have done. It almost made me feel sorry for him. *Almost.*

"So where did you go, anyway? Where'd you disappear to?" I set my elbow in the sticky spot again.

"I didn't go anywhere."

"You mean you were here in town? This whole time? You just changed hotels?" I closed my eyes and shook my head. I'd pictured him in New York, Atlantic City, maybe San Francisco. I don't know why it stung, but knowing he'd been here all along cut me deeply.

"I kept tabs on you, though," he said. "I heard you married Shep." He took another drag off his cigarette and gave me one of his long looks. "So," he said finally, "how's the kid?"

The kid? I could have smacked him for that. "The *kid* has a name."

"Well?" He hiked up his eyebrows.

"Her name's Hannah." I reached for his pack of cigarettes.

"So, is she mine?"

"What difference does it make now? She has a father and she sure as hell doesn't need you."

"Well, her so-called father seems to be incarcerated at the moment." He smiled.

"Oh, shut it." The bourbon hit me and hit me hard. I fished out a cigarette from his pack.

Tony leaned in and lit it for me. "Tell me something. And be honest with me."

"You want me to be honest? That's rich, coming from you." I inhaled hard off my cigarette and took another gulp of bourbon.

"Do you love Shep Green?"

"Yes. I love him. I love him more now than ever."

He ran a finger along the inside of his collar and finished off the rest of his drink. "Don't you wanna know if I still love you?" I knew where he was going. I could hear it in his voice. "Because aside from whatever you *think* you feel for Shep, I know you still love me."

"Don't flatter yourself."

"Oh," he said with a laugh, "you do love me, Vera. You love me so much you can't see straight."

"You have a real high opinion of yourself, don't you?" This conversation was a mistake. I reached for my pocketbook and gave the ashtray a shove. "Swell seeing you again, Tony." I stood up and as I turned to storm off, he reached out, grabbed my arm, and pulled me onto his lap.

"Don't go!" His tone changed and now he sounded desperate. "Don't leave me, Vera. I never meant to hurt you. I swear I didn't."

For the first time, I saw his gorgeous brown eyes glass over. "You think it hasn't torn me up inside? What I did to you?" He shook his head, looked around the bar and back at me. "I wanted to come back to you so many times, but I heard you got married and there was nothing I could do. But when I saw you last night, I knew there was no way I could stay away from you. Why do you think I came looking for you today? Why do you think I let you go last night? I love you, Vera. I've always loved you."

My heart was beating fast. I was losing myself just looking into his eyes. Before I could say anything, he kissed me, and son of a bitch, he was right. I couldn't see straight.

THE ACCOMPLICE

Now that it was summertime, beer gardens and outdoor cafés were open and business was busier than ever. Evelyn and I had just gotten back after delivering an extra sixty cases of whiskey to a warehouse up north for Felix Marvin. It was our third run that week.

After the night Tony had spotted us in my mother's truck, Evelyn and I were too afraid to take it out again, so we bought a new truck—a business expense. It was another Ford Runabout, but plain black and unmarked—without any Abramowitz Meats signage on it. Our new truck looked just like a hundred other black trucks on the road, which was exactly what we wanted. In between runs we kept it parked out back behind Evelyn's building since it would have been too conspicuous in my neighborhood.

It had been a smooth run, as most of them were, but I was tired. As I was sorting through the mail, Drucci called with an update on Shep's case.

"The lawyer's still working on the appeal," Drucci said. He

must have been calling from a phone booth. I could hear street traffic rumbling by in the background.

"Vinny, it's June already and Shep's been in the penitentiary for six months. He spent three months in jail up here before that. At this rate he's going to end up serving the whole sentence." I shuffled through the envelopes.

"I know it seems like that," said Drucci as a streetcar clanked by in the background. "But we're working on it."

"I feel like there's something you're not telling me."

"You know as much as we do. I promise you."

"Please, Vinny. Don't insult me." I pressed my fingertips to my head and closed my eyes. "All I want to know is when my husband's coming home!"

I hung up the telephone and tossed the stack of envelopes onto the desk. Bills and more bills but not a single letter from Shep.

Shep's *going away* had set off a chain of events that I could never have seen coming, not in a million years. Drucci, Bugs and the others offered little comfort. Comfort was what I needed. And Tony Liolli was there to provide it.

In many ways it seemed like Tony and I had never been apart. He had a room at the Plymouth Hotel where we'd meet in the afternoons. Moments after I'd arrive, my clothes would be tangled in a pile on the floor. I was helpless when it came to him. No one but Tony had ever made me feel so defenseless. And his kisses . . . I hadn't been kissed in so long. I hadn't felt that surge of excitement rush through my body since forever. He left me drenched in sweat, panting for breath, my mouth gaping open, my legs so shaky I didn't think they could hold me up.

But when he was finished with me, there was a shift in me, as if a switch had been flipped. All I could think about then was Shep passing his days inside a prison cell.

One afternoon, Tony lay stretched out on his back, practicing a new trick of making a coin appear and disappear from one hand to the other. I collected my clothes off the floor and worked my way into my dress. I could feel his eyes on me, watching me, willing me to come back to bed. He had wanted me to stay, but I was antsy. After he'd drained the heat out of me I had shut down. I didn't want to think about what we'd just done, didn't want to bask in the afterglow. No, all I wanted was to go home, make dinner for my daughter, tuck her into bed and read to her.

Tony reached for a cigarette, striking a match on the underside of the night table. He took a drag and stretched back out on the bed, exhaling toward the ceiling. "Get your fine behind back over here," he said with a laugh, when he saw I was just about dressed.

"I can't." I stared at the clock on the nightstand to keep from looking at him. "Really, Tony. I do have to go." I clipped on my earrings and slipped into my pumps, using my finger as a shoehorn. "I'll see you on Thursday. I promise." I was reaching for my pocketbook when he got off the bed, came over and kissed me, long and deep. I closed my eyes, not out of passion but out of disgust. With myself. I felt like I was suffocating. It was the kiss good-bye that was the hardest for me, always tasting bitter on my tongue.

I slipped out of his room and called for the elevator. Stepping into the lobby, I checked around, looking left and right. No one seemed familiar. A man I'd never seen before made eye contact with me and I looked away, walking as fast as I could and almost bumping into one of the bellhops. Once I cleared the front doors and made it around the corner, I let myself breathe. Everywhere but inside Tony's hotel room, I was still Shep Green's wife.

And Hannah's mother.

That night, as I was putting Hannah to bed, reading her a

bedtime story, she was chatty. She pointed to her quilt and said, "That's my bankie. That's my bankie."

"Yes, that is your blankie."

As I was putting the book back on the shelf, I heard her say, "Mama, bahdol, bahdol." My heart stopped. I turned around and she was smiling, proud of herself, pointing to her bottle. But what I heard, what I swore I heard her say was, "Mama bad girl. Bad girl." I thought she could feel my guilt when I held her, could hear it in my voice when I read to her.

"Yes, that is your bottle," I said, trying to recover.

After I got her to sleep, I sat down and wrote Shep a six-page letter.

Two days later, I woke up thinking about Tony, feeling all that heat building up inside me again. I got aroused just thinking about being with him. Six more hours and I would see him again.

And that was how the days and weeks were passing. I was raising my child alone, because my husband was in jail, and I was transporting illegal liquor while carrying on a passionate affair with another man. Who was this woman? How did I get so far off-track? This wasn't the life I'd planned on leading.

Later that night Evelyn telephoned me, hysterical. It took several minutes to calm her down enough for her to tell me what had happened.

"I did it, Vera. Oh, my God, I didn't mean to but I did it."

"What? What did you do?"

"Oh, God! I shot him. I shot Izzy. I think he's . . . he's dead. I think I killed him."

I dropped Hannah off at Dora's place, and when I got to Evelyn's apartment, I knocked. I could hear her breathing on the other side of the door.

"Who is it?"

"It's okay, Ev. It's me."

She cracked the door a slice, her eyes shifting from left to right before she let me inside. She was pale and trembling. Blood was splattered on her forehead and cheeks. She was still holding on to the gun—Shep's six-shooter that I'd given her for our liquor runs. I wasn't sure if she was drunk but I could smell the whiskey coming off of her.

"I didn't mean to do it. He was yelling at me and calling me names and I . . . I just snapped and the gun was right there and I . . . I shot him."

"Where is he?" I asked, prying the gun from her fingers, setting it on the table.

She pointed toward the bedroom door. "I just wanted to shut him up."

I held my breath as I crept into the bedroom. The first thing I saw was the broken lightbulb and the base of the lamp shattered on the floor. There was blood sprayed across the wall and drenching the bedsheets. I let my gaze fall on Izzy. His face was frozen with one eye closed, his mouth gaping open. She'd shut him up all right.

I ran out of the room, thinking I would be sick. I gripped onto the back of the sofa until the nausea passed, until I was able to speak. I blew out a couple deep breaths and got my brain working again. Evelyn was a wreck, and I knew I had to be the cool and calm one. "We have to get him out of here."

"I didn't mean to do it. I don't want to go to jail."

"You're not going to jail. We just have to figure this out." I reached for a cigarette, my hands shaking so I could barely get the match lit. I went over by the window. *Think, Vera! Think!* We needed to get help; we couldn't move him alone. I didn't know if Basha and Dora would know what to do. Cecelia was our best bet, but she would tell Drucci, and that could spell disaster for Evelyn. Actually, Basha and Dora would have surely said something to Squeak and Knuckles, too.

There was only one person I knew who could help us.

I finished my cigarette thinking of every reason why I shouldn't make the call. Then I went to the telephone and dialed Tony's hotel.

I didn't tell him anything over the phone other than that I was in trouble and needed him. I gave him Evelyn's address and poured myself a drink.

Halfway through my bourbon, I started explaining why I called Tony. "Do you remember that night when we got stopped on our way back from Milwaukee? Remember the man who let us go . . . ?"

Evelyn was still in shock over what she'd done to Izzy and though I was painting a pretty obvious picture, I knew she wasn't putting the pieces together. Still, I had to tell her, and I had to trust her with my secret.

When Tony showed up, he took one look at me and then at Evelyn. "What's going on here?"

"There was an accident." I pointed toward the bedroom.

Tony went inside and a few minutes later he came out and planted his hands on his hips. "Izzy Seltzer?" He looked at me, dumbfounded. "You *whacked* Izzy?"

"It was an accident," I said, shaking my head. "It was self-defense."

Evelyn wasn't saying a word. She was seated on the edge of an ottoman, rocking back and forth like she was in a trance.

"What do we do now?" I asked him.

"We gotta make him disappear. Give me a second here." He went over to the bar and poured himself a drink, and after a few sips, he said, "But before we go any further, whatever happens here tonight, no one—you hear me"—he pointed to Evelyn—"no one can know I had *anything* to do with this."

He went back in the bedroom for a few minutes, and when he came out, he had a plan. "Get me some sheets and blankets," he said to Evelyn. "As many as you have. You still have your truck?" he asked me.

"It's out back."

"Go get it and park it in the alley."

The rest was a blur. I raced down the back stairwell to avoid the doorman and ran out back where we kept our truck.

By the time I got back upstairs, Tony had already wrapped up Izzy's body, and Evelyn had collected all the blood-soaked bed linens. When it came time to move him, Evelyn couldn't bring herself to touch Izzy's body. I grabbed hold of one end, Tony had the other, and together we walked what was left of Izzy down the back stairs. His hand was sticking out of the bloody sheets, hanging there, bobbing like a tree branch. I could see where Tony had removed Izzy's ring and probably any other jewelry that could have identified him. Tony had hold of most of him, but still, Izzy's body felt like a side of beef. When we hefted him up and hurled him into the truck, he landed in the cargo box with a thud.

Without a word, I handed the keys to Tony. Evelyn and I slid in close together, all three of us riding in the front seat. It was hot inside the cab and we rolled down the windows, finding little relief from the stagnant nighttime air.

We drove through downtown, the streetlights glowing beneath the skyscrapers and along the bridges. People were out walking along the sidewalks, coming in and out of restaurants and hotels. We cut west on Randolph and then south onto Halsted. Evelyn kept her eyes shut for most of the ride while I smoked one cigarette after another. Tony was quiet, concentrating, still working out the details of how we were going to get rid of Izzy.

As we headed farther south, the stench began wafting in through the windows and I realized where we were heading. With each passing mile the stink intensified.

A sick feeling was mounting in my gut, but I didn't say a word as he drove up to the stone archway of the Union Stock Yards.

"Which way?" He looked left, then right.

"To where?" I held my breath, knowing where he was going.

"Abramowitz Meats."

"Oh, no. Tony, please not there. Please—"

"You want this handled? He can't be buried. We can't dump him into the lake. We can't risk having him wash up. He can't be found. Izzy needs to disappear. Vanish."

I sighed and squeezed Evelyn's hand. "Go left and at the end of this road make a right. It's the red building at the end."

We left Evelyn out in the truck with Izzy's body while Tony and I got the spare key that my mother kept hidden around the back of the building and we went inside. It was cold on the kill floor, about forty degrees cooler than it was outside. Even from the entrance there was dried blood splattered on the walls and some still puddled in spots where the floor wasn't level, the aftermath from the slaughtering that had taken place earlier that day. Half a dozen skinned cattle carcasses were still strung up, hanging from the meat hooks in the ceiling.

"Where are the cleavers?"

I couldn't speak as we worked our way past the crates piled high with skinned heads, eyeballs bulging from their sockets, tongues hanging out, resting against a rake of teeth.

Tony grabbed the biggest cleaver hanging off the back wall, the one with the twelve-inch blade. We went back out to the truck and drove around to the edge of Bubbly Creek. Tony and I dragged Izzy's body out of the back of the truck, watching as the blood-drenched bedsheets fell to the ground. The sound of cicadas and other insects buzzed as a swarm of mosquitoes hovered over the churning, murky waters.

Evelyn couldn't watch. She crouched in the corner, her back toward us, her hands covering her ears. I stood transfixed, unable to turn away. I half expected to hear Izzy scream when Tony first lifted up the cleaver and, with two whacks, severed the head. I thought there would be a fresh spray of blood, but Izzy's blood had long since stopped circulating. My father flashed through my mind. Was he already dead before the Black Hand butchered him? I'd never thought of that before. *Please, God, let him have already been dead.* One more thrust and Tony cracked the skull in two. That one made even Tony pause and take a deep breath. He was covered in blood. I was standing back but even so, every few whacks, the blood sprayed over me like a mist. Next was the breastbone. We heard it split. One more whack and it went right through the heart, shooting out blood clots the size of chicken livers. With each new thwack, I shuddered and gagged. The whole thing—the dismembering of Izzy Seltzer—could have taken an hour, maybe less, maybe more. I was in a fog, unaware of time passing.

Part by part, Tony heaved Izzy's pieces into Bubbly Creek. We watched them sink to the bottom, the gurgling bubbles popping up along the surface.

Once it was over, I vaguely remembered us hosing down the back of the truck along with the cleaver before hanging it back on the wall. The only thing left was the blood-soaked bedsheets and blankets. Tony found an old milk crate and shoved them inside before stowing them in the cargo box. It was going on four in the morning, and we had to hurry before the first shift came on.

None of us said a word on the way back downtown. Tony pulled up to a giant trash bin outside of Cook County Hospital—the same hospital they'd taken Izzy to the night he'd been shot—and there he disposed of the bloody bedsheets along with the milk crate.

When we arrived outside Evelyn's apartment, Tony threw the truck in park and handed me the keys.

Before heading toward his car, parked around the block, he said, "You know what you have to do now?" I nodded, and just in case he thought I'd forgotten, he pointed to the third floor apartment. "You gotta clean up every trace of blood, every broken piece of glass. You gotta make it look picture-perfect. Like nothing happened. You understand? And you"—he said to Evelyn— "you get on the phone tomorrow morning and start acting like the concerned girlfriend. You don't know where he is. You're scared. You got that?"

Evelyn nodded.

"Let's just hope they pin this on Capone." He leaned over, gave my cheek a kiss. "You call me if you need me."

I grabbed hold of his collar. I did need him now, didn't he know that! I didn't want to let him go.

"You're gonna be okay. I can't risk sticking around here. Just remember what I told you to do and everything'll be fine."

He kissed me again and then disappeared around the corner. As soon as he was out of sight, I felt abandoned. And terrified. Evelyn was still in shock. I was on my own now and the clock was ticking. We were operating in real time and every step, every move counted. We had to do everything just right.

Evelyn's apartment smelled like death when we walked inside. The sun was just coming up, sending faint bands of daylight through the windows. The bedroom door had been left ajar. Neither one of us wanted to go inside, so we stalled for as long as we could, doing everything *but*. Evelyn poured us both a drink and we smoked a couple cigarettes. Eventually we filled buckets with soap and water and tore her tablecloth into rags. We couldn't bring ourselves to speak.

The worst was behind us, but still, we had to finish the job. With just my knuckles, I pushed open the bedroom door. It looked even more gruesome in the daylight.

We shoved the bed aside and swept up the broken glass before we got down on our hands and knees and began to scrub. Every once in a while, one of us would start to gag. The buckets of suds had turned from pink to crimson. We must have dumped those buckets down the tub and refilled them two dozen times. Evelyn kept breaking down and sobbing, muttering, "I can't believe it. I just can't believe what I've done. . . ."

She said that so many times, over and over again, as if she were in a trance. The sound of her voice was pulling me in, too. What had we done?

It was almost ten in the morning by the time we'd finished and I left Evelyn. I had called Dora earlier and asked if she could keep Hannah for a few more hours. I couldn't face my child right then. All I wanted was to go home, strip off my clothes, take a bath, as hot as I could stand it, and sleep until I'd be able to convince myself that it had all been a bad dream.

When I made it up the front steps of the house, the door was unlocked. I thought maybe in my haste I'd left it that way the night before. But I should have known better.

I stepped inside and ten months later, there he was. Home again.

"Hello, Dollface."

THE HOMECOMING

"Well, don't just stand there." Shep held his arms open but I hesitated. How could I go to him knowing I had his best friend's blood on me?

I covered my eyes with my hands and began to cry. "You're home? Oh, Shep, you're really home? Why didn't Drucci tell me?"

"I didn't want to get your hopes up in case things fell through." He walked over to me and as he came closer, his expression changed. Reaching for my blood-speckled sleeve, he looked at me. "What happened here?"

"Oh." I closed my eyes and shook my head, sending my mind spinning. "Just some trouble down at the slaughterhouse. I've been down there all morning. I'm just going to run upstairs and bathe and—"

"Hold on. Wait a minute." Reaching around my waist, he pulled me toward him. "Come here first. Let me hold you." He kissed me and held me tight.

I squirmed in his arms like a girl on a bad first date. "I'm a mess. I stink."

"I don't care." He kissed me again. "Don't you know how much I've missed you, Dollface."

With my palms plastered to his shoulders, I pried myself out of his embrace. "Just let me freshen up first, okay? I'll only be a minute." Before he could protest I scurried away, stopping at the top of the stairs to look back. Shep didn't resemble the man I'd seen in prison. He was dressed in a beautiful double-breasted suit, clean-shaven, hair slicked back, exposing his widow's peak. Aside from being a bit thinner, he looked the same, as if he'd never *gone away.* "I've missed you too, Shep."

I drew the bath, scalding hot, and submerged myself. My mind was racing, spinning with what-ifs. Izzy had a habit of staying out all night, so it wasn't unusual for Evelyn to call around looking for him. . . . But still, I knew it was only a matter of time before the others noticed him missing, too. . . . I could hear the clock ticking out in the bedroom. With each passing second, I grew more anxious.

As soon as the water covered my shoulders, I sank down in the tub until my entire face was underwater. At first I held my breath, my eyes wide open, staring at the ripples along the ceiling. But then I thought about what was left of Izzy, lying on the bottom of Bubbly Creek, and I bolted up, sitting in the tub, shivering as I began to gag.

Later that day, with Shep home and in my bed, I felt him curl his body around my backside, his lips grazing my shoulder and the back of my neck. I was glad he was out of jail, yet I couldn't say I was relieved to have him home. I'd always thought that once Shep was here with me again I would relax, let my shoulders drop, that I would be the Vera I was before he went away. But with him home, I felt more tense than ever. I was hiding so many things. So much had changed while he was away. Including me. I wanted to put everything back the way it was before he went away, but it was too late for that.

"Do you want to talk about it?" I asked finally, clutching his fingers.

"It's over," he murmured. "The past is in the past."

"Was it awful?" I guess I was the one who wanted to talk about it.

"It wasn't so bad. I'm just glad to be home."

"That was the longest ten months of my life," I said. "Hannah and I were so lost without you here. The guys tried to help us out, but after Hymie was killed . . ."

"I know. Vinny told me he did the best he could, but I know it wasn't enough. It was killing me to think about you and Hannah having to go without. How did you manage?"

"I cut back wherever I could. I put Hannah in secondhand clothes. Had to let the housekeeper go. Had to let a lot of things go. . . ."

"I'm going to make it up to you. Just let me get back on my feet and I promise I'll make it up to you."

"You don't need to make it up to me. I'm just glad you're home." There was a long pause. "Did you get my letters?"

He kissed my shoulder.

"I wrote to you. Almost every day. Why didn't you ever write me back?"

"They only let us write once a week."

"And?" I turned and looked at him.

He closed his eyes. "C'mon, you know I'm no good at writing."

"I wasn't looking for poetry."

"I just . . . I couldn't do it, okay?"

"Shep, don't get upset."

"Don't you think I feel guilty enough as it is?"

"I'm not trying to make you feel guilty. I was lonely. I was worried about you. I wanted to hear from you because I missed you, that's all."

He got up, lit a cigarette and walked over to the windows. It was only then that I could see his ribs and just how much weight he'd lost in prison.

I closed my eyes and lay back. My mind drifted; glimpses of that severed head came rushing back to me. Sometimes I saw Izzy's face clear as day; other times the face I saw belonged to my father. My God, could I ever get myself past this? Would I go to hell for it? Had I gone too far to protect Evelyn? I could go to jail. I was guilty. I had no defense.

"New drapes, huh?" he said.

"What?" I opened my eyes and propped myself up on one elbow.

"I see you got some new drapes in here for the bedroom."

"The other ones were never really the right shade. . . ."

He reached over and ran his fingers along the fabric. "They're nice. . . ." He continued to study the draperies. "Things must not have been all that tight while I was away." He took another drag off his cigarette and fingered the drapes while streams of smoke curled past his shoulder. "I noticed you had some new dresses in the closet. You hired the housekeeper back, too. How'd all that happen?"

I didn't say anything. I wanted so badly to come clean, to tell him everything and be rid of my guilt. The bootlegging was minor compared to everything else. How could I begin to tell Shep that I'd been an accomplice in his best friend's murder, that I'd brought in a rival gang member to help dispose of the body, a rival who also happened to be a man I was having an affair with. Even if Shep could have gotten past all that, was it fair to heap that much on him when he'd just gotten out of prison? I couldn't ask Shep to be my confessor and absolve me of my sins. I couldn't expect him to forgive me when I couldn't forgive myself.

"You were broke," he said, a little louder this time. "How were you able to do all that and make ends meet?"

"I did what I had to do."

"And what was that?"

"Nothing you would have approved of."

I saw the muscles along his shoulders flex. "Is there someone else?" He turned and looked at me. "Has someone else been taking care of you?"

A wave of guilt blasted me. I got out of bed and went to him, looping my arms about his waist. "I'd never want to betray you. Don't you know that? And you're home now. You're back home, and that's all that matters."

"If there's something I should know, you need to tell me."

I shook my head and squeezed him tighter. I loved Shep. What good was the truth? It wouldn't change a thing. It could only crush him. "You have to trust me, Shep."

"I want to trust you, but it doesn't wash, Vera. Someone had to be helping you out."

"It was hard while you were gone but no one helped me out." That was the truth. I'd made every cent on my own. "I swear. No one helped me." I kissed his shoulder. "I don't want to fight about this. Or anything. Can't we just have this time together?" I felt his arms circle around me and I closed my eyes. "I love you, Shep. You don't ever have to question that. Not ever."

After Dora brought Hannah back to the house that afternoon, Shep couldn't get over how much his daughter had changed. She was talking in full sentences now. And running and going up and down the stairs, too. He crouched down for her, like a catcher waiting for a fastball, but instead Hannah ran to me. I wasn't surprised. Why would she go to him? Despite all the pictures I'd shown her, all the stories I'd told her, she didn't know this man in her living room. She'd no sooner warm to him than she would a total stranger.

"Just give her some time," I said, looking at Shep's wounded expression, remembering how I'd felt the day Hannah had run to Dora instead of me.

After ten months of his being *away*, Hannah may not have known her father, but when I saw the two of them together, side by side, their dark hair and eyes, the shape of their mouths, there was no doubt in my mind who her father was.

"Here," I said, handing him an oversize picture book. "Why don't you read her a story? She loves it when you read to her. This one's your favorite, isn't it?" I said to Hannah as I scooped her up in my arms and placed her in Shep's lap.

Shep hesitated and then opened the book. Hannah broke into a smile, her fingers pointing to the pictures. According to the grandfather clock in the corner, it was almost three. Enough time had passed. Someone was bound to notice Izzy missing. Any second now I expected the phone to ring—someone looking for him.

Hannah giggled, clapping her hands while Shep thumbed through a few pages before he closed the book and set it on the table. "You don't want to hear this same story again. How about I tell you a story instead?"

Hannah's eyes were locked on the book, her tiny hands groping for it, her face scrunching up as her lungs gathered steam for a crying bout.

I picked up the book and handed it back to her, and that seemed to pacify her for the moment.

"I told you it's her favorite. . . ." I leaned over and kissed the top of his head. "Daddy's tired, honey. Mama will read to you later."

I spent the rest of the day reminding myself that Shep was back home. I had grown so accustomed to managing without him. It didn't occur to me to ask for his help when I was on my tiptoes, reaching for a bowl on the top shelf, or straining to open a jar.

While I was in the kitchen cooking, Hannah began warming up to Shep. Soon the two of them were in the drawing room and she was showing him her toys while I made Shep's favorite dinner, a standing rib roast and scalloped potatoes. My family was reunited. I'd waited so long for this and yet I couldn't take it in. I was a wreck inside.

The next day, Shep attempted to get his life back to normal. He put a call in for Izzy and I froze, praying that Evelyn was convincing on the other end. He didn't seem fazed when he hung up and said he was going to stop by the cemetery to visit his mother's grave and then he'd be back.

"Aren't you going to stop by Schofield's?" I asked.

He paused and gave me a curious look. "You trying to get rid of me already?"

"Don't be silly."

"I've been away for a long time. Schofield's can wait." He kissed me on the cheek. "I'll be back in an hour."

As soon as he was gone, I got busy trying to clean up the mess I'd made while he was away. After our exchange in the bedroom, Shep hadn't pressed me again about how I'd managed while he was away. It was clear that part of him didn't want to know. Evelyn and I were supposed to make a liquor run that day, but given the Izzy situation and Shep's being back home, there was no way we could do it.

When I telephoned Warren Steel, his voice was tight, polite but with an edge.

"What do you mean, your circumstances have *changed*?"

"I'm afraid I won't be doing any more selling for you."

His tone turned cold and brittle. "You realize that you had me order another two hundred cases for you."

"I know, but you see—"

"Listen to me, Miss Abramowitz, I don't care if you sell those cases or not—that's your business—but either way, you owe me five thousand dollars."

I was shaking when I hung up the phone.

The next call with Felix Marvin didn't go much better.

"And this news you tell me over the telephone? I'm sorry to hear this. This upsets me. But you should know that I've already committed to my people. They're expecting a delivery. I need at least a hundred cases. I would hope that a nice girl like you wouldn't leave me high and dry."

I was already doing the math in my head. Even if Evelyn and I managed one last run, that would have satisfied Felix, but it still left Warren with a hundred cases to move, and us twenty-five hundred dollars short. I had about half that stashed away, but with Izzy dead, Evelyn was going to need every penny she'd earned the past few months. And realistically there was no way we could make that last run. Shep didn't have the Meridian anymore and that meant he'd be home all the time—at least for the time being.

It had never occurred to me that getting out of the liquor trade would be harder than getting into it.

The next day I told Shep I had to run an errand and went straight to Tony's hotel room. I was barely inside his room before he kissed me, told me he'd been going crazy thinking about me. He kissed me again and started to unbutton my dress.

"Wait—I can't." I twisted myself away from him. "I have to get back home."

"What? You just got here." He stood back and jangled some coins in his front pocket.

"Oh, Tony." I swallowed hard. "We have to talk."

"What's the problem?"

"Shep's back. He's home."

He studied my face for a moment and shoved a matchstick in the corner of his mouth, his jaw twitching back and forth. "Well, we knew he was coming back sooner or later."

I glanced at my hands. My wedding ring was glaring at me. "We just have to be careful, that's all."

I shook my head. "He's my husband, Tony. I can't. I can't do this anymore."

"Yeah, well, he was your husband while he was away, too. That didn't stop you." He pulled the matchstick from his mouth and pitched it onto the bureau.

"That was different and you know it." It sounded like the right thing to say, but it was still a betrayal.

We both grew silent, and Tony turned his back to me. "So he's in and I'm out. Is that it? You expect me to just walk away. Bow out?"

I didn't say anything.

With one step he was at my side. He grabbed me, pulled me close, and kissed me.

"Tony, no! I mean it!" I twisted out of his arms.

"So you're just gonna throw it all away." Tony slammed his fist to the wall. "You really love to jerk me around, don't you."

"That's not true."

"You've been doing it to me from the very start. 'I can't see you anymore, Tony. Go away—I'm scared we'll get caught. Come back to me, Tony—I miss you. I love you.' "

He wasn't wrong about that. I never saw it from his point of view before, but he was right. I pushed him away and pulled him to me, only to push him away again.

"Make up your goddamn mind, Vera. Or better yet, you know what—just do me a favor and leave. Go on. Just get the hell out of here. And the next time you have a body to get rid of, tell your husband to take care of it. Not me."

I let myself out of his room. He never even said good-bye.

I was too upset to go home and face Shep so I drifted along the sidewalks, past the shops and street vendors. I never meant to hurt Tony. I never meant to hurt anyone. Eventually I made my way up to Grant Park. The sunlight was blinding, and I found a shaded bench beneath a giant oak tree, where I sat and cried, ignoring the passersby who stopped and stared, asking if I was okay. . . .

I cried for Tony. For Shep. I cried for myself and even for Evelyn and Izzy. Everything was coming to a head and I was responsible for so much pain, so much damage. If it weren't for Hannah, I would have given anything to turn back the clock, to be in my mother's house again with a chance to start over. Maybe I could have persuaded Shep to get out of the rackets, to become a legitimate businessman. Maybe I wouldn't have fallen in love with him in the first place. All I knew was that I'd wasted my time chasing after all the wrong things. I had money now and a big house, I had more fancy clothes than I knew what to do with and none of it meant a thing.

I dried my eyes, blew my nose and took out my compact to retouch my makeup.

When I came through the front door that afternoon, Shep was working in his study. I stepped inside without knocking and when he looked up, he leaned back in his chair and smiled.

I sat in his lap and wrapped my arms around him. Despite

it all, I wasn't sorry I'd fallen in love with him. "Let's start over, you and me, huh? Let's forget about the time you were away and let's just start fresh again. Can we do that?" I kissed him and rested my head on his shoulder. We'd both come back home now.

MORE SECRETS TO KEEP

It had been three days. Three days since Shep had come home. Three days past due for Warren Steel and Felix Marvin. And three days since anyone had heard from or seen Izzy—though I thought I'd seen him plenty of times. If a man with dark hair was seated in a café, or walked across the street, or went by on the trolley and the sunlight hit him just right, my heart would stop and I'd do a double take. I'd need ten minutes after that for my pulse to stop jumping.

In the days that followed, just as Tony had hoped, the members of the North Side Gang were convinced that Capone was responsible for whatever had happened to Izzy. No one suspected Evelyn. The girls and even the men all rallied around her. Evelyn turned out to be quite the actress, impressively shedding tears at just the mention of Izzy's name. Only I knew what fueled her outbursts.

Unlike Evelyn, Shep was gripped with genuine grief. Each day that passed with no sign of Izzy compounded his agony. He combed Izzy's hangouts looking for him, asking questions. He and the guys scoured the lakefront, back alleys and quarries searching for Izzy.

One night, as soon as Shep walked through the door, I knew something was up. I was worried that they'd found some part of Izzy. Or maybe they'd found his ring. Tony said he'd get rid of it, but what if they'd found it?

Shep fixed himself a drink and handed me the late edition of the *Daily Herald*. "Do me a favor," he said, pointing to the photo of Izzy on the front page. "Read that. Tell me what it says."

Though he'd sold papers as a kid, Shep was never one to read newspapers. Until he met me, he never even had a paper in his house. He said they were filled with lies. Nothing but yellow journalism. So I was surprised that this time he wanted to know what it said. I thought maybe he had handed the task over to me because he was too distraught to read it himself.

"Just tell me what it says, huh?" His jaw was set, his eyes focused on the newsprint.

I sat down and began to read:

Search Is On for Missing Gangster

A citywide search continues for Isiah "Izzy" Seltzer, a top lieutenant of the so-called North Side Gang. Last seen on July 18, 1927, the twenty-six-year-old missing gangster is a close associate of gang leader Vincent "Schemer" Drucci, George "Bugs" Moran, and convicted mobster Shepherd "Shep" Green. . . .

When I finished reading the article, Shep dropped into the chair opposite me. "Anything else in there about him? Does it say anything about Capone?"

He got up and paced while I leafed through the pages of the

front section, scanning the columns. "I don't see anything. Here," I said, handing him the paper, "see if I missed anything."

Shep shook his head and backed away with his hands up like I was tossing him a bomb. "I can't . . . I can't read that." A deep crease formed along his brow, and if I didn't know better, I would have thought he was about to cry.

"It's okay," I said, setting down the newspaper.

"No! It's not okay! It's not okay, goddammit!"

In all the years I'd known Shep, I could have counted the times he'd raised his voice on one hand. "What is it? What's wrong?"

"Don't do this to me."

"Shep—"

"You really want to break me? Now? Of all times?"

"Shep . . ."

He was panting hard, like he'd just run a mile. "Don't make me say it. Do you really need to hear me say it out loud?"

"Say what? Why are you getting so angry with me?"

"I'm not angry with you. I'm angry with myself. Jesus . . ." He ran his fingers through his hair and tried to calm himself.

I didn't know what we were fighting about.

He turned his back and muttered, "I can't read that paper. Okay. I can't read *any* paper."

"What?" I still didn't get it.

"Why the hell do you think I never wrote to you when I was away? Why do you think I don't read to Hannah?"

I sank down on the sofa, dumbfounded. Shep still had his back to me, his shoulders rounded and slumped forward. I thought about all his books, how he had arranged them according to color and size, not by author or even subject. . . . How he always wanted me to read to him . . . I thought about the files I'd found in his drawer—how everything had been typed by someone, but there was no handwriting. It struck me then that aside from his signature, I'd never seen Shep's handwriting. It was all making sense. It should have made sense all along.

He came and sat next to me, but still, he wouldn't look me in the eye. "I hate this about myself."

"Don't say that." I leaned over and rubbed his shoulders.

"I had to drop out of school when I was just a kid. Hell, I never even made it past the first grade. I can do numbers. They come easy to me. They make sense. But words—letters—they just never did." He hung his head and I began to massage his neck.

"How come you never told me this before?"

"I didn't want you to think you married some stupid loser."

"I never would have thought that. Look at you. Look at what you've accomplished."

"Yeah, look at what I've accomplished." He laughed bitterly. "I've done a lot of things I'm not too proud of. And now half my friends are dead because of it." He polished off his drink, got up and poured himself another. "I just can't keep this up anymore."

"You've done great, Shep. I know men with a wall of diplomas who aren't half as smart as you. So what if you can't read. If you can't write." He winced when I said that. "You don't have anything to be ashamed of."

"I never wanted you to know. I never wanted anyone to know. Izzy . . . He was the only one I ever told."

"Izzy?" Just the mention of his name flooded me with guilt.

"He used to do all my reading for me. My writing, too." He blew out a sigh and rubbed his temples. "I don't know how I'm gonna manage without him."

I leaned over and cupped his face in my hands. "You have me now. I'll help you. Whatever you need. You bring it to me."

He turned away and looked at the bookcases. When we

moved into the house I had the housekeeper alphabetize the volumes. I remember when he saw them rearranged, he said they looked sloppy.

"Dion always said it was important to surround yourself with good books. I always thought someday I'd get to read them."

"You will." I wrapped my arms around him. "I know you—I know the kind of man you are, and someday, I know you'll read every one of those books."

PAYBACK TIME

Evelyn and I made two failed attempts to square our business with Felix Marvin and Warren Steel. Both were interrupted by funerals of two North Siders, one found in the trunk of his car, the other shot two days later on the front steps of his house.

Still, Evelyn and I were able to pull together twelve hundred and fifty dollars of the twenty-five hundred owed—but that was based on if we could deliver the hundred cases to Felix. We were hoping that if we could meet with both parties, face-to-face, and hand over the liquor to Felix and the money to Warren, then Warren might pardon the remaining twenty-five hundred dollars. I couldn't think about the other twenty-five hundred dollars I owed him on top of that.

But with Shep back and working the phones from his office at home, it was impossible for me to disappear for the ten or twelve hours it would take to get up to Milwaukee, meet with Warren Steel, make the delivery to Felix and get back home.

While Shep was down at Schofield's one afternoon, I telephoned Warren, hoping to buy us more time.

"I'm a patient man, Miss Abramowitz. But even I have my limits. You're testing me—you should know that."

"I can give you about half the money now and—"

"I'm not interested in half."

"But I promise—"

"You keep promising but not delivering. I trust this is the last time we'll have this conversation."

Before I could say anything more, the telephone line went dead.

About a week later, I was standing at Dearborn and Division, waiting for a taxicab. It was a hot, balmy afternoon, and the sky was a sheet of uninterrupted blue. Pigeons waddled about, pecking at the sidewalk. I fanned myself with a magazine and squinted as the sunbeams bounced off the windows, shiny hoods and fenders of the motorcars parked along the street.

I'd been waiting for nearly ten minutes when a familiar voice coming from behind said, "I told you, I have my limits."

I turned around and there was Warren Steel, puffing on his pipe. He was standing next to a short woman who was broad across the shoulders and had the ruddy complexion of a fisherman who'd been at sea too long. I had no idea how he'd managed to find me.

"You decide you're done with the liquor trade and think it's all right to leave me with a warehouse full of whiskey? That doesn't make for good business, Miss Abramowitz."

"I'm working on it."

A streetcar passed before us, the conductor clanking the bell.

"What is there to work on?" he asked. "I'm getting tired of hearing that." He and the woman took a step forward that drove me one step backward.

"I just don't have the money right now. I have about half, but—"

"I'm not looking for half the money." Warren and the woman advanced another step while I retreated from the sidewalk into the alley. "I don't do business this way. I didn't think you did, either." He looked at his companion and nodded.

I didn't see the woman's hand come up, but I sure did feel it. She knocked me backward. I saw a flash of white and before I could steady myself, she came at me again, tore the pocketbook from my hand and cracked me across the jaw with it. I tasted blood as it filled my mouth. She charged at me again with a force that knocked the wind out of me as she pushed me into a row of garbage cans. I doubled over, lost my balance, and landed on my side. The putrid smell of spoiled food filled my nostrils as more blood trickled from my lip. I started to get up and she was on me, pounding me with her fists as a string of bloody spittle spewed from my mouth. She hit me again and again. I cowered with my hands up, trying to shield my face. I didn't even put up a fight.

Before they turned and left me, Warren said, "I'll expect my money by the end of the day tomorrow."

My lip was sliced open and my knees and shoulder throbbed from where I'd hit the ground. A pigeon hobbled at my side, cooing. Pages of the magazine I'd been carrying lay scattered about the alley. Everything in my pocketbook had spilled out onto the ground. My lipstick, hairbrush, and compact were lying in a pool of slop. I crawled over to my pocketbook lying next to a coal chute with the grate unhinged. Warren hadn't even bothered with the few dollars I'd had tucked inside. Staggering toward the curb, I found a taxicab and headed home.

The cabbie turned around and looked at me. "Miss, you okay? You sure you don't need to go to the hospital?"

"I'm fine," I said, trying to wipe away the blood running down my chin. "Just take me home."

The housekeeper gasped when I stepped inside. She helped

me upstairs, helped me clean off the blood. I looked in the mirror and saw that the bruises, red and plum colored, were already coming up. She worried that I needed stitches and telephoned Shep down at Schofield's. He rushed home and found me in bed, holding Hannah in my arms.

"What happened?" His expression turned from concern to alarm when he bent over and got a closer look.

Hannah pointed to the ice pack on my lip. "Mama got boo-booed."

"Yeah, she sure did." He leaned over and scooped her up in his arms. "Why don't you go downstairs and see what Daddy brought you and let me talk to Mama." He set Hannah down and nodded to the housekeeper.

Once they were out of the room, Shep closed the door and sat on the edge of the bed, brushing the hair from my eyes. "What in the hell happened?"

I lowered my eyes and studied the backs of my hands. From where I sat now, I realized what a foolish move this had been. I wasn't cut out to be a bootlegger. And now that I'd gotten in over my head, I was terrified to tell Shep I needed him to step in and save me.

Shep leaned in closer, gently lifting my chin, forcing me to look him in the eye. "Who did this to you?"

"Oh, Shep." I began to cry. "I'm in trouble."

That night, while the doctor came to the house to put a few stitches in my lip, Shep and Squeak headed for Milwaukee to pay Warren Steel a visit. Evelyn came and stayed with me. Even though the doctor gave me something to make me sleep, I fought it all the way. My mind was so keyed up, I wasn't even groggy. Not even a bottle of whiskey could have put me out.

"You did the right thing," Evelyn said, lighting a cigarette off the one she was about to rub out. Dark circles had settled beneath her eyes and her skin had a dull, grayish cast to it. Everyone mistook that haggard guise of hers for grief.

She'd wasted no time finding a new place to live, a small efficiency with a Murphy bed and one tiny window with a cracked pane of glass. She'd moved out of the apartment she'd once shared with Izzy, and closing the door, she put what she'd done behind her. Evelyn had been questioned so many times by the guys and then the police that she had her story down. It was like the lie you tell yourself over and over again until it becomes your new truth. I knew that, because I'd been doing the same thing.

For two girls who had grown up discussing everything from first kisses to our monthly cycles, we never talked about that night with Izzy. She never mentioned Tony Liolli either. We had swept the entire incident from our minds, but there was no denying what she'd done, what I had done. You couldn't do something like that without being changed forever. I knew there would be payback for this somewhere down the line. There was no way Evelyn and I could walk away from this scot-free. Life didn't work that way. I still closed my eyes at night and saw Tony with that cleaver. I could still smell the blood. I still saw Izzy's mouth gaping wide for his last gasp of breath, one eye shut, the other open, watching the whole thing.

By the time Shep got home, Evelyn had dozed off on the divan, but I was still wide awake.

"What happened?" I asked. "What did you say to him?"

Shep removed his hat and set it on the hook on the back of the closet door. I couldn't read him. Couldn't tell if he was angry, tired, or just disappointed in me. At least he knew that no one else had been providing for us while he was away, though that didn't change the fact that I'd had an affair with Tony.

"A debt is a debt," Shep said finally. "And yes, I could have bartered with him, could have sold the liquor for him myself, but thank God, I don't need to do business with a *shtoonk* like Warren Steel." Shep went over to the bar and poured himself a drink. "But I've never chiseled a man in my life and I wasn't about to start now. So I paid him his five grand."

"Oh, Shep, I'm sorry." He'd barely been home for a month and I figured that I'd just taken a big bite out of whatever money he'd been able to make since. And then some. "How did you even manage to get hold of that kind of money?"

"Let's just say I'd rather owe Vinny a few bucks than that putz Warren Steel."

Evelyn began to stir, her eyes fluttering open.

"I squared away with your buddy Felix, too."

Evelyn was awake now, sitting up, reaching for a cigarette.

Shep came back over and sat down. "Now would be an excellent time to tell me if there's anything else you ladies have been up to while I was away."

I couldn't look at Evelyn. I just shook my head.

"So it's over?" asked Evelyn.

"For now." Shep swept his hair off his forehead, exposing his widow's peak. "Tomorrow Squeak and Knuckles are going to sit down with Mr. Steel and teach him a thing or two about how to treat a woman." Shep raised his glass and took a sip. "And from now on, ladies, you two are officially out of business."

RETURN TO MOUNT CARMEL

The next day I got a frantic telephone call from Basha. I'd just walked into the house and she was jabbering a mile a minute.

"Slow down, Basha." I held the receiver to my ear while I worked my way out of my coat. My lip was still swollen and it hurt to talk. "I can't understand a word you're saying."

"They got him. They shot him."

My thoughts went straight to Izzy. My heart took off, pounding away. *I knew we'd get caught. I knew it!*

"Cecelia's a mess."

"Cecelia?"

"Didn't you hear what I said? They got him. They shot Vinny. . . ."

Vinny! I nearly dropped the phone. Everything in the room turned hazy and dark. Not another one. Each man we lost brought the danger that much closer to home. If they could kill Vinny, was Shep next?

I still couldn't believe it. Vincent "Schemer" Drucci, gunned down and dead at the age of twenty-nine. He was killed in broad

daylight at Wacker and Clark. As it turned out, Capone and the
South Siders weren't responsible. Not directly anyway. This time
the bullets belonged to a Sergeant Dan Healy. But no one doubted
that Capone had paid him plenty to pull the trigger.

I was numb for days. It was as if I were only going through
the motions when we attended the wake and then the funeral.

"Poor Cecelia," I said, as we girls rode in the back of the limo
out to Mount Carmel for the funeral. The fellas were in the car
ahead of ours.

"We're losing all our men," said Basha.

Dora nodded. "Doesn't it feel like we were just here?"

"I had to buy a new black dress just for this one," said Basha.

I took a long draw off my cigarette. The violence wasn't just
getting to the North Siders. The whole city was on edge, bracing
itself for the next round of gunfire. Some of Capone's men had set
off a bomb at a speakeasy on State and Division, not far from our
house. The week before, they shot up a barbershop because Capone thought Bugs was inside, getting a haircut and a shave.
What was next? Were tommy guns going to turn up in the
dance halls, in restaurants and movie houses? I was afraid to
pick up a newspaper anymore. It seemed like somebody we knew
was either washing up in Lake Michigan or found in an alley or
the trunk of a car.

I opened my compact and looked at my bruises. Even though
they were fading, hidden beneath my makeup, I didn't look like
myself. I had too many different faces: wife, mother, accessory to
murder, former bootlegger, former adulterer. I didn't know which
one was the real me anymore.

"It's a shame," Evelyn said, gazing out the window at rows
and rows of headstones. "Vinny was a good guy."

"They were all good guys," said Dora. "Even Hymie. When
he liked you, he was good to you."

I nodded, detached from it all. I'd seen too much blood lately, been to too many burials, told too many widows and gun molls how sorry I was. At times I thought I was losing the ability to feel anything at all. Everything was unraveling. I didn't recognize my own life anymore.

"I don't know how Schofield's can keep up with these funerals. Did you see all those flowers back at the chapel?" said Basha. "I heard they cost something like thirty grand."

When we arrived at Mount Carmel there were two rows of limos and cars stretching a quarter mile down the drive, leading from the cemetery back to the main street. It was a sunny afternoon and breezy. Someone had dropped a handkerchief and I watched it get carried off by a wind gust, cartwheeling over the grounds.

Drucci's funeral had plenty of fanfare. Thousands of people turned out to pay their final respects: friends, relatives, city officials, policemen, and every crime reporter in town. Drucci had served in the navy during World War I, and the police figured since one of their own had done the shooting, it was only proper to give the Schemer a twenty-one-gun salute.

I never got used to the idea that the very people who killed you, or wished they had, turned up at your funeral. The tent where Drucci's casket sat waiting to be lowered into his grave was reserved for family, close friends and gang members, with everyone else standing outside, looking on.

As I stepped inside the tent with Shep I glanced around; one dark suit butted up against another. And there, just six feet away from us, on the opposite side of Drucci's casket, stood a band of South Side Gang members: Al Capone, "Machine Gun" Jack McGurn, Antonio Lombardo, and next to him, Tony Liolli.

Tony saw me and when our eyes locked, all the blood rushed to my head. My heart took off, beating fast. I never expected to see him again after that day in his hotel room. And I never expected that the three of us—Tony, Shep and me—would ever be in the same place at the same time, breathing the same air. It shook me. I wasn't a good enough actress to pull this off.

While the priest conducted the service, Cecelia sobbed, breaking down in Bugs's arms, shrieking, "Oh, no, not my Vinny—they killed my Vinny!" It took both Bugs and Knuckles to hold her up during the ceremony.

She reminded me of Viola O'Banion, so brokenhearted at Dion's burial that she had to be carried away from his grave at the end. We could see Dion's tombstone from where we stood. It was the tallest monument in the cemetery and came to a sharp point at the top. It was near Hymie Weiss's mausoleum.

Cecelia let out another agonized sob and I looked away. But I couldn't keep from glancing back at Tony, just to see if he was still looking at me. He was.

All through Drucci's burial, Tony Liolli and I stole glances, but I couldn't tell if he was still angry with me for walking out of his hotel room, or if he still wanted me.

Shep reached for my hand and laced his fingers through mine, squeezing tight. Tony looked away. He had me feeling sorry for him and that made me angry. I knew it was painful for him to see me with Shep, but Tony had had his chance. He chose to walk out on me when I needed him most. I couldn't look at him anymore. Instead I watched Drucci's casket being lowered into his grave, going down, disappearing below the earth's surface.

THE HATBOX TRICK

The days following Drucci's funeral were grim. Shep moved about the house in a listless state with his shirttails sticking out, his suspenders hanging down. He hadn't shaved or combed his hair and the last time I'd seen him looking so unkempt was when I'd visited him in jail.

I tried reading to him, but could tell by the way he gazed out the window that he wasn't listening. I couldn't reach him no matter how I tried. Even Hannah, who always found a way inside, would tug at his pant leg, crying, "Daddy! Daddy, come play!" only to have him smile and tell her to run along before he'd go into his study and shut the door. Other times he paced endlessly.

"You're wearing a hole in the carpet," I said without getting so much as a grin in return.

It seemed he always had a drink in his hand and I couldn't remember the last time he'd eaten a real meal. It went on like that for days, for weeks.

At night he worried in his sleep, thrashing about in the covers, waking in a cold sweat, bolting straight up in bed, gasping.

"What is it? What's the matter?" I'd ask, turning on the lamp on the nightstand.

He'd run his hands through his hair, catch his breath, and say, "It's nothing. Go back to bed."

One morning, Shep came down to the kitchen with flecks of blood on his chin from where he nicked himself shaving. He sat at the table, picking at his breakfast. I looked at the dark circles under his eyes and the stress written across his face.

"Another bad night, huh?" I asked, wiping my hands on a dish towel.

"Did I keep you awake?"

"It's okay." I poured him a cup of coffee and opened the icebox. "How do you want your eggs?"

"I'll stay in the guest room tonight."

"No, you won't." I closed the icebox door. "I want you to stay with me." I went and stood behind him, massaging his shoulders, shocked by how tight his muscles were. "You can talk to me, you know. I won't break. You can tell me what's going on."

"I wish I could. I wouldn't even know where to begin." He leaned back and sighed.

"You need to relax."

He rubbed a hand over his face and scratched the whiskers along his jaw. "I don't remember how to relax."

"I'll help you." I leaned forward, resting my chin on the crown of his head as I ran my hands over his chest and shoulders. "That's it. Just relax." For a minute I felt him give in to my touch, easing back into my fingers. "Now tell me what's going on."

The moment I said that, his shoulders stiffened and he shrugged away from me. "I gotta get going."

After he left, I went upstairs, and as I was sorting through his clothes to take to the cleaner's, I found a forgotten ten-dollar bill in the pocket of his trousers. I clutched the ten and went to my closet, where I kept a hatbox hidden in the back. Inside was a pouch filled with the forgotten bills I'd found in Shep's coat pockets or suit jackets, and lying on the bedroom dresser. I took the ten and added it to the mix. I felt guilty taking his money like that—especially when all I had to do was ask. But I couldn't resist setting a few dollars aside for myself, just in case.

After Shep came home from prison, I swore I'd never be without money again. If something ever happened to him in the future, I wanted to be prepared. I knew if I had to, I could take care of myself but I wouldn't take the kinds of risks I had before. I wouldn't do anything that would put Hannah or myself in jeopardy again.

Apparently Evelyn had learned that lesson, too. She had taken what little money she'd found of Izzy's and was investing it in the stock market. She seemed to have a knack for it and swore it was almost as easy to make money in the market as it was from the liquor trade.

"Only it's not nearly as much fun," she'd said to me once.

I fingered the scar along my lip, wondering how she would have felt if she'd been slapped around. I sorted through the money in the hatbox, the singles, the five- and ten-dollar bills—the occasional twenty. I didn't have more than five hundred dollars total but I'd been watching Evelyn work the stock market. I was thinking she could help me, teach me the ropes. It was something I'd been considering.

I looked at my salvaged money, remembering the days when I counted the five-hundred-dollar bills first, then the hundreds, fifties and twenties. I didn't have anything smaller than that.

I had to admit part of me missed the liquor trade. Those drives back and forth to Milwaukee did something for me. I loved how Steel's men waited for us outside the warehouse, how they lifted those boxes and set them down according to our instructions. And, of course, Felix's men were always waiting for us on the other end, not making a move until we told them to.

A big day for me now was reading the newspaper and the mail to Shep, writing out his correspondence for him, maybe preparing a new recipe or having lunch with the girls downtown. I'd spent more time waiting around the house for the doctor to come when Hannah had an earache or a cough. A challenge was fixing her doll's arm or picking out a new book to read to her. There were only so many fashion magazines I could leaf through, only so many dresses to buy, only so much time I could spend at the beauty parlor. I hated being confined to the mundane tasks of wife and mother. I'd run my own business before for God's sake. I'd been important then. I was the decision maker and the moneymaker. All I felt now was boredom. Denying that I needed more, that I was capable of more, may have kept my husband comfortable but it stymied me.

One night I sat at the dinner table, looking at Shep and Hannah while my mind drifted, taking my thoughts to places they shouldn't have gone. All Basha wanted was to be Squeak's wife. All Dora wanted was a baby. Cecelia and Viola had lost their husbands and Evelyn was alone. I should have been so grateful. According to Dora, I had it all. But it wasn't enough. I still craved excitement, the kind of excitement that had gotten me into trouble in the first place. Something was missing. I knew what it was and I hated myself for missing it.

I was restless that night, unable to sleep. The next afternoon, once Shep had left the house to meet with Bugs, and Hannah was upstairs in her room with the housekeeper, I picked up the telephone. A band of sweat broke out across my brow, and my voice trembled when I asked to be connected. As soon as I heard Tony's voice, I froze.

"Hello? Hello? Is someone there?"

I hung up and backed away from the telephone and went into the parlor where I sat in the dark until I stopped shaking.

ROOTING FOR BOTH SIDES

Summer dragged on. The hot, humid days melded together, one after another, until it was autumn. The weeks of not sleeping, not eating were taking their toll on Shep. For the first time I noticed a couple strands of gray at the tip of his widow's peak. One night I found him pacing in the upstairs hallway, like a sleepwalker. Lately, instead of working from home, he'd been leaving the house earlier in the mornings and returning later at night. I didn't want to add to his troubles. I tried to be a good wife, understanding and patient. I slammed cupboards and doors only after he'd left the house. He hadn't touched me since Drucci was killed. And I didn't have it in me to reach for him again, not after the last time, when he took my hand away and told me he was too tired.

One evening while I was in the kitchen, drying the dinner dishes, I overheard Shep on the telephone with Bugs. "Where was this . . . ? How long ago . . . ? Are you sure it was him . . . ? Who's with him besides Liolli . . . ?"

Liolli? I froze and nearly dropped the plate in my hand. The blood started pounding inside my head.

"Okay . . . Get Squeak and Knuckles. I'm on my way. . . ."

I slung the dish towel over my shoulder and leaned against the counter. "You're going out?" I asked when he came into the kitchen. My voice was quaking. I couldn't help it.

"Just for a little bit." He bent down and kissed Hannah, who was still in her booster chair playing with an empty bowl, dancing it across the table.

"What's going on? What did Bugs want that's so urgent?"

Shep straightened up and looked at me, his eyes growing narrow.

I knew better than to ask about his business, but I couldn't help myself. "I don't want you going out there tonight. You're exhausted. You need to start taking care of yourself." I glanced over at Hannah, happily sliding her bowl about the table.

He reached for a bottle of cooking oil and unscrewed the cap. "I'll be back in a couple of hours." He took a swig of oil. "It's no big deal."

"It is a big deal to me." The tears were building but I swallowed them back.

"Aw, here we go again." He shook his head. "You have no idea what I'm up against. This whole organization is riding on my shoulders."

"I've never asked you for anything before. Please—please don't go out there tonight. If you won't do it for me, do it for her." I reached over for Hannah and hoisted her into my arms. "Please, Shep. Please . . . ?" My voice trailed off.

"Don't do this to me. I gotta go out there and do what I do. You know what Capone did to my best friends. I can't let that go, Vera. I'm never gonna let it go."

"Not even for me?"

"Don't ask me that. You can't ever ask me that. I'm leaving. I have to." He turned, reached for his overcoat and walked out, closing the door so hard behind him the chandelier in the foyer clinked back and forth like wind chimes.

"There, there, Mama," Hannah said after Shep left, patting my hair, because that was what I always did to soothe her. "It'll be okay. I promise."

Seeing that little face of hers, the rosy, chubby cheeks and those outstretched fingers, lifted my heart a million miles off the ground. Only she could do that for me. Only she could take my mind off what was going on out there in the streets. I smiled as we played peekaboo and patty-cake, and after I'd given her a bath, I cuddled with her, letting the scent of her hair, fresh from the tub, circle around me.

I had put it all out of my mind until after I'd gotten Hannah to bed. That's when the telephone calls started. First it was Basha calling and then Dora. Whenever the men went out looking for Capone, we girls stayed on the telephone, or else gathered at someone's house to wait it out. We'd compare notes, speculating what-ifs. If they weren't home by such-and-such an hour, that meant X, and if they hadn't shown up at Schofield's, that meant Y.

"Have you heard anything yet?" Dora asked.

"No. Not a word. You? Do you know who's with Capone?"

Dora went silent. It was a dumb question, something I never should have asked. We weren't supposed to care about the other guys, but that night I was rooting for both sides. I reached for a cigarette, struggling to get the match lit.

As soon as I got off the line with Dora, my mind started to unravel, my thoughts spiraling to the grimmest possibilities. What if Capone and his men retaliated? They were all armed and all it took was one shot, one wrong step. I feared the next call would be Bugs or Knuckles, telling me Shep was in the hospital, or else—God forbid—dead.

I got up and fixed myself a drink and took a big, burning

gulp and then another. If things went the other way and they killed Capone, then Tony would be dead, or at the very least, wounded. Once I got that thought into my head, I couldn't shake it. I smoked another cigarette, picturing Tony with a gunshot to the abdomen or maybe the shoulder. I could see him hobbling his way back to the Plymouth, hiding his blood-soaked shirt beneath his overcoat.

I drew down hard on my cigarette just as a new fear came to me. I knew how Tony was—stubborn and foolish. He would rather bleed to death in his hotel room than take himself to a doctor or the hospital. He'd collapse on the floor and no one would know he was in there dying. I crushed out the cigarette and reached for another. Suddenly keeping Tony alive became my responsibility. It was up to me to save him somehow.

I was still awake when Shep came home. It was after three in the morning. The sound of his key turning the lock sent a rush of relief through my body. He was safe. Bolting up in bed, I pulled back the covers and ran to see that he was really okay.

"I'm fine. Everything's fine," he said, walking me back upstairs.

What did *fine* mean? I searched his face, trying to read his expression. His eyes were heavy, his coloring off. He went into the bathroom and I crawled back on the bed, hugging my knees to my chest. When he came out he was guzzling a bottle of bicarbonate. Was his stomach upset because he'd just gone on a shooting spree, or was his stomach upset because Capone and his men got away?

"Go back to sleep," he said. "It's late."

The next morning I frantically searched the newspapers. I couldn't find anything on Capone, but maybe it hadn't made the morning edition yet. I wanted to call the hospitals, but I couldn't risk it. Not with Shep upstairs sleeping.

Not knowing whether Tony was dead or alive and not being able to ask anyone about it was eating me up. Regardless of what had passed between us, he was still a human being, and he had been there for me. He had saved me on that snow-covered road; he had saved me the night Evelyn killed Izzy. I couldn't leave him to bleed to death inside his hotel room.

As soon as the housekeeper arrived, I quickly got dressed and stepped outside to hail a taxicab.

The driver turned to me. "Where to, lady?"

Where to? I didn't know if I was doing the right thing or not. I looked back at the house. The ivy crawling up the side needed scaling back. The front gate with its black finials needed painting, too. . . .

"Lady, the meter's running. . . . Lady?" The driver looked at me through the rearview mirror. "You okay?"

Reluctantly I gave him the address, and twenty minutes later he dropped me off in front of the Plymouth Hotel.

My heart was pounding as I rode the elevator, my eyes locked on the iron gate as the car rose to the eighth floor. I knocked on Tony's door, wondering what I would do if there was no answer. Would I tell the desk clerk? How could I do that without getting myself involved? I knocked again. I would call from a pay phone and have them check in on him. . . .

Finally on the third knock I heard footsteps on the other side of the door, staggering across the floor. My chest grew heavy as I pictured Tony struggling, dragging himself to the door. I heard the chain latch slide and braced myself.

Tony opened his door. He was bare chested, his trousers barely up on his hips. I looked for blood, for bandages. He was fine. Relief spread through me, and then I realized what a fool I'd been.

He looked at me, confused. He was still half asleep. "What are you doing here?"

I couldn't tell him why I was there. No way could I say that Shep and the others had gone after him and Capone.

"Vera?"

"I just . . . I just . . ." He smiled and reached for my hand, pulling me inside. He tried to kiss me and I squirmed away. "No, Tony . . . No . . ." I wasn't there for that, but just the touch of his hand, the brush of his lips had already begun to wear me down. He pressed his body up against mine, my back against the door as he moved in closer still, his thigh spreading my legs apart. Was I fooling myself, acting so concerned about him? Or was that just a convenient excuse? Was this what I'd really come here for all along? He kissed me again, and this time he had me. I couldn't fight it anymore.

"I knew sooner or later you'd come back to me," he said.

BOOK THREE

1928–1929

EVERY TIME WAS
THE LAST TIME

I promised myself. I swore every time it would be the last time. And yet there I was again in Tony Liolli's hotel room, in his bed and in his arms.

I had one leg thrown over his thigh with the bedsheets twisted about our bodies. Just an hour before I couldn't wait to see him, and now I couldn't wait to leave him. It was storming outside, one of those September rains that carried a cold, penetrating chill. We lay in bed smoking cigarettes, listening to the rain pelting against the windows. Every now and then a flash of lighting streaked across the sky, followed by the rumble of thunder. I promised myself I'd leave as soon as the storm let up.

"Been thinking about getting out of the rackets," he said.

"Oh?" I reached across his chest and crushed out my cigarette in the ashtray on the nightstand. I'd heard this from him before and knew it was just talk.

"Maybe I'll start a business. A legit one. And I'm going to

give up the ponies and the dice games, too. I owe a lot of people a lot of money right now."

"Who do you owe?"

"The question is, who don't I owe?" He laughed as if it were an accomplishment rather than an embarrassment. He pulled back the covers and wandered into the bathroom, still talking to me over the sound of his urine splashing into the bowl. "I should have listened to Torrio. He said I was too smart for this racket and that . . ." The last of what he said was drowned out by the flush of the toilet.

He came back out, sat in the chair, and grabbed a cigarette, lighting it off a candle on the nightstand. "It drives Capone crazy that I *chose* this life. He says I'm soft. Thinks I was born with a silver spoon in my mouth." He reached up and ran his fingers through his hair, sending that one rebellious lock onto his forehead. "I'm smarter than Capone. I could run this town better than he does." He took another drag off his cigarette and exhaled toward the ceiling.

I got off the bed and searched the floor for my stockings but he grabbed me and pulled me to him. God, he knew how to heat me up again. I sat on his lap, facing him, looping my legs about his waist, letting them dangle down the back of his chair. He wrapped his arms around me and pulled me closer to him. It had stopped raining but I couldn't leave, not yet. Not when every time was the last time.

When I arrived home later that afternoon, Shep was in his study, leaning forward in his chair, his whiskey glass pressed to his forehead. The top button of his shirt was undone and he'd loosened his tie. He was supposed to be down at Schofield's all day. What was he doing home so early? It wasn't even six o'clock.

"Where ya been, Vera?" His voice sounded strange, tight. Something was wrong.

"Just out." I cleared my throat and inched my way closer to him. He looked at me as if he were searching for something. Did he know where I was all afternoon? *How could he possibly know?* I turned away and futzed with a vase of flowers on the edge of his desk, keeping my back toward him.

"Did you see Basha today?"

It felt like a trap. I had to stop and think this one through. I rearranged a daisy, stalling.

"Vera?"

"No, why?"

"So you haven't heard?"

"Heard what?" I looked back at him from over my shoulder.

He came over to me, wrapping his arms around me from behind. "It's Squeak." Shep pulled me closer. "He's gone. They shot him. He died on the way to the hospital."

I heard myself gasp as I covered my face with my hands and sank down into his body.

"I'm losing everybody, Vera," he said, his breath hot against my neck. "Dion. Then Hymie and Vinny. Izzy. Now Squeak. They're all gone."

My eyes turned glassy and a lump gathered in my throat. "I don't know what to say. I'm sorry, Shep. I'm just so sorry. If I could undo it all, I would."

"I know you would, Dollface. I know you would. . . ."

I wasn't sure if I was talking about Squeak or Izzy or everything else.

Mrs. Squeak wanted Basha to leave the wake, and that caused some scene. Shep and Bugs tried to reason with Basha, explaining that the family found her presence there inappropriate.

"Inappropriate?" Basha looked at them through the black

netting on her hat hanging down past her eyes. "You've got to be kidding me."

Shep shook his head and took hold of her arm, coaxing her toward the door. "I'm sorry, Basha, but it's a request from the family. And at a time like this, I think we have to respect the family's wishes."

"Family? What fuckin' family?" She jerked her arm out of his grip. "I was Squeak's family. I'm the one who belongs here. Not her!"

Everyone in the chapel turned and looked. It was obvious by the way they whispered and made faces that they all knew she was Squeak's gun moll.

Dora, Evelyn and I stood to the side, watching.

"Should we say something to her?" Evelyn asked.

"I'm not opening my trap—no way." I shook my head.

"Let the fellas handle her," Dora said, staring straight ahead at the casket.

"C'mon, Basha," said Bugs. "What do you expect? You've been screwing her husband for the past ten years. Plus, you took a shot at her once."

"Yeah, and I should have killed the stupid bitch when I had the chance!" Basha glared at the row of mourners staring at her. "What do you think you're all looking at?"

"See, now, your little outbursts are one of the reasons why they don't want you here," said Bugs.

Shep stepped in. "Basha, c'mon now. Either you let us walk you out with some dignity. Or else—"

"Or else what?"

"Or else I'm afraid Squeak's wife's going to have the cops arrest you."

"These are my freakin' choices?"

"I'm afraid so."

"What the hell can she have me arrested for?"

"Disrupting the peace, for starters."

Basha contemplated this for a moment. "Can I at least view the body? Can I at least say good-bye?"

Shep thought this was a reasonable request and went to talk to the family. Mrs. Squeak begrudgingly agreed, so Basha went up to see Squeak one last time. With Bugs and Shep on either side of her, she placed her hands on the edge of the casket and leaned forward, resting her head on Squeak's chest.

"What the hell is she doing now?" asked Dora. "Is she gonna climb in there with him?"

Basha broke down, weeping all over Squeak, mumbling louder and louder, "I love you, baby. I love you, baby. I love you. I love you, baby. . . ."

Mrs. Squeak broke that up, pulling Shep aside. "Okay, that's enough! Get her out of here! Out! I want her out of here. Now!"

That's when Basha took a swing at Mrs. Squeak and almost knocked over one of the candles at the head of Squeak's casket. Bugs grabbed Basha from behind, locked her in his arms.

She squirmed and struggled, yelling, "I'm not going any-where."

Basha bucked and snorted like a horse being broken when the cops put the handcuffs on her.

Bugs and Shep worked their magic, pulled some strings and got her out on bail just in time for an encore performance two days later at Squeak's funeral.

SOUTH SIDE BLUNDERS

How could two men love me when I hated myself so much? I didn't deserve to be loved. I'd look at Cecelia and Basha. They were suffering so over losing their men when I was the one who should have been without love, not them.

Poor Basha. Her grief was thick as tar and just as black. After Squeak's funeral, when she wouldn't answer her telephone, Evelyn and I went to her apartment. We found her sitting in the dark in her bathrobe, drinking and smoking cigarette after cigarette. Her hair was stringy and dirty and I could smell her body odor, sour and rank.

"C'mon, now," I said, after I'd run the bath for her. "You need to get cleaned up and get dressed. You'll feel better."

"I don't wanna feel better. I wanna die."

Evelyn and I looked at each other. I grabbed one arm, she took the other and together we lifted Basha up.

"Let me *go!*" Basha kicked and screamed, trying to twist away. "Goddammit! Let go of me! Let me die!"

Basha couldn't have weighed more than a hundred pounds, but she was strong. She gripped onto the door and I had to pry her fingers off the glass knob, one at a time. "Goddammit! I said let me go!"

The water sloshed back and forth like an angry sea as we hefted her into the tub. Basha tried to fight it, but even as she splashed and told us to "go to hell," I saw her eyes close. Then her jaw went slack and her shoulders sank below the water's surface as the steam rose up around her like fog. "I hate you both," she said in a lazy drawl.

I was soaking wet. So was Evelyn. We grabbed some bath towels and dried ourselves off while Basha leaned back in the tub, muttering, "Why did they have to kill him? Why?"

An hour later, she was dressed and even managed to nibble a slice of toast.

After that, I looked in on her every day, opening the drapes to let some daylight in and making sure she at least tried to eat something. It wasn't until she ran out of cigarettes and gin that I convinced her to venture outside her apartment.

"What am I gonna do without him?" She pushed her dark glasses up on her nose. It was a beautiful fall day, leaves changing colors, swaying in an easy breeze, but Basha wasn't seeing any of it. "I thought I was lonely before whenever he was with *her*. Now I don't even get the crumbs anymore. I'm telling you, I don't wanna live without him."

"Don't talk like that. You're going to be okay." I put my arm around her shoulder, offering her a half hug. "It just takes time. It's only been a few weeks."

"I just hope to God you know how lucky you are. You got a man to go home to. A man who loves you. And only you. You don't have to worry about sharing him with somebody else."

Just as she said that, I stepped down wrong on a break in the sidewalk and lost my balance in a graceless stumble. I took it as a sign. God was watching.

It was Indian summer. The sky was a brilliant blue without a hint of clouds. The fruit stands and flower pushcarts were out on State Street for the last time before they'd close down for the winter. Buckingham Fountain was turned off for the season, always a sign of the city bracing itself for the coming cold. Like everyone else, I wanted to take advantage of the beautiful weather, and the steady breeze made me feel like walking.

It was about half past eleven, and I was heading for Tony's hotel down on the south side of town. As soon as I rounded the corner at the Plymouth, I stopped in my tracks. Through a haze of sunlight, I spotted Cecelia and Dora coming down the sidewalk. Dora was wrestling with her packages, switching the bags from her left hand to her right while Cecelia chattered on.

Just when I thought maybe they hadn't seen me, Cecelia looked up in surprise.

"Hey, toots—that is you! What are you doing all the way down here?"

"I'm just . . . There was a shop I wanted to visit . . . that's all. . . ." The words circled inside my head, and I wasn't sure if I'd actually spoken at all. My pulse raced and I felt clammy, even a little dizzy. A streetcar hurtled past us, bells clanking as sparks shot off the overhead cables. I finally managed to ask what they were doing on that side of town.

"Guess what?" Dora reached into her bag and pulled out a baby rattle. "Guess who's having a baby!"

"You?" I smiled, or maybe I just stared. My thoughts weren't attached to the rest of me.

She nodded and hugged me. "Can you believe it! After all

these years of trying, it happened. I just found out yesterday. I was gonna call and tell you later."

"Look how happy she is," Cecelia said with a shrug. "Personally, I don't get it, but if it makes her happy, then God bless, right?"

I smiled. Was it my imagination or were they looking at me funny? My mind went to every bad place. Did they come all this way just to shop or were they checking up on me? Maybe they'd followed me earlier in the day. Maybe they suspected what I was up to. My breathing turned shallow.

"C'mon, we're gonna grab some lunch. There's a great little café around the corner."

I had no choice. I had to go with them.

I was a nervous wreck, looking all over the place for Tony, catching my breath each time I saw anyone who resembled a man about his age, about his height. I fidgeted with the menu, with the silverware, with anything I could find. Eating was next to impossible. Each time they asked me a question, I wondered if they were probing, trying to trip me up.

At one point Cecelia excused herself and went to the ladies' room, and that gave me a chance to steer the conversation toward Dora's pregnancy.

"How are you feeling?" I asked.

"I feel terrific. Never better." She nodded, contemplated a sip of coffee and then set her cup back down on the saucer. "So let me ask you something. Woman to woman."

"Okay." I swallowed hard and braced myself. *This is it.*

"When you were pregnant, were you scared? You know, about having a baby?"

"It doesn't hurt." I smiled, relieved. "They'll put you to sleep. You'll be sore afterward but you won't feel anything while it's happening. You wake up and there's your baby."

"No, I'm not talking about the labor. I mean, were you scared? You know, with all the killing going on, all the violence. I don't know if I want to bring a child into all this."

I smoothed the napkin across my lap. There was a time when I felt threatened by Dora, worried that she'd steal my daughter's love out from under me. But now she was reaching out to me, one mother to another. There was a new bond between us.

"Everything's gotten so violent," Dora continued. "It frightens me. How do you deal with it?"

"It was different when I had Hannah. We'd lost Dion, but it was nothing like it is out there now. We didn't know how bad things were going to get." I ran my fingers over the napkin again. "Frankly, the hardest part is trying to raise Hannah in a *normal* household when I don't know what normal is. As a mother, I don't know what I'm doing. I make it up as I go and I'm sure I'm doing it all wrong."

"No, you're not."

"Oh, yes, I am. She wants an extra cookie and I let her have it and then I think I shouldn't have. When I give her a bath, I worry if the water's too hot, too cold. Honestly, I never know if I'm doing anything right. The only thing I know for sure is that I don't want her to grow up the way I did."

"But let's face it, she's Shep Green's daughter. She's not going to grow up like you did. She was born into a family of privilege."

"And a family of crime."

Dora sighed. "I guess that's what I'm worried about. How do you bring a child into a world with such violence . . . ?"

What do you do? You learn to cook and you set the table every night and you make the beds and do the laundry and pretend that you're no different from any other family. But you know you're living under glass. You know it can all be shattered in an instant.

Cecelia came back to the table and the interrogation picked back up. What was the name of the shop I wanted to visit? How did I discover it? Where were my packages? What a shame that I'd come all this way and hadn't bought anything. . . .

After lunch, as Cecelia flagged down a taxicab, they offered me a ride back up north but I begged off.

"I think I'll stick around down here. You two run along. There's some more shopping I want to do. You know, since I never, *ever* get down this way . . ."

I waited on the sidewalk until their taxicab drove out of view, and then I took off in the opposite direction.

"You're late." Tony was leaning against the doorjamb, his shirt unbuttoned, his hair rumpled. If he wasn't drunk already, then he was on his way. "I've been waiting here for you for over an hour."

I pushed past him and tossed my pocketbook on the dresser. "I ran into Cecelia Drucci and Knuckles's wife right outside your hotel."

"Did they see you come in?"

"No."

"So what are you worried about?"

I poured myself a drink and spilled half of it. My hands were shaking. "You should have heard me trying to explain what I'm doing down on this side of town. I could barely get a sentence out. I wouldn't have believed me."

"Relax. You're overreacting. They just caught you off guard, that's all."

I looked at him, exasperated. "That's easy for you to say."

"You're making a big deal out of nothing. You've got just as much right to be down here as they do."

Maybe he was right. Maybe I was overreacting. I glanced at the clock on the nightstand. "I have to be back home by three. Should we still do this or not?"

The mood was shot. We both knew it. Still, he took off his shirt and unbuttoned his trousers while I slithered out of my dress, folding it neatly and setting it on the dresser. Usually our clothes ended up in a tangled pile on the floor. But not that day they didn't. Once I was undressed I slid under the bedsheets, waiting for him. He wasn't even aroused when he climbed on top of me, crushing my leg with his thigh. His breath was sour and smelled of cigarettes and whiskey. We barely kissed at all, and when it was over, I felt dirty and couldn't wait to bathe the last half hour away.

THE HOLIDAY BLUES

Shep sat behind his desk, fiddling with his cuff link. He couldn't look at me when I read to him anymore. Even if it was from a novel. And that day I was sorting through scraps of paper and cocktail napkins and anything else that Bugs had found to write on. I read them to Shep one by one. Some were dropoff points. Others were instructions for Knuckles and some of the others like Frank and Peter Gusenberg. Another was a list of repairs for a truck that John May needed to fix.

I was let in on Shep's business now but only because he needed me. It reminded me vaguely of my own bootlegging days.

"You know," I said, "it would make a lot more sense if Bugs had Frank stay back at the warehouse and he sent Peter to—"

"Is there anything else there?" Shep asked, letting me know my opinion wasn't needed.

"That's it." I handed him Bugs's notes. There was a definite cutoff point to my usefulness.

He nodded, got up from his desk and reached for his hat. "I'll be back late. Don't wait up." He walked out of the room.

Sometimes I didn't feel like his wife, but more like his underling. It had been weeks since he'd held me or kissed me, let alone made love to me. I missed him, and the more he shut me out, the more I justified my running back to Tony.

The next morning I went to Tony's hotel. Capone was sending him out of town for a few weeks the following day and the two of us went at it, hoping it would sustain us while he was gone. I'd lost all track of time and was more than thirty minutes late meeting the girls for lunch.

"Have you ordered yet?" I asked, rushing into the Walnut Room.

"Just waiting on you." Evelyn shot me a look and raised her menu.

"Maybe now we can order. We're starving." Basha snapped her fingers to signal the waitress.

"Oh c'mon, I'm not *that* late," I lied as I settled in, shrugging off my overcoat, resting it on the back of my chair.

"So where were you, anyway?" Evelyn asked, her eyes locked on her menu. It was like she knew I was keeping something from her.

"I had to take Hannah shopping for shoes."

"I thought you did that yesterday," said Basha.

"It, ah, well, we started to and then something happened and . . ." God, I couldn't keep my stories straight. I shifted in my chair. I was still wet from Tony.

"It's okay. You're here now." Dora smiled. She was pregnant and not about to let anything get her down.

"No Cecelia today?" I asked, looking at the empty chair.

"She sends her regrets." Evelyn pinched open her pocketbook for a cigarette.

"It was their anniversary the other day," Dora said. "It knocked her for a loop. Some days she seems like her old self and some days she's a wreck. Poor thing."

"Poor all of us." Basha reached inside her pocketbook for her flask and poured some gin into her coffee cup. I couldn't remember the last time I'd seen Basha sober. Now that she was no longer plotting Mrs. Squeak's demise, she didn't know what to do with herself. It was as if her favorite hobby had been taken away.

"Do you believe this," I said, trying to lighten the mood as I gestured toward the garlands and big red bows wrapped around the pillars. "We just got through celebrating Thanksgiving last week and they're already putting up Christmas decorations. It gets earlier and earlier each year, doesn't it? Sheesh."

"Thanksgiving? What's there to be thankful for?" Basha rolled her eyes. "You know, it wasn't supposed to be like this. We weren't supposed to end up alone." Basha took a sip of her gin. "I hate those goddamn greaseballs—every last one of them. May they all be gunned down!"

Evelyn nodded. "May they all rot in hell!" She had the victim role down.

I couldn't look at Evelyn for fear she'd read my face. She knew about Tony. Though she'd never said a word, she knew. *She knew.* And if any of the others had known I was involved with a member of the South Side Gang it would have been the end of me.

I opened my menu and closed it again. I couldn't eat. My stomach was in knots. I wasn't just two-timing my husband; I was two-timing my girlfriends and the entire North Side Gang.

This affair was exhausting. I was tired of saying I was with the girls when I was at the Plymouth Hotel. And because Tony would get jealous over Shep, I'd tell him I was with my mother when I was at home with Shep. I didn't know what I was doing with Tony. Some days, like that morning, I couldn't get enough of him. But other times I knew it wasn't worth the risk.

With each passing day, I had a sinking feeling that I was going to get caught. But still, I couldn't bring myself to end it with Tony. Each time I tried, I grew weak. In so many ways he knew me better than Shep. He knew my darkest, blackest secrets—things that would have turned Shep away from me. Maybe I deserved a cheater like Tony after all. I knew I didn't deserve Shep.

I t was two days before Christmas when we got the news. Three months into her pregnancy and Dora lost the baby. Evelyn and I went to see her, bringing her flowers and magazines, hoping to cheer her up.

When Knuckles answered the door, we were shocked. Their usually pristine house was cluttered with newspapers, dirty dishes, laundry strewn about the sofa and chairs. Their Christmas tree was in the corner waiting to be trimmed, the floor covered with boxes of bulbs and a tangle of lights.

Knuckles looked like he hadn't slept in days. Warning us, he said, "She's in a bad way. I can't even talk to her."

While Evelyn went into the kitchen to wash the dishes and straighten up, I ventured into the bedroom. I sat on the edge of the bed, but couldn't get Dora to look at me. She stared straight ahead. It was the first time I'd ever seen her without any makeup. Her skin was pale; her lips were thin and chapped. I was surprised by how young and innocent she looked.

"The doctor said you're going to be fine. You can try again. You're still young enough."

She turned to me in anger, her blue eyes rimmed with tears. "Easy for you to say! You still have your baby. I never even got to hold mine!" She rolled over with her back toward me. "Go away," she said. "You're the last person I want to see right now. Just leave me alone."

I reached out to stroke her shoulder but stopped myself. She didn't want me there. That was clear. There was nothing I could say to take away her pain and apparently my very presence was making it worse.

I eased up off the bed and showed myself out. She didn't stir. I wasn't even sure if she knew I was gone.

After we left Dora and Knuckles, Evelyn and I made our way over to State Street. Snow was falling, turning downtown Chicago white and picturesque. It was beautiful with all the storefronts decorated in their garlands and twinkling lights. Christmas carolers stood on the street corner, their voices trailing behind us as we cut over to Washington.

As Evelyn and I pushed through the revolving door, a store greeter in his red vest welcomed us to Marshall Field's. We dusted snow off our coats and stomped the slush free from our boots before heading to the glove display.

Evelyn stuffed her hands inside a pair joined at the wrist by a string. "Ooh, these are nice. Irwin would love these." She'd started seeing Irwin just a few weeks before, and already she was smitten. "Oh, or look at these!" She held up another pair. "Before I forget, do you and Shep want to join us for dinner Saturday night? Irwin wanted me to ask you."

"Yeah. Sure. I have to check with Shep, but it sounds swell." I moved over to the scarves. "So this is getting serious with you and Irwin, huh?"

"Isn't it crazy?" She beamed. "What is it about me and men whose names start with the letter *I*?"

I paused over a blue satin scarf. This was the first time I'd heard Evelyn make even the slightest reference to Izzy.

"I'm just head over heels about Irwin. I love him, Vera. I really do. And not like before. This time it's real."

I smiled and squeezed her hand. "He's a good man. He truly is. Too bad he's in such a lousy business."

"Making brassieres?"

RENÉE ROSEN

I gave her a look. "I meant his *other* business."

"Oh." Evelyn frowned and set one hand on her hip. "So I've been thinking. . . ."

"What about?"

"Well, you know, I trust Irwin. I trust him in ways I never trusted Izzy. And I think it's important that Irwin knows he can trust me, too. So . . . I've decided that I can't have any secrets from him."

"What do you mean by secrets?"

"You know," she said, drumming her fingertips along the countertop. "I want to come clean."

"About?"

"You know *what* about."

"Evelyn!" I could feel my eyes bulging out of their sockets. "Are you crazy?"

"How am I supposed to have an honest relationship with him if I've got this huge secret between us? It's been eating me up alive. I need to get this off my chest."

"Ev—"

"He loves me—he'll understand."

"Have you lost your mind?" I tossed the scarf onto the counter and pulled her aside. "You can't tell Irwin. You can't tell *anyone*. Not ever!"

"But he'll understand. He really loves me."

"I don't care how much he loves you. Listen to me." I grabbed her hands and forced her to look me in the eye. "Those guys— our men—they may love us, but their number one priority— their number one loyalty—is to each other. You can't come clean to Irwin without dragging me into this. How do you think it's going to sit with him that you killed one of his best friends?"

"It was an accident. Self-defense. You said so yourself."

"You think that's going to matter to them? And what exactly

are you going to tell Irwin when he asks what you did with Izzy's body?"

"I don't know . . . I could—"

"Are you prepared to tell Irwin that a member of the South Side Gang helped you and *me*? You're going to drag me into this! You can't do that. I helped you—you can't turn around and ruin my life. Shep doesn't know anything about Tony Liolli."

Evelyn looked like I'd just smacked her. "Okay, okay—I'm sorry. I wasn't thinking of it like that."

"No, you sure weren't!"

"I get it. Okay. I won't tell him. I promise. But don't forget, Shep was away when it happened. And besides, it's not like you're still seeing Tony." She looked at me and I watched her expression change. "Oh my God! Vera, are you still seeing him? You're not, are you?"

My eyes glazed over. "God, no. What do you think I am, crazy?"

A NEW YEAR'S RESOLUTION

Dora and I sat side by side at the beauty parlor, waiting to have our nails done. It was the first time I'd seen her since she'd lost the baby. We'd gone for coffee earlier and then wandered through a couple stores. I kept expecting her to apologize for what she'd said that day in her bedroom but it never came up.

"What's taking them so damn long?" I asked, watching one beautician scurrying about with a basket of curlers and another picking up a handful of bobby pins she'd dropped on the floor near us.

"Relax. Tomorrow's New Year's Eve. Every place in town is packed. What's your hurry?"

"Nothing." I eased back in my chair and crossed my legs, letting my top one swing back and forth. "I just have a lot of errands to run." I didn't have any errands. I was late. Tony was expecting me at his hotel at two o'clock and it was already a quarter past.

"I know we always go to the Palmer House for New Year's Eve, but I'd love to skip the party this year," she said.

"Is Basha going?"

"No. Neither is Viola. Or Cecilia."

"It's been a rough year for everyone, hasn't it?" I said.

"You can say that again. At least you've got Shep back home now. But for the rest of us, what the hell is there to celebrate? Good riddance to 1928. . . ."

I gazed at the photographs on the wall opposite us: one of a woman with a shingle bob, one with an Eton crop and one with a finger hairdo. All the while I was thinking about Tony. I hadn't seen him in more than two weeks. He'd been in New York the week before, and now Capone wanted him down in Florida after New Year's.

"Boy, are you ever fidgety today," she said, placing her hand on my knee to stop my leg from swinging. "What's eating you?"

"Me? Nothing." I shook my head and willed my leg to stay put. "I've got a lot on my mind is all." I thought about Tony, waiting for me in his hotel room, wondering what was keeping me. "I'll be right back," I said, bolting out of my chair. "I just have to make a quick call."

The front of the salon was crowded with women draped in dark capes, sitting in a row of swivel chairs, waiting to be shampooed or cut or dyed. Others had their heads tucked inside the drying machines or hooked up to the permanent-wave contraptions. The air smelled of perfume, borax, setting lotions and nail polish remover. I made my way over to a dainty desk with a telephone reserved for clients. Another woman was sitting in the sweetheart chair, already on the line, confirming her plans for New Year's Eve at the Blackstone Hotel. I folded my arms across my chest and tapped my foot, glancing around to make sure I didn't recognize anyone standing nearby. As soon as the telephone was free, I sat down and dialed. The line was ringing and I anxiously looked around the beauty parlor until finally the front desk answered.

"Plymouth Hotel."

"Can you please put me through to Tony Liolli's room . . . room eight twenty-seven. . . . Yes. Liolli with an *L*." I was waiting to be connected when someone tapped me on the shoulder. I turned and my heart clamped down.

Dora was standing over me. Her blue eyes narrowed as she studied my face. "They're ready for us now," she said.

"Oh. Okay. Swell." I tried to keep my voice steady and hung up, barely able to get the receiver placed back on the hook, my hands were shaking so. It was noisy in the beauty parlor and it was possible that Dora hadn't overheard me asking for Tony Liolli.

She walked away and I followed her into the private room where they took care of special customers like us.

As soon as we were inside, Dora turned to me. "Liolli? Tony Liolli? Dear God, tell me he's not the errand you need to run this afternoon."

I closed my eyes and cursed under my breath.

"Spill it, Vera. What the hell are you up to?"

"Dora, please." I still couldn't look at her.

"Uh-uh. Something's going on and you'd better tell me what it is."

I tried stalling again, but Dora pressed harder. "Okay," I said, finally letting my eyes meet hers, "but you can't tell anyone."

She gave me an indignant glare. "Who am I going to tell?"

"Just promise me."

Two beauticians appeared in the doorway with their nail files and polish. Dora shooed them away. "And close the door behind you." Turning back to me, she said, "I promise. I swear I won't tell anyone. Now spill it."

I lowered my head to my hands, perspiring. I could feel Dora's eyes on me, wearing me down.

"I mean it," she said. "Tell me what the hell's going on."

I felt myself cracking, slipping, the words rising up in me like bile.

"Vera!"

"Oh, Dora," I blurted out, "I'm in love."

"What!"

"I'm in love. I'm in love with him." I held my breath, waiting for something awful to happen. Shouldn't the sky have fallen? Shouldn't the earth have given way beneath me?

"You're in love with Tony Liolli?" Dora's mouth dropped open. She leaned back in her chair looking like she'd just had the wind knocked out of her. "Aw, Jesus! Tell me you're not serious."

"I love him, Dora. I do."

"Oh, honey, you gotta end it. You can't be fooling around with Tony Liolli. That guy's a loose cannon. He's trouble with a capital *T*. And you'd better hope he keeps his trap shut. If it gets out about you and him, you'll both be six feet under. You should know better. You're Shep Green's wife. You can't be two-timing him with one of Capone's men. Jesus, Vera, use your head. Who else knows about this?"

I thought of Evelyn. "No one. God, I've never told anyone. You're not going to say anything, are you?"

"What? And get myself killed, too? Not only am I not gonna say anything, I'm gonna forget you even told me about it. And what you're gonna do is end it with Liolli, you got that?"

I nodded and pressed my fingers to my temples. My head was pounding.

"You know what kills me," said Dora, pursing her lips, her voice taking on a definite edge. "You have everything. A loving husband, a beautiful, healthy daughter, and you're willing to piss it all away on some greaseball who probably whacked half your husband's best friends."

"I know it's wrong. I know it doesn't make any sense."

"So you are gonna end it with him, right?"

I nodded, barely able to breathe, knowing that I'd just made the worst mistake of my life.

left Dora and on one of the coldest days of the year I decided to walk. Block after block, with no destination in mind, I wandered, heading north, oblivious to the automobiles and trolley cars whirling past me. I stepped into an intersection and a driver blasted his horn and skidded to a stop, missing me by less than half a foot. I kept walking, drifting along Michigan Avenue past the Wrigley Building, the Tribune Tower and onward past the pumping stations housed inside the water towers that looked like stone castles.

When I could no longer feel my toes or my fingers, I stepped inside the Drake to warm myself. The footman held the door for me as the luxury of the grand hotel welcomed me inside.

Entering the marble lobby, I passed by the bellhops and chambermaids and handsomely dressed couples walking along the corridor. It took me back to my first visit to the Drake, the night I modeled jewelry for Mr. Borowitz. I'd so desperately wanted to be in that world of glitz and glamour. I got glitz and glamour, all right, but I also got gore and carnage. I had escaped the rotting stink of the slaughterhouse, the blood and guts of the kill floor, and look where I'd run to. I'd landed in the middle of a world that was far more violent than the Union Stock Yards.

I kept walking and came to the spot where years before I'd first met Shep Green. That night it was Shep who had stepped in to save me from Mr. Borowitz. And in a way, he'd been saving me ever since. How could I have betrayed him like this?

Maybe it was a good thing that Dora found out about Tony. Maybe it would force me to do the right thing. God, I was tired of it all. It used to be the anticipation that made me hunger for

Tony. Before the hotel door was even locked, we'd be devouring each other until my body shook and my throat was raw from crying out. Then I was empty, the lust and desire all burned out of me only to start slowly gathering strength again the minute I left him. That was the pattern, but now it had been interrupted. Tony had been out of town so much lately that already things had changed between us. At first the separation was excruciating but now it was a dull ache, fading more and more the longer I'd stayed away from him.

Standing in the hotel lobby, I felt as if a switch had been thrown and the lights were all on. I could see now that Tony had become a habit I'd grown addicted to. I'd loved Tony once—of that I was certain—but not anymore. I hadn't realized this until that very moment.

I went to a phone booth and rang his hotel. "I can't make it over there today," I said, leaning my forehead against the glass panel, feeling the coolness spread across my skin. ". . . Yeah, sure, I'll see you when you get back. . . ." I hung up and wiped my eyes with the back of my hand. These weren't tears of heartache. They were tears of relief.

THE KISS OF DEATH

It was a Wednesday afternoon, February 13, the day before Valentine's Day. I passed by a store window filled with red hearts and strings of cupids stretched from one end to the other. It was cold outside, the temperature dipping down into the teens. The ground was frozen, the snow was old and dirty now, and even if a fresh inch or two fell and covered it up, you'd always know what was lying below the surface.

Dora asked about Tony only one other time. All she said was, "Did you take care of that problem of yours?"

I looked her right in the eye and said, "Yes."

But I hadn't ended it with Tony. And not because I didn't want to. But because I hadn't seen him. Tony had been down in Florida for most of January and when he was back in town for a few days, I made excuses, afraid that if I saw him, I'd lose my nerve. But I was ready now.

A chill swept through the air and I turned up my collar. I boarded the southbound el train and rode it down to the Fifteenth Street stop, just a few blocks away from the Plymouth Hotel.

When I keyed into the hotel room, I was surprised that Tony wasn't there, especially since he knew I was coming over. I sat on the side of the bed, waiting for him. I had my compact out, passing the mirror over my face. I looked like hell. My eyes were bloodshot, my skin was gray and my expression was sad even when I forced a smile. I used to shine, like I was something special. How did I get to look so old at twenty-three?

I heard someone out in the hallway. I looked up, expecting Tony to come through the door, but whoever it was kept walking. I lit a cigarette and helped myself to the bourbon he kept stashed in the bottom of the nightstand. With my drink in one hand and a cigarette in the other, I lay back against the pillows, knowing that this was the last time I'd ever be in his bed.

After I finished my cigarette, Tony showed up. He was wearing a pin-striped suit, a wide-brimmed hat and white leather spats with black buttons. He was suntanned from being down in Florida and looked every bit as handsome as he had the first time I'd seen him at the Five Star. But still, something inside me had shifted. And he could sense it.

I sat up on the side of the bed when he kissed me. "There's something I need to talk to you about," I said, watching him toss his hat onto the dresser.

He came over and sat beside me, placing his hand over mine. "There's something I gotta say first, though. You have to hear me out." He reached for a cigarette, lit it and chucked the burning match into the ashtray. I waited, holding my breath, while he drew a deep puff. "I did a lot of thinking while I was away." He got up, poured a couple drinks and handed one to me. "I love you, Vera. I want you with me. Not just for a few hours here and there. But every day, you and me."

"Tony, that's what I need to talk to you a—"

"I'm getting out of the rackets. For real this time. No more talk. I'm gonna leave town and start over. And I want you to come with me."

"What?" I was there to end it, not run away with him. "I can't go with you."

He shook his head, sending that strand of hair onto his forehead. "You. Me. Hannah—we'll hop a train, or we'll jump in the car and head to Mexico and we can start over. We'll hide out in Tijuana or Mexico City. No one'll find us there."

"I can't leave Shep. You know that."

He took a pull from his drink and fixed his eyes on me. "I'm gonna tell you something. And you can't say a word—not to anyone—you understand? If I didn't hate Capone—if I had a shred of loyalty left for him—and if I didn't love you as much as I do, I wouldn't be telling you this. And if you breathe a word of this, I'm a dead man, you got that?"

I took a long sip from my drink.

"When I was down in Florida with Capone, I was let in on some business, and it has to do with Bugs Moran and Shep."

"What?"

"He had someone contact Bugs and Shep—they think they've got a lorry of whiskey coming to their garage on Clark Street tomorrow morning. And as soon as they show up, Capone's gonna take them out. Both of them."

I looked at him in shock, trying to make sense of what he'd just said. "What? Why Shep?"

"Why? Because, next to Bugs Moran, the one person Capone wants dead is your husband."

"What are you saying?" My voice was cracking. "I don't understand—why? Why is he going to kill Shep?"

"I can't tell you any more than what I already have." He got up and paced like a madman. "Jesus, I'm talking way the hell out of school, do you get that?"

I just stared at him, still in shock.

"You gotta keep your mouth shut about this, Vera. I mean it."

"How can you expect me to keep my mouth shut? You just told me they're going to kill my husband and you expect me not to say anything?"

He came over to my side, grabbed my chin and forced my eyes to meet his. "If anyone knew I was telling you this, they'd kill me. You want that?"

I sat on the edge of the bed, resting my head against the heels of my hands.

"I mean it, Vera. The only reason I'm telling you is because I'm leaving town and I want to take you with me. And I don't wanna scare you, but I don't think you should stick around town anyway. Somebody connects the two of us and you're as good as gone. You're a traitor in their eyes. And it won't just be the South Siders after you—the North Siders'll probably wipe you out before Capone's boys even get a chance."

I couldn't breathe. I started rocking back and forth, cradling my head in my hands.

Tony came over and crouched down before me, taking hold of both my hands. "I gotta take care of a few things and then we can go. I can pick you up in the morning and we'll be gone."

I shook my head. I couldn't think.

"You gotta come with me. It's the only way. We'll get out of town and we'll do it now."

I pressed my fingertips against my eyes. They burned. My shoulders ached. Everything ached. I kept my eyes closed. I couldn't look at Tony.

"Listen to me—Shep's going down—you can't save him. Shep's got a hit coming, and that makes you a widow."

"This is all happening too fast."

"We don't have a choice. So here's what we're gonna do. Tomorrow morning, when Shep leaves for the garage, I'll swing by your house. I'll come get you and Hannah and we'll be on our way."

I opened my eyes and looked away. How could I not tell Shep he was in danger? Yet if I said anything, if I even hinted, he'd know that someone had told me. Even if I didn't serve up Tony's name, he'd figure it out. The cigar man, hotel clerks, the Four Deuces barkeeper, Dora, even Evelyn—they all flashed through my mind. It wouldn't take long to find the trail that led from me to Tony. I needed time to think but there was no time. I doubled over, feeling like I'd swallowed snakes. I covered my mouth with both hands. The chills took over my body as I rocked back and forth.

Tony grabbed me by the shoulders, trying to hold me still. "Say you'll do it. Tell me you'll come with me."

I couldn't answer. I could barely breathe. I didn't know what I was going to do the next minute, let alone the next morning.

He asked again if I'd come with him. When I didn't respond he said, "It's gonna be okay. I promise you. You gotta trust me on this, okay? You do trust me, don't you?"

I nodded. My head was spinning. If I told Shep about the hit, they'd kill Tony. If I didn't say anything, they'd kill Shep. There was no way out of this.

When I left the hotel, I was light-headed and shaky. People on the streets went about their business as if everything were normal, but I knew the world was about to end. At least, for me it was.

I walked nine or ten blocks in the bitter cold. I didn't know if I could run away with Tony, but I did know that I couldn't live with myself if I didn't warn Shep. I picked up my pace, flagged down a cab. I had him take me straight to Schofield's.

"Shep? Shep?" I barged into the flower shop, panting as if I'd run the whole way. It was dark inside, and after the bright winter light outside I was blinded. Once my eyes adjusted, I saw a couple of the Little Pishers looking up from their card game in back. I couldn't make out their faces.

"He's not here," one of them said.

"Where is he? Did he say when he'd be back?"

The boy shrugged. "I don't know nothin'. Sorry."

I raced home after that, but Shep wasn't there, either. After I sent the housekeeper home, I telephoned Dora. "Can you watch Hannah for me?"

"What's wrong?" Dora asked as soon as she heard my voice. "Are you okay?"

"I'm fine. Everything's fine." I didn't know what was going to happen when I told Shep, but I knew I didn't want Hannah home to witness it. I cleared my throat, steadied my voice. "It would be a big help if Hannah could stay with you tonight."

Before we left the house, I brushed Hannah's hair aside and studied her face. She was so young, just four years old, the same age I was when my father was killed. I couldn't let that happen to her.

When I dropped Hannah off, Dora stood in the doorway wearing an apron, holding a wooden spoon in her hand. "Is everything okay? You don't look so good, Vera. Come inside and let's talk. Something's up, I can tell."

"It's nothing. Really." I forced a smile. I couldn't tell her. She already knew too much as it was. "I'm just in a hurry," I said, pointing back to the cab idling at the curb. "The driver's waiting for me." I kissed Hannah and started to walk away.

"Vera, wait!"

I froze in place for a minute but couldn't turn back. "I have to go. I'm late."

"Vera—Vera, come back here."

I heard her footsteps on the sidewalk coming after me, but I kept walking and was back inside the cab before she could stop me.

When I got home, Shep still wasn't there. I poured myself a drink and smoked a cigarette, rehearsing what I'd say when he came through the door. I knew Tony said there was nothing I could do to stop Capone, but Shep was smart—he'd find a way out. But he had to know what he was walking into.

The sun had gone down and daylight had left the room hours before. I sat in the dark, hardly stirring at all. Even after I'd spilled half my drink down the front of my dress, I sat and finished what was in my glass. I didn't get up again until it was time to fix myself the next drink, light the next cigarette. At seven o'clock I called Schofield's but they still hadn't seen Shep.

"Will you tell him I need to speak with him? Tell him it's important," I said.

A few hours later I called again, but the line was busy. I telephoned every five minutes until I finally got through, but there was no answer. The phone just rang and rang.

I turned on a lamp and looked at the clock. It was half past eleven. Where was Shep? And what was I supposed to do now? I knew that as soon as I told Shep about the Capone hit, my life would never be the same. Shep had a better chance of dodging his killers than I had of saving my marriage. There was a good chance he'd throw me out of the house. What would I do then? Get Hannah and then what? Where would we go? Would I call Tony and tell him to come get us? Could I really do that? Run away with Tony? Forever?

I went upstairs to the bedroom and sat on the side of the bed, thinking that I should have had the housekeeper turn the mattress. I couldn't remember the last time I'd had her do that. With everything else on my mind, turning the mattress became a concern. It was a problem I knew how to solve.

I slipped out of my dress and slung it over the back of the chair. I wandered into the bathroom, going through the motions as I slathered cold cream onto my face, deliberately not looking in the mirror. I couldn't bear to look into my own eyes. I crawled into bed and lay there, staring at the ceiling, rehearsing what I'd say to Shep. The hardest part was knowing where to start.

I dozed off and when I opened my eyes it was half past three. Shep still wasn't home. The sheets were cold when I slid my hand over to his side. Most wives would have worried that their husband was with another woman, but not me. I never doubted Shep's fidelity. Shep Green was a good man and I couldn't have said that for the others, even his beloved Dion O'Banion. Sometimes I thought Shep should have let Dion take his sins with him to his grave. I knew I was being superstitious, but I wished Shep had never eaten that sin cake. And I wished I had never been involved in Izzy's murder.

A tear trailed down my cheek and landed on my lips. I rolled onto my side and begged God for forgiveness. Then I prayed for a miracle.

MY VALENTINE

When I woke up the next morning, the sheets on Shep's side of the bed were still untouched. His robe was hanging on the back of the closet door. He never made it home last night, and all I could think was, *It's already happened. Shep's dead. Capone killed him.*

I looked at the bedside clock; it was half past eight. I threw off the covers and reached for the same dress I'd worn the day before. It was where I'd left it on the chair. I got dressed and caught a glimpse of myself in the mirror. I looked like hell. A crease had formed across my cheek from the pillowcase. My dress was wrinkled and stained from the drink I'd spilled on it.

As I reached for the door, Shep surprised me, coming into the bedroom with his hands behind his back.

"Oh, you're home! Thank God!" I splayed my open fingers across my pounding heart. I went to throw my arms around him and he presented me with a bouquet of roses.

"For you!" he said.

"For me? Why?" I looked at him, confused.

"Valentine's Day, Dollface. Today's Valentine's Day." His tone was off. Or maybe it was me who was off.

I thanked him and mumbled something about putting the flowers in water. I headed out of the bedroom with him close on my heels, following me down the stairs and into the kitchen. I knew I had to tell him about Capone, but I didn't know where to start. I still didn't know what those first few words should be.

"You were out all night," I said, keeping my eyes on the roses. "That's not like you. I was worried. Where were you?"

"You really want to know where I was all night?" He leaned against the counter, watching me reach for a vase. His tone of voice was odd. "I'll tell you where I was. I was out looking for your boyfriend."

I nearly dropped the vase. "My *what*?" The moment the words left my mouth, I regretted them. I was ashamed that my first impulse was to deny it.

"Your boyfriend. Liolli. Tony Liolli." Shep had thunder in his voice.

I tried but couldn't look at him. My heart raced and my hands shook as I stuffed the roses inside a vase that was too small. Some of the petals came off, falling onto the counter.

"You want to tell me why Knuckles knows about this and I don't?"

Dora! I squeezed my eyes shut. I knew it. My worst fear: Dora had told Knuckles. Shep moved in closer and I flinched, blocking my face with my hands.

"What's the matter, Vera? You scared of me? You think I'm gonna hurt you?" He was back in control. His voice now had an eerie calmness to it.

"Shep . . ." My chin trembled. I was already crying, looking at him through a blur of tears.

"Oh, I'm not going to hurt you—you don't need to worry your pretty little head about that."

"Shep"—I was panting as I spoke—"you're in trouble—Capone's after you."

"Tell me something I don't know. Like tell me what the hell's going on with you and that scumbag Liolli?"

I took a deep breath and went over to the table, pulled out a chair and sat down. It was time to come clean. I told Shep *everything*, beginning with the news that Capone was planning to murder him.

". . . I don't know all the specifics," I said after explaining all that Tony had told me. "But I do know that Capone'll kill you if you go to that garage today."

"Well, that would be very convenient for you and Liolli, wouldn't it?"

"Oh, Shep, you have to believe me. It's a setup. I swear it is."

"I don't give a damn about Capone right now. What I want to know is what the hell's going on between you and Liolli?"

I tried to warn him again about Capone but he wasn't hearing me. He just kept asking about Tony and me. So I started from the beginning. As I was talking, I heard this voice coming from me, but it didn't sound like it belonged to me. "*. . . I met Tony before I even knew you. . . . And then you were away for so long. . . .*" It was as if someone else were telling the story. There was no emotion. I was tapped out. "*. . . We'd meet at his hotel room. Twice, sometimes three times a week . . .*"

Shep was standing, leaning against the counter next to me. He closed his eyes and rubbed his forehead.

". . . I don't know what I was thinking," I said. "It was a mistake from the start. I was just so lonely when you went away, and even after you were back home, you were never around and I was scared and I know it was wrong. I just couldn't figure out how to get out of it. . . ."

Shep's jaw stiffened. He twisted his wedding band and clenched his fist.

"Shep . . ." I reached for his hand but he pulled away from me.

"I'm not sure I want to know the answer to this," he said, "but I have to ask you—is Hannah even mine? Is she my daughter?"

"Of course she's yours." My eyes glassed up. "You're her father. I swear it. You have to believe me—"

Shep held up a hand to silence me. "What makes you think I could ever believe anything you say to me again?"

"Because I love you, and you have to believe what I told you about Capone or else he's going to kill you. I'm telling you the truth, Shep. They're coming for you at the garage on Clark Street later today—he said there was nothing I could do to stop it. He told me we had to go away and start over. He wanted to take me to Mexico. But I'm not going. I'm not. I couldn't."

"You wouldn't get too far anyway," he said, checking his pocket watch, "because I've already got a tail on your boy Liolli. Did that as soon as Knuckles told me what was going on. I'm watching every move that greaseball makes. If he hadn't been hiding out at the Four Deuces all night, I would have finished him off by now."

"Oh, God!" The knots in my stomach pulled tighter.

Shep reached for his overcoat and shrugged it on. "I'm late. We'll finish this when I get back." He set his fedora on his head and made his way to the front door.

"No, Shep, please! You can't go down there. They're waiting for you at the garage. I swear it. They're going to kill you there." I chased after him, squeezing my way between him and the front door, blocking him from leaving. "No, Shep—please." With my body still pressed against the door trying to stop him, he reached for the knob, and when he pulled the door open I lost my balance and fell in the corner. I was stunned for a moment and when I looked up, Shep was already heading out the door.

"Shep! *Shep!*" I ran after him out the front door, a rush of freezing air stinging my cheeks. "Shep, wait."

Shep stopped. I stood frozen too. A new panic rushed through my veins. There was Knuckles, standing outside the front gate with his pistol drawn, pointed at Tony Liolli's back. Tony's gloved hands gripped onto the black finials of the gate for support. He didn't speak but I could see his breath against the frigid air, coming out fast and hard. His car was still running, idling at the curb. Knuckles's car was right behind his, doing the same.

I'd never had the chance to call and tell Tony I wasn't going with him. I was so worried all night about Shep, calling Tony was the farthest thing from my mind. He must have come here to get me, assuming Shep had already left for the garage. He had no way of knowing Shep was running late.

"Well, well, well." Shep started down the steps. "Look who's here." His voice was so calm, so void of emotion, it was unnerving.

Shep walked past the gate and over to Knuckles. "I'll take care of it from here," Shep said. "This one's personal. This one's mine."

Knuckles nodded and put the gun back in his pocket as he backed away.

Tony was dumbfounded. He turned toward Shep and then toward me. The look in his eyes said it all. He'd never expected me to say anything to warn Shep. Tony really believed that I would have just let my husband die.

"You're just in time," said Shep, still in a tranquil, even tone. "I was just leaving. She's all yours."

"Let's not jump to conclusions here," Tony said, trying to sound just as composed as Shep. "This isn't what you think." He acted like he was ignoring everything Shep had just said, but I heard the tremor in Tony's voice. He knew what was really going on here.

Shep let out one sharp laugh. "First you fuck my wife and now you insult my intelligence. Get in the car, Liolli." He was so in control, so smooth in his delivery that it took a moment before I realized he'd reached for his gun.

"Shep, *no!*" I raced down the steps, heading for the gate, but Knuckles rushed in and grabbed me, holding me back just as Tony lunged for Shep. I screamed as he drove Shep back into the gate, going for his gun. "No! Stop it! Stop it!" I was struggling against Knuckles, trying to break free, when I heard the gun go off.

Shep and Tony stood still. A wind gust kicked up, sending a mist of snow all around them. The white powder sparkled and glistened in the air while Tony began to stumble forward. As soon as Shep stepped away, I saw the blood and saw Tony sink down into a snowdrift. His eyes went wide as his hand reached up to his chest, blood gushing over his fingers. He tried to get up but Shep fired again, and this one hit Tony in the forehead, sending a spray of blood and gore out the back of his head and onto the snow-covered ground.

I screamed again and tried to break free, but Knuckles still had a firm hold on me and my feet were slipping on the ice. I couldn't get to Shep or Tony.

Shep gave Tony a nudge with his shoe before he called to Knuckles. "Get rid of him," he said as he headed for his motorcar.

Knuckles nodded, and as soon as he let me go I ran after

Shep, stumbling over the ice and snow. "Shep! Shep, no! Wait—you can't go!"

By the time I reached his car, Shep was already in the driver's seat and starting the engine.

"No! Shep! Don't! Don't go!" I was pounding on the door, running alongside the car as Shep pulled away. I slipped and fell into the snowbank at the curb just as a neighbor across the way opened her front door and then closed it fast. I dropped my head to my hands and sobbed.

I stayed like that, stunned and paralyzed, until I was finally able to push myself up against the snowbank and get up. I couldn't speak or look at Tony as I made my way back toward the house. I stood, holding on to one of the limestone pillars. The wind was blowing the snow up around my legs. I watched, horrified, as Knuckles dragged Tony's blood-soaked body away from the gate, his lifeless head slumped forward. I closed my eyes and turned away. I couldn't watch anymore. It was bad enough when I heard the thud of Tony's body landing inside the trunk of his car. I forced myself back inside the house, and when I finally looked out through the front window, I saw that Knuckles had covered the bloody ground beneath a fresh blanket of snow. He was already behind the wheel of Tony's automobile, driving the body away.

Everything turned quiet then. I was alone, and that's when my legs gave out beneath me and I collapsed, weeping into the crook of my arm. My body shook while everything spun inside my head. Tony was dead. He was dead because of me. My husband murdered him. My husband—was he ever coming back to me? He was walking into a deathtrap.

I had to stop him. I had to. I couldn't let him go down to the garage to meet Bugs.

. . .

was still in shock as I ran back inside the house and got my coat and pocketbook. I rushed back outside to hail a taxicab. It felt like an eternity before one stopped for me. Finally I was heading north, praying that I'd get to the garage in time. I kept searching out the window but Shep's Cadillac was nowhere in sight.

I had the taxicab drop me on the east side of the street, at the corner of Dickens and Clark. Snow was coming down, and the sidewalks were slippery. I passed a man outside his hardware store, shoveling the walkway out front, when I spotted Shep rounding the corner.

I ran toward him, sliding over the snow and patches of ice. As soon as Shep saw me, he grew angry. "What the hell are you doing here?"

"You can't go in there! You have to believe me." I stood in front of him with my hands out, trying to stop him, the words running loose—I couldn't get them out fast enough.

He stopped and gave me a look that was so cold and hateful, it wounded me more than his fist ever could have. "Go home. Get the hell out of here." He stepped around me and kept walking.

"Please. You can't go in there. Not now. I'm telling you. It's a trap! It is!"

"Go home, Vera. You don't belong here. Just go!" He kept walking.

I trailed after him, trying to keep up, calling to him, but he wouldn't listen. There were motorcars and trucks rumbling up and down Clark Street and he darted in between them, crossing to the west side of the street. The traffic was too heavy and I couldn't make it across in time. All I could do was stand helplessly, watching him head toward the S.M.C. Cartage Company garage. A German shepherd chained to the post out front let out a yelp when he saw Shep. I called to him one last time as he disappeared through the side door.

I didn't know what to do. I couldn't leave with him in there. The wind howled as it whipped in and around the buildings. I turned to shield my face and noticed Bugs walking down the sidewalk. He was less than half a block away when a police car pulled up in front of the garage. When I looked again for Bugs, he was gone. He must have seen the cops and darted inside a building on the corner.

Four men got out of the squad car: Two were policemen; two were dressed in dark overcoats.

A raid? Shep was being raided! Capone couldn't carry out a hit if the garage was being raided. I didn't care if they arrested Shep and put him back in jail, just as long as Capone didn't kill him.

It was freezing outside, the temperature barely in the teens. I couldn't feel my feet or fingers anymore and ducked inside the coffee shop across the street from the garage to wait it out. A string of bells chimed when I stepped inside, bringing a gust of wind in with me. A handful of customers seated at the counter, still with their coats on, looked up at me. I took a front table by the windows. An inch or so of snow had piled up on the ledge and the glass was frosted over from the cold. A half curtain hung down, doing a poor job of blocking the draft.

As I was staring out through the parting in the curtain, the waitress came by and asked if I was okay. I didn't answer and instead ordered a cup of coffee and as she was filling my cup, a loud noise bellowed out from across the way. It sounded like an eruption, followed by a couple of loud booms, one right after the other.

My heart stopped. The waitress flinched and missed my cup, spilling coffee on the table instead. Everyone in the coffee shop looked up, their forks and spoons suspended above their plates for a moment, before they returned to their meals and conversations. I peered through the parting of the curtain and everything seemed fine, normal. A few people walking by outside had stopped when they heard the noise, but then kept going.

The waitress was still wiping up the spill when I looked up and saw the cops walking out of the garage with their machine guns pressed to the spines of the two men who had gone into the garage with them earlier. I'd never seen either of them before but whoever they were, they weren't members of the North Side Gang. The men they'd arrested had their hands in the air as the police put them into the back of the car and drove off, the exhaust billowing out against the cold as their car disappeared down Clark Street.

I began to breathe again and leaned back in my chair, looking out the parting in the curtain every few minutes, watching for Shep. *Thank you, God, for not letting him get arrested. Thank you.* I thought the police must have come for someone else, not Shep. Although I didn't understand why they had left with the same men they'd arrived with. It nagged at me, but I couldn't think about it, because just then the sight of Tony lying bloody in the snow flashed through my mind. I closed my eyes, trying to clear the image. Then all I could think about was Shep. My thoughts rapidly shifted back and forth between the two: What had I done to Tony, and how could I salvage my marriage. I heard the faint whine of sirens off in the distance when the waitress came by again, and I ordered a refill of coffee.

What would Knuckles do with Tony? Would Shep be charged with his murder . . . ?

The sirens were drawing closer, their shrill squeal drowning out my thoughts. I pulled back the curtain just as two police cars drove up in front of the S.M.C. garage. Everyone inside the coffee shop rushed to the windows, their faces pressed to the glass, looking to see what was happening. The neighbors lurked in their doorways, while passersby gathered out in front of the garage.

My pulse quickened. Someone let out a round of screams so piercing it cut through the sound of the sirens. I screamed, too, as I grabbed my pocketbook, jumped up and raced out of the coffee shop.

Before I'd even made it across the street, the entranceway of the garage was crowded with gapers, people with hands clasped over their mouths, the shock visible on every face. A photographer was already on the scene with his camera raised, trying for the first pictures. There was chaos with everyone shouting, hollering all at once. I pushed and shoved my way toward the front. The German shepherd was still chained to the post outside, baring its teeth. A man who had just come from inside the garage brushed past me, shaking his head, a hand pressed to his forehead.

I stopped him, grabbing hold of his arm. Even though I knew, I still had to ask. There was a sliver of hope that maybe, just maybe, I was wrong. "What's happened? What's going on?"

"It's awful," the man said, removing his hat, smoothing down his hair. "All those men in there—everyone inside—they've all been shot. They're all dead."

He said something else to me but I just held on to his arm. I could barely breathe. I was aware of people rushing back and forth, but everything—all the sounds, all the movement—was distorted, until eventually, everything around me grew small and quiet and dark.

THE DRY SPELL
HAS BEEN BROKEN

REPEAL, 1933

Hannah sits on the side of the bed waiting patiently while I scoot my way behind her to finish braiding her hair. It's thick and shiny and long enough so she can wear it any way she wants. Mine was just like it when I was a young girl. "You're lucky," I tell her. "You're gonna thank me for this hair someday."

"Oh, Mama, you always say that."

"Say what?" I lean forward to get a good look at her.

"'Oh, Hannah,'" she mimics me, "'you're gonna thank me for your eyes. For that nose. Oh, and of course'"—she rolls her eyes—"'for that charming and delightful personality.'" She leans back against me, giggling.

She turns nine this year, nine going on twenty-nine. She's wiser than I was back then, but she looks just like me when I was her age. She's feisty, too. Feistier than I was at her age, though my mother disagrees.

I tie two satin ribbons to the ends of her braids and give her a squeeze from behind.

"Help, help!" she teases, flailing her arms. "I can't breathe. You're suffocating me!"

"You want to pick out what I should wear today?"

She lights up. She started doing this when she was six or seven, thinking it was only fair that since I picked out her school clothes, she should pick out my work clothes. We go into my room and she races to the wardrobe in the corner. "How about this?" She pulls out a red gown with a cape collar and circular flounces.

"Don't you think that's a little fancy for work?"

"But it's so purdy." She places her hands primly beneath her chin and bats her long lashes.

"What do you think of this?" I hold up a steel gray peplum frock.

Hannah tilts her head and contemplates. "Do you think you'll be warm enough? It's going to be cold today."

Always, from the time she was a baby, Hannah in her own way has taken care of me. It's instinctive in her. She must have gotten it from Shep, because I know she didn't get it from me.

"I think I'll be fine." I slip into the dress and my shoes before we head down to the kitchen for breakfast. While I put on the percolator for coffee, I peer out the window. The trees out back are bare and the sky is gray. There's a chill inside the house but I don't dare fire up the furnace. We're rationing coal, trying to save it for the truly cold winter days ahead.

I fix Hannah's breakfast and pour my coffee. She reaches for the toast as I butter it and takes a bite. "Uh, uh, uh—sit down at the table."

She goes to where her place is set and takes a sip of milk.

After breakfast, I walk Hannah to the schoolyard and bend

down while she wraps her arms around me. She gives me a kiss and says, "Now go have a good day."

I look back and wave. She's standing where I left her, at the edge of the schoolyard, watching, waving back. I walk a few more feet and turn around and she's still there, waving to me again. This is what we do. Every morning. I know that she'll stand there and wave to me until I turn the corner. Then in her mind, I'm safely on my way to the streetcar. As soon as she's out of sight, I start to miss her.

Once on board I take a seat toward the back and look out the window. We pass one bungalow after another, and somewhere beyond the horizon, in the distance, I picture the Wrigley Building and the downtown skyscrapers towering over the city. I miss the hustle-bustle of downtown and think about moving back all the time, but my mother needs me right now. It's the least I can do, since she was there for me after Shep's murder. My mother, more than anyone else, knew what I was going through.

After the massacre on Clark Street I was in shock. I hadn't even had a chance to absorb what had happened to Tony when I found out about Shep. If it weren't for my mother and Hannah, I don't think I could have gone on. For Hannah's sake I had to pull myself together. And it was only then that I realized that when my father died, my mother never let me see her broken. I had to be just as strong.

I remember I wouldn't look at the newspapers until after Hannah was in bed asleep. The next day the *Chicago Tribune* had photos of Shep and all the other victims, along with pictures of the crowds gathered outside the S.M.C. Cartage Company garage. The headline split me down the center:

North Side Gangsters Gunned Down in Cold Blood

The reporter had coined the phrase "the St. Valentine's Day Massacre," and according to him, "The bloodbath was a carefully orchestrated scheme, designed to execute key members of the North Side Gang." Apparently those weren't real police officers who raided the garage. They were gangsters—presumably Capone's men—dressed in police uniforms, out for slaughter. It was all staged. There was no raid.

I tore up every newspaper, every article. I still haven't told Hannah exactly what happened to her father. There's time for that, and hopefully by then, I'll find the words to explain it all to her.

The conductor calls out my stop, and I get off the streetcar and pass through the giant limestone gate along with the other workers heading in for another day. It's mostly men in tattered overcoats with some teenage boys and a few women mixed in. Ever since the stock market crash a lot of people are out of work, but you wouldn't know it down here at the Union Stock Yards. Money is tight for everyone now but people still have to eat.

I step inside the main office and Ida Brech looks up from her typewriter. "You're in early today," she says, handing me a stack of messages.

I shuffle through them while Ida preps me for the day ahead. I have two appointments with cattle salesmen and one with a new salt vendor. I pour myself a cup of coffee and sit at my desk, returning to the stack of messages, deciding who to deal with first.

I call Otto at the tannery down the street. "Tell him it's Vera with Abramowitz Meats." Two seconds later, Otto's on the line. ". . . Yeah, Otto, you bet I'm not happy. You're chiseling me. . . ." I look at Ida and roll my eyes. "Listen, we had an agreement and I expect you to honor that. End of story . . ." He's yapping on and I'm making notes for my next call. "Well, now," I say with a laugh, giving Ida a wink, "that's more like it. Just don't let it happen again. . . ."

No sooner do I end my call than I hear Ida say, "Well, look who's here."

I glance up and set the telephone back down. There is my mother coming through the doorway. "Ma, what are you doing? You need to rest."

"*Feh!*" She shakes her head and leans on her cane as she makes her way across the room, favoring her right side. I get up from the desk and help her into the chair. This is the first time she's been back to Abramowitz Meats since her stroke in August. That was when I sold the house and Hannah and I moved back home so I could take care of her. I worried that Hannah wouldn't want to move to Brighton Park, but when I told her, she sprang to her feet and said, "Really? We get to go live in the same house you grew up in?"

I see where my mother's missed a couple buttons on her dress and I reach over and make it right. She's never gotten her full strength back, and fastening a button can be as monumental a task as opening a jar.

"How are you feeling, Mrs. Abramowitz?" Ida gets up to fix her a cup of coffee.

"I'm managing just fine," she insists. "I'll be back here before you know it."

Ida looks at me, and all I can do is shrug.

"Let me see the ledger." My mother motions to me. "Let me see what you've been up to while I've been gone."

I pull out the leather-bound book and place it in her lap. With her finger, she traces over the numbers and mumbles something to herself. At least her nails are clean now. She finally let me file them and remove the dirt underneath. Maybe one day she'll even let me polish them. Looking up, she smiles at me with half her face; the other half is frozen. "You've done good," she says.

And so I have, even during these tough times. Last month I purchased a machine that does the work of six men. I've also cut a few good deals with our vendors. It's gritty and nasty as ever down at Abramowitz Meats, but it doesn't bother me as much anymore. Maybe it's because I'm older now. Or maybe because I've seen things much uglier and darker than the Union Stock Yards.

My mother lowers her head as a strand of drool lands on the open pages of the ledger. She doesn't notice it. I reach for my handkerchief to wipe her mouth, but she swats my hand away. She's proud. I have to respect that.

make my way out to the theater lobby, waiting while my eyes adjust to the light. I've just seen *42nd Street* with Bebe Daniels and Ginger Rogers for the third time.

When I step outside the movie palace I hear the paperboys shouting the headlines from every street corner: "Extra, extra—read all about it! 'Prohibition Ends Tonight! Liquor to Flow Again! The Dry Spell Has Been Broken!'"

It's official. After thirteen years, the "Noble Experiment" has proven to be nothing but a colossal joke. Everyone knew the Volstead Act was going to be repealed and now they're all getting ready to celebrate. All the downtown hotels, dance halls, and cabarets are throwing big bashes.

The December wind is lashing out with all its fury. I turn away with my back toward the lake, facing the patina clock outside of Marshall Field's. It's after four o'clock and I need to get home. Hannah and I are going to bake cookies later.

The sun is setting and I walk by a speakeasy just as the doors fly open, letting a cluster of people empty out onto the sidewalk.

A man motions to me from the doorway, holding a martini glass in one hand and a bottle of gin in the other. "C'mon in, doll!"

It gives me a shiver when he calls me that because it's so close, too close, and I know no one will ever call me Dollface again. I shake my head and keep walking past a dozen or so taverns and saloons, officially back open for business. I look in the picture window of a restaurant and see people pouring champagne freely, clinking their fluted glasses in toast after toast.

A couple of drunks in front of me weave their way back and forth down the sidewalk with their arms thrown over each other's shoulders, singing, "Oh, how are you goin' to wet your whistle when the whole darn world goes dry . . ."

You would think it was New Year's Eve, the way people are carrying on. Everyone's blotto.

Everyone but me.

When I get home that night, I feed my mother and give her a sponge bath. Hannah and I make snickerdoodles and sugar cookies for her to take to school. After she's in bed, I clean up the kitchen and change into my bathrobe and nurse a bourbon while I listen to the festivities over the radio, coming live from the Knickerbocker, the Palmer House and every other hotel in town.

It's the end of an era and I can't let the moment pass without remembering the good times we had, despite it all. I can't help it; it chokes me up, and I wipe a tear rolling down my cheek.

"Don't cry, Mama." Hannah comes and sits next to me.

"What are you still doing up?" I clear my throat and drag my hand across my cheek.

"I thought you seemed lonely tonight."

"Now, how can I be lonely, huh? I've got you."

She comes and sits next to me and rests her head on my chest. I brush my hand through her hair, pushing her bangs back off her forehead. That's when I glance down and see what can only be the start of a widow's peak. Just like her father's.

She snuggles in closer and says, "If you want, you can go ahead and suffocate me again."

I wrap my arms around her and squeeze with all my heart.

"Well, what do you think?" Evelyn holds out her hand, showing me her engagement ring.

"It's beautiful," I tell her, holding her hand in mine. "I'm glad to see that after four years he's finally making an honest woman out of you. I'm happy for you." And I am. Irwin's one of the good ones. And he's out of the rackets now, doing what he can to keep his factory doors open and his workers employed. "It figures," I say, "you and your big boobs would end up marrying a man who makes brassieres."

Evelyn laughs. We're sitting in the parlor at my mother's house, just like we used to do when we were girls. She reaches inside her pocketbook for a roll of Necco wafers and tells me about the wedding plans.

"Wow. That's soon," I say when she tells me the date.

"I know, but like you said, after four years, it's time already." Peeling away the waxed-paper wrapper, she pops a lime candy in her mouth and hands the roll to me. "But it's gonna be a small wedding. You'll come, won't you?"

"Of course. Wouldn't miss it."

"You know the others'll be there."

"I know, but that's my problem, not yours." I don't keep up with the girls anymore. Dora ratted me out, so there's no love lost there. I heard she had a couple more miscarriages and I think she always resented me because I'd had a baby and she couldn't. The other girls don't bother with me now, either.

"Is Basha still dating that old guy?" I ask.

Evelyn laughs. "Wait till you meet him. You'll die. He's old enough to be her father."

"Yeah, but I hear he's rich." I laugh, imagining what it will be like to come face-to-face with the old gang again, after all these years. "Aw, we had some good times for a while there, didn't we?"

She nods. "Absolutely."

I place a clove Necco disk on my tongue and let it dissolve. "Feels like a lifetime ago." After the massacre there was nothing left of the North Side Gang. Capone had broken them that day on Clark Street. They didn't have the time or the men or even the heart to rebuild. I bite down on my wafer, cracking it in two. "What do you hear from the fellas?" I ask, dusting the Necco powder off my fingers. "Do they still keep in touch?"

"Yeah, but it's not the same. Irwin told me Bugs is back to safecracking and that Knuckles is knocking off jewelry stores with a couple of the Little Pishers." She fluffs her hair off her neck. She offers me another Necco before she opens her pocketbook and drops the roll inside. "You know Irwin's friend David will be at the wedding. And he's coming alone."

I smile. "I'm not ready for anything like that. Not yet." I look out the window at the old neighborhood. I do think someday I'll meet someone. A nice man who'll be a good father for Hannah. I imagine we'll have a nice place to live. We'll go see some shows, take in a movie now and then. We'll be just another regular married couple. We'll have holiday dinners together and plan a family vacation to the beach every summer. We'll watch Hannah grow up and argue over how she is wearing her hair, or the length of her skirts, or which boys she wants to date. We'll make nice, respectful love once, maybe twice a week. Maybe I'll even have another child someday. I'm twenty-seven now, almost twenty-eight, but who knows? Could still happen . . .

When I lay it all out like that, normal doesn't sound like such a bad life. It sounds kinda nice. And nice doesn't sound so dull anymore, either.

AUTHOR'S NOTE

One of the luxuries of being a fiction writer is that we can take creative license, which I've done consciously throughout this novel. Having far too much respect for historians and nonfiction authors, I present *Dollface* not as a work of historical fact, but as one of fiction based on historical fact. Those well versed in the history of Chicago and Prohibition will see where I've altered some events and time lines. These include the Sieben Brewery Raid, which occurred in May 1924, as opposed to March 1924. This was a pivotal event in which Dion O'Banion set up a double cross that landed Johnny Torrio in jail and was the impetus for O'Banion's murder. The North Siders vowed to seek revenge, resulting in Chicago's infamous Beer Wars. The Hawthorne Arms shooting was in September 1927, not August 1927. Vincent Drucci was ironically buried with military honors for his service during World War I; however, he was murdered in April 1927 rather than August 1927. Seven members of the North Side Gang were murdered in the St. Valentine's Day Massacre. For the purpose of this novel, I added an eighth member by having Shep Green perish in the massacre as well.

AUTHOR'S NOTE

Many real-life gangsters and gun molls from the 1920s are featured in *Dollface.* They include Al Capone, Johnny Torrio, Dion O'Banion, Hymie Weiss, Vincent Drucci, George "Bugs" Moran, Cecelia Drucci, and Viola O'Banion. The female bootleggers were based loosely on the famous female rumrunner Mrs. Willie Carter Sharpe. All other characters are fictional.

While conducting my research I read a great deal of fiction and nonfiction and want to pay credit to the following: *City of the Century,* by Donald L. Miller; *Outlaws of the Lakes: Bootlegging & Smuggling from Colonial Times to Prohibition,* by Edwards Butts; *Chicago Gang Wars,* author unknown; *The Jungle,* by Upton Sinclair; *1929,* by Frederick Turner; *Oh, Play That Thing,* by Roddy Doyle; and *The Wettest County in the World,* by Matt Bondurant.

I also made use of other sources while writing this novel, including the Harold Washington Library Chicago newspaper microfilm holdings and the Untouchables Tours in Chicago, hosted by Craig Alton, who was also kind enough to give me a guided tour of the Back of the Yards and what remains of the Union Stock Yards. He also arranged for a tour of Chiappetti's, one of the last standing slaughterhouses in Chicago. Additional inspirations and factual content came from the following: *The Speakeasy* and *The St. Valentine's Day Massacre,* both produced by the History Channel, and *Chicago's Gangland Graves,* produced by Untouchable Tours, with David Gault. There are also countless Web sites devoted to the 1920s and Chicago's gangland activities of that era. The following sites were particularly helpful: Crime Magazine: An Encyclopedia of Crime (www.crimemagazine.com), "Whacked by the Good Guys" by Allan May (crimemagazine.com/whacked-good -guys), the Lawless Decade by Paul Sann (www.lawlessdecade .net), Hymie Weiss (www.hymieweiss.com), and My Al Capone Museum (www.myalcaponemuseum.com).

Photo by Charles Osgood

Renée Rosen is a freelance writer and the author of *Every Crooked Pot*. She lives in Chicago, where she is at work on her next novel.

CONNECT ONLINE

www.reneerosen.com

DOLLFACE

A NOVEL OF THE ROARING TWENTIES

RENÉE ROSEN

QUESTIONS FOR DISCUSSION

1. The Jazz Age was a time of prosperity and wild abandon. There was a lot of experimentation, sexual expression, and new independence for women. Lately there's been renewed interest in the Roaring Twenties. What is it about this period that intrigues people? Is it the music, the clothes, the social mores? Or is it something else?

2. Throughout history, people have been fascinated by gangsters, particularly those of the Prohibition era. Organized crime has been glamorized in movies and fiction, and many of the most violent figures enjoyed more celebrity than the Hollywood stars of their day. Their mystique seems to eclipse the fact that they were ruthless killers. What is it about gangsters that makes them so intriguing and appealing?

3. Friendship and loyalty are strong themes in *Dollface*. Is there a difference between friendship and loyalty, or do you see them as the same? Is it possible to be loyal to someone you don't consider a friend? Maybe a boss or a coworker? Do you think you can take loyalty too far? Would you remain loyal to

a friend even though you knew they'd done something illegal or morally wrong?

4. Aside from the obvious bond between Vera and Evelyn, what other characters in the novel share an equally strong connection? Do you think the men valued their relationships with one another as much as the women did? How do you think men's friendships differ from female friendships?

5. From the opening of the novel till the end, Vera undergoes a transformation. What do you think caused her to shed her frivolous flapper facade? What factors do you think contributed to the changes in her character? Was it the obvious milestones she experienced, such as marriage and motherhood, or did you sense that there was something else that accounted for her growth and maturation?

6. The twenties were a liberating time for women. If you had lived during the days of Prohibition, do you think you would have been a flapper or would you have been more conservative?

7. In the twenties, women cutting their hair, wearing makeup, and smoking and drinking in public were all signs of rebellion and independence. What sorts of things do progressive young women do today that would be considered comparable? What kinds of things have you done to show your independence?

8. Vera is involved with two men throughout the novel. Do you think it's possible to be in love with two people at the same time? How was her relationship with Tony different

from her relationship with Shep? Which man do you think she loved more? Would she have been happier with one man over the other in the long run?

9. Women's groups and organizations were popular during this era. In the case of *Dollface*, Vera chose to align herself with the Jewish Women's Council, but was later expelled when the members learned that her husband was a gangster. Did you feel the women's council treated her fairly, or should they have allowed Vera to continue participating in the group? Why do you think it was important for Vera to belong to such a club in the first place?

10. Thirteen years after it was enacted, the Volstead Act was repealed and Prohibition was deemed a failure. In today's society, can you identify any movements to ban certain items or behaviors that echo those of Prohibition? And if enforced, what do you think the outcome would be? What lessons did our nation learn from Prohibition, and are there any obvious mistakes that we as a society continue to make?

11. When she was a young girl, Vera's father was brutally murdered by the Black Hand Gang, a deadly extortionist group that gave way to the Mafia after it was disbanded in the early twentieth century. How did the murder of her father influence Vera's life? Do you think his murder had anything to do with her choice of men and the path she ended up taking?

12. Do you think Vera knew in the beginning of the novel that Shep and Tony were gangsters, or was she just naive? Once it

was obvious that they were both gang members, how did she justify their actions to herself and others?

13. Mother and daughter relationships factor strongly into this novel. Vera's complicated relationship with her mother undergoes a major shift through the course of the story. What do you think accounts for this change? How is Vera's relationship with her mother different from Vera's relationship with Hannah?

14. When Shep was incarcerated, Vera found herself in survival mode. Do you agree with the choices she made? Do you think she was courageous or reckless to enter into her own bootlegging operation?

15. The women in *Dollface* represent flappers, gun molls, and mob wives. How do you think Vera, Evelyn, Dora, and Basha are similar? How are they different? Was there one character that you identified with more than the others?

16. Vera suffers a great deal of pain and loss at the end of the novel. Did you feel sorry for her or did you think she got what she deserved?